THE
POPE
MUST DIE

DONALD ANDERSON

HANOVER PRESS

Published in the United States of America by Hanover Press.

ISBN: 978-0-9961534-2-3 (paperback)

Ebook ISBN: 978-0-9961534-3-0

Book Cover by Landô

CAST OF CHARACTERS

AMANDA O'BRIEN: CIA officer

JORDAN HARRISON: FBI agent

SIXTUS VI: Supreme pontiff of the Roman Catholic Church. Born Nicholas Cassella

JOSÉ EUSEBIO BARRANCA: Vatican Secretary of State

AHMED BENSAÏD: Jordanian businessman

KHALID ZAHIR: Kuwaiti billionaire

FOSTER: President of the United States

RICHTER: General Secretary of the Vatican

PERKINS: U.S. ambassador to Italy

BRIAN WILSON: American embassy attaché

VALERIE COHEN: National Security Adviser

OROZCO: Secretary of Defense

ALEJANDRO GÓMEZ: Jesuit priest

GIUSEPPE FALZONE: Sicilian mafioso

SIMA: former MI6 agent

VIOLETA MANOLOV: Bulgarian terrorist

PETAR TODOROV: Bulgarian terrorist

SISTER SOFIJA: Vatican nun

PILAR: Spanish bartender

GENERAL JEFFERSON CHEEKS: Director of National Intelligence

IGLESIAS: Algeciras port administrator

TIGRE: Algeciras port worker

VIVIANA: Algeciras port worker

MONICA: CIA officer

VITALY CHERTKOV: Russian ambassador to the Vatican

BOB GOODMAN: CIA officer

SVETLANA: tattoo parlor owner

ZHYULI: Svetlana's girlfriend

DMITRY: Russian counterfeiter

YURI: captain of *Das Kapital*

VERONICA (V): CIA officer

MRS. WU: British Chinese woman

NANCY WU: Mrs. Wu's daughter

HRISTOV: captain of *The Grindon*

BUCK: captain of the *USS Franklin*

THE
POPE
MUST
DIE

Chapter 1

He had hardly wanted to be a priest; yet, somehow, he became pope.

He had taken the name of Sixtus VI – Sixtus the Sixth – because the number six held a special meaning to him. He was born on the sixth of June, the sixth month of the year. When the digits of his birth year, 1977, were summed in numerological fashion, one plus nine plus seven plus seven, they equaled six.

"Your eminence," the newly appointed Vatican Secretary of State José Eusebio Barranca announced in his accented English, "Mr. Bensaïd is here."

"Please send him in." Sixtus was always mindful of the power of a *please*.

Cardinal Barranca left Sixtus's private office, leaving the door open for Bensaïd. Bensaïd kissed the pope's ring – the traditional, gold Fisherman's Ring depicting Peter casting his net with the pontiff's name inscribed. "Your Holiness. Thank you for seeing me."

"I always have time for my most cherished patron." Sixtus watched as Barranca closed the door, leaving them alone. He had met Ahmed Bensaïd when he was sixteen and known by the Christian name of Nicholas Cassella. He had been working part-time as a kitchen aide in a state-run institution for the developmentally disabled when Bensaïd appeared one day, gifting a large sum to the institution. Rumors had circulated that he was related to one of the residents. One evening, while Nicholas was on a picnic bench on the wooded campus, Bensaïd introduced himself. He gave Nicholas his card, told him that he had heard great things about him, and mentioned a scholarship program that his 'team' sponsored at Williams College. The scholarship provided a full grant for the study of religion. Bensaïd asked if he was Catholic. Nicholas was surprised by the question, as he assumed Bensaïd was Muslim by his appearance. Bensaïd seemed to acknowledge his surprise. He told him he was Muslim but that he found Catholicism "a very fine religion." He said it was important to learn about the religions of the world "to find one's place in life." The expression stuck with him.

"I trust you have received the funds," Bensaïd said.

"I never had a doubt. You have always been a man of your word." Sixtus was telling the truth. He had never had a want at Williams or later, when he went to Harvard Divinity School for his master's and doctoral degrees. He even had had enough to send money home to his mother, who worked as a waitress.

"It is our pleasure."

"And the cardinals who voted for me?" Sixtus asked, referring to the College of Cardinals members who had been paid off as part of the campaign.

"They each received a million as we agreed."

Only thirty of the cardinals had to be bribed. Along with the five million that Sixtus had been paid, the total investment to ordain him was less than planned. A bargain, in the words of Bensaïd's benefactor, Khalid Zahir.

Barranca was not among those bought off.

Bensaïd glanced at the *New York Times* and *International Herald*

Tribune newspapers splayed on Sixtus's desk, each heralding Sixtus as the first American pope and one of the youngest. At forty-eight, Sixtus was the youngest pontiff elected since Leo X in the fifteenth century. American media celebrated Sixtus's origins as an Italian American, a bridge between cultures, the European homeland and the newly settled America. His great-grandparents had emigrated to America during World War I. "Your ascendancy has been historic. A true blessing."

"I couldn't have done it without you."

"You've always been so modest." Bensaïd pronounced his statement without the slightest hint of irony, even though he knew that Sixtus was quite arrogant. That lust for power, that unbridled sense of destiny, was what made the young Nicholas Cassella stand out. Bensaïd had compiled a detailed personality profile of Nicholas, noting his need for respect, his desire for control, his appetite for power, before awarding him the scholarship to Williams. Because he recognized these traits at an early stage, he was able to train him to sublimate these qualities so that his ambitions didn't threaten his competitors or derail his purpose.

"World leaders have been calling to pay their respects," Sixtus said.

"As they should."

"But not the American president."

"Barranca has made inquiries?"

"Yes. But I don't trust him. He is too subservient. They all need to kiss the ring, even President Foster. Perhaps he thinks that because I am an American, I am beholden to him. But I am not. Barranca hasn't properly conveyed that message."

"Barranca is harmless," Bensaïd said. "He wants to be pope one day. He knows how to be diplomatic."

"I would have preferred Richter." Sixtus was referring to the right-leaning German cardinal.

"We don't want to raise suspicion," Bensaïd said. "These internal posts are not that important to our plan. We will deal with Foster soon enough. That's why I have come. You must extend an olive branch. Send him a personal note. A gift of some sort. Perhaps something for him and his wife. He knows he needs Catholic support. Let him believe that you will help corral support behind him."

"What do I ask for in return?" For Sixtus, everything was a quid pro quo.

"Nothing at all. Because in just a matter of weeks, in addition to pope, you will be president."

Chapter 2

José Eusebio Barranca was born to a middle-class family in Cuenca, Ecuador. *Middle class* in Ecuadorian terms meant that the family had household help – a full-time maid, a thrice-weekly gardener, even an occasional driver at their beck and call. His mother didn't work; his father was an agricultural minister who had business connections throughout the country. José and his three brothers and sisters all received a university education; his sister had a Ph.D. in biochemistry and was employed by a multinational pharmaceutical company. Two of his brothers were lawyers. When José's father had first learned that his eldest son wanted to be a priest, he was disappointed. He felt that José could rise to the heights of power, either as a captain of industry or a politician. In time, however, as his son rose through the ranks of the Catholic Church, he became quite proud of him, as his son's religious connections opened doors. Now, as secretary of state, Barranca had a direct line to the president of Ecuador, as well as to leading politicians and diplomats throughout Latin

America, the United States, and Europe. There was no end to papal power. The Vatican made conglomerates like Google and Amazon and heads of state from countries like Brazil, India, even France, seem like small potatoes. The Church possessed assets in the trillions of dollars, all of it tax-free, growing annually, astronomically, with compound interest.

While Sixtus did not trust Barranca, Barranca also felt that something was off with the new pope. It was as if he had been primed for the role, for decades. If he had noticed it, why couldn't others? Or did they not care? Were they just like Cassella?

Since there wasn't a blemish on Cassella's record, there was little reason, except for inexperience and his younger age, that anyone would vote against him. Sixtus had won election from the College of Cardinals on the rare first vote. It was as if he had been pre-ordained, the vote a mere formality. Every cardinal, including Barranca, was an automaton adhering to the orders of some invisible puppet master pulling the strings, forcing them all to write *Cassella* on the white, linen paper ballots.

Barranca realized he was jealous. He also knew that one day he could be pope. He was the same age as Cassella. However, he didn't have the same American lineage. While Cassella grew up poor, Barranca had benefited from privilege. In today's world, this entitlement worked against him. The Church needed the poor. They were the ones who would tithe, who would obey, who would blindly adhere to any edict the Church made. The needy were the blind faithful. They were the army of tomorrow.

Barranca feared that perhaps there was something under the surface that prevented his own rise. That lover from Idaho that he took while at the University of Notre Dame – that sinewy young American who taught him so much about himself, about the human body, about love. How he still sometimes longed for his touch, even though they hadn't seen each other for decades. They had been discreet, but still: Did the Jesuits at Notre Dame turn a blind eye, knowing that they could hold the intelligence over him? Cassella had no such skeletons in his closet, at least that anyone knew about.

José Eusebio Barranca sat in his office reviewing his emails. More congratulations for Sixtus came in from leaders of war-torn Africa, from Muslim leaders in Malaysia and Indonesia, requesting an audience. Sixtus's trusted aide, Cardinal Richter, who was appointed general secretary of the Vatican, entered without knocking. He stood on legs so thin they were like stilts pegged at the hip. How could those rickety sticks even support his body?

Richter glared at the pile of papers on Barranca's plain, wooden desk. He addressed him in his brusque, German-accented Italian. "His Holiness needs a gift for the American president and his wife." Richter looked around the small room, the white walls, the simply framed pictures of Mother Theresa, Jesus, and Pope John Paul II.

So, he was relegated to being a personal shopper. "Of course. Anything in mind?"

"No idea. That's why we have come to you."

Barranca noted the use of the royal *we*. Richter couldn't control his imperious bearing. "When do you need it by?"

"Thursday."

It was Monday, and he had several days. He appreciated the advance notice.

"Make it personal. Something Foster would hold in esteem."

"We will ship this?"

"*I* will," Richter replied, correctly his impertinent use of the royal *we*. "You just need to find the right token. This is the Holy Father's first request of you. Please do not disappoint." He twisted his thin hips and exited the office.

Barranca knew that he was not in the pontiff's inner circle. But what made Sixtus appoint him to such an important post as secretary of state in the first place? Did he want to keep him close so that he could keep an eye on him? Or did he know that in such a position he could easily be made irrelevant?

Chapter 3

Barranca's mission was precarious. President Foster was fickle. A bit materialistic. Transactional. Something personal to him would be a luxury trinket one could find on the Via dei Condotti in Rome. Something anyone with enough money could buy. A high-end wallet; a lighter he could use to light up those Cuban cigars smoked in secret; an expensive Bulgari or Panerai watch that his son or daughter could pawn.

What would the First Lady appreciate? Of course, high fashion. Designer anything. She had no taste but knew how to look the part. They were both picture-perfect, the articulate American couple posing as regal laureates with a divine right to rule, WASPs to the end. The only thing the two would truly appreciate was another four-year term.

At midday, Barranca changed into street clothes. He preferred to roam the streets of Rome as an ordinary man. A navy polo shirt, gray slacks, a pair of handcrafted Belgian loafers – an indulgence, but one he felt was worth the expenditure. When he would trot off to Brussels to have them fitted, he'd buy extra pairs for his brothers and father, all made with molds that the shoemaker kept on file. He was determined that the Barranca men be eminently heeled.

José sauntered to the subway stop nearest the Vatican, passing a sundry line of elderly women walking their dogs while holding small plastic baggies to pick up their droppings. Seeing the dogs, he recalled his days at university back in Quito, when strays would roam the streets and deposit their delights on the sidewalks. As annoying as their turds were, he missed those dogs. They looked as healthy as the ones cared for by Rome's tony ladies who tugged at the fine leather leashes. While the canines of his homeland may not have had owners, they were loved.

As he hopped on the metro, he enjoyed the fact that no one had any clue who he was. While his name was mentioned in the paper, his face was not known. Besides, it was rather nondescript. The caramel tone of his skin blended well with the tones found in the Mediterranean. His chocolate brown eyes were hardly extraordinary. Pale skin. Besides, being a man of a certain age – in his late forties – he found that people barely paid attention to him.

Or so he thought.

A young man in gym gear graciously moved his legs to allow Barranca to sit next to him. The bank of seats by the door was designated for the handicapped or elderly. Barranca was reluctant to sit there, but he was tired from the walk. He wasn't getting as much exercise as he used to. The wines and flamboyant dinners were starting to take their toll on his once-athletic physique. He told himself that he would get up if a needy woman entered the rail car.

The train roared on, and soon, he took his exit at Termini station, the central train station where locals and tourists milled about, hustling around each other as they darted to and fro to find their next point of departure. Barranca would be taking the B line to Barberini. From there, he would walk to the American embassy, where he had an appointment with an attaché, Mr. Bersch. He knew he could easily take a cab for the trip. It would be fully paid for on his 'company' card. But he needed to stretch his legs, to let his mind wander, to cogitate on his mission. He knew God would lead him.

A man who had been riding on the same car as him – this man had entered the train car at the same time as him at Cipro station – stopped in his path. He seemed to growl something. He looked Eastern European. He was not well dressed. In fact, he had a bit of a homeless air. His hair was disheveled; his black beard was dark, with random, unkempt, gray whiskers.

Barranca tried to go around him, but the man put up his arm.

"Stop," he said in harshly accented Italian. He was carrying a newspaper against his side.

"Excuse me," Barranca replied politely. "I must be on my way."

The man put his hand on José's arm, grasping it tightly. "They are planning something."

"Yes, well, no thank you," Barranca replied, flustered.

"You mustn't let them get to America," the man said.

"Who?"

"I know who you are," the man said, squeezing his forearm vigorously.

"Who are you?" Barranca asked impatiently.

"I'm nobody," he said. "I'm just a fisherman."

The reference made Barranca think of the four fishermen whom Jesus surrounded himself at Lake Galilee, primary among them Peter, who was then known as Simon. "Please, I must be going."

Instantly, the man tumbled into him, a crowd of passersby rushing alongside them. The man took his newspaper and handed it to José. It was covered in blood. The man was bleeding profusely from the side and fell to the ground. A woman who passed by screamed as he fell to the floor. More people stopped around them, watching the man writhe in pain, taking his last breaths. Barranca was frozen in shock; he didn't know what to do. A young woman took him by the arm, gently pushing him away from the throng. "Come with me," she said.

Chapter 4

The woman had an American accent. She steered him to the doors of Termini station that led outside, where dozens of travelers were coming and going, many transporting luggage. "Don't turn around," she said. "Pretend nothing has happened."

"We have to help that man," Barranca said.

As he started to turn back, she pulled his arm. Her strength startled him. For such a slender woman, she was able to pull her into him with little effort.

"There is nothing we can do," she said. "The police will take care of it." She raised her hand to hail a cab. One stopped immediately. The advantages of being a blonde in her late twenties.

"Via del Moro in Trastevere," she told the cab driver in Italian.

"Where are we going?" Barranca asked.

"Someplace safe," she said.

"Who are you?" Barranca asked.

"Signore Barranca, I am Amanda."

"How do you know who I am?" José demanded, his voice tense.

"Is everything okay back there?" the taxi driver asked in Italian.

"*Sì tutto bene,*" Amanda said back in Italian. *All good.*

"I'm not okay!" José Eusebio retorted.

"Mr. Barranca," Amanda said in English. "I assure you are safe."

"I don't feel safe! I don't know you!"

"I can bring you to the police," the cabbie said.

"Yes, the police, please," José Eusebio shot back.

"The police are not necessary," Amanda said back in Italian. "There's a misunderstanding."

As the cab stopped at a light, Barranca quickly opened the door and rushed out.

"Goddamn it!" she said in English. She took a twenty-euro bill from her pocket and handed it to the cab driver. *"Grazie. Mi dispiace." Thank you. I'm sorry.* She rushed out the back door after Barranca. He was heading down an alleyway off the main road.

"Mr. Barranca, please," she called after him. "I'm here to protect you."

He started walking faster.

She had no trouble catching up to him.

He could hear her footsteps behind him, and he started to look into a doorway. He tried to open the door, but it was locked. She stood behind him. As he turned around, she held a gun to him.

Chapter 5

Staring at the gun pointed towards him, his mouth agape, Barranca stood, frozen. His limbs went numb.

"I will give you anything you want," he said to her. "Please don't hurt me."

"I'm not going to hurt you," Amanda answered. "I only need you to come with me." She lowered the gun. She could see him investigate around her, behind her, as if trying to scout an escape. "Don't run. You won't get away. I'm highly trained." She took out a card and handed it to him.

Amanda O'Brien. Special Attaché, American Embassy. A gold, embossed eagle was featured centered at the top. Braille lettering was stenciled in the card. He recognized the card as a legitimate business card from the embassy.

"You know Ambassador Perkins?" she asked. "I work for him."

"Prove it," he said.

She took out her cell phone. It was a small model, about half the size of typical cell phones. It folded in half, like those models from a decade or two ago. She pressed a few buttons and then handed the phone to Barranca.

"Amanda?" the voice answered.

It was a direct line to the ambassador.

Barranca didn't reply.

"Amanda, are you okay?"

"Excuse me, whom am I speaking with?" Barranca asked. He had met the ambassador previously, and he thought he recognized the voice, but he couldn't be sure.

"This is Ambassador Perkins. Is this Secretary Barranca?"

"It is."

"May I speak to Amanda?" he asked.

The cardinal handed the phone back to Amanda, who listened for a moment.

"Yes, everything is all right," she said. "We had a little bit of a disturbance. I will brief him." She hung up the phone.

"Do you believe me now?" She didn't attempt to conceal the exasperation in her voice.

* * *

Amanda hailed another cab and again, with hardly a wait, a cab came to retrieve her and the cardinal. They headed to Trastevere, a trendy neighborhood with shops and restaurants. She had the driver stop at a street corner near a cafe; then she and Barranca walked a couple of blocks into the residential area. She pressed a series of numbers on an intercom, and the front door buzzed them in.

"I really am running late," Barranca said, looking at his watch. He twisted his other hand over it, as if the twisting could alter, or turn back, time. The panic hadn't subsided. He wasn't used to this frantic pace, and the image of the dead man at Termini station still haunted him.

"You were going to the American embassy, were you not?" she asked while leading him through the door. The hallway was austere, completely white, about twenty-feet square. An interior wooden door stood opposite the front door. It looked heavy, and it had another intercom attached to the wall.

"How do you know?"

"You made an appointment with Attaché Bersch."

"Are you spying on me?" He paused, his eyes bearing into her. "Are you with the CIA?"

"You know I can't answer that. I'm with the American embassy. I'm a special attaché."

He laughed. "I know what that means."

She punched a dozen more numbers into the intercom, and the wooden door buzzed. "This is a safe house. We'll be free to speak here. I'll need your phone."

Chapter 6

Amanda O'Brien had joined the Central Intelligence Agency eight years ago, having recently graduated from Cornell University. Ever since she was a child, she had wanted to be a spy. She was an introvert; yet the possibility of the unknown, of being thrust into situations beyond her control, excited her. She had watched spy movies, spy TV series, read the novels of John Le Carre, Graham Greene, Helen MacInnes, and Frederick Forsyth. Most of what she watched and read featured men; women were often only in supporting roles. She didn't know what the future would hold for her, but as she approached her thirtieth year, she was hopeful. One day, she'd make a difference. She felt she had already done so in Afghanistan, where she recruited a young Afghan teenager who served as a conduit passing critical information to the Americans. As a result of the information, drone strikes were carried out causing the deaths of over a dozen terrorists. She received commendations for her work. Still, she knew she was merely beginning to scratch the surface of what she could accomplish.

She had been assigned to Rome practically against her will. It was supposed to be a vacation of sorts after having been posted for many years in Afghanistan and the Middle East. While her Arabic became flawless, the Agency felt that she needed a breather. Rome would be the location where she could unwind, lose herself in the impeccably simple but tasty cuisine, and perhaps begin to have some semblance of a social life.

Amanda would have none of it.

From the moment she arrived in Rome after spending a year back at Langley, she sought a new adventure. She was determined that whatever she undertook would have some meaning, some relevance, some way to change the world in which we lived. She was an idealist, but she was also relentlessly practical. When she learned that a highly enriched uranium had been sold by the Pakistanis to middlemen connected to Yemenis, and when she learned that this group had ties to Khalid Zahir of Kuwait, the oil tycoon who over the last several years had branched out into illicit arms purchases, her interest became piqued. When intelligence reported that the boat carrying the radioactive material was said to be coming to Italy and then to be transported among consumer goods to the United States, she became even more interested. When she learned that Zahir had funneled millions of dollars to support the election of Pope Sixtus VI, she felt that she was pursuing the most consequential case of her career. But she always felt that way. Everything she did was imbued with the essence that the world's future was at stake.

The safe house was adequately furnished in case any officer or subject needed to hide out for a few days, a week, even a month or two. The pantry cabinets in the kitchen were stocked with canned foods, many of them organic, which the station in Rome checked periodically for expiration dates. The team was known occasionally to take home cans of cannelloni beans, fine minestrone soups, and other assorted gourmet items and then make notes for their replenishment. The house was hardly used. Some officers thought of using it as a tryst pad, but they knew that it was monitored centrally at the station. Live feeds were recorded and kept for at least thirty days. Artificial intelligence software, trained to spot any unusual activity, scanned the recordings nightly. Today's meeting between Amanda and Barranca would be one such occurrence that it would flag.

She led Barranca to the kitchen, where she placed his turned-off cell phone in a Faraday bag which she retrieved from a drawer. The bag would prevent the cell phone from being picked up by nearby cell towers. She then placed the bag in a metal cabinet that was three inches thick. The magnetized cabinet would thwart any attempt to listen through the phone's microphone or watch through its camera lenses remotely.

"Could I have some water?" Barranca asked her. He was still holding the newspaper that the man at Termini station had given him.

"Of course." She opened the refrigerator door, noticing how well furnished the commercial-sized fridge was. Various European beers and wine spritzers lined the drawers. "Flat or sparkling?" She almost laughed as she asked the question.

"Flat, please."

She grabbed two bottles, one for each of them. "Let's sit down?" She handed him the glass bottle and went into the living room. She was careful not to turn her back to him, as she knew the bottle could be used as a weapon. Fully trained in taekwondo, she was prepared for an offensive move should he wish to challenge her. At the Farm, the CIA's training facility at Camp Peary in Virginia, she had routinely managed to take down men twice her weight with a pair of moves. And she never had to make the acquaintance of their testicles.

José didn't make any sudden moves. He sat on the sofa in the living room.

Amanda sat opposite him in a modern armchair. "What did that man give you?"

"Nothing," he said, shrugging.

She nodded to the newspaper in his hand. "What is that?"

"Oh, this newspaper? Nothing. It's nothing at all." He held it up, letting the paper unfold in landscape fashion before her. Blood covered the bottom quarter, which the man must have held against his side.

"There's blood on it," she said.

Turning to look at the paper, Barranca gasped. "I didn't even notice it."

"Can I take a look?"

He handed her the paper. She didn't touch the part with the blood, but she carefully turned the pages, inspecting the newsprint for any handwriting and, at the same time, watching to see if anything might fall from inside.

"What is it?" he asked.

She continued to turn the pages until the end. "Just a newspaper." She stopped to look at the story on the last page. A color picture of Sixtus graced half the page. Under it, chronological tables in Italian gave his life story. Pictures of him as a baby were displayed, along with his high school senior portrait. "Have you read this?" she asked.

"No. Why?"

"I don't know. Perhaps it contains something important. Some clue. The man apparently wanted you to have the paper for some reason."

"Maybe he was just bleeding and he dropped it. I was the closest to him."

"He was stabbed in front of you," Amanda said.

"I didn't see anyone stab him."

"We're checking the surveillance cameras. But we're certain he was stabbed intentionally. This was not a random act."

Barranca sat, shocked, his lips parting as his brow furrowed. How could he, the secretary of state of Vatican City, be involved with something like this? His mere presence at the scene could cause an international stir. Questions would be raised – such as, Why did he leave the scene so quickly? *What was he hiding?*

"He sought you out for a reason," Amanda said. "What was it that he said to you?"

"Nothing."

"Nothing? You exchanged words, didn't you?"

"Yes, but nothing of importance."

"Come now, cardinal. You must remember what he said."

"He said, 'Don't let them get to America.' Barranca corrected himself. "No. He said, 'You mustn't let them get to America."

"Who did he mean by *them*?"

"I have no idea."

"Is anyone from the church planning on going? Is Sixtus?"

"At some point, I'm sure he will. But nothing is planned for the moment."

Amanda noted that Barranca's name was mentioned in the article, along with General Secretary Richter. "What's your relationship with Cardinal Richter?"

"Professional."

"Professional-professional? Or cordial?"

"Merely professional. I wouldn't say we see eye to eye on many things."

"Like what?"

"The power of the papacy. The ability of the church to forgive sins. Modern reform. The usual."

She knew the answers to the questions she was asking. She was testing him as to how truthful he'd be to her. Perhaps he knew this and was answering in kind. "Is it true that you're in favor of women becoming ordained as priests?"

"It's His Holiness's decision. I don't really have a position on the matter."

"Surely, if you were pope, you would change things."

"But I am not."

"Yet," she said.

"It's unlikely I ever will be. Sixtus is young. He will live a long time."

"Unless someone wants to assassinate him."

"Is that what you think that man wanted? To kill His Holiness?"

"I don't know. I was hoping you could shed some light on things."

"I'm afraid I can't." He exhaled. "I really must be going. Is there anything else you need from me?"

"Just a few more questions," she said. "Why did you take the train?"

"I like to walk. I don't get much exercise. I'm trying to get more sun, too. I'm quite pale as you can see."

She could see that his skin was indeed quite washed out. "Don't you stroll through the gardens at the Vatican?"

"Not as much as I would like. Are you insinuating that I met that man on purpose?"

"I don't know," she said. "Did you?"

"Of course not," he scoffed. "I've never seen him in my life."

"He's an Albanian citizen," she said.

"He said he was a fisherman."

"He boarded a boat and landed in Brandisi. We tracked him here to Rome."

"Why were you watching him?"

"Because he contacted us," she said.

Chapter 7

"He contacted you?" José Eusebio Barranca asked with an incredulous tone.

"Yes. I'm trying to learn why he was following you."

"He was *following* me?"

"He was tracking you from the Vatican. You didn't notice him, did you?"

"I thought I recognized him when I saw him at Termini Station. I didn't think anything of it. It seemed like pure coincidence."

Amanda decided to take a risk. She would lay some of her cards on the table. "What do you know of Khalid Zahir?"

"The oil tycoon?"

"Yes, from Kuwait." She would say no more. She wanted to see what Barranca would reveal.

"Even though he is a Muslim, he is a friend of the church. He supports Sixtus's mission to spread Catholicism."

"Has he been to see the pope?"

"No."

"Has he called?"

"To congratulate him, of course."

"Why do you say, '*of course*'?"

"Well, naturally, they have a long history, a relationship that goes way back."

"How far back?"

"Don't you know this?"

"Know what?"

"The history between them?"

"I don't." In part, she was lying. She knew that Zahir was a strong supporter of Sixtus, but she couldn't assume to know whatever Barranca did.

"They say that Zahir has been funding Sixtus's rise through the Catholic Church. That he supported his family, gave him grants, allowed him to pursue his life-long, theological studies. That sort of thing."

"Who are *they*?"

"The other cardinals, of course. Naturally, some of it is gossip. Many are jealous. One doesn't know for sure, you know?" He took a sip of his water. "Zahir's aide, Ahmed Bensaïd, has been more on the frontlines, you could say. He handles most of his business with Sixtus. He visited Sixtus today."

Amanda had read a profile of Bensaïd. He was the consummate diplomat, educated at Oxford, born to a wealthy family in Jordan, unmarried with no children. Rumored to be homosexual, he spoke several languages; besides Arabic and English, he was fluent in Spanish, French, and Italian. He had homes on the Cote d'Azur in Southern France, apartments in Amman, Paris, Rome, London, and New York. His net worth was estimated at over five hundred million dollars. His family had been wealthy, but not nearly that wealthy. They had perhaps a few million dollars when he was born. Now, they were worth a hundred times that amount, primarily due to their connections to

Khalid Zahir and the business opportunities he presented. Bensaïd flew around the world on a Dussault Falcon 10X, one of Zahir's private jets.

"What did they talk about?" Amanda asked.

"I don't know. I wasn't invited to the meeting. However, I was tasked to find a gift for the U.S. president shortly thereafter."

"That's why I was heading to the U.S. embassy. I wanted to get some more ideas." At that moment, his cell phone buzzed. He answered the call, which was from Attaché Bersch, his contact at the embassy. Bersch was asking if he was on his way. Barranca turned to Amanda. "I'm late for my appointment with Signor Bersch. He's expecting me."

"Cancel," she said. "I know exactly what you should give him."

Chapter 8

Jordan Harrison strolled out of the gym in Foggy Bottom, the neighborhood in Washington, D.C. that was home to George Washington University and wasn't far from his office at the Federal Bureau of Investigation. Four to five days a week, after finishing his duties as Special Agent at the FBI, he would go to the gym, both to decompress and to work on his physique. He was in phenomenal shape – six feet two, 190 pounds. He was a one-time, though second-string, tight end in college. His quasi-action-figure build, achieved naturally and without any stimulants beyond caffeine, garnered admiration from men and women alike. As a thirty-one-year-old Black man, often wearing custom-tailored suits that couldn't help but emphasize his broad shoulders, he frequently got glances from young ladies who would make excuses to ask him questions. Questions like the time, where he was from, whether he had a girlfriend, whether he was gay.

Five-thirty. Atlanta. No. No.

Usually there were additional questions. Where'd you go to school?

What brought you up to D.C.?

Georgia Tech. Work.

They'd say, "You must be smart. What do you do for work?"

He wouldn't mention that he was an FBI agent. He didn't want to attract attention and advertise to the world what he was doing. He'd say he worked in the tech field, on databases. That usually shut down the conversation about work.

If he found the girl particularly attractive, he'd sometimes add a little more. Such as, "I'm from a small town near Tennessee."

"A small-town boy!" they'd coo.

He knew how to charm.

As he made his way back to his apartment, he received an unexpected text from his boss, Larry. Larry never bothered him outside the office. Larry was in his early fifties and nearing retirement; thinning, graying hair; barrel-chested and barrel-waisted, from ever-increasing Low T and a steady intake of beer. "Call me ASAP," the message read.

Jordan saw that Larry had sent the message about forty-five minutes ago, while he was inside the gym. The coverage there was notoriously spotty.

He dialed Larry. "Hey boss," he said.

"I was wondering when I was going to hear from you." Normally, Larry had a sheepish demeanor, but this evening, something had ticked him off.

Jordan, as the youngest person and lowest-ranking member of the team, adopted his usual deferential tone. "Sorry, sir. I didn't get your message until just now. I was at the gym."

"I need you to go on assignment."

The idea galvanized him. He hadn't traveled outside of the Beltway since he had joined the Bureau. "Where to?"

"Spain."

"Spain?" Jordan asked incredulously. While he worked in counterterrorism, the FBI was a domestic agency and most of its investigations centered on local threats.

"You got a problem with that?"

"No, not at all. I've never been." Jordan wasn't accustomed to such a crusty Larry.

"I need you there tomorrow. There's a plane tonight. Be on it."

* * *

"Forget Bersch," Amanda said to Barranca. "Go back to the Vatican and get something there."

"Some of those items are quite priceless."

"You don't need to go that far. But President Foster and his wife appreciate history. American and European history. They like to think of themselves in the center of it all, like we're at a crossroads in our history."

"I see," Cardinal Barranca said. "Perhaps a papal bull that he could frame. It would probably be a reproduction."

"Something related to Martin Luther would be nice. The Fosters are Lutheran, after all." Foster was, in fact, America's first Lutheran president.

"I don't know why I didn't think of that. Thank you so much." Barranca seemed genuinely thankful and happy to be in Amanda's presence for the first time since he had met her. "What will happen to that man?" he asked.

"We're investigating it. I'll keep you posted."

"So, this isn't the last time we'll meet?"

"I'm afraid we're just beginning."

Chapter 9

Jordan Harrison took the red eye from Dulles Airport in Virginia to Madrid, arriving in the early morning. He didn't have clear orders on what to do or where to go – Larry told him that he would receive further instructions on arrival.

Even at this early morning hour, the airport – Europe's second largest behind Paris's Charles de Gaulle – was a beehive of activity. A driver with a placard containing the initials "J.H." greeted him. The town car escorted him to Old Town, a central neighborhood not far from the Royal Palace, the largest royal palace in Europe. The car stopped on a quiet tree-lined street, where a row of town houses stood. The driver waited for Jordan to exit, not saying anything.

"Is this it?" Jordan asked.

"This is the address," he answered.

Jordan handed the driver a tip. The driver waived it off. Jordan wondered whether the American five-dollar bill turned him off. He wasn't aware that the driver was employed by the *Centro Nacional de*

Inteligencia, Spain's domestic and foreign intelligence agency, which was a cross between the FBI and the CIA.

He took his bag and exited the car. In a moment, he heard the front door buzz. He understood this was his clue to open the door and enter.

* * *

Sitting at the foot of his bed in his modest room in the private quarters of the Vatican, José Eusebio Barranca scoured the daily newspapers. First *La Repubblica,* then *Il Messaggero,* then *Corriere della Sera.* He was trying to find a mention of the man who was killed at Termini Station. He looked through page after page, column after column; there was no mention. It was as if he didn't exist. Stabbings in Rome were common, but they still received coverage. Was the man that non-consequential, that unimportant?

Barranca opened his laptop and searched the internet. Again, there was no mention of the man.

A crowd had gathered at Termini. A woman had screamed. Surely, the police must have come. But he didn't remember hearing any sirens. People saw the blood. The outside of the newspaper he had given him was covered in blood. Amanda had taken it. Was that her way of erasing the incident, scraping it entirely from having ever occurred?

José Eusebio peered out the window that overlooked the courtyard. Amanda had said the man had been following him. Why? He wanted to tell him something. He had been tracking him from the time he left the Vatican. But he had waited to approach him until he reached Termini. Why didn't he approach him earlier? He had patiently marked time until he was far away from the Vatican.

"You mustn't let them get to America." The man's words echoed through Barranca. Why? Who? Was it someone at the Vatican? There was more than one person. It was a *they,* not a *he* or a *she.*

José Eusebio went to his closet and looked at the sport jacket he was wearing yesterday. Some blood smeared against the lapel. It trailed toward the pocket. Then José placed his hand in the pocket of the jacket where he found something unexpected.

Chapter 10

President Foster sat at the Resolute desk in the Oval Office, surrounded by several advisers – his chief of staff, the national security adviser, the secretary of defense, and the head of the CIA.

Valerie Cohen, the national security adviser, sat on a sofa, looking toward the president. Foster got up from his desk as he perused a report and sat amongst his advisers on a Federal-style armchair. Cohen spoke:

"Sir, we've sent an agent to monitor the shipment that we discussed yesterday."

"I don't understand how it could have fallen in the wrong hands."

"We understand the purchasers have very deep pockets. They have paid a billion dollars for the materials."

"Fully assembled?"

"Not completely. That will take a little more effort. But we estimate it's something they can accomplish in a matter of a couple of days with the right expertise."

"And who did you say is behind this?" the president asked.

"We suspect it's a group aligned with Islamic radicals. It's being funded by Khalid Zahir," Cohen said.

"Isn't he a friendly?"

"He was. But you know how times change."

"What's in it for him?"

"We don't know."

"Is he going to attack Israel?"

"That's the typical play. None of those Arabs really want Israel in their midst anyway, even if they don't fully support the Palestinians."

Foster thought for a moment. "You need to make sure those weapons can't be launched against the state of Israel. Do whatever it takes. Blow them up in the middle of the Mediterranean. I don't care who the collateral damage is."

"These materials can be unstable," Secretary of Defense Orozco said. Orozco was a first-generation American who had risen to the rank of general before being appointed to head the DoD. "We could trigger a nuclear explosion in civilian territory."

"I thought they weren't operational!" the president roared.

"Yes, that's correct," Orozco explained patiently. "They can't be deployed. However, they can explode. And that explosion can be substantial. We're talking about the mother of all bombs."

"Well, fuck me," Foster said.

* * *

Jordan Harrison entered the townhouse on Avenida La Celestina in the heart of Madrid, closing the door behind him. The interior of the apartment was completely quiet. The space was well furnished; old, Spanish master paintings – replicas, of course – lined the hallways. Antique furniture – Baroque in style – adorned the living room. The floor-to-ceiling curtains were drawn. He turned on a switch, which lit a silver chandelier hanging from the center of the fifteen-foot ceiling.

His cell phone rang. He recognized the number as a European area code. "Hello," he said, answering.

"Jordan?" a woman's voice asked.

"Yes."

"I see you've arrived. My name is Amanda O'Brien. I'll be your contact. I'm afraid I couldn't be there in person. Perhaps you could log onto your computer, and we can do a face-to-face call. I'll send you the link via text."

"Okay," he said, hanging up. He looked around the room. Were there cameras watching him?

* * *

José Eusebio held a piece of paper that was folded into a small square. He didn't recognize the paper at all. He noticed a dried, bloody thumbprint on it. He placed his jacket back on the hanger and put it in the closet. He sat at the foot of his bed and unfolded the paper. One corner of the paper was stuck together on account of the blood. He carefully examined the paper, which was a letter-sized document titled "Bill of Lading." The contents were listed as an electromagnet scope and various parts. The destination was Johns Hopkins University School of Medicine in Baltimore, Maryland. A large warning was noted under the contents: "Contains radioactive devices. Proper handling required."

Is this what that CIA officer Amanda O'Brien was looking for? Should he call her and let her know what he found?

The place of origin on the notice was listed as the University of Granada in Spain. Then he noticed something peculiar: the transmittal letter had today's date on it. If it was just dated today, how would the man at Termini Station have had it, yesterday? It had to have been printed ahead of time and post-dated. It was as if the shipment was planned ahead of time.

José Eusebio knew he had something important, but he didn't know why the transmittal letter was important. An electromagnet scope – what was that exactly? The man at Termini Station intentionally wanted him to have the notice. He had made a point of obfuscating the transfer of the paper, concealing the trade by pushing the bloody newspaper in José's hand.

José could put the paper back in his jacket, but his intuition told him the paper wouldn't be safe there. Someone might come looking for it. Or worse, someone might send the jacket to dry cleaning, and the paper would be lost, thrown away or ruined by the laundering chemicals. He needed to hide the piece of paper. There were few places in his room where he could hide things – that was by design. He could place it in his Bible. That might the first place the nosy cardinals and nuns who were asked to spy on him would look. He could take a picture of it on his cell phone and destroy the paper, flushing it in the toilet. That was an option. He would ponder more before taking that step. He could fold it back up, not as small as it was previously but about two or three times its size. Then he could fit it under the wooden post of his bed. He folded the paper, lifted the bed by its post, and placed the paper on the rug where the bedpost would fit over it. Yes, that worked. This would keep the paper safe from prying eyes, at least for a day or two.

So he hoped.

* * *

Jordan Harrison had unpacked his laptop and launched the secure, Zoom-like app that the National Security Agency had deployed on government computers for staff of the NSA, FBI, and CIA. All communications on the app were heavily encrypted. Audio-jamming software was built into the application so that if someone tried to surreptitiously record a meeting, even via cell phone, the contents would be scrambled and undecipherable, even by a supercomputer that could spend a week trying to reduce all the added noise and sound distortions. He carefully entered the fifteen-digit ID that Amanda had texted him into the app to connect.

A ringtone sounded, and within seconds, Amanda connected. She was much younger than he had thought – about his age. He was used to dealing with mostly white men in their fifties, and the sight of a thirtyish, attractive blonde was a welcome change.

"Hi, Jordan," she said. "I'm Amanda."

"Nice to meet you. I wasn't expecting to be contacted so soon."

"We don't like to waste time around here. Sorry for all the secrecy, but I didn't want to inform the home team what was going on. Leaks, you know?"

The frank way she talked surprised him. "You're with the Bureau?"

"No. The Agency."

"The Agency? The CIA?"

"Yes. You're at one of our safe houses. This is a CIA mission. You're kind of on-loan to us. To me."

"Why is that?"

"There's a domestic connection to what's happening. Or so I think. Since we can't operate within U.S. borders, we had to loop in the Bureau."

"I see. I'm not accustomed to operating outside the States."

"Hopefully, you won't be here long."

"Can you tell me what's going on?"

"We have information that a nuclear weapon is being transported to the United States. We need to intercept it."

"Where is it?"

"We don't know. That's why I need you, to help me locate it. I suspect it's still here in Europe and will soon be on its way across the Atlantic."

"It's being shipped by boat?"

"Yes. That's always the safest way. The easiest way to avoid detection. It can be slipped into the cargo of some commercial ship."

"Is that all we have to go on?"

"I'm afraid so. We expect it's on a smaller ship now and will be transferred to a larger vessel in the next day or two. That will make its voyage across the pond safer."

"Do we know where it's headed?"

"Your guess is as good as mine. I'm guessing somewhere along the Eastern seaboard."

"That doesn't give us anything concrete. Why Madrid?" he asked.

"Good question. I don't suspect you'll be there long. Our intelligence tells us the boat went from Montenegro across the Adriatic to Italy. If it's on the way to the United States, it will either make a long trip through the Suez Canal, which is risky given all the military patrols there. It's more likely it's going to pass through the Mediterranean to Spain and then go through Gibraltar before heading to the States."

"I'll be heading south?"

"Yes, you'll appreciate the weather there."

"Who's behind this?"

"We don't know. The money seems to have come from Khalid Zahir. He's an Arab billionaire. His money is in Kuwaiti oil. He's only trafficked in small arms sales before, mostly to help the Houthis and Hamas. By small arms, I mean the usual Kalashnikov assault rifles, sniper rifles, grenades, and PKP machine guns from Russia. The typical tools of the trade. Nothing extraordinary. It's unusual that he seems to have stepped up his game. Moving into nuclear is a bold move for anyone."

"How do you know it's him?"

"That's something we need to discuss in person."

"This is a secure line, isn't it?"

"It is. But it involves highly sensitive intelligence. The windows in the safe house are protected from eavesdropping. There's even a transmitter on the roof to scramble communications. But even with that, I can't risk our sources and methods. I have a couple of things I need to wrap up here. I'm in Rome, did I tell you?"

Jordan had assumed she was in Spain. "No."

"We'll be able to meet in a day or two. It's your pick where to go. Even shot between the port at Valencia or Algeciras. Algeciras is near Málaga, in the south near Gibraltar."

"You did say the weather's nice down south, right?"

* * *

As José Eusebio Barranca made his way to the Collections Room in the Vatican – the vast, library-sized archive that contained tens of thousands of historical artifacts related to the Catholic Church and which rivaled the top museums of the world – the Louvre, the British Museum, the Smithsonian – his mind sifted over his find. Johns

Hopkins University School of Medicine, the University of Granada, the electromagnet scope. He didn't know what to make of it all. And then meeting Amanda, a CIA agent. Having practically been kidnapped by her. He didn't like this world of gray. The only unknowns he could endure were those at the level of God, faith, the spirit, and life everlasting. Murder – the ultimate sin – was not in his vernacular. A man of the cloth, he had little interest in worldly affairs, despite being the Vatican's secretary of state. Perhaps that is why they chose him. They knew he didn't really care about politics and foreign relations. He could be controlled. Yes, that is why Richter allowed Sixtus to put him in that post. He would be a minor inconvenience, someone they could push into the shadows, control like a puppet obeying his master's commands. Whenever he'd voice an opinion, it would have the force of a peep from a mouse. They knew him well. He was starting to know himself as well.

Barranca reached the basement of the Vatican's administration building, the Palazzo del Santo Uffizio. A guard was posted at the entrance. He was a member of the Swiss Guard, the security force that protected the pope and Vatican City since the time of Julius II in the sixteenth century. The Swiss Guard was the world's oldest army, and the personnel assigned to the Holy See were all practicing Catholics. They were known for their loyalty to the pope, their discipline, and their bravery.

Barranca made his way through the corridors where expansive metal storage cabinets twenty feet tall stood. Nothing was under lock and key, and there were no cameras in the Collections Room. Word of honor was the code, and the few that had unfettered access – cardinals, primarily – wouldn't dare steal an item, unless, of course, they had been instructed to do so, perhaps to hide some incriminating piece of Catholic history. But for the most part, the documents and artifacts that were stored were harmless, having meaning only to the clergy, theologians, and historians. Yet for that audience, that meaning had the equivalency of life and death.

Barranca proceeded past the file cabinets to the area where museum-like glass and wood cases housed additional items that had more visual appeal than yellowed pieces of paper. Sometimes, foreign dignitaries would receive private tours of the collection, showcasing armor from the Middle Ages, jewels that rivaled the British crown jewels, artwork from Michelangelo, DaVinci, all the way to Picasso and de Kooning – artwork that the Vatican didn't want to display to the public but wanted to flaunt to those it wished to impress. In many cases, the framed art was piled up against each other amidst statues by Rodin, Bernini, Koons, and Polykleitos. Once, a British prince was said to have commented, "These works are absolutely priceless." The cardinal guiding the tour replied, "Everything has its price." Soon, after a wire was received, one of the Kandinskys made its way to a palace in Scotland, allegedly acquired from "a private collection." In turn, the papal financial advisors, acting on a tip, used the proceeds to make an early investment in Nvidia, making over a billion dollars profit from a mere twenty-million-dollar stock purchase.

A second security officer, also a member of the Swiss Guard, strolled through the area, avoiding eye contact with Barranca while observing him nonetheless. The lighting in the cavernous hall was dim, to limit potential damage to the collection. Museum lights shone indirect light near some items. The air was temperate, perfectly moderated, and free of any moisture.

José Eusebio made his way to the displays which contained historical items related to Martin Luther. Unlike the artwork stored in every nook and cranny, as if these temporal curios could come and go as easily as ladies talking of Michelangelo, all the items in the cases bore index cards and were strictly catalogued, noting the date of the item and its historical significance. Many of the items were letters or small works of art. A copy of the *Exsurge Domine,* the papal bull that threatened to excommunicate Luther if he did not recant his heresies within sixty days, was framed in a locked Lucite cabinet. Among his heresies were his criticisms that the indulgences that people bought from the clergy could rightfully absolve them of sin. When Luther refused to denounce his writings, he was, several months later, excommunicated. After several minutes of searching and reading through the artifacts related to the bull, Barranca found an item that intrigued him. It was a letter written by Cardinal Cajetan, who was ordered to arrest Luther if he did not recant. Barranca read the letter carefully. Cajetan wrote to Pope Leo X that Luther's arrest might spark demonstrations and further resistance to the Church, causing the spread of Lutheranism in Saxony, the area of the Holy Roman Empire where he lived and preached. The letter was dated June 30, 1520, two weeks after *Exsurge Domine* was issued.

Barranca had never heard of this part of the story. He had been taught that the church was united in their effort to oppose Luther. The letter contradicted that thesis.

He felt he had what he was looking for. He anticipated that the item would hold special significance for President Foster. The letter would show that within the Catholic Church, there was a call for some leniency toward Luther. It was a prized possession, and while the original letter would not be given to Foster, Barranca would have Church scribes reproduce it faithfully. He knew the perfect place: the well-trained hands of the Franciscan friars at the Convent of Amadori ai Frati outside of Florence in Tuscany.

As he took the letter from the case, he heard a noise on the other side of the room. He looked, expecting to see the security officer. The Swiss Guard was gone. Barranca heard the noise again. Then the lights were turned off, and he was left in darkness. "Hello?" he called out.

He heard footsteps. Soft footfalls stamping the concrete floor. "Hello?" he called again. "Who is there?"

There was no answer.

In the dark, Barranca shifted against the curio cabinet and made his way back to the entrance. Across the room, he saw a dim light flash toward him and then disappear. It was as if someone was trying to light the room to see where he was going. He heard a bang, as if the person had unexpectedly bumped into something.

"Who is there?" Barranca shouted.

Still, there was no answer.

He anxiously made his way around the room. He bumped into a cabinet, and he hurt his toe. Alarmed, he withheld the cry he wanted to emit. Someone was watching him. Who could it have been? Was it Richter? Would he have turned the lights off on him, to punish him? To force him to find his way in the dark, as punishment for being around?

His blood pressure rose. He made his way toward the wall. There, he was able to follow it until he reached a large cabinet. Another sharp noise, and his panic heightened. He tried to open the cabinet door, but it was stuck. The clanging echoed through the room. He quickly stepped along the wall. All he could think of was that man in Termini Station who had been stabbed. He could see him hand him the newspaper. Perhaps someone knew he had given him something. Perhaps they had already found it under the foot of his bed.

His breathing heavy, he reached another cabinet. He unlatched the door; the handle didn't move. He tugged and shoved it back and forth. The rattling clanged in the hall. He tried to make less noise as he pulled on the handle. The door opened. He let out a sigh of relief. He stepped inside.

As he stepped inside the cabinet, he could feel long hair covering his face. It seemed like a wig. He brushed the hair out of his eyes, and he stepped back, letting his head fit under the wig as if he was placing it on his head. He quickly closed his eyes, attempting to slow his breathing. As he stood in the closet, he realized he had dropped the letter! It must be on the floor outside the cabinet. Christ, he thought. How had he dropped it? Now, the man pursuing him would certainly know where he was hiding. He closed his eyes again and said a short prayer. "Please God. Do not allow them to get me. Please spare me. I am a faithful servant. Protect me."

The door to the cabinet opened and Barranca opened his eyes. He screamed. He couldn't control himself. "God no!" he shouted.

A boy looked at him curiously. He was about fifteen years old. He was wearing a red robe and a white surplice over it. "Your Excellency. I'm sorry. I didn't mean to scare you."

Barranca could feel tears rushing down his face. While they were tears of fear, a slight sense of joy overcame him. He didn't recognize the boy, but he had a sweet, angelic face. He had to have been an altar boy, one of a couple of dozen that the papacy employed for helping hands throughout the year. They served as interns.

"What are you doing here? Why did you turn out the lights?"

The boy held out his hand. "I was asked to bring you to see His Holiness?"

"Why are the lights off?" Barranca demanded.

"I don't know. They just turned off when I entered the room."

"Get them back on."

The boy knelt. "You dropped something."

"Don't touch that!" Barranca hollered. "Get me some light!"

In an instant, as if God himself were overhearing his command, the lights in the Collections Room came back on. The Swiss Guard yelled from the entryway. "Sorry about that, your Excellency. We had a power generator fail. All is working now."

As the boy looked back up at the secretary of state, he could see a large wet stain on the crotch of his scarlet cassock. The cardinal had pissed himself!

"Goddamn it!" Barranca said.

The boy's face turned pale. He had never heard a cardinal curse before.

Chapter 11

From the Madrid safe house, Jordan sent a message to Larry on Rebar, the secure, NSA messaging app that they used. Rebar had been developed in the post-Snowden years to track cell phone data. The development team had wanted to call the application *Rebus,* but that name had been used for an obsolete and unrelated program. So they chose *Rebar* when the project manager saw steel reinforcements being laid in concrete during a construction project at NSA's Fort Meade headquarters. She had asked what the steel was used for and learned that it helped create tension and forced the concrete to adhere better. The name stuck.

"Arrived in Madrid. Heard from my contact, Amanda. Heading to Algeciras," he wrote.

He could see that the message was received, and, through the animated ellipses that danced in a bubble, that Larry was typing. "Keep me updated" came the reply.

Short and sweet. It was just like Larry not to offer any warmth or ask questions. Jordan doubted Larry even knew who Amanda was. Jordan didn't consider him a force multiplier.

Jordan debated whether to unpack any items. He decided he'd only change clothes. He took off his shirt and tie; his suit jacket was already hanging on the back of a chair. He customarily wore suits when he traveled, to give himself a professional air to counteract any potential annoyances he might encounter. He put on a T-shirt. He researched the trains that departed for Algeciras from Madrid and found they ran on a regular schedule, about twice an hour. He could leave at any time. He took another glance around the room, looking for hidden cameras. He didn't spot any, but he was sure they were lurking behind the antique clocks on the mantel, on the lights hovering over artwork, in the edges of the curtain rods, or dozens of other places to keep a bird's-eye view of all goings-on. He changed into a pair of jeans, not bothering to go into the bathroom, where he assumed there would be no cameras. Let them look, he thought. It wouldn't be the first time the powers-that-be saw a man in boxer briefs.

* * *

Cardinal Barranca had also gone to his room to change robes before meeting Sixtus. On his way back to his room, he had held the letter in front of his crotch so that no one saw the pee stain. He was embarrassed when he had to hand the letter to the security guard so that he could check out the document. He hoped the Swiss Guard hadn't noticed the wet spot.

He made his way to Sixtus's office. Once there, the archbishop who served as one of his chief assistants told him to wait. The archbishop sat quietly, reading his Bible. Barranca was reminded of Pope John XXIII's comment when asked how many people worked at the Vatican. Rather than giving a number, as in "about 3,000," he answered, "About half."

After a couple of minutes, the phone rang, and the archbishop picked up. "He's here." Then he hung up. "He's waiting for you in the courtyard."

Terrific, José Eusebio thought. He was already late from having changed; now, he was just sitting around. The pontiff wouldn't be pleased to have been kept waiting.

José made his way outside. The weather was blissful – sunny and warm. Warblers, sparrows, and robins flurried in the olive and lemon trees and bougainvillea that dotted the plaza.

He saw Sixtus sitting on a cement bench next to Richter. Of course, Cardinal Richter would be there with him. A private meeting was out of the question.

He bowed before the pope, who held out his hand. He expected Barranca to kiss his ring. This was a new behest. The cardinal dutifully obeyed, and he noticed a small smile creep over Richter's lips as he watched Barranca bend down.

Such a pompous, power-hungry man, thought José Eusebio.

"What have you found for Foster?" Sixtus asked.

He had just given him the assignment and already expected results! Did he know that he had had the run-in at Termini Station, where a man had been killed? Did he even care? No, he only wanted what he wanted. "I found a letter that I think will be of value. It's from Cardinal Cajetan, telling Leo X that he didn't want to arrest Luther."

"Disobeying the pope?" Sixtus scoffed.

Richter joined in with a soft rebuff.

"Cajetan felt it would cause further schisms in Saxony. I don't agree, but..."

"I don't care whether you agree or not," Sixtus interjected. "I don't need a history lesson, least of all by you."

Barranca felt his patience tested. "President Foster would appreciate such a gesture, as he is a Lutheran."

"I know he's a Lutheran!" Sixtus rejoined.

"Perhaps it is a wise choice," Richter said. "It would appease him to some degree and show that we're not afraid of the past."

"We should have arrested and executed Luther," Sixtus said adamantly.

"I couldn't agree more," said Richter. "But it might behoove us to take a more neutral stance with Foster, at least for the moment."

"Politics," Sixtus said derisively. "We have God on our side."

"As always," Richter acquiesced.

"You're not giving him the original," Sixtus said to Barranca.

"No, of course not. I'll have a copy made."

"I need it tomorrow."

"That will be impossible, Your Holiness. I haven't sent it to the scribes yet."

"What are you waiting for?"

Barranca stood with his mouth agape. Sixtus eyed him, thinking that the cardinal might say something. "That is all," he said dismissively.

Barranca knew that he was being excused. Richter seemed to enjoy watching him being heeled. He walked back toward his office. It was already late afternoon. As much as he wanted to investigate the bill of lading originating out of Granada, Spain, he knew where he had to go.

Chapter 12

Jordan Harrison had taken an early train from Madrid to Algeciras. While on the train, he made reservations at a hotel in the center of the city. He sent Amanda a text via Rebar when he was en route. "I'll text you when I arrive," he wrote.

She replied quickly. "I'll try to make it there tomorrow."

* * *

Cardinal Barranca hailed one of the Jesuit priests who were assigned to the Vatican. They were younger men, in their early twenties, many of them students of history, philosophy, and theology that the church would place as professors in universities worldwide. They mostly had their days to themselves, to study, research, and write. But today, Barranca had a chore for one of them. He wanted to be driven to Florence.

The papacy had a fleet of cars available. As secretary of state, Barranca had his choice. He selected a BMW sedan, a 7-series. "Make sure it's gas," he told the priest. "We don't have time to recharge."

The drive took a little over three hours, not including a stop they made for lunch at a delicious trattoria in Orvieto. He learned the Jesuit priest was Mexican American and named Alejandro. They spoke Spanish during the entire ride. He was studying for a doctorate in philosophy at the Pontifical Gregorian University in Rome, a Jesuit institution. The university's alumni included seventeen popes and about a third of the current College of the Cardinals. During much of the ride, José Eusebio's mind was on the bill of lading and a feeling that he should have gone to Granada, Spain to investigate. As they arrived on the outskirts of Florence, he asked Alejandro to stop for a rest. They took the next exit off the highway and were led to a small vineyard. "This is fine," José Eusebio said. When the car pulled over, he explained that he was going to stretch his legs. He told Alejandro to go inside and buy some wine. The Jesuit scholar obeyed.

José walked outside the vineyard's main office and tasting area. He took out his cell phone and dialed Amanda, using the telephone number she had given him. "Hello, Amanda?" he said when she answered.

"Cardinal?" she responded.

"Yes. You told me to contact you if I learned something."

"What is it?"

At that moment, a car pulled up behind him and two men quickly emerged from the car, a late-model, black Mercedes sedan. They pointed submachine guns at him.

Chapter 13

Within a matter of moments, José Eusebio was silently ordered, via the men's hand motions, to drop his phone. He slowly bent down to place it on the ground. He did not hang up the line.

"Cardinal?" Amanda said. "Are you there?"

One of the men motioned for José to come to them. He proceeded to walk toward them on the paved driveway. As he walked, he turned toward the entrance of the tasting room, looking for Alejandro, his Jesuit chauffeur. There was no sign of him.

The other man went to pick up the cardinal's cell phone. With gloves covering his hands, he disconnected the call. Then he turned the phone off. While it was shutting down, he removed the SIM card.

The men ushered Barranca into the backseat of the Mercedes. They proceeded to sit in the front of the car. The sedan quickly sped off.

Alejandro emerged from the tasting room holding a box containing several bottles of wine. He looked around, perplexed, wondering where the cardinal had gone. He caught a glimpse of the sedan as it disappeared beyond a hill on the winding country road.

* * *

Amanda, who had been in Bari when she received the call from Barranca, stood, hanging onto her phone while she watched the boats in the harbor. What had happened to the cardinal? He didn't hang up on her immediately, though she had heard nothing after he stopped talking. She had driven to Bari that morning, acting on information that the boat carrying the radioactive weapon might have landed there from Montenegro. She was waiting to catch up with a Signore Puzzi, a local merchant that invariably was on the payroll of the Mafia as well as the CIA. She opened the Rebar application on her phone. She had been tracking Barranca for days. It showed his location at a vineyard in Impruneta. The *Fattoria Fedele.* The Faithful Farm.

She zoomed in on the location for Impruneta. She saw that it was on the outskirts of Florence. What was Barranca doing there?

She looked around the harbor. She had been looking forward to her day trip to Bari. She recalled hearing about the city in the movie *The Bridges of Madison County.* Meryl Streep's character was from Bari, and while it had a certain romantic, Old World charm, the area of the port had an industrial and desolate air. Exhaust from boats and cars passing on the street filled the air with semi-toxic fumes. Municipal garbage cans overflowed with refuse. Sad-looking men – some of them Italian, some immigrants – who had lost their way idled along the streets, in search of something. Drugs? Alcohol? A woman? Some respect? Sympathy perhaps. Amanda pretended not to see them, not because she didn't care, but because she didn't want to engage with them. She was working. She couldn't blow her cover. She was even tempted to say hello in Arabic – *mrban* – to a few of them, but this would only intrigue them. They'd want to know how she knew Arabic, which she could speak fluently. She couldn't tell them she'd spent years in Afghanistan, Iraq, and Syria – working for the CIA. No, she didn't have a character she could slip into, a cover, which she would have had she been stationed in one of those countries to give some plausible explanation for her presence, her actions, her interest. For now, the men had to be invisible, wandering, and desperate angels in search of something to save them from themselves.

She called Barranca back. An automated message from the mobile carrier answered, saying that the phone number was unavailable. That would happen when the SIM card was removed. She hung up.

So strange. He had said he had learned something. What?

She stood at a railing separating the land from the sea. She scrolled through Rebar and reviewed the tracking of Barranca's locations over the past day. He had been at the Vatican the whole time, except from this morning when it showed him going up to Florence. From all the locations captured, it looked like he had driven.

Could the people pursuing the man at Termini Station have trailed him? She had suspected they might. She should have warned him. She should have told him not to travel. But would he have listened? He was secretary of state of the Vatican.

A man put a hand on her shoulder, startling her. Her body froze, her breathing went fast, and her mouth fell open. As she turned, she saw Signore Puzzi.

"*Mi scusi,*" – Excuse me. "I didn't mean to frighten you," he continued in Italian.

She laughed. "I didn't see you behind me."

"I thought all you spies had eyes on the back of your heads," he said, his bloodshot eyes bugging out from under bushy eyebrows.

* * *

Jordan Harrison arrived in Algeciras just as Barranca was being abducted. Amanda O'Brien was right: the weather in the south of Spain was beautiful. The sun shone brightly overhead, and crisp air from the Mediterranean coursed through the sleeves and pant legs of his suit. He was tempted to remove his jacket but thought better: He'd keep it on until he checked in at the hotel where he'd change into something more comfortable.

He took a cab from the train station to the hotel. At the station, he was accosted in Spanish and English by numerous men who offered him hashish, *coca* – cocaine, tours around the city. Most of them looked like they came from Arab countries; Morocco was just a stone's throw from the city. He ignored them all.

He checked into a modest hotel. He didn't want to attract attention to himself as a 'rich' American, and he knew the bureaucrats might complain if he spent too much on a room. The area looked relatively safe. He sent Larry a text on Rebar that he arrived in Algeciras. He told him he was going to use the secure messaging app from now on to communicate. He received no response.

He sent Amanda a text on Rebar also, giving her the name of his hotel. He didn't hear back from her either.

He didn't know what to do. This mission was unlike any that he had been on before. Usually, he had clear orders – find this person, surveil the goings-on at this location, write a report on this or that. He had now entered another world – the gray world of espionage where there were no written rules, no expectations, no clearly defined actions that he was to take, no deliverables. It didn't feel right to sit back and wait for something to happen. He knew that's when the worst things were bound to happen, when you just sat back, ready to take it. He saw this from his father, who had been wiped out of a sheet-metal factory job after a decade or so and then learned a second trade, auto mechanics. He still worked at the Ford dealership repairing cars. He was going to keep that job until he retired, even though arthritis was slowing his hands and he could no longer slip under the chassis of vehicles as easily as he could twenty years ago. But he said he had five more years, and then he'd call it quits. His pension and Social Security would be enough. His mother still worked as a nurse. His four brothers and two sisters had all moved on from Whistlewood, Georgia and were professionals like himself. His father didn't need to work to support them, but after having to work for so many years out of necessity, to feed seven hungry children, he couldn't yet bring himself to stop.

Jordan himself had this mission to work instilled in him, too. He couldn't sit idle. There had to be something to do. But what? He checked Rebar again. Not even a thumb's-up from Larry or Amanda.

He unpacked his suitcase and took off his suit. The hotel didn't have a gym, and he improvised a quick workout, wearing only his boxers. After he exhausted his abs and chest from crunches and pushups, he took a quick shower and changed into a polo and shorts. Then he realized something was missing. Despite his new attire, he felt naked. He didn't have his FBI-issued SIG Sauer P226 by his side.

He should have taken one from the safe house in Madrid. Surely, there would have been a small arsenal there that he could have plundered. It was too late now.

He sent a message to Amanda. "Is there a place I can get a piece around here?"

He waited for a response. None came. That would be something he could do: He could find a piece.

* * *

"*Che cosa? Che cosa stai facendo?*" José Eusebio kept saying. *What is this? What is going on?*

He was sitting in the backseat of the Mercedes sedan while the car raced through the hills of Tuscany. José wasn't sure if they spoke Italian; so, he resorted to English. "Where are we going?"

The man in the passenger seat turned around and said, "Be still."

He had an accent; yes, he was not a native speaker of English. He could be German, Russian, from one of the Slavic states.

"Why are you taking me?" Barranca pleaded.

"Quiet!" the man shot back.

José squirmed in his seat. The car had that new car smell – the odor of leather from the seats permeated the air. The windows still had stickers on them, and the back pouch of the front passenger seat had what looked like an instructional card lodged inside. The card was laminated, and for a moment, José thought he could use the sharp edges of the card as a weapon. Perhaps he could stick it in the eyes of his assailant and blind him. He cursed himself at the thought. They had guns that could shoot him to pieces in an instant. They were at least ten to twenty years younger than he was, and much stronger. They had effortlessly plopped him in the back of the car. He was no match for their physical fitness. Such was the life of a man of the cloth who only had God on his side.

God, yes. He said a silent prayer. *Save me from these men. Deliver me to safety. Let them do me no harm.*

When Barranca opened his eyes, the man in the passenger seat was staring at him, and he laughed. "You think God will help you?" he asked, as if he could read José's mind. "You have no God anymore. You have sacrificed him."

"What do you mean?" asked José.

The man laughed again, and the driver joined in. The man in the passenger seat said something – it sounded like Russian. They jabbered back and forth a bit. Barranca had a keen ear for languages, having traveled all over the world. He heard several *da*'s – yeses, but there seemed to be a hint of Turkish or something else in what they said. The driver kept saying *si*. That wasn't a *yes*. And they didn't say *nyet* for no. They seemed to be saying *ne* for *no*. And when the passenger said *ne*, he shook his head up and down, nodding. That was the movement Westerners would make to signal yes or agreement. But when the driver said *da*, he would shake his head from side to side. For these men, the movements were the opposite of what we do in Western cultures.

Then it dawned on Barranca. The man was saying no while his head moved in the yes motion. A tell-tale sign.

They were Bulgarian.

Chapter 14

Amanda O'Brien stood in the office of a small warehouse on the Bari docks. Signore Puzzi was showing her a handful of papers from the Queen of Spades Transport Company based in Sofia, Bulgaria. Various shipments were originating from Burgas, Bulgaria on the Black Sea to Istanbul. All the papers had a black-and-white logo of the Queen of Spades.

On a computer screen, he illustrated the trajectory: "The ships pass from Istanbul to the Sea of Marmara to the Aegean Sea." He drew a finger around Greece. "Then they go around Greece, undetected, and stop in one of a dozen cities along the Albanian coast. There are many men like me who are happy to accept shipments of any kind, for the right price. That's how we make our living."

"Yes, of course," Amanda said.

"You have my money, no?"

"I will have it wired to you."

"No, cash."

"You know we don't deal in cash," she said. "It's too risky."

"So be it," he said. "Twenty thousand, correct?"

"Yes," she said. "In Euros."

"Very good. They're harder to trace, you know?"

"Yes, I know."

"You Americans are always so agreeable."

Amanda knew that Puzzi was playing with her, practically taunting her. She knew better than to take the bait. "Where did this information come from?"

"You know I can't reveal my sources."

"I need to know how reliable it is."

"It's from the same group that lets me know when the cocaine is coming through."

"I need a name," Amanda demanded. "You know we can shut them down in an instant."

Puzzi's eyes and lips twitched in a sign of nervousness. "*Il Leopardo.* The Leopard. Mr. Falzone, out of Sicily. He runs the operation. You can't let him know you got the information from me. He owns half of Queen of Spades. He'll kill me if he finds out."

"He won't," Amanda said. "You have my word."

"Thank you," Puzzi said in relief.

* * *

Jordan Harrison had debated between going back to the train station or heading to Algeciras's port. He knew that either place would lead him to what he wanted: a weapon. Railway terminals and ports of call in Europe were notorious for being the center of illicit activity. He opted for the port, as it would serve a dual purpose: to scope out where he would potentially intercept the arms shipment as well as fulfill his immediate goal of procuring a gun.

When he arrived at the port, he was accosted by an Arab-looking man who offered him cocaine, hashish, fentanyl, and other drugs. "I lost my ID," Jordan said.

The man smiled, in a cross of satisfaction and disbelief. He spoke to him in broken English. "Around the way, up the stairs." He pointed to a building across the street.

Jordan handed him twenty euros and headed across the street.

The office building was as seedy as they came. Scantily dressed, gypsy-looking women hung about the stair railings, peppering him with sultry looks and clucking their tongues as they shot him some phrases in Spanish. He assumed they were soliciting him. He ignored them as he went upstairs.

There, he found a heavy-set man with an unkempt grayish-black beard and a cigarette dangling from his mouth. Stale smoke filled the air. "Do you speak English?" Jordan asked.

"Yes. What do you want?" he said gruffly.

"I lost my ID," Jordan said.

"You have a passport?"

"No. I lost that too."

"Too bad," the man answered.

"I just need a local ID," Jordan said.

"It will cost you."

"How much?"

"One thousand."

"How long will it take?"

The man stood. His shirt – an FC Barcelona soccer team jersey – rose over his hairy, burgeoning belly. "Fifteen minutes."

Jordan handed him the cash, and the man's sandals dragged over the floor as he puttered to the front of the office. "Stand over here," he said.

Jordan obliged. In a matter of seconds, the man snapped a photo of Jordan using his cell phone. Jordan was a bit stunned. He likely had a pathetic expression on his face when the man snapped his picture. "Can we do it again?"

"No need." The man he sauntered to the backroom, breathing heavily as if he were doing a heavy workout on a treadmill.

At that moment, a text notification popped up on his cell phone. He knew it was from Rebar, as it was disguised as a generic system notice that read "Updates Pending." He opened Rebar, and a message from Amanda appeared:

"Won't be there until tomorrow. Have to see a Mr. Falzone in Sicily."

She said nothing about a gun. He figured he was on the right course.

* * *

José Eusebio Barranca tried to discern snippets of the conversation between two Bulgarians, but his knowledge of Bulgarian was far too limited. He couldn't make out anything they were saying. He resorted to reading body language for clues. However, they merely glanced at one another with snarled lips. Their black eyes barely met.

"I am late for an appointment. They will come looking for me."

The Bulgarian in the passenger seat laughed. "No one will come looking for you. They know you are with us."

Did Richter order his kidnapping? "I am the secretary of state," Barranca countered.

"We know who you are," the Bulgarian replied. "We're almost there."

"Where are you taking me?"

The Bulgarian tossed a piece of black cloth at the cardinal. "Tie this around your head. You don't need to see where we're going."

Barranca held it before his chest, pondering whether to comply.

"Tie it tight. We don't want to see you peeking."

* * *

Amanda had chartered a helicopter to take her from Bari to Sicily – such was the benefit of having the largely unlimited, covert budget of the CIA at her disposal. The flight took a little over an hour. While she was enthralled by the breathtaking beauty of Italy's mountains and the Mediterranean, her mind was never far from her mission. She called Cardinal Barranca again. Still, she received a message that the phone was not in service. NSA's Rebar showed no change in location from where he was tracked last, outside of Florence. She could call his office, but she doubted anyone there would give her any information.

The helicopter landed at a private helipad in Taormina, on the eastern coast of Sicily, where large cliffs towered over the sea. Mount Etna loomed in the background. She had heard reports about how the volcano had been spewing fiery lava and ash over the past year. Etna was the most active volcano in Europe. Scientists predicted that the spate of constant activity indicated it might burst at any moment, leaving the nearby posh resorts in rubble. But no one seemed to care. The luxury hotels and spas were brimming with tourists, enjoying the picturesque views of the crystalline water, frothy waves, rocky shoreline, and the sun.

At the helipad, which was outfitted for the fancy billionaire class, with al fresco dining, a wine cellar, and solarium, she rented a car. While she had the choice of a Ferrari SUV – the Purosangue, she chose a more modest Maserati GranTurismo coupe. The car retailed for well over a hundred grand, but the rental charge wasn't that bad, even with the comprehensive insurance. She knew the folks back in Langley accounting wouldn't raise a fuss. When it came to operational matters, they never did. However, if she were back in the States, they'd nickel her to death. So instead, she took the tack that most other operational officers did: Spend Uncle Sam's money like water whenever she could because the pay she received was a pittance for all the hours she worked. While she was on duty in Afghanistan, one month she tracked how much she worked and then calculated what her hourly wage would be. Even with the bonus that she ultimately received, her earnings fell far below the federal minimum wage. But this was love, she told herself, and in the game of love, money was just an aphrodisiac.

* * *

Just as he thought it would be, his picture on his new Spanish identification card was atrocious. He had a surprised grimace, the type you give when you aren't ready to have your picture taken. He noticed that instead of the navy polo he wore, the ID picture showed him in a loose-fitting sweater with a collared shirt poking from underneath. The photo had clearly been altered, and this shop was certainly sophisticated to have turned around such a realistic picture in a matter of minutes.

Before he left, he asked the heavy-set, sandaled owner where he could buy a gun. The man said, "One hundred euros."

Everything was a shakedown here. Jordan complied by giving him a hundred-euro bill. The shopkeeper then handed Jordan a business card that read *Tatuajes del Sol.* For its logo, the card had a sketch of a hand-drawn, bright sun with a face inside the circle, like you would see on a tarot card.

Jordan translated the name of the business, recalling his high school and college Spanish. *Tattoos of the Sun.* "Who should I ask for?"

"Rafa," the owner growled with a thick accent.

"Rafa," Jordan repeated.

"Like the tennis player." He was referring to the shortened form of Rafael, often used affectionately for Rafael Nadal.

Jordan took a cab to the *Tatuajes del Sol* parlor, where the same logo that was on the business card was emblazoned on a sign over the front door. The shop had no customers inside. A wiry, tattooed man wearing a vintage Ozzy Osbourne concert T-shirt came from the backroom to the counter when Jordan entered. He had multiple piercings – through his nose, his earlobes, his lips. On his hand, he wore several large rings. He was a forty-something rock star who had never reached his glory.

"I want to see Rafa," Jordan said in his makeshift Spanish.

The man gave him a puzzled look. He replied in English: "There is no Rafa here."

"I am sure he said *Rafa.* Like Nadal."

"Oh, you want to see Rafael Nadal? You're in the wrong place. He's retired."

He was being a wiseass. Jordan took out the ID that he had just purchased. "I need something to go with this."

The man took the ID and inspected it. "Very good work." He proceeded to walk toward the backroom. Where was he going with his ID? Jordan was about to grab him by the neck.

The tattoo artist left the door to the backroom open and said,

"Follow me."

* * *

Barranca was driven in darkness for another twenty minutes. He tried to remain calm, even tried to doze off. But he couldn't sleep. Every time the Mercedes hit a bump in the road or maneuvered along the roadway – usually at a high speed – he could feel his usual world of peace and comfort slipping away. What had he done to deserve this? He had tried to be good to Sixtus. Richter, of course, had had it out for him from the start, but Sixtus – why was he so nasty? What was he trying to prove? That Barranca would, could, never be pope? Would he resort to killing him to prevent this from ever happening?

The car pulled onto a bumpy road. It seemed like the passage was paved with stones. The suspension of the Mercedes did little to stop the wavy tossing and turning. Barranca felt like retching. The taste of that delicious *amatriciana* turned nasty as it started to rise in his throat, along with the *guanciale.* Suddenly, the car came to a stop, and José was sure he was about to vomit into the seatback as he lurched forward. He felt like he was on a plane that had abruptly come to a harsh landing.

The passenger door opened, and the Bulgarian grabbed him. "Out!" He wrenched José out of the car and practically pushed him along, almost causing him to lose his balance as he made his way over the rocks.

His eyes still covered by the blindfold, José Eusebio sniffed. He could smell something distinct, perhaps oil, grease, grime. He caught his balance and stood still. In a flash, he felt the Bulgarian's hand on his back, jerking him forward.

"Move!"

* * *

Amanda O'Brien arrived in the vicinity of Falzone's residence about a half hour after landing. She enjoyed taking the sporty Maserati through the roadway, rapidly passing other cars, trying not to be too obnoxious doing so, and handily mounting the hillside terrain. The radio blared an old Adele song – "Set Fire to the Rain," and she sang along. She told herself the sedan wasn't too ostentatious; it was a bright, metallic blue. She loved how the sunlight cascaded over the hood. This was the life.

According to the GPS, Falzone's mansion was up the hill about a kilometer away. As she approached, two motorcycles came in opposite directions – one towards her, the other behind her. They were both riding Ducatis. She turned off the radio. Suddenly, the motorcycle behind her ran up to her side, driving alongside her. She looked in the rearview mirror. The motorcycle going in the opposite direction turned around and started following her. Then, ahead of her, a black SUV came barreling down the hill, towards her. The SUV crossed into her lane!

She had been trained in evasive maneuvers at the Farm. The man in the motorcycle waved his arm at her, apparently wanting her to stop or slow down. He was wearing a leather jacket and a helmet, indistinguishable under his gear.

Amanda hastily slowed to a speed of about 40 kilometers per hour, from 110. The motorcycle then ended up well ahead of her, and the one trailing her had to pull to the other lane to avoid colliding with her. Then she charged forward, toward the SUV. She zipped between both lanes, back and forth, so that the SUV couldn't tell where she was going to go. They headed straight for one another. It was a little game of chicken. A risky move, certainly, but one that she hoped would pay off. The SUV veered into the opposite lane to avoid a collision, and then Amanda raced forward, trekking up the hill back to her speed of 110 kph.

As she passed the SUV, another black SUV, a twin of the other, came towards her from around the hill. The other SUV turned around to chase her, and the two motorcycles were also in pursuit. The motorcycles got closer, and one of the riders took out a gun. Then she knew she was in trouble. Big trouble. The rider shot at one of her rear tires, causing a blowout. The Maserati swerved. She had to slow down, considerably. Then a shot from the other motorcyclist took out her front passenger tire. She was dead; there was no point in trying to evade the pursuit. Up ahead, she could see the gate of Falzone's estate. A huge villa towered on the hillside, looking down below at her car and the men who now circled her.

She grabbed her revolver as she exited the car.

Chapter 15

As Barranca waddled forward blindfolded, the Bulgarians abruptly stopped him. He could hear the clanging of a metal door opening. Where were they taking him? He could smell the odor of grease and grime. This had to be some sort of industrial building.

They ushered him into the building; he heard the echo of footsteps. From the sounds that reverberated, he fathomed the ceilings were quite high, perhaps twenty, thirty feet. He heard the Bulgarians open another door which clanked loudly, as if it was on rusty hinges. They pushed him through. The door closed in a thud behind him. They led him forward, poking at his back. One of them said, "Sit down." He could tell by the voice it was the man in the passenger seat.

He crouched his knees, not knowing exactly where to sit. In a flash, the blindfold was removed from his eyes. The room was dim, but his eyes needed a moment to adjust to the faint light.

Relieved, he sat on the metal chair, one of those stackable, folding types. Instantly, the Bulgarian started to lift the shirt over Barranca's head, undressing him. Then he started to undo José's belt. Barranca cried out: "What are you doing?"

The Bulgarian pulled at José's pant legs. "Take it off! Take it all off!"

José stretched his legs forward to allow the man to remove his pants. All that remained were his briefs.

"Those too," the Bulgarian said.

* * *

In the backroom of the tattoo parlor, Jordan Harrison observed several cabinets resting against the wall. Entering a combination in a lock, the tattoo shop owner opened one of the cabinets. Each of the doors had numerous semiautomatic rifles hanging inside. The closet was outfitted with numerous drawers; the owner pulled out one of them. Beneath locked glass cases lay pistols of various makes. Jordan recognized several of them: Berettas, Colts, Smith and Wessons, Rugers. Some were brand new, others looked used. The closet was a veritable candy store for the hunting-inclined man. There were several that Jordan didn't recognize; he assumed they might be shadow or ghost guns, homemade through 3D printers.

"I'm looking for a Sig Sauer P226," Jordan said.

"Are you a pig?" the owner snorted.

"No, I'm not a fucking pig!" Jordan snapped back.

"You look like a pig," the owner barked. "You come in here with your fake ID and think you can set me the fuck up." His hand slide behind his lower back – Jordan knew the maneuver. The owner brandished a .44 Magnum and pointed it at Jordan's face.

"What the fuck, man."

"Tell me you're not a fucking pig."

"I'm not a pig."

The owner pointed the tip of the gun slightly toward the corner of the ceiling behind Jordan. "Well, you're on video and they're watching you. So don't try shit with me or I'll make sure they slice your pretty face up real good before they send you back home." He motioned with the

Magnum for Jordan to move away from him. Then he went to the other closet and entered a combination in the digital lock. As he had his back turned, Jordan thought how easily he could grab him by behind and snap his neck. In one quick twist, he'd be dead. The fool had no idea who he was dealing with. How well-trained he was, how strong he was, how observant he could be. He had noticed the camera before the owner had pointed it out. There was another one in the other corner of the room, too. It would have made more sense for the owner to point that one out because it would have exposed Jordan's weaker, left flank. But he wasn't thinking. He was too busy being macho and enjoying his control trip.

This other closet contained AK-47s and military grade weapons in its doorways. The owner unlocked a case where an array of revolvers was displayed. He looked at them briefly. "Looks like we're out of the pig special."

"I'll take the Glock," said Jordan.

"That's a thousand. Dollars."

"Fine."

* * *

Sixtus sat in his private quarters. While the papacy had trillions in assets, the accommodations for its leaders were incredibly modest: a simple desk along with a few chairs in the office area. In the adjoining sleeping area: a bed, nightstand, a bookcase that held religious texts and scholarly documents, and a *prie-dieu*, a *pray-to-God*. The prie-dieu was a kneeling bench used for prayer; it had a shelf where the supplicant could rest his elbows while beseeching the Lord. This prie-dieu dated back to the fourteenth century, to the time of Clement V, when the papacy was moved from Rome to Avignon, France. It was made of oak native to the Provence region, and while it had wear, from dozens of popes who had kneeled before it, it did a fine job concealing its age.

As Sixtus knelt, a crow appeared at the window that overlooked St. Peter's Square. Sixtus watched as the bird turned its head to the side, and with one eye, observed him. Sixtus closed his eyes. Rather than placing his elbows on the shelf of the prie-dieu, with one hand he drew a small circle on the shelf. Lifting his finger, he then proceeded to draw in the air a five-pointed star. It was a pentagram. These words he said to himself:

"Satan, please hear me. I've done all that you've asked. Is there anything more you need from me? Please tell me."

He waited for an answer. He was accustomed to sitting in silence while he thought he heard messages back. When he was a boy, he was never certain if he heard actual responses or if he was imagining the words. He had a similar reaction whether he was praying to God or to Satan. Was anyone there? Was his mind playing tricks on him? How could anyone be certain that what they heard was true? Despite all his years of praying, he still had doubts. Lack of conviction. Unknowing. He never felt anything after he prayed. Years later, when he was in the seminary, his fellow priests seemed to report of feelings, validations that gave meaning to the messages. At the time, he wondered: Were they putting him on? He would tell both God and Satan to pinch him slightly on the arm to let him know either one was there. *Do not let my name be mocked!* would come a response. But was it a real voice? Was it just an interior monologue in his head?

Sixtus continued to kneel in silence. No response came. "Tell me, dear Satan. I have obeyed you since I was a boy. Tell me what I must do."

"But you have also prayed to God, have you not?"

What was that voice? Again, was it just his own musing?

"I only wanted to validate that I was talking to the one true Satan. I need to know you are real."

"You should never doubt me. Do you doubt God?"

"I doubt everything. I don't know what is true. I place myself in your hands."

"But you would place yourself in God's hands if he answered also, wouldn't you?"

"I would never."

"You lie! You are an opportunist!"

"I'm trying to serve you," Sixtus said back in prayer.

"You want to serve me?" He asked. "Then I demand blood. Go to the window and let me drink of your blood."

Once the command came, there was silence in his head. He had an order, and he knew what he had to do. He went to his desk and opened the drawer. Pens, pencils, rubber bands, and then he found what he was looking for. He took the paper clip and bent it so that it could no longer hold paper. The sharp chrome edge he lodged into the tip of his index finger. He didn't gasp; he didn't feel any pain. He felt a sense of duty. As blood trickled from his finger, he went to the window where the crow was. It had now darted off. He turned the crank on the window to open it. Noise from the crowd below increased. Someone had seen him; the faithful knew where the pope's private quarters were, and they cheered. He waved his hand. Blood was dripping from his other hand, his left hand. As he waved to the crowd, giving a cordial, thankful smile, he let the blood flow onto the ledge. He continued to wave while he pressed his index finger into the stone. He glanced quickly at the stone and saw that a small pool of blood had formed there. Looking out onto the crowd, he saw a crow perched on one of the hundred-forty-odd statues that lined the roof of the balustrade that encircled the plaza. The crow chose a statue close to the pope's quarters. Apparently noticing him, it twisted its head this way and then that. Then it flew off onto the top of the obelisk in the center of the square. Sixtus V had had this obelisk moved from Egypt to the Vatican in the sixteenth century. Through the gentle din of the admiring crowd, he heard the crow give one single, loud caw. Yes, that was the sign he was looking for. He gave a final wave and closed the window. A louder cheer thundered then faded. Sixtus VI gave one final look at the blood on the windowsill. He looked quickly at the crowd, and there, a nun was observing him. He didn't recognize her. Her face looked blank, almost as if she had no face at all under her veil. Her head cocked, she stood in silence. A feeling of enmity overcame him, and he transferred this hostility to her, mentally, as if he could transmit his thoughts to another person and have them feel what he wanted them to feel. He wanted her to feel ill; he sent disapproval, antagonism.

He turned away from the window and went to the bathroom where he ran water over his bloody, dirty finger. In the medicine cabinet, he found a Band-Aid and wrapped it around his finger, tightly, and he pressed his thumb against the bandage. He looked at his face in the mirror. "I have done what you asked," he said to himself, but he was not saying this to himself but to some Other.

When he returned to the sleeping area, he saw the crow on the window ledge, pecking at the small puddle of blood. The crow cocked its head upward, to let the blood slide into its throat. The one eye of the crow that Sixtus could see blinked rapidly.

* * *

Amanda O'Brien stood in the street, holding her Glock and aiming it squarely at one of the men who had exited the black SUV. He pointed a semiautomatic rifle at her, as did a man from the other SUV. "Put your gun down!" he thundered. "We're all armed!"

She knew she didn't stand a chance. They outnumbered her. They had more weapons. They could easily overpower her. Yet she knew she also held a trump card: "I'm an American diplomat. Put your guns down."

The man laughed at her. "I don't care who you are."

She didn't need to tell them she was CIA. They had probably assumed that was the case when she said she was a diplomat. "I'm with the American embassy, in Rome. My name is Amanda O'Brien. If I don't return, there will be hell to pay."

"Mistakes happen," the man shrugged.

"This isn't a mistake," she said. "I'm live streaming this as we speak." She motioned her wrist up in the air, where she had a watch. "I've told you who I am and my status. I'm here on a diplomatic mission to see Signore Falzone."

"He's not here."

"I know for a fact he is here."

"How do you know?" the other man scoffed.

"Do you have an appointment?" the other assailant joined in.

"How could I have an appointment if he wasn't here? I know he's here. I told you as much. Now put your guns down and tell him Amanda O'Brien from the American embassy is here to see him." She had employed the commanding tone that the instructors at the Farm had taught her. Do not let your voice quaver; be firm; be respectful; yet demand compliance. The human voice was a weapon, one of the most powerful known to man, they had drilled into her.

"You put your gun down," one of the men said.

"I will, and you will follow me."

The men laughed to each other. *Who does she think she is?* they must have thought.

She had a moment of doubt, and she quickly dispelled it from her mind. She knew that a single grain of doubt could create a deadly situation for her. This was no time for equivocation; they would do what she told them to do. "I'm putting my gun down," she said as she slowly lowered her gun. At that moment, the driver of one of the SUVs came out of the car. Amanda could see that he was listening to an earpiece. He announced, "Put your guns down. We're taking her to the fortress."

A sense of relief overcame Amanda. Her gambit had worked. The fortress was what they called Signore Falzone's lair.

Chapter 16

Jordan Harrison sat on a park bench in Algeciras, scrolling through his cell phone. Now that he had bought a gun, which he had securely tucked into the waistband of his shorts under his polo shirt, he didn't have much to do but wait. He saw a text from his mother. "Son, you didn't tell me you landed okay. All good?" she wrote. She was always worrying about him; she didn't like that he traveled. "Be careful," she would say. "There a lot of bad people in the world." He would say that he knew that, and that's why he joined the FBI, to track and jail criminals and make the world a safer place. She would say, "There are always others who will take their place." She was much more fatalistic than he was. In a text, he dashed a reply: "Sorry. Got in last night. Doing good."

He searched the internet for "Falzone in Sicily." Dozens of results were returned. He learned that Giuseppe Falzone was an Italian industrialist who had made his money in, among all things, tires. According to internet lore, his business was a front for the Sicilian

Mafia. Falzone Motors had strongarmed all the major Italian automobile manufacturers into using it for their new cars. Meanwhile, Falzone served as a conduit for the Colombian cartels who imported cocaine into Europe. Naturally, Falzone took a substantial cut. In more recent years, he was investigated for manufacturing amphetamines in Estonia and Poland and distributing them throughout the European Union. These investigations went nowhere. Throughout his entire life, he had never been charged with a crime. "Not even jaywalking," his lawyer was once quoted as saying.

Even though he had received no word from her since his last ping, Jordan sent a message to Amanda on Rebar: "Everything okay? I see this Falzone is one bad..." He hesitated while typing. He didn't know the Italian word for *man,* so he put in what he was thinking: "*hombre.*"

He continued: "Let me know if I can help."

He had a bad feeling. Intuition, his mother would call it. Always follow your gut, his father would say. Both were semi-superstitious people. Borderline conspiracy theorists, especially his mom. He hadn't inherited those traits. But he did keep a certain measure of caution and listened to whatever his inner voice told him. It couldn't hurt, he told himself, especially if he didn't share his thoughts with anyone else.

He watched boats pass through the harbor, and he got up to take a closer look. After a while, he went to a small coffee shop where the locals fraternized, smoking and shooting the breeze. He thought he might pick up some info while hanging about. Many of the men were immigrants from European nations. Besides Spanish, he heard Arabic, Eastern European languages, even what sounded like Greek. Some even seemed to be speaking Portuguese and Italian. It was a real melting pot.

While sipping a coffee, a woman approached him. "Are you looking for someone?" she asked in English.

He shook his head. "No."

She stared at him intently, as if to ask, "Are you sure?" But she didn't say anything. She was quite beautiful – exotic-looking, with perfect push-up hair. She looked Arab, and she had an English accent. Then she said: "*I* am looking for someone."

Was she propositioning him? He was careful not to indicate any interest. That could only lead to trouble, despite his boredom and her obvious attractiveness.

"You might be able to help me find him. Mr. Korelov." She raised an eyebrow as she said the last name, as if to prompt some sort of recognition from him.

"I don't know him."

"He's an associate of Mr. Falzone. Surely, you must know him," she said.

"Falzone? I've heard of him. Are you meeting him?"

"He doesn't have time for me. He keeps his hands clean, if you know what I mean. He always sends one of his vassals."

"You're in business with him?" Jordan asked.

"I'm trying to be. You're American, aren't you?"

"Yes." His alarm bells were going off. Had she approached him on purpose, targeting him for some reason? Was this a set up? It couldn't have been a coincidence that Amanda was meeting with Falzone and then, the same day, within hours, a stranger comes up and asks if he knew him. It seemed like this was a maneuver of some sort.

"You know," she said quietly. "The man at the tattoo parlor, he showed me your picture and told me you bought a gun."

So now he was in the tattoo shop owner's personal database of illicit arms patrons. Was she an undercover police officer? She did have an air of authority, like law enforcement personnel. "No, I think you're mistaken."

She pulled out her phone and showed him the picture that the shop owner had taken of him in the waiting area. It was just a picture of his face, not of the full identification card.

There certainly was some sort of coordinated activity on the part of the tattoo shop and this woman. Who was she? What did she want? He had committed a crime in Spain buying a gun illegally; while he knew he could get off the hook with some calls from the Bureau, it would be a hassle, the operation would be stalled, and his credibility diminished. "Why are you following me?" he asked.

"I thought you might lead me to Korelov." She held out her hand. "My name is Sima, by the way."

He took her hand and shook it. He contemplated giving her a fake name, but he thought she may have seen his false identification card with his name on it. "Jordan."

Just at that moment, a man came up behind Sima and appeared to stick something in her back.

Jordan saw that he was holding a gun.

"Don't try anything. You're coming with me. Both of you," the man said.

* * *

A woman entered the darkened room where José Eusebio Barranca, stripped naked, sat on a chair. She handed him his pants, underwear, and shirt. As he took the clothing and dressed himself, she didn't take his eyes off him.

"Can't you at least turn around?" the cardinal said.

"When was the last time a woman saw you naked?" she asked. "Your mother?"

She had an Eastern European accent. She could have been Bulgarian, too. "Who are you? Why am I here?"

"The man at Termini Station gave you something. Where is it?"

"He gave me a newspaper. That's all."

"You're lying." As he stood before her, she took his hand and twisted it.

He screeched in pain, grimacing while he crouched over his arm.

"This will get a lot worse if you don't tell me."

A rush of adrenaline coursed through him. "There was nothing!" He pulled his hand away from her. He was tempted to strike her, to defend himself, but held himself back.

"I know there was something. They're turning your room upside down now at the Vatican. They will find it."

He didn't accept what she was saying. If they had searched his room thoroughly, they would have found what they were looking for. They had to have moved the bed. She was bluffing. They had taken all his clothes to inspect them carefully. They hadn't found anything; so now, they were taking things to the next level. An interrogation. Perhaps torture. The thought sent shivers through his spine.

She put a hand on his shoulder to try to force him to sit down. He stood his ground and didn't move.

Who was this woman – this relatively small, 130-pound female – to physically coerce him into compliance?

She stepped back and took out what looked like a Taser. "You don't want to cooperate? I'll see to it that you tell me what I want to know."

"Fuck you!" Barranca didn't normally swear, but the words burst out of him.

She laughed.

"I demand that you let me go!"

She laughed even harder.

"They will come looking for me."

"They don't give a shit about you!"

"You son of a bitch!" He leaped towards her, and at that very moment, she pulled the trigger on the gun, and it shot forth a zap that sent him bowling over in pain to the floor.

Reeling in pain, José managed to pull himself off the floor and lunge at her. Taken completely by surprise, she shrieked as he wrestled her to the concrete floor. They pushed and pulled at each other for several seconds when he succeeded in taking the stun gun from her. He pointed it at her when the Bulgarian men who had taken him hostage came rushing through the door. Barranca didn't hesitate; he aimed the stun gun at the woman on the floor and pulled the trigger.

* * *

Falzone's henchmen escorted Amanda to the magnate's hilltop compound. They had asked for her Glock; when she refused, their earbuds buzzed, and the voice on the other end told them to drop the matter. Amanda assumed they had figured out that she was a CIA officer. She would never admit to them that she was, as she was operating under cover, but she knew where the kid-glove treatment came from.

The pair of black SUVs passed without issue through the manned security gates. The motorcycles tailed closely behind. The estate was massive. As the car wound up the hill, she glimpsed spectacular views of the Mediterranean. The property was meant to intimidate; she knew the type. Falzone wanted to give a warning shot to any potential adversary that might enter the gates that his power was vast and far-reaching.

A small vineyard lay near the foothills at the base of the house. The SUV pulled up to the front door and a security officer opened the rear door. "Ms. O'Brien," he said in English. "Mr. Falzone welcomes you to his home. He apologizes for the inconvenience. If only next time, you could make an appointment."

"I'll keep that in mind," she answered.

He led her into the home, where staircases on each side of the colossal foyer led to the upper floor. The ceilings had to be thirty feet high. The security officer showed Amanda to a sitting room off the entryway. Ornate, gilded Italian furniture glittered under the light of dueling chandeliers which brightly lit the room. The shimmer and shine would have made Donald Trump envious, she thought. A huge oil painting of a leopard hung over the fireplace, with Falzone's face superimposed where the head of the leopard would be. A homage to himself, she thought, Falzone "*The Leopard.*"

A maid brought a silver tray with coffee and tea service. She asked what Amanda preferred, and Amanda said she would take tea. She handed her a fine porcelain cup and saucer laden with green leaves and a gold and brown handle that resembled a branch. When she left, Amanda peered at the bottom of the demitasse: *Royal Copenhagen Denmark,* it read.

She took a sip, and Signore Falzone entered. She stood. The security officer closed the massive oak doors behind him, leaving them in sparkling silence. Falzone was immaculately dressed in a finely tailored gray suit. His white shirt was neatly pressed; his tie – a vintage, yellow-and-blue Versace with a medusa – was perfectly knotted. He looked as if he was ready to go to a fine restaurant, and he was enraptured by the young, nubile date before him whom he would ravish post-dessert. She wondered whether he had changed into such fine attire upon hearing of her visit or if he always wandered around his estate dressed like this.

"I'm sorry about the misunderstanding," he said, taking her hand but not shaking it. It was a more intimate gesture – a holding, and he didn't want to let go. "A man in my position must always be careful."

"I understand," she said.

"I'm making sure your car is repaired."

"Thank you."

"Please have a seat. Tell me what I can do for you. You have come alone, correct?"

Why was he verifying that she was alone? He had to know that there was no one with her. "My team is awaiting my return," she said.

"Of course."

"I understand you are connected to the Queen of Spades shipping company."

"I'm not familiar with it. I don't deny it, but I have many holding companies. Is there a matter?"

"A shipment is being sent through it. I need to know where it came from, where it is, and where it is going."

"And you came all this way?" he asked with slight derision.

"I didn't have a choice. It seems that everything is secretive, so closely guarded."

"Of course, you know a man in my position must be very careful."

"Of course." She took out her phone and showed him the picture of the shipping notice.

"Where did you get this?"

"It's not very hard for us." She let the *us* linger in the air, to resonate with him, so that he would infer that she was referring to the Agency.

"Of course. May I see?"

She handed him her phone so he could inspect the image more closely.

"Enzo," he said, barely raising his voice. In a beat, the security officer opened the massive oak doors. He was obviously standing by and could hear everything they were saying. "Could you get this fine lady information details on this shipment?"

He raised her phone, and she followed by reaching for it. "I can't let my phone leave my sight."

"Of course," Falzone said.

"I'll take a picture," interjected Enzo.

"That wasn't so difficult, was it?" Falzone chimed.

"It depends on what information I'm given," she said, raising her eyebrows.

"I will tell you everything I know," he said smarmily.

* * *

Jordan and Sima walked along the harbor as the man with the gun directed them. "This way," he said, pointing the gun in the direction of a waiting car. Jordan saw a black sedan with tinted windows waiting a block ahead. He knew the risks of entering a vehicle; it was, perhaps, one of the riskiest things that a person could do, whether you were law enforcement or an innocent bystander. It would put him at the mercy of his captors.

"We are we going?" Jordan asked.

"Don't you mind," the man said.

Jordan was asking to find out more about the man. He could tell from his accent that he was likely Spanish. His pronunciation had a lilting sound, commonly heard among native Spanish-speakers. He had commonly heard this manner of speaking among illegal immigrants in the United States. While Spaniards had a harsher accent – more guttural, more rigid, there was a similarity.

As they approached, Jordan saw a small stand on the sidewalk selling street food. A couple of workers were eating there. While they couldn't be depended on for help in deterring the assailant, or for being trustworthy witnesses, he had to use them to his advantage.

They neared the food stand. A graying man with a scruffy beard was selling the food. "We're stopping for food!" Jordan shouted in English.

He was taking the tactic of causing a commotion. The workers eating at the stand looked up at him. Jordan knew his assailant wasn't aware that he was also armed.

"Get a move on," the man with the gun said. He lowered his pistol so that it wouldn't be visible to the men at the stand.

Jordan reached in and grabbed a plate of food that one of the workers was eating. It was a kebab with rice and hummus. "Hey!" the man yelled in Spanish.

"It's good?" Jordan asked in an animated fashion, acting like a crazy man.

The other workers listened and watched in confusion.

Jordan took the plate and threw it in the face of the man with the gun. The hummus flew in his eyes. Jordan reached around Sima and pushed her out of the way. Jordan tackled the man, wrestling the gun from his hands. It dropped to the ground, and a bullet shot off. The workers at the stand freaked out. They mumbled something and scurried off. The gray-haired man stood behind the stand in shock, not aware what was going on. Sima snatched a couple of the plates that the workers left and threw them at the man with the gun. His face and shirt were covered with garbanzo beans, pieces of chicken, relishes that accompanied the food. Then she took a plastic squeeze bottle and squirted it in his eyes. It was a hot sauce. The man cried out. She kicked him.

Jordan seized the gun and shot the tires of the black sedan that was waiting for them. Other workers and passers-by on the sidewalk started shouting and running. A driver came out of the sedan. Sima screamed, "Watch out!"

Jordan fired towards the man but intentionally missed him. The driver ducked behind the car.

"We need to get out of here," Jordan said to Sima.

"I have a car around the block," she said.

He debated for a moment: Was it safe to go with her or should he stay on his own? He looked around the harbor. The commotion around them was still ongoing, but it would soon dwindle down. He knew the lack of a crowd would leave him at risk. "Okay, let's go." He held the assailant's gun and signaled it upwards for Sima to lead the way. He figured if he didn't like the looks of the vehicle, he could always make a last-minute dash or create some other diversion to escape again.

Jordan followed behind Sima as she rushed down the street toward the side of a building. Suddenly, Jordan's stomach fell into a pit: Was she leading him to a trap? He didn't know this woman at all. He slowed down.

She looked back towards him. "What's the matter?"

He couldn't help but give her a forlorn, lost gaze. He felt at her mercy, and he knew this was not a good position to be in.

"Come on!" she said, egging him forward. She continued down the sidewalk alongside the brick building. Jordan trotted behind, ploddingly catching up to her. Then he saw a white car that looked out of place for the surroundings. It was a Range Rover. Jordan hadn't seen any of these British imports in the country; they were clearly a luxury. She did have an English accent; the car was fitting.

She went to the driver's side of the car as he reached the vehicle. He hopped into the passenger seat. She turned the ignition over and expertly maneuvered the car in a U-turn at high speed. This woman knew how to drive.

"What's a G-man doing in Algeciras?" she asked, flooring the gas.

Chapter 17

After being slapped around for having tasered the woman who was interrogating him, José Eusebio Barranca sat in the metal chair. One of the Bulgarians had placed a zip tie around his wrist and looped it through the frame of the chair. Having his arm twisted behind him hurt; it was the same hand that the woman had twisted, and he felt it going numb. Fortunately, he had one arm free and was able to scratch those pesky itches that came over his face, shoulder, and head. He felt as if he was being attacked by microscopic bugs. In the dim light, he couldn't see any. Perhaps it was just his mind, his nerves, playing tricks on him. "What do you want from me?" he cried out.

The Bulgarian man laughed. Whatever José said, he seemed to laugh in reply.

The woman who had been tased re-entered the room. José suddenly got more anxious. What might she do to him in retaliation? "Don't let her touch me!" he shouted.

She laughed.

All these Bulgarians could do was laugh. It was as if they enjoyed the power they held over him. "I don't know anything."

"You're lying," she retorted. "You know how I can tell you're lying?"

"How?"

"Because you just admitted it."

"Just let me go. I'll give you what you want."

"Now we're talking."

"It's under my bed."

"Under your bed?"

"Yes, under the bedpost."

"What are we talking about?"

"A piece of paper."

"That's all you have?"

"Yes, that's all he gave me. A newspaper and a piece of paper."

"Where is the newspaper?"

"I don't have it. I gave it to a woman at the embassy. Amanda is her name."

"An American?"

"Yes. It had blood all over it. Amanda looked at it and found nothing."

"I've heard that before," she scoffed, her eyes narrowing in disbelief. "How do you know this woman?"

"I don't. She was there at the station when the man was stabbed."

"How convenient."

"She'll be looking for me."

"I'm sure she will. Where do you think she'll find the body?"

"Excuse me?"

The woman laughed, her gaze slowly traveling up and down him. "What is this piece of paper you're referring to?"

"It's a shipping notice."

She stuck her face in his, with a menacing smile. "Tell me!"

"I didn't do anything with it!" Barranca yelped. "I just stuck it under the bed."

"So that no one could find it?"

"Yes. I thought it might be important."

"Now I know you're telling me the truth. You know how?"

"No. How?" Barranca said.

She laughed. "Because you've pissed your pants and you didn't even notice it."

Barranca looked down at his waist, ashamed. He saw the stain over his crotch. Is that why they were constantly laughing at him? "What are you going to do?" His eyes widened in panic.

"We're going to get the piece of paper," she said.

"From Richter?"

"Richter?"

"Yes, is he working with you?"

"Don't worry," she said. "We have someone on the inside."

* * *

"I was asked to do a favor," Falzone explained to Amanda.

"A favor?"

"Yes. To provide a secure means of transport for something highly sensitive."

"You weren't told the contents?"

"I didn't want to know. Plausible deniability, as they say."

"Of course. Who asked this favor of you?"

He squirmed in the chair. "That question makes me uncomfortable."

"That's how I felt when your security team shot out the tires of my Maserati."

He couldn't help but emit a chuckle. "You are a charming woman, Ms. O'Brien. But I'm afraid that charm has its limits."

"How much did they pay you?"

"Two million dollars?"

"To bring it where to where?"

"From Montenegro to Valencia to Algeciras. And from there, it will change into someone else's hands and make its way to America."

"Do you understand that this is a weapon that's being transported?"

"As I said, I know nothing about the contents."

"I need the name of the man who hired you," she demanded.

He slid a finger under the collar of his shirt, as if trying to loosen its hold on him.

Amanda interpreted this as a sign that he would talk. He had something more to say. It was time to turn up the heat. "This entire operation of yours could come crumbling down."

"What is said stays between us, no?"

"I'm afraid everything is being transmitted back to the embassy." She removed her cell phone from her pants pocket. "They have been listening to everything we're saying. It's the latest technology."

"I thought you came to me as an honest woman," he said.

"I have. That's why I'm telling you this. I've come for information. That information is what I need." She knew how to put the pressure on a subject: continually raise the stakes until he was cornered. Always leave them room for self-respect, for self-preservation. But ensure that the target could not evade the desired result. "You have my word that we will not compromise you as the source of the information. This little rendezvous that we have had will remain confidential."

"Something for my file?" he proffered. "I know where those files can end up."

"We have no interest in starting a war with the Sicilian Mafia. Your status as a confidential informant will remain strictly confidential. You won't be the first mafioso that we've done business with."

"No, I know there is a long history, dating all the way back to the assassination of John F. Kennedy. I just want that on the record." He gave a Cheshire-Cat-like smile.

"Duly noted."

"She said her name was Violeta."

Amanda was surprised that it was a woman who ordered the shipment. "She was Russian?"

"No, Bulgarian. Or so she said. She could have been lying for all I know. But she came through with the money. Bitcoin transferred to my account."

"The one in the Seychelles?"

"You do your homework. I'm impressed." He paused as he took a sip of tea from the Royal Copenhagen teacup. "My mother always wanted a service like this. It's a shame she couldn't live to see it. All of this," he said, raising his hands toward the ceiling, "is for her. We must do it for someone, you know? Who do you do it for, Ms. O'Brien?"

"For my country," she answered.

"But there has to be someone else. Someone deep down that you are trying to please, to satisfy. Is it your mother?"

"No, she couldn't care less. She doesn't even know what I do for a living."

"She thinks you work for the State Department?"

"Something like that."

"Then who? Your father?"

"I never really knew him." She was being completely truthful. He died when she was eighteen, during her freshman year at Cornell. She had only seen him a dozen or so times, starting when she was a teenager.

"Ah, then that is it. You're filling the void of your father. Uncle Sam has replaced him. How noble of him."

"I suppose." She thought Falzone had a point.

"Let me give you a piece of advice." He placed the cup back on the saucer. "It never works out that way. You always end up trying to please someone who can't be pleased. They don't want the same things you do. They want you to be happy, but their vision of happiness will never be the same as yours. Do what makes you happy, Amanda. You don't mind if I call you by your first name, do you?"

"No, in fact I prefer it."

"Likewise. Call me Giuseppe. Mr. Falzone makes me feel old."

"What is Violeta's last name?"

"I don't know."

She surmised he was being truthful. "What is her contact information?"

He took out his phone. There, he opened his Signal application and showed her the contact entry along with a telephone number.

She didn't recognize the area code. She took her cell phone and snapped a picture of it. "The chat history is all gone."

"We tend to like those disappearing chats, you know?" he answered.

"You could make my life easy. Could I have the confirmation of the Bitcoin transfer?"

"The account details? Sure, they must be here somewhere." He scrolled through his phone. As he thumbed through various pictures, without lifting his head, he said, "Remember, Amanda. Your father only wants you to be happy. He doesn't care if you save your country. He only wants you to save yourself."

She tried not to wriggle in her seat. She didn't want to let on that he had gotten to her, and that, uncontrollably, her spirits were sinking. She didn't like to be reminded of her childhood.

"Here it is. I can send it to you. I do wish you had called beforehand. We could have avoided all that unpleasantry. I'm told your car is ready. The rental car agency won't suspect a thing."

"I'll take a picture of that." She snapped a picture of his screenshot of the transaction confirming the Bitcoin transfer. She handed him her card. "This is the best way to reach me."

"Headquarters will be satisfied. I take it they have it in their possession already." He was referring to the photograph she had taken. He was suggesting that all her phone activity was being monitored in real time by the Agency.

"That's how things work." Even though the Agency wasn't watching her phone, they did have the ability to access it remotely. She wanted Falzone to think that they had her back, so that he wouldn't try anything untoward.

"I take it you have everything you came for?" he asked.

"I do. I'll be in touch if I need anything else. Thank you for the Early Grey."

* * *

"What makes you think I'm with the FBI?" Jordan asked Sima as she pulled onto a side street of the port.

"The way you handled the gun. It was very precise. Only the most highly trained handle weapons like that."

"I'm with MI6," she stated confidently.

"I wouldn't have guessed until I saw how you drive."

She whipped around a corner at high speed, expertly throttling the SUV down and then racing it as she rounded the bend. She watched as Jordan braced himself against the dashboard.

"I don't think they're following us," he said.

"You can never be too sure."

"Who were they?"

"Someone who didn't want us to meet."

"Is the gun shop owner working with you?"

"No. We have his operation under surveillance. We get a digital snapshot of every ID he creates. He doesn't have a clue."

She continued toward the center of the city, and then suddenly took a U-turn to go back in the direction she came from. Jordan knew she was taking evasive maneuvers. He too was trained to switch directions randomly, to head off potential tracking.

"This your first operation?" she asked.

"How can you tell?"

"The way your knuckles change color. I can tell you're not used to this."

"How did you know I was here?"

"I didn't until I saw your ID. It's not often clean-cut guys like you are buying weapons and fake IDs. You probably could have contacted MI5. They would have set you up." She was referring to the United Kingdom's equivalent of the FBI. She headed onto the highway that led to the outskirts of the city.

"I'll remember that next time."

"You're optimistic," she quipped, suggesting that there wouldn't be a next time.

"What are you doing here?" he asked.

"Same thing as you."

"Which is?"

Her brow raised, she shot him a look. "Tracking a shipment, right?"

So, they were on the same page. Before he could answer, she quickly moved through a couple of lanes of traffic to exit the highway. His body lurched forward and sideways as the Range Rover gripped the pavement.

"The Agency enlisted our help," Sima said. "We have a lot of operatives on the ground. It's all-hands-on-deck." She slowed as she drove down the road along the highway, passing a line of numerous parked cars. Some of the cars had for-sale signs on them. She slowed, and then she pulled over. "It's time to change vehicles."

Having parked the car, she stepped out. She took out her phone and pointed it at a gray Volkswagen sedan. Punching in a few numbers, Jordan heard the car unlock. She reached under the driver's seat and grabbed the key fob.

"Where are we going?" Jordan asked.

Without hesitating, she started the car and put it into gear.

Chapter 18

Sister Sofija made her way through the poorly lit hallways of the private quarters of the Vatican. She swore that one day, some elderly cardinal would trip and fall in the darkness, perhaps to a tragic end. She herself was in her late sixties and had spent her whole life serving God, at least she told herself. She was an Augustinian nun, and while the Augustinians prided themselves on their commitment to poverty, Sister Sofija had managed to evade this vow. She had come from Lithuania and had grown up under Soviet rule. While the country was now fully independent and a member of the European Union, her upbringing had instilled in her the need to hustle, swindle, and steal. Yet she only managed to achieve a modest standard of living. "Everything, everyone, is for sale," her mother used to tell her. "Be good. Devote yourself to the Church and you will always have bread." Lithuania was a predominantly Catholic country, and before she came of age, she was living among the Augustinian nuns who schooled her. Unfortunately, she ran across Sister Gabija who, like

Sofija's mother, was fully indoctrinated in the wiles to which Lithuanian women resorted to find food, comfort, and lodging for her family. She was rumored to be the lover of the wife of a party leader. Gabija even sent Sofija to satisfy her on occasion. The woman paid well, and while Sofija did not receive her share of the proceeds, she had made a valuable connection in the party official, who also came to abuse her. She became a conduit of information, passing valuable state secrets via Church channels between Communist officials and the West. It was a vast network, and while suspicion was always cast at the Church, it had more freedom than any other organization in the country before the fall of the Iron Curtain.

This afternoon, Sister Sofija was on another errand. Once the work of party leaders had dried up, she had to find meaningful employment elsewhere. Previously, she had sent home her earnings to dear mother; but since her death, she was now on her known. And with the fall of the Communist empire, she had access to Western banking. Through her schemes, she had managed to amass savings in the six figures. Bitcoin made things easier. What would she do with all this money, she would occasionally ask herself. She told herself she would retire to Hawaii. She wanted nothing more than to go to Hawaii and eat pupu platters. She had seen pictures of those platters in women's magazines as a child, and she would continue to scour the internet for preternatural images such as on Pinterest in later years, if only to long. She wasn't a glutton like Gabija, she told herself; she just wanted something moderately worthwhile to satisfy a humble appetite.

No one was around. None of the doors to any of the cardinals' rooms were locked. There was no need for privacy at the Vatican. Even the pope's quarters were rarely locked, until Sixtus came along. She entered Barranca's room. The bed was made. She closed the door behind her. If anyone found her inside, she would tell them that she was lost. She knew how to play like an old woman slightly off her rocker. She would faint a little; she would scream; she would laugh; she would plead; she would kick her legs back and forth like a child and clap her hands in triumph. She might be sent for evaluation, but that was the least of her worries. Gone were the days when she could have offered sexual favors to get out of a bind; that was her usual go-to, though she never had to resort to such a measure. Who would want a gray-haired old lady? These cunts wouldn't even let her dye her hair.

If Sixtus hadn't locked his doors, she could probably leave this godforsaken Church sooner than planned.

Violeta had ten thousand dollars in Bitcoin waiting to be transferred to her account. Information on Sixtus had a price tag of twenty-five thousand. If only an assignment like that would come her way.

Now, all she had to do was lift the bed and find the piece of paper. She first lifted the corner near the window. How heavy it was. She felt a strain in her back. The oak frame was solid. She wasn't built for this kind of work anymore. All she had to do was to tell her superiors that she was sick and needed to go off on her own. They would let her escape.

She again tried to lift the post. She couldn't find the strength. She would have to take the mattress off. She started with the pillows, throwing them on the floor. Then she pushed the top mattress off the box spring. The mattress wasn't that heavy. The Church was so cheap in that regard. They could afford the finest mattresses; instead, they cut corners everywhere. Even growing up at home she had a more comfortable bed than this.

She took another attempt at lifting the post. No avail. She popped the box spring up from the frame, taking some weight off it. She tried again to lift the bed. It came up an inch and then fell back into the carpet. She could kill Barranca. She loathed Violeta, who could have paid her more. But ten thousand dollars for maybe twenty minutes of work? Who else but God could command such rates?

She got on the floor and lay by the foot of the bed. She wasn't a big woman, but she was a bit over 180 pounds the last time she weighed herself. Most of the mass was in her hips. Facing the bed from the floor, she pushed with all her might to lift the frame while at the same time craning her neck so that she could see underneath the bedpost. She saw nothing but carpet. She let the bed down and before she got up, she thought she heard some noise in the corridor. Footsteps. Nerves overcame her. Should she hide under the bed? Then there was silence. She proceeded to get up and move to the other side of the bed. There, she followed the same procedure, lifting the bedpost, grunting so. This time, she saw a folded piece of paper. She was going to grab it, but when she removed her arm, the bed fell back to the floor with a thud. It was heavy; she couldn't keep it up with just one arm.

Taking a long exhalation, she lifted the frame again. She blew at the piece of paper. Puff, puff, puff. It moved an inch. Puff, puff, puff. It moved some more. Now, it looked to be away from the reach of the post, and she let the bed fall in a thud. She hastily grabbed the folded paper and opened it. It was titled *Bill of Lading;* the notice meant nothing to her. She would have to research what *lading* meant. She placed it on the comforter and, with her phone, snapped a picture of it. She shoved it into her pocket. At that moment, the door to Barranca's door opened. It was Richter.

"Sister Sofija, what are you doing in the cardinal's room?"

"Your Excellency," she gasped.

"What are you doing on the floor? Why is the mattress like that?"

"I don't know," she said. "I just knocked and I found the room like this. I wanted to put it back together before he came back. Forgive me."

He gave her a stern, though confused, look.

She couldn't tell whether he believed her.

"Why would you come into his room?" he demanded with an accusatory tone.

"I heard some noise when I was in the hallway. A bit of a ruckus. I didn't give it a thought, but then I came back and knocked and didn't hear anything. I wanted to make sure Cardinal Barranca was okay. I haven't seen him all day. Then I found the room like this. You don't think anything has happened to him, do you?"

"He went up to Florence." He took a breath. "I'm not sure if I believe you. Come speak to me later. Get this room fixed."

"I'm not sure if I can. This is very heavy."

"Get some help then."

"Okay," she answered meekly.

He left the room. She had completed her mission.

* * *

An hour later, as Cardinal Barranca sat in the darkened room – sweaty, panicked, his arm still zip-tied to the chair, wondering what he should do – he again said a prayer to God. "Please save me," he implored. "Let me out of this place." If he could cry in prayer, the tears would have flown down his face and created a puddle that he could swim in. But there were no tears, merely entreaties that were perhaps more hopeless than they were hopeful. As he prayed and prayed, he became filled with more self-pity. Feeling this way wasn't like him, not since his days at Notre Dame when he told himself it wasn't fair that he couldn't walk the grounds of campus holding the hands of Joseph, his beloved. "Joe," his friend told him to call him. But José Eusebio, who had the same given name but in Spanish – how they were twins, fraternal, or perhaps brothers, in some odd way – would only call him "Joseph." He preferred the biblical reference; there was no "Joe" in the Bible, and his love for him was sacred. José Eusebio found himself thinking of Joe – Joseph – during his prayers. He could free him. Could God send him to console him, to hold him, to treasure him? It was all wrong, he knew. It was blasphemy. But he knew better. Times would change, and they would be free.

He opened his eyes, and a semblance of a tear, a drop, covered the iris of his left eye. Only one eye had moisture; the other was dry. He was two halves of a singular self. Two parts that talked to each other but that were not the same. Like he and Joseph. The realization caused him to gasp. What had he done to his life? He had forsaken love to continue to serve God. Wasn't God his one true love? No. The tear trickled down his left cheek, stopping just as it reached the ridge of his cheekbone. As he felt it, it continued to roll a bit further down his face. Then he pulled up his untethered arm and wiped it. *Stop feeling sorry for yourself,* he said in silent admonition. The sacrifice was minimal, the memory sublime.

He wouldn't be in this situation if it weren't for that encounter with the man at Termini Station. Why had he been following him? He had targeted the cardinal, following him from the Vatican to the train station, as if there was some connection between the two of them. He had wanted him to know something. He had given him the transmittal slip. But it all seemed inconsequential and unrelated to him. Barranca ruminated: Couldn't the man have gone to the police? Maybe they wouldn't have investigated. But what could a cardinal do? And then the CIA investigating. A tinge of regret gripped him. He should have told Amanda O'Brien that he found the shipping notice. Then he wouldn't be here, held captive in the dark, waiting helplessly. He had made a colossal mistake, and now he was paying the price.

Violeta entered the room, turning on the lights, startling him from his reverie. Her footsteps resounded against the cement. A wave of panic waved through him. What might she do in retaliation for his having tased her? A look of quiet satisfaction seemed to pour over her face as she approached him. She bent forward near him, putting her face directly in front of his. He wanted to spit at her; it wasn't like him to spit, but he felt that she deserved this comportment. She was an evil woman. He could see it in her small, brown-blackish eyes, eyes the size of a coffee bean and so dark, her irises and pupils melded. She had no feelings. She had no soul that she hadn't given up years ago, probably when she was a little girl.

"You've been crying," she whispered. A smile overcame her mouth as she continued staring at him. She kept her face inches from his.

He wanted to spit more. He had a hard time restraining himself. He felt like an animal, half-caged, half-free.

"You poor baby."

She took a cell phone from her pocket. It was the cardinal's. She waved it before his face to unlock it. She scrolled through the numbers he had dialed. "You think you're so important." Then she went to his photos and scrolled through them. She went to the very top, the earliest photo stored in the phone. There were several pictures of Joseph, his Notre Dame lover, sitting on the edge of a bed in José Eusebio's dorm room; another of him on a bench on campus; a final one of him at a restaurant with a tall pint of beer before him on a high-top table. He was alone in all three of them. She held out the picture of Joseph sitting in the tavern before Barranca. He was surprised that all the data was still on the phone, after the SIM card was removed. But he didn't know much about technology. Joseph's blue eyes gleamed red in the photo, they were so pale. "He must be very special. What's his name?"

"Joseph," he said.

She laughed. "So much like you fairies. If you don't dress or look alike, you have the same name. You're always looking in the mirror, searching for someone just like you."

"He's nothing like me," José Eusebio countered.

"You loved him. But did he love you?"

"Of course."

She laughed, this time even more loudly. "Such faggots! It's a shame you will never see him again."

"Let me go! I didn't do anything to you! I can't cause you any harm!"

She laughed again, in a scoffing sort of way. "We don't have any more use for you."

"Then let me go."

She smiled. "I will." She took a knife from her pocket. The blade shimmered in the light before him. In a flash, she slid it across his throat.

Chapter 19

Sima pulled the Range Rover through a gate onto a stone-covered driveway. A Spanish villa was set behind thick, scarlet bougainvillea. Large agave plants covered the adobe facade and windows. Some of the vines nestled underneath the roof's clay tiles. As she stopped the car, a notification appeared on Jordan's cell phone. It was a non-descript notice, and he knew it was from Rebar. He opened the app and saw the message from Amanda. "Call me," it said.

"This is our safe house." Sima got out of the car, and Jordan stepped out also. He stood by the car.

The front door opened, and a burly man, about 250 pounds, six feet three, with unkempt black hair and a bushy beard, stood before it. He was holding an automatic rifle.

"It's okay," Sima said to her burly body man. "He's FBI."

The man lowered the gun.

"I'm going to make a phone call," Jordan said.

"Be my guest," she said. "We'll be inside."

He stood outside the villa, amidst the tropical landscape. Everything looked benign, almost resort-like. But how safe was he here? Who were these people? How could he count on her really being MI6? This man didn't really look like British intelligence. But maybe that was the point: he didn't look the part. From what he saw of her on their video call, few would suspect Amanda of being a CIA officer either.

Jordan pressed the call button within Rebar to dial Amanda. All calls were routed through local networks but masked through special technology that concealed the caller's cell phone information, such as the IMEI and SSID numbers, from the network.

As the phone rang, he thought he saw the burly man peering out the window through the bougainvillea, watching him.

"Jordan," Amanda said.

"How did everything go with Falzone?"

"Okay. I got some info on the shipment. He said it's going to Valencia and then will go through Algeciras. He was a little short on the details. I got the funding source and I'm having that investigated now. Where are you?"

"I'm in Algeciras. I'm with a woman who says she's with MI6. Can you check her out for me? Says her name is Sima. She has a big bodyguard who's staring me down. I don't know if it's safe here."

"You get a last name?"

"No." He casually snapped a picture of the license plate of her car. "I'm going to send you this license plate too. It was the getaway car we slipped into."

"Getaway? You run into some trouble?"

"Kind of. I bought an unmarked Glock, and she was following me. She said she was meeting someone named Korelov who's an associate of Falzone. She thought I was meeting him."

"This was just out of the blue?"

"Yeah, crazy, I know. It seems like too much of a coincidence. Then, right after I meet her, we get attacked by a couple of guys at the harbor."

"You think it was a setup?"

"Possibly. She had a car around the corner, which makes sense. But then we switch to another car after we get away. What I can't figure out is why she'd target me."

"You're FBI," Amanda said.

"Yeah, but no one knows I'm here. I used a fake name on my ID. I just used my real first name. She said MI6 is watching the gun shop. So she had my ID on file."

"There's facial recognition. Some of the more advanced criminal groups are using it to target law enforcement and high net-worth individuals for ransom."

"She said the Agency asked for MI6's help."

"To do what?"

"I'm not sure. To find this guy Korelov, I guess."

"Anyone associated with Falzone wouldn't be on anyone's radar but mine. This sounds fishy. Send me your location. I'll do some snooping. You should get back to the hotel. I'm not going to be able to get there today. I need to go to Florence. The secretary of state of the Vatican has disappeared."

What did the Vatican's secretary of state have to do with them? He didn't ask. All these events and circumstances were new to him. He had entered a different world, one that he wasn't trained for. He was about to ask Amanda what was going on, but she had already disconnected. She must be in a hurry. He then sent her his location. He also sent via Rebar the photo of the Volkswagen's license plate.

Sima came to the front door. "Are you coming in?"

Pretending to look at his phone, Jordan stealthily took a picture of her at the doorway. "Yeah, I'm just finishing up." He tapped at the screen, sending the photo to Amanda while closing Rebar.

* * *

Cardinal Richter knocked on the pope's office door. While the pope had a private study, where only senior officials had access, the more official office downstairs was more accessible. Nuns, altar boys, lower-level priests, foreign dignitaries, high-profile Vatican visitors, clerks, were apt to pass through the halls. At any moment, they might cross paths with the pope, though it was unlikely because the pope was known to keep the doors to the suite closed and Swiss Guard security was posted outside. A private elevator connected the office to the upper chambers, and only a handful of Sixtus's most senior staff had access to stop at the pope's suite. Richter was one such official.

"Yes," Sixtus answered.

Richter heard the response and opened the door. "Your Excellency, I'm afraid there's been a security breach."

Sixtus looked concerned. But he said nothing.

"I found Sister Sofija in Cardinal Barranca's room earlier today."

"The Lithuanian? The Augustinian?"

"Yes, the same."

"What was she doing there?"

"She said she heard a noise. His bed was taken apart. She was looking for something."

"Could it be the Americans? Or the Russians? Could they have sent one of their spies to search his room?"

Richter was taken aback by Sixtus's sudden, paranoid turn. Why would the Americans or Russians be involved, in something relatively mundane involving a trespassing nun? "Why would they do that?"

"He is secretary of state. Perhaps they are looking for information on our foreign policy."

"With all due respect, Your Excellency, our foreign policy is minimal. All we do is make pronouncements and advocate for peace throughout the world. There is nothing secretive about it."

"But they know all that is changing," Sixtus said.

"Yes, but that will take time."

"They don't want to wait. Speaking of waiting, where is that letter that Barranca was having transcribed?"

"He went to Florence this morning."

A papal assistant – another cardinal – entered the room. "Excuse me, I apologize for the intrusion."

"What is it?" Richter demanded.

"There has been an incident."

"Speak!" Richter hollered.

"Cardinal Barranca's been kidnapped."

"Kidnapped?" Richter was astonished. Even the pope's face fell to the floor.

"I have Father Gómez sitting outside. He is quite shaken up."

"Send him in," Sixtus said.

"This can't be a coincidence," Richter said as the cardinal left the office.

"No," Sixtus agreed.

Father Alejandro Gómez, who had accompanied Barranca to Florence, appeared in the doorway.

"Please, have a seat," Sixtus said.

Gómez and Richter both took a seat on the sofa by the white marble fireplace. The fire was unlit. The pope came round his desk and sat opposite Richter in an upholstered white chair, near Father Gómez. Gómez was quite nervous; it was evident he had been crying. "Would you like some coffee or tea?" Sixtus asked him.

Gómez declined. He spoke in English. "No, thank you, Your Excellency. I don't know what happened. We were on our way to the Convent of Amadori ai Frati when we stopped at a vineyard for a little rest. We had been driving all day." He took a prolonged pause.

"Yes." Sixtus's tone suggested the priest should continue.

"When we were leaving, we were ambushed." While his English was quite good, he pronounced 'ambush' with a terrible accent – like *amboosh*.

"Ambushed?" Sixtus repeated.

"All I saw was that the cardinal was taken away when I came out of the store."

"He wasn't with you?"

"No, he wanted some air. To stretch his legs. It was a black Mercedes."

"What does that tell us?"

Gómez shook his head. "That's all I know."

"You haven't heard from him?"

"No. I tried calling, but the calls didn't go through."

"Why didn't you call and give us the news? Why did you wait until you got here?" Richter asked.

"I was scared. I didn't know what to do."

"So you drove all the way back from Florence without telling anybody?" Sixtus's tone was more patient than Richter's.

"I didn't want to stop. I was afraid of what might happen. I wanted to get out of there."

"And the letter?" Sixtus asked. "You didn't bring it to the convent?"

"No. It's still in the car."

"My God," Sixtus said, doing the sign of the cross. "God be with him. God be with us all."

"I haven't done anything wrong, have I, Your Holiness?"

Richter didn't allow Sixtus to answer – "An investigation will determine that. Is that all you saw? Nothing else that would give us a clue?"

"They looked like professionals," Gómez said.

"Professional what?" Richter asked.

"Assassins."

Chapter 20

Pope Sixtus VI sat in his office alone after Richter and Father Gómez had left. He hated this office, which had no windows facing outside. Security had advised him that it was safer that way, as bullets couldn't wander in unannounced. If he were ever to be killed in the office, it would be an inside job. Someone who had access to the inner sanctum, some cardinal who had gone postal, some clerk or Swiss Guard who had been paid off. More than likely, his security team explained, he would be poisoned or given some medication that would cause his untimely demise. He would be victim of the Church's massive bureaucracy, its Deep State.

He had had bulbs installed that gave the appearance of daylight, but they too emitted an artificial glow. He was certain that the lack of sunlight, a natural source of vitamin D, would lead to ill health. But no one seemed to listen. Everyone nodded and said, "I understand," to placate him. He was supposed to respond in kind when they asked him to sign some important pronouncement or declare something in a speech that he didn't fully agree with. This papacy wasn't meant for the independent-minded. It was designed to carry on tradition, to watch guard over the inevitable decay, and to offer smiles and waves whenever the camera was on.

What a farce.

From his office phone – the cardinals didn't allow him to have a cell phone – he dialed Ahmed Bensaïd.

"Your Holiness," Bensaïd answered, recognizing the direct line from which Sixtus called. "How good to hear from you."

"We have a situation," Sixtus said.

"You're referring to Barranca?" Bensaïd said.

"Yes. What happened?"

"Most unfortunate, I know. It couldn't be helped."

"How are we going to deal with him?"

"Deal with him? What do you mean? He's dead."

"Dead?" Sixtus exclaimed. "That can't be."

"I thought you heard. Listen, it's best we do not talk here. I can be in Rome this evening. May we meet tonight?"

"We better." Sixtus hung up the phone. A dead cardinal on his hands? How was he going to coordinate the news? Barranca was much loved; several of the cardinals had even voted for him as pope, presumable as an obstacle to Sixtus's own ascendancy. This seemed a completely unnecessary move, something that could have serious repercussions and which might cast suspicion on him. It was well known in inner circles that Sixtus didn't care much personally for Barranca; but his appointment of Barranca as secretary of state was a bit of a detente. To the College of Cardinals, they had found a working rhythm. Now, it had all been disrupted.

He buzzed his secretary. "Can you send Richter in, please?"

* * *

Amanda O'Brien had taken a commercial flight from Palermo's Catania airport to Florence, arriving just before 6 p.m. The middle-aged Italian man sitting next to her kept trying to make chit-chat, but she politely told him, in Italian, that she had had a long day with her husband and child and needed to sleep. He looked at her hand where she wore a simple gold wedding band, something she would carry and use now and then to deter the predators who, like mosquitoes to warm flesh, invariably gravitated toward her.

Upon landing, she received a message from Riccardo, a contact at the AISE, Italy's intelligence agency. "A body has been found. Call me *pronto*," read his message.

While in the taxi on her way to town, she called him.

"I'm afraid it's very bad news." Riccardo had a thick, sing-song accent as he spoke English. "The body of Cardinal Barranca has been found near the Bilancino Dam."

"What happened?"

"His throat was slashed and his body wrapped in a blanket. The state police received a call an hour ago saying a jogger found the body. It's an artificial lake with tourists and locals in the area hiking and enjoying the outdoors."

"An anonymous call, I presume?"

"Yes, untraceable too."

"Are the police there now?"

"They've secured the area and have taken his body to the morgue. The pope has been notified."

"Was his cell phone on him?"

"Yes. But the SIM card was removed. Pieces of that were found at a winery in Impruneta not far away. The Vatican called us saying that the cardinal was abducted. He was with a priest who was unharmed."

"His name?"

"Alejandro Gómez. The dam isn't far from the convent where they were headed. They took a rest and that's when the kidnapping occurred."

"The police weren't notified until now?"

"Gómez was scared and waited until he got back to the Vatican. You know how those priests are."

"Skittish."

"Cardinal Richter called himself to tell us about the kidnapping. I just informed him that the body had been found. He doesn't want to put out a press release until they notify his family."

"Listen, I need you to make sure all his personal effects remain intact. I'll be at the morgue in half an hour."

* * *

Sima had prepared sandwiches for Jordan and her burly body man. Jordan noticed that she was remarkably calm considering the attempt on her life. Perhaps this was just the proverbial 'stiff upper lip' that the Brits were famous for. He had told her he needed to go back to the hotel, but he could tell she was stalling him. He offered to take a cab, but she insisted that she would drive him. It was too much of a security risk to allow any lay personnel on the safe house's grounds. While he understood this rationale – and he would have found any lack of objection on her part to be disconcerting, the notion of having to spend more time alone with them, vulnerable, at their mercy, didn't sit well with him. Who were they? How and why did she really target him?

As they ate and chatted, he couldn't help but show his discomfort at being there. "I really do have to get back."

"No worries," she replied.

Despite her agreement, she exhibited showed no signs of rushing along.

"You mentioned Korelov. Who is he?"

"He's someone we've been targeting. He coordinates all the shipments through Spain for Falzone. We got word there's a very important piece coming through any day now."

He would play dumb. "What is it?"

"Weapons," she said. "Very sophisticated, military-grade weapons. We think they came from Qatar, via Russia or Syria. We need to make sure they don't leave Europe."

Their assignment sounded the same as his. "How are you going to stop them?"

"We have contacts at the port. Intelligence assets embedded within the service. It's not hard for us to stop a boat."

He had never asked Amanda how they would stop the shipment, but he assumed it was through similar means. Everything seemed to be adding up. He took another bite of his sandwich. The ham was quite tasty – salty, but that made up for the lack of chips. He received a notification on his cell phone. It was Rebar. He opened the app as Sima asked him some personal questions, like where he was from and how long he had been with the FBI. The message was from Amanda:

"There is no MI6 safe house at the location you gave me. They're still running the check on the photo of Sima you sent me. The car isn't in their database. The fake plates would be."

Every alarm bell suddenly went off. Instinctually, he tried not to convey any concern. He stared at his phone while he tried to quell his breathing. Then he exited out of Rebar, not merely by closing the app but by signing out. He wanted to make sure that if someone were to get possession of his phone, they couldn't simply open the application and access it. Doing this was standard protocol.

"Is there something the matter?" Sima asked.

He noticed as she turned to the counter that she placed a knife that she had used to slice the crusty, artisanal bread in the sink.

"No, nothing at all."

"You're sure? You need to get going, right?" She had taken her cell phone and tapped at the screen. Before he could answer, the burly man entered the front door. Jordan did not see any weapons in his hands or waistband. Without hesitating, he threw the remainder of his sandwich at Sima because he knew she had a gun and close access to the knife in the sink. It was a foolhardy attempt to blind her, but he knew that any distraction was a good one. He raced down the hall toward the back, his adrenaline pumping. He darted so fast that his body slammed against the plaster. The self-induced pummeling didn't affect him, and all his sensations were heightened. He was in fight-or-flight mode. He could hear the burly man rush after him. Without a doubt, he didn't want to fight him, though at a solid, jacked, 190 pounds, he could hold his own and inflict serious damage. Plus, he still had his Glock.

As he made his way to the back of the house, into a bedroom that looked like the master, he retrieved the Glock from his waist. Glocks didn't have manual safeties; so the gun would be ready to fire whenever he needed it.

The bedroom had French doors that led to the back. They had better be unlocked. He turned the knob as he heard the burly man enter the room.

"Stop!" the man shouted.

The doorknob turned, and Jordan opened the door, barely looking behind. A bullet was fired, and as he heard the blast, he dove toward the ground at the side of the house. He didn't go to the ground, though, and instead lifted himself slightly in a crouching position as he barreled toward a masonry wall. As he sprinted toward the wall, which stood about five feet high, he pushed against his heels with all his might to lunge to the top. As he jumped, another bullet careened against the ground. His hands gripped the top of the wall, and he pushed against it as a gymnast would against a pummel horse. He bounded over it. He heard another bullet ricochet against the stone wall.

He was in another person's yard. He scanned what looked like a chicken coop. Then he heard the chickens raise a fuss and scatter in the yard, startled by the foreign presence. He heard the burly man struggle as he tried to jump atop the wall. Jordan hurtled through the yard when an elderly man, perhaps in his early seventies, wearing well-worn overalls, came out a side door. He garbled something unintelligible in thickly accented Castilian.

"Your car," Jordan yelled. "I need your car."

The man looked at him blankly.

"*Su auto! Su carro!*" Jordan held his Glock toward him.

The man understood and reached into his pocket, dangling his keychain. Jordan grabbed the keys and headed to the front of the house where he saw a white Toyota pick-up. The truck looked like it was twenty years old. Jordan jumped into it; it started perfectly; and he sped off. He looked in the rearview mirror towards the wall between the two properties and saw no sign of the burly henchman.

As he bolted down the gravel driveway onto the paved road, he searched for signs of Sima or anyone else following him. He had paid attention to his location when Sima had driven him to the 'safe house.' He knew the highway wasn't far off. He lowered the window and could hear the faint hum of traffic in the background. He was getting closer. It was just a matter of finding the entrance. He coursed through the mostly residential neighborhood where houses stood far back from the road behind thick shrubbery, trees, and fences. When he looked ahead, he spotted what looked like an entrance to the highway. As he surged toward it, all of a sudden he heard a bullet fire behind him. It was Sima, in the gray Volkswagen sedan! She was driving, and the burly body man was in the passenger seat with his hand out the window, aiming a gun at his truck!

Without stopping, Jordan pulled alongside another car waiting at a light to enter the highway. He didn't bother yielding and bounded onto the thoroughfare, planting his vehicle directly ahead of a much larger truck that slammed on its brakes. Jordan managed to get ahead, watching as the larger truck fishtailed in the lanes behind him, slowing Sima and the other cars who were waiting to merge onto the highway. He weaved this way and that between cars to get further ahead. He looked in the rearview mirror and didn't spot the VW behind him. He seemed to have lost her.

He passed the next exit and realized he was heading away from Algeciras, toward the north of Spain. As he drove by the off-ramp, traffic lightened up, and there, amid the cars that he passed, was the gray Volkswagen! Sima was catching up to him. Another exit was approaching. He moved into the middle lane of the expressway, and then to the right lane, and then back to the middle lane. Then he moved to the fast lane. Each time he switched lanes, Sima followed in suit, performing the same maneuvers. The exit was a few hundred yards ahead. He increased his speed. The truck's speedometer said he was going 160 kilometers per hour. That must have been about 100 miles per hour! As the Toyota came closer to the exit, he increased his speed even further, to 175 kilometers per hour, rapidly moving across the middle and slow lanes and onto the exit ramp. As he crossed traffic, horns blared and brakes screeched. In the VW, Sima tried to mimic his maneuver, but she couldn't keep up. He slowed on the exit ramp, praying there wasn't a sharp corner or curve, but instead a straight roadway that would allow him to slow down more safely. His prayers were answered. He saw a linear path ahead and braked to eighty, and then seventy, kilometers per hour. He watched as Sima continued on the expressway. Before he had driven off the highway, he had noticed that the next exit was five kilometers ahead. The VW would need to reach that exit and then turn back to the exit Jordan had taken. He would have a ten-minute advantage over her.

While he had managed to shake her off, he didn't feel out of the woods. He knew it wouldn't take much effort to catch up. Time was not on his side. He continued to drive east. And he wondered: What if they had called more lackeys who were trailing him?

Chapter 21

Sixtus's assistant buzzed the pontiff to announce Richter's arrival. "Send him in," Sixtus said curtly.

Richter had a look of disbelief, of intense sorrow. As much as he personally didn't care for Barranca, the news of his death struck him to the core. "Your Excellency, I am so sorry."

"Sorry for what?" Sixtus demanded.

Richter stammered; he was at a loss for words. "Cardinal Barranca, Excellency."

"You didn't have anything to do with it, did you?"

"No, of course not."

"Then why be sorry?"

"It's just that..."

Sixtus interrupted – "There has been a change in plans. We were going to send a facsimile of the letter to President Foster. I don't want to delay things any longer. Gómez aid he has the original in the car."

How cavalierly he would part with the Vatican's priceless treasures, its history. "You want to send the original letter?" Richter asked incredulously.

"Why not? What good does it do for us sitting in our vault? The president will enjoy it and appreciate the historic value. Go get it and write something cordial for the president."

"Don't you want to write it yourself, Your Excellency?"

"Why would I want to do that? Just draft something and I'll sign it. Make sure it's not too unctuous. I don't want to come across as obsequious. Perhaps mention that he might want to keep it in the Smithsonian for safekeeping after he leaves office."

"Certainly, Your Holiness. And what are we to do about Barranca?"

Sixtus stared at the blank, white walls. In times like these, he would truly appreciate a window, if only to afford him some perspective. "We'll need a press release drafted. I don't want anything to go out until tomorrow."

"Why the wait?"

"We must notify his family. There's no rush. I'd like the investigation to proceed without scrutiny. Do you see any downside to that?"

Richter observed that Sixtus's demeanor was sharper than usual. Sixtus would usually speak to Barranca in the way he was now being spoken to. He was beginning to regret having supported Sixtus for the post. However, the million dollars in his secret Swiss account kept him in line. "None, Your Holiness. Where is his body being held?"

"At the morgue, I presume."

"Should we send someone?"

"Why?"

"I don't know, I just thought..."

Sixtus interrupted again – "When we get in touch with his family, we'll see what they want to do with the body. It's out of our hands."

Richter was confused. Many cardinals were buried at St. Peter's Basilica. Was Sixtus saying he wouldn't be buried at the Vatican? "Are we going to have a funeral service here?"

"I don't see why we should. He was always an Ecuadorian at heart.

He was a bishop there. Let his family take care of it."

"What about the other cardinals? It might be perceived as a slight."

"Fine. We can have a wake here and then ship his body off. Just tell them that's what his family wanted. I'm sure they'd want him closer to home."

"Of course, Your Holiness." He hesitated for a moment. "Do we know what happened?"

"It was rather gruesome. He had his throat slashed."

Richter covered his mouth in shock. "Who would do that?"

"We need to be extremely careful from now on. There's going to be a lot of negative press. The good thing is, if they start digging into Barranca's background, they won't find much."

"What about that boy?"

"The one from Notre Dame?"

"Yes."

"They won't find out anything about that. We've managed to keep it hidden for years. Unless there's a leak from inside, there's nothing to worry about."

"Do you think this has anything to do with Sister Sofija being in his room?"

"You think she could be connected to his murder?"

"I don't know," Richter replied. "But it seems a strange coincidence that she was in his room looking for something the same day he was killed."

Sixtus reflected for a moment, looking over Richter's shoulder. Again, he was searching for a window, some source of light. This room wasn't conducive to his best thinking. The office was only temporary, he reminded himself. "You may be right. Let's keep an eye on her."

* * *

Amanda arrived at the morgue at 7:30 p.m. While it had officially closed, Riccardo met her at the entrance. Using his clout as an officer of AISE, *Agenzia Informazioni e Sicurezza Esterna*, he managed to get them access. The AISE wasn't known as a powerhouse in intelligence circles, but domestically, it held its own and could instill fear in any red-blooded Italian. The days of Mussolini, though many decades in the past, still echoed, and the Italian citizenry was aware of its tendencies toward fascism. It was as if they wanted someone else – some strong man – to solve their problems, rather than trying to find solutions on their own.

"*Scusi. Scusi,*" Riccardo said, fending off the media who had already assembled at the front door to the morgue, a brick building from the sixteenth century that was once a mill. It stood on the outskirts of the city, away from the hustle and bustle of all the tourists. But today, with the paparazzi in full force, having smelled blood, the tumult here was as great as at the Duomo on a Sunday afternoon.

Amanda had thrown a scarf over her head and let it drape over her face. She didn't want to be photographed because her cover could be jeopardized. She wore large Ferragamo sunglasses that had been gifted to her by a friend back at Langley when she got the assignment to Rome. With all the accoutrements, you could hardly tell she was a blonde, let alone a CIA spy.

Truth be told, this was the part she loved most about being a spy: making herself invisible.

"*Scusi, scusi,*" Riccardo yawped at the throng as he ushered Amanda to the front door. Amanda noted that much of his kvetching was for show: The paparazzi were cordoned off from the sidewalk and weren't in their way at all.

"*Chi è morto?*" – Who has died? – piped a female reporter's high-pitched voice which rose above the din.

Amanda could hear Riccardo groan as he closed the door behind them. As much as she enjoyed making herself invisible, as if she were some important, coveted prey, she could tell that Riccardo enjoyed the attention of the masses.

"I'm sorry about that," he said to her in his heavily accented English.

"They don't know it's Barranca?"

"I don't think so. There are some rumors, some rumblings, as we have leaks inside the morgue. We have leaks all over Italy. We are like a sieve filled with pasta and drip, drip goes the water as it drains out. I can't help it."

She wondered if he might have been the source of some of the rumors. Perhaps he was lining his pocket on the side. His expensive Persol glasses, finely tailored Italian suit, and sleek black shoes might be difficult to pull off on a civil servant's salary, even with mama's help.

He escorted Amanda down one hall and then another. He certainly knew his way around the building. A couple of female attendants whispered to each other as Amanda passed. She had removed her sunglasses and scarf. Though her Italian was excellent, she couldn't decipher what the women were saying, their voices were so hushed.

He led her to an elevator, and they went to the basement. This must be where the newly arrived bodies were taken, she thought. The air was cool, so cool that Amanda shivered, and she deliberately jerked her head to attempt to shake off the chill that had invaded her. It didn't work, and she felt her teeth chattering. This flimsy clothing that she wore, so thin, such unnatural fibers, perfect in the Roman sun, did little to shelter her from the frosty onslaught.

A Swiss Guard stood at the entrance to the building. The Vatican had surely sent him. Could the media have seen him enter the morgue? Perhaps someone at the Vatican was on the take, too. While the Vatican was technically its own sovereign country, with its own laws, culturally, it was as Italian as pizza.

The guard did not make eye contact with Amanda or Riccardo. Nonetheless, she was sure that he could describe her *a fagiolo* – literally, to a bean or, more commonly, to a tee – down to her chattering, perfectly symmetrical, American-polished teeth and her shoulder-length, blonde hair that framed her oval face and brown eyes, giving her a wholesome air that belied the Italian garb that she used to disguise herself. Riccardo stopped at a metal door that had a small window for an opening. It was the type you'd see at a butchery where all the meat was stored. A sign read *Sala Autoptica* – Autopsy Room. Without Riccardo's having to say a word, the Swiss Guard policing the door opened it.

Upon entering, Amanda immediately took her scarf to cover her mouth and nose. The smell of chemicals was overwhelming. She looked at the corners of the ceiling; only a small window at ground level let in a sliver of natural light and no fresh air. Riccardo flipped the switches and with a large click, an array of fluorescent light brightened the room overhead. The lights momentarily flickered, and Amanda presumed they were straining the circuits. Italy was known as much for its food as for its notoriously faulty electrical systems. The lights calmed down and maintained a steady state as she and Riccardo approached the body.

She had no desire to look at the corpse. As a teenager, she had read enough Patricia Cornwell novels to know that a dead body offered nothing but puzzles that only scientists were interested in solving. She had no such curiosity. A dead body was a dead body. But she had come because she did want to learn one thing: how brutal was the kill.

Riccardo lifted the off-white cloth that covered the torso.

She saw a gash on Barranca's neck. The skin was reddened where a scar would form if he were still alive. The edges of the wound appeared to have been scraped thoroughly – for evidence of some sort – DNA, foreign matter, et cetera. Amanda had seen enough to know that it was a serious knife wound but not one that had been overly vicious. She had seen much worse, edge to edge, sometimes like a smile, or so deeply puncturing the skin that the larynx was exposed along with the Adam's apple. The assailant had taken a little care to be gentle with Barranca's neck. There was almost a motherly touch. The person who killed the cardinal had some care for him, or at least, sympathy. It was likely a woman, she surmised.

Riccardo took out his cell phone and snapped a picture. Was he going to sell it on the underground?

"I don't think we should be taking pictures," Amanda said.

"For the office," he said. "They will want to see."

She gave a noncommittal 'uh-huh' to signal disbelief and doubt.

He was going to take one from another angle. She stopped him. "One's enough."

"Yes, of course."

He was probably regretting taking her with him, but she didn't care. She looked at the body, noticing that one of his wrists had red welts. Someone had handcuffed him. She went to the other side of his body and lifted the cloth covering that remained over his left arm. Examining that wrist, she saw no markings, no sign of restraint. Kay Scarpetta would have been proud.

"I've seen enough," she said.

"Don't you want to see the rest of his body?" Riccardo asked. Without hesitating, he reached over to pull the entire cloth off Barranca's body, as a magician would when making a big reveal. When he lifted the cloth, her eyes couldn't help but gravitate over the lower part of his exposed body. Then, she saw what she really didn't want to see and knew that she wouldn't be able to unsee.

"*Che culo,*" Riccardo smirked in admiration and without any hint of irony. How lucky.

Amanda turned to a clear plastic bag situated on a nearby stainless-steel table. It was marked 'Barranca' with a black Sharpie and contained his clothing – the same suit that he had worn the day she met him. He might have only owned a couple, she thought. Despite the extreme wealth of the church, even the cardinals were held to a tight budget when it came to worldly possessions. She opened the bag and slid her hand in the pockets.

"What are you looking for?" asked Riccardo.

She didn't answer. She was looking for anything, in fact. Anything that would give her some clue as to why he was so brutally murdered. She knew there was a connection to the shipment and the man he had run into at Termini Station. She wanted something that would help her determine who was responsible for slashing his throat. She continued to rifle through his pockets, hoping to find something. There was a wallet, embossed with his initials, J-B-E. Inside were his Vatican identification card; a couple of hundred euros; two credit cards, one looked personal, the other the official card he would use for Holy See business; an ATM card; a driver's license from Indiana, with an address at an apartment in South Bend. The University of Notre Dame was located next to that city, and she knew he had studied and taught there years ago. Funny how he hadn't gotten an Italian driver's license. Perhaps there was no need, with all the drivers at his disposal. The Indiana license had expired a few years ago. In the billfold compartment, she found a picture of what looked like his mother in Ecuador, wearing a rosary. Amanda thought of what she didn't see: There were no pictures of his father or brothers. No picture of Sixtus or any pope for that matter. Nothing that truly connected him to the church.

She went through each of the pockets – in his sport coat, in his pants. In a second bag, his shoes and socks were held. The shoes were expensive black leather loafers with only slight wear. The socks matched the brown color of his pants. Nothing was hidden inside them.

A third bag contained his underwear. On the front of the white briefs, there was a large stain, from urine. His death wasn't pleasant; but there were no signs of outright torture, only mistreatment and neglect.

A watch – there was no watch. She looked back at his wrists. There was no watch there either, only welts. The wallet had remained in his pants pocket; the watch should be somewhere. Did his captors take it? She knew he wore a wristwatch. She saw it yesterday. It had a gold face and a black leather band. He had twisted the band around his wrist. Had the Italian police taken it, as the spoils of their murder investigation?

"Is something the matter?" Riccardo asked.

"No, nothing." She hadn't found any additional clues. "Is he wearing a ring?"

Riccardo looked at Barranca's hands. On his left hand, he saw a gold ring. "Yes, it is his cardinal's ring. It has St. Peter and Paul on it, with a star. It's called the Cardinalate."

She was impressed how much some Italians knew of their faith. She had noticed the same ring yesterday but hadn't gotten a close look. "Can you take it off?"

Riccardo looked not the slightest bit uncomfortable as he took Barranca's hand and tried to twist the ring off. Rigor mortis had already set in. "He's so stiff."

"Does the ring look tight?"

Riccardo saw a roll of flesh on each side of the ring. "Yes, his finger does look fat. Should we have them take it off for us?"

"No. That's up to his family or the Vatican." So, they had taken his watch but not his papal ring? The captors might have left the ring to ensure that he was identified properly as a cardinal. The police might have realized they couldn't take it off because it was stuck on his finger. But one of the officers might have been tempted by the wristwatch; it would have been easy to unfasten the band and snatch the watch.

Amanda looked at the bags of clothing she had scattered on the table. She could sense Riccardo observing her, waiting for some finding, some pronouncement. But she had nothing. Nothing more than a cadaver. On top of it all, she had a distinct sense of guilt. She could have warned Barranca not to travel. She could have told him his life was in grave danger. She could have offered to escort him to the convent. But she had failed to protect him, and now he lay still, at God's mercy.

* * *

Jordan continued to drive at a rapid pace through the small village. In a short amount of time, he came across another highway. He risked heading onto it, the A-381 autoroute to Cadiz. He constantly looked in his rearview mirror for any sign of the gray Volkswagen. Every car in a similar shade of gray sent alarm bells up his spine; he was relieved each time when he realized it wasn't Sima's car. But still, he had the sensation that someone was following him, watching his every move. He had never been in a shootout before. Even with his training at Quantico, where they simulated chases, kidnappings, hostage situations, robberies, and the like, he hadn't been prepared for actual gunfire. He could have been killed. He could have been taken hostage. And while he had fortunately sent the location of the "safe house" to Amanda – as a precaution, who knows what would have happened to him had Sima and her burly goon managed to subdue him. He had wanted to call his family – to say something to his father, if only to say, "Hello, I'm here, how are you?" He wanted to hear his father's calming, reassuring voice. He wanted to be consoled. He wanted to be comforted, with his father's hands on his shoulders, telling him not to worry, that he had done good, that he'd have another chance, that he was proud of him, son. Words he'd hear as a young child. Words that would encourage him on. Words that had propelled him to Georgia Tech, to the FBI. Words that echoed in his mind whenever he doubted himself. Words that made him try harder. Words that made him reap the benefits of success. Words that were now conspicuously absent.

He couldn't risk calling his father. He knew enough about cell phones to know that he might be tracked somehow. He was beginning to feel paranoid. He wasn't the fearful type, but his antennae had not only been raised, they had been twisted and bent this way and that, pointing in all directions except home. He was in foreign territory, literally. He had never felt so alone, so vulnerable. So this is what life as a spy was like. He preferred the team environment of his mustachioed mates back at FBI headquarters.

As he drove onward, he reached a mountainous area. It was Los Alcornocales Natural Park. He passed through stone tunnels carved in hillsides. The radio turned to static. He continued to drive in this westerly direction. He realized he had made a mistake. He had driven into the middle of nowhere. There were few cars on the road. Anyone could come up behind him, shoot his tires out, and leave him for dead on the side of the highway. He had committed the cardinal sin. He had driven without objective, without a plan. He had wanted to escape. Now, he was trapped in his freedom.

The truck went up and down the mountainsides. He looked at the fuel gauge. He had less than a quarter of a tank of gas. He doubted there were any stations for miles. Damn, he needed to hear his father's voice! But he couldn't bring himself to call, to admit he needed him, to tell him how scared he was. *Someone else might be listening.* But who, he asked himself. MI6? God?

A steep hill lay ahead. He pressed on the gas to keep going at his steady clip. He could feel the fuel gauge becoming more depleted by the second. *So God,* he asked, *is this it?*

He was being overly dramatic, he told himself. That's what his father would say. Yes, this wasn't the end of the world. Not quite. He took his cell phone as he steadied the truck around a curve and opened Rebar, struggling to sign in and maneuver the truck at the same time. He called Amanda. The phone rang. Answer, answer, he told himself. Then a voice came on the other line:

"Jordan," she said. "Did you get my message?"

"Did I ever."

"What happened?"

"I almost got killed."

"I'll head there tonight."

"Where?" he asked.

"Algeciras."

"I'm in the mountains now. I'm heading towards Cadiz."

"You're getting around."

"I didn't have a choice."

"Listen, I'm grabbing a flight to Madrid tonight. We've got to meet somewhere."

"I'm not even sure I'll make it to Cadiz. My tank's running empty."

"Keep your phone charged. I can always track you down via Rebar." Amanda paused. "I'm afraid I have some bad news. We lost Cardinal Barranca. He was the secretary of state for the Vatican. He was murdered."

"They were looking for information on the shipment?"

"They probably wanted to know what he knew. I don't know what they learned. He wasn't tortured, so I assume he told them what he knew."

"He didn't know much, did he?"

"Not that he revealed to me. But you never know. If they're willing to kill a cardinal, there's no limit to how far they'll go."

"That's for sure. I barely escaped alive."

"You're going to have to head back to Algeciras, you know?"

"I hope you have some weapons."

"I do. And some extra tricks up my sleeve too. I'll call in some back-up. This is too high priority to let things slip to chance."

"I never asked you," Jordan said. "Why did you want the FBI's help?"

"If we can't stop the shipment, we're going to need someone who can legally operate onshore. It's better to have someone who's already read in."

"You think we might have missed the boat, literally?"

She chuckled at his pun. "I don't know. I should have been there today. I just wanted to check on the cardinal. I was too late."

"I hope you're not too late for me."

"I suggest you change cars as soon as you can. I haven't received the report on Sima yet. I don't know what's taking them so long. I'll let you know when we have it. I'll see if we have a safe house in Cadiz. But find a non-descript hotel. That works just as well. The key is to blend in."

Blending in: It was the story of Jordan Harrison's life. But it wasn't easy when you were an African American living in predominantly white, Hispanic, and Arab Spain. "I'll do my best."

* * *

Amanda sat in the boarding gate of Florence's Amerigo Vespucci Airport, waiting for her flight to Madrid. She was connected to a private VPN that the CIA used throughout Europe, and through that VPN, another connection was made to a satellite for ultrasecure communications. The IP addresses and routing were continually updated to prevent hacking, and the system was monitored twenty-four/seven by the NSA. The IMEI of every cell phone and the MAC address of every computer were meticulously tracked in a database and cross-referenced against known devices to detect intrusion. Every year, under the auspices of the Office of the Defense Intelligence Agency, the umbrella organization that oversees the CIA, the NSA, and the other American intelligency community at large, IMEI and MAC IDs were changed on the devices so that cloning or masking couldn't be used to infiltrate the system.

For the most part, Amanda entered her activities in Rebar, giving her superiors an update on the murder of Barranca and the attack on

Jordan. She constantly edited her comments so as not to appear completely clueless, but the fact was, she hadn't made a whole lot of progress. She was able to document the location of the supposed 'safe house' that Jordan escaped from, as well as the license plate number of Sima's getaway car. Her account wasn't totally useless, she told herself. She also requested back-up in Spain – any officers that could be spared to assist. As she hit *send*, a man and a woman caught her eye. They didn't take seats, though there were plenty available. The couple stood at the edge of the waiting area, in the aisle and in the way of other travelers who were passing through. Perhaps they were oblivious, self-centered travelers. The woman had short, dark hair; was thin; looked to be in her fifties. She was Caucasian but had an Eastern European air. Next to her was a man in his mid-to-late thirties. Tall, strapping, with a thick but trimmed beard. He also looked Eastern European. They didn't look related. They were too mismatched to be boyfriend and girlfriend. They didn't have the air of business travelers – salespeople or colleagues who worked together.

While tapping at her phone, Amanda took her hand and brushed her hair, playing with it, pretending to stretch and relax her neck as she rocked her head back. What the man and woman didn't know was that Amanda was recording them with her digital watch, which had a camera that was attached to her phone. Could this woman be the Violeta that Falzone said had ordered the shipment? Amanda had her telephone number. She could try to call her. But no. She should wait. She didn't want to raise any suspicion before they arrived in Madrid. The woman was a pro, and she might realize she was being followed.

Amanda tried to appear relaxed, imagining she was on social media watching some nonsense videos. Meanwhile, she put an urgent request of the home office into Rebar. She wanted the full passenger list of the flight. She would be boarding any minute.

Chapter 22

Amanda's flight departed at 9 p.m. and was scheduled to arrive just before midnight. She would have preferred to flight directly into Algeciras or Malaga, a Spanish city close to the port, or even Cadiz, but none of the flights were direct. She would have been routed through Stockholm or some other far-away city that had more transport options than Florence's mid-size Amerigo Vespucci Airport. She told herself that flying to Madrid wasn't such a bad option after all. She wasn't sure where she'd be able to connect with Jordan. From Madrid, she could get anywhere, easily, as it was the undisputed hub of the Iberian Peninsula.

The passengers were mostly Spanish, with a smattering of Italians. Amanda and the Eastern European couple stood out in the cabin of the Airbus 319, which held about 150 passengers and crew. The flight was only half full; there was ample space to spread out in the rows.

Fog had set in and caused a delay with departure. The pilot announced, in Italian, that he would try to arrive on time by increasing speed. Amanda took the opportunity to check Rebar. A response came in from the home office regarding her request for the flight manifest.

"What operation is this for?" the message read.

Such bureaucracy, she thought. No one in government could, or would, lift a finger unless there was some official policy, procedure, or op to record activities against. It was a way of ensuring that everything was officially sanctioned, even though in the world of clandestine ops, nothing was truly sanctioned. At least eighty percent of what undercover officers like Amanda did was fly-by-night improvisation guided by intuition and instinct. The officer who asked could have easily looked up the information if he or she had an iota of motivation. Lack of initiative was probably why those folks were sitting at desks anyway.

"Double Bogey," she wrote back. Many of the chiefs at Langley were intensely interested in their golf game, and they needed something to amuse themselves, especially if things went sideways. At the same time, she sent the video of the Eastern European pair asking them to use facial recognition to determine who the couple was.

Shortly, the plane took off, and while she was in the air, she would have no connection. Staff weren't allowed to access Rebar through airplane Wi-Fi. She didn't fully understand why, but the Cyber Command geeks at Fort Meade had deemed it too much of a security risk. She would have to wait until the plane landed around midnight. It would only be about 6 p.m. then in Washington. Still plenty early, but just around the time when shifts would start to change. Some person completely unfamiliar with her requests would respond. That person would probably be a contractor who was just trying to earn some experience before he could hop over to Booz Allen or Deloitte and double his salary, all on the taxpayer's dime. These contractors were the new, less dangerous breed of Edward Snowden.

* * *

After dinner and prayers, Cardinal Richter stopped at the nuns' quarters where he was hoping to see Sister Sofija. He had noticed she hadn't eaten with the rest of the nuns in the dining hall. She missed out on a gorgeous, slow-roasted leg of lamb accompanied by a fine Piedmont Barolo. The church deemed their premium victuals as necessary tributes to the Son of God. Whatever that might be criticized for its excess could be justified by invoking Jesus and his disciples. Saying a few holy words made the rationalization so.

Richter stopped at Sofija's room and knocked. No answer. Another nun came down the hall. "Do you know where she is?" he demanded.

"I haven't seen her all day," whimpered the nun, her feeble voice trembling. Everyone was afraid of Richter. He had that demeanor, that authoritative baritone that could exorcize a demonic spirit within fifteen feet. "It's not like her to disappear like this."

"Call me when she gets back."

"If it's late?" the nun asked meekly.

"I don't care," he snapped. "I want to see her."

"Yes, Your Excellency."

* * *

Sixtus sat alone in a private garden of the Apostolic Palace. The story of his life was that he was always alone, having only occasional passersby and interlopers who needed him or whom he needed. The most consistent presence in his life, other than his mother until her death, was Bensaïd. The garden was illuminated by a few heating lamps that a Swiss Guard had turned on when the pope expressed his wish to rest there. Sixtus asked the guard to leave him alone, but he stood at attention at a side entrance to the palace about twenty meters away. He would keep his voice quiet. It was times like these that he hated Pope Francis more than ever; he had given up the Papal Palace of Castel Gandolfo where for centuries popes had taken summer vacations. Francis wanted to democratize the church, to shorn it of its elegant trappings at least from a public perspective. So Gandolfo was opened to the public and made into a tourist attraction. Meanwhile, Sixtus and all of Francis's successors were left with no privacy, no place to think and be by themselves. Perhaps that was the point. Francis didn't want any pope to be able to think independently or to secure too much power. The power would be concentrated in the hands of many, not a few, and the papacy would be no more than a committee, like a board that governed a major corporation, and the pope was no more than a chief executive officer who could be dismissed by majority vote of the board. Hogwash, he thought. He wasn't going to end up like Benedict and be forced to resign. Francis should have been hanged for blasphemy. In Sixtus's eyes, he did more damage to the papacy than any modern pope, and he was determined to undo that damage.

As he sat with his cell phone in hand, dimly lighting his face, checking his schedule for tomorrow and seeing all the meetings that had been planned for him but not by him, he asked whether the White House would be any different. He would be a prisoner there, too. But at least he'd be able to shuffle back and forth between Washington and Rome, and he'd have Camp David and other retreats he could retire to. He knew he'd have to play the game a little longer and not raise suspicion. He had managed to win over Francis with his do-good, globalist bullshit, and he was certain he could keep the current cardinals in line. After all, most had been bribed, and Bensaïd had the receipts.

Still, he was worried about what had happened with Barranca. Murder was a step too far.

Sixtus heard low voices where the side entrance was, and Bensaïd approached. Sixtus extended his hand so that Bensaïd could kiss his Fisherman's Ring, a trivial formality but one for which they had to maintain the pretense.

"May I sit?" Bensaïd asked while making a mental note that the guard had retreated to the entrance.

"Please." Sixtus pointed his finger to a spot on the stone bench near him.

"I know this news is troubling," Bensaïd said.

"You said he was harmless," Sixtus interrupted.

Sixtus's shortness surprised him. "Your Holiness, there was no other way. He was getting too close."

"But why?"

"The man at the train station gave him information that put the entire operation at risk. All he had to do was make one phone call and we would have been set back years, if not forever."

The prospect of several more years of this charade didn't sit well with Sixtus. "But how do we know it hasn't already been jeopardized?"

"Because we now have the evidence." Bensaïd took a piece of paper from his coat pocket and showed it to Sixtus. It was the shipping transmittal that Barranca had hidden under his bedpost.

Sixtus glanced at it as if he didn't want to see it, then looked up at the palace to see if any windows nearby were lit. Could anyone be watching them?

Bensaïd stood and moved toward the heating lamp. He slipped the edge of the paper into the flame, and it caught fire. He let it burn, and when the flames got too close to his fingers, he dropped it to the ground. He watched it disappear into ash by his feet, then he stomped it, dissolving the ash into the cobblestone.

"If you got the evidence, why did you have to kill him?"

"I told you there would be casualties."

"Yes, but not so close to home. I don't want anything that could be pointed back at me."

"Ultimately, everything will point to you, Pontiff. You had better get used to it."

Sixtus reflected for a moment. He knew that without Bensaïd, without the secret patronage of Khalid Zahir, he wouldn't be pope. But now, he was starting to feel even more isolated. Richter had become suspicious. Every cardinal and archbishop would be on alert; every nun in fact. All roads led to Rome. And he had no leverage over Bensaïd or Zahir. He couldn't protect himself. The only possible way was through Richter, and even then, the two were no match against the money and connections that Bensaïd and Zahir had. His only option was to call things off, and he couldn't do that. He was too close. Once he seized the reins of power, he could make his move. Bensaïd and Zahir would be at his mercy then. He could bend them at will. "How do you know he didn't pass on the information?"

"I can't be one hundred percent sure. But we have operatives working to ensure the safe passage of the materials. They will go through tomorrow. If anyone stands in our way, they will be killed also."

Sixtus heard shuffling on the other side of the garden. Startled, he looked behind him toward the hedge. He signaled for Bensaïd to inspect. Bensaïd stood and peered through the privet. It was so thick he couldn't make out anything. He shrugged.

People were always spying on one another here, thought Sixtus. No one had enough to do. Everything was a game of one-upmanship when it came to information. What did you know that others didn't, and how that knowledge could be leveraged and parlayed into power. Sixtus himself hadn't had to play that game; as a trusted favorite of the hierarchy, he was always privy to inside information. But now, the intrigues centered around him and everything he said or did. How did the other popes cope? Did they ignore the whispering, the conniving, the backstabbing? Sometimes they put a tighter lid on information, closing the circle on some so that they would be less of a threat. Yet that didn't reduce the resistance, the perpetual currying of favor. Sixtus had had to jockey for position; as an assertive type, it wasn't hard for him to do. Still, he knew that many would like to see him fail, if only to use that as reasoning to elect them as the next pope. Barranca fell into that category. Perhaps he deserved to die, if only for his covetousness. He wasn't certain about Richter. But Sixtus knew one thing: There wasn't going to be another pope.

Chapter 23

When the plane landed in Madrid and taxied to the terminal, Amanda checked Rebar and saw that she had received a report from the home office. Sima was a gun for hire. For the past fifteen years, she had done a lot of odd jobs throughout Europe. Most were related to industrial espionage. She was sophisticated and fit into high-end circles. Many of her targets were wealthy businessmen who were being blackmailed or coerced into taking certain actions. She was a kind of 'honey pot' without the sex. She could lure anybody. She was completely self-taught and had started in this line of work after a nasty divorce from a wealthy businessman who had left her with nothing on account of a prenup. She had no formal intelligence training. Illegal arms shipments were not her specialty. She had probably taken the assignment because of the high pay. The greater the risk, the greater the reward.

Amanda forwarded the report to Jordan. She took her time deboarding. She wanted to follow behind the Eastern European couple, although they were seated behind her in the plane. She foraged inside her bag, pretending to look for something. But as time passed, and as she let other passengers move ahead of her, she knew that she might attract suspicion, particularly from the Eastern European pair. She would have to get off the plane. But now she had something in her hand that could lead her to them which would help her track them. It was a pen. To the casual observer, it looked like any old pen with three different color inks. But the pen could shoot its ink a few feet ahead, and when two of the inks combined, they created a third substance that was largely invisible against dark backgrounds, such as black or navy clothing. The inks would congeal into a photovoltaic spot that could be tracked electronically.

She walked off the plane, thanking the crew and heading into the crowded airport. There, she checked Rebar for any information on the couple. Nothing yet. The couple passed by her. She took out a folio and scratched it with the pen. She turned the pen into position as the couple proceeded ahead. She was several yards behind them. Numerous targets presented themselves: the dark blue blouse that the woman wore; the man's blue jeans; his gray canvas backpack; the black suitcase that the woman rolled. Amanda had never used the pen before. In demonstrations, she saw that the force could be considerable, and officers were advised to use caution when administering the shots to someone's clothing. Personal effects raised less suspicion. She got closer to the woman. The suitcase zigzagged beside her, sometimes trailing her. Amanda managed to shoot the first ink against the rectangular side, about a third of the way up. The ink became barely discernible.

The couple said something to one another, and suddenly, the man went in one direction across the hall and the woman turned back from where they had come. What were they doing? Amanda sauntered on a bit; then she saw that the man was heading into the men's room across the aisle. She presumed the woman was headed into the women's restroom. She continued to walk a little further; then she looked behind. The woman was gone. Yes, she too had gone into the restroom. Amanda quickly made her way back down the hallway and proceeded into the women's room.

As she went inside, she saw about a dozen stalls lined up against the wall. She walked by them, looking at each doorway to see if she noticed a black rollaway case. There! She spotted it, right against the doorway in the middle of the stalls. Amanda wanted to enter the stall next to it, but it was occupied. At the end of the row, another woman exited a stall. Amanda quickly scooted inside, taking her place behind the door so that her shoes wouldn't be visible from the common area. She heard a toilet flush; a door opened; a suitcase was being wheeled across the tiled floor. She heard the faucet run. She peered from the crack of the door. Now that she was connected to Rebar, she placed a call to the number Falzone had given her for Violeta.

Amanda's volume was completely muted, but in an instant, she heard the woman's cell phone ring with a sci-fi melody. Yes, it was Violeta!

Amanda watched as Violeta looked at the phone, puzzled by the unknown number. She pressed a button to ignore and silence the call; then she proceeded to the exit.

Moving steadily and with deliberation, Amanda emerged from the stall and went to the stall. With Violeta's back towards her as she proceeded through the exit, Amanda fired the pen at the suitcase, hitting it precisely at the spot that she had hit before.

Amanda stood at the vanity, grabbing a paper towel, turning her back to the door. Then she retreated to the stall area. She gave a moment to listen to see if the woman was going to return for some reason. Amanda was practicing the tradecraft she had been taught: Never assume that you are in the clear after completing an operational hurdle. The target can always come back.

After a few moments, she exited the bathroom, looking at her phone, in part to appear distracted, but also to avoid potential eye contact with the target. From the corners of her eyes, she didn't see the Eastern Europeans. Nonetheless, she didn't look up.

She clicked the tracking icon within Rebar and saw the dot at the Madrid-Barajas Airport. She zoomed in; a large plot showed facsimiles of the terminals, runways, and parking areas. The dot was in the center of one of the terminals. The tracking worked! But she knew it had a shelf life. In less than a day, the tracking would be less reliable and disappear.

Chapter 24

Jordan Harrison had managed to pass through to the other side of the forest where there was a semblance of civilization. His gas gauge teetered on empty as he entered a small village. He knew that at any moment, the truck might stop. He pulled to the side of the road, near a local pub/restaurant. The sign outside the bar caught his eye: It said *'El Lince'* and had the face of a tiger-like cat with pointy ears and a spotted face in the background, all in gold and white. He looked up *El Lince* on Rebar's secure browser. *El Lince* meant 'the lynx' in Spanish. He learned that the Iberian lynx was the national animal of Spain. The area was deserted, with few cars on the road and fewer lights on in the surrounding buildings. If Sima or her henchman followed him there, he would be a sitting duck. He knew he shouldn't stay. But he could use a beer. He entered the pub. Spanish music played faintly in the background. A woman in her late twenties or early thirties was cleaning the bar. She had numerous piercings in her nose and along the helices of her ears. She wore pronounced, black eyeliner that gave her eyes a winged, elongated shape, like a cat's. She looked like a grown-up goth girl. There were no patrons inside. Jordan didn't know what she was cleaning exactly. Perhaps she was bored.

"*Hola,*" he said in Spanish.

She said something back in Spanish very rapidly with a thick Castilian accent. He didn't understand but asked for a beer: "*Una cerveza, por favor.*"

"American?" she asked in English.

"Yes."

"What kind would you like? I have several craft beers."

"Anything local?"

It took her a moment to understand, to translate what he was asking in her head. Then she smiled and took a beer from underneath the counter, exhibiting it for him.

The bottle had a very colorful label; there appeared to be a man on a horse. Sancho Panza, perhaps, from *Don Quixote.* "That would be great. Thank you."

She popped the bottle cap off and handed it to him. "Where are you coming from?"

"I'm just driving through from Malaga," he answered, lying.

"Going to Cadiz?"

"I think I might head back to Madrid." He didn't want to leave any clear clues where he was going in case Sima caught up to him and interrogated the bartender.

"Well, you're a way off. You need to head back up north. This road will lead west."

"Yes, I was going to turn up ahead. I just had to get through the mountains." He took a swig of the beer. "This is really good."

"My cousins make it." She had a pleased look on her face, and her Spanish pride beamed. She retreated to the other side of the bar.

Jordan checked Rebar and, in the darkened bar, read the intelligence report on Sima. It seemed to sum her up well. But it still gave him no idea how she had managed to identify him. Was it purely through her connection to the gun dealer? That was certainly a possibility. She could have been hired to watch all gun purchases to see if anyone might potentially interfere with the shipment. But that would be a lot of people, and a mountain of work. It didn't seem feasible. To Jordan, it seemed as if she had somehow been tipped off to his presence.

The bartender returned, drying a glass with a towel. "You ready for another one?"

"I better take it easy tonight. Listen, my truck has pretty much run out of gas. Is there a gas station around here?"

"Yes, a couple of kilometers down the street, near the edge of town."

He twirled the bottle on the countertop. It was a miraculous piece of black, burnished wood that looked centuries old. "I'm not sure if I'll make it."

"I'm closing soon," she said. "I can give you a lift."

"My name's Jordan, by the way."

"Pilar."

"What's this town called?"

"We gave it a nickname. *Sincojones.* Without Balls." She laughed. "It's Sincona."

* * *

Amanda watched Rebar as she saw the Eastern European couple navigate through the airport, making their way to a rental car agency. She knew she had to do the same. She hadn't made a car reservation herself and instead headed to the transportation section of the terminal to reserve one. She had accounts at all the major agencies; she chose one that the Europeans weren't using. With her platinum status, she had no problem getting a car. While she waited for the shuttle transport to bring her to the car pick-up location, she saw that Violeta and her companion were driving along the highway.

They were heading south. Algeciras, she thought.

She sent Jordan a message via Rebar: "Just landed in Madrid. Are you in Cadiz yet? I might have to go directly to Algeciras." She didn't want to lose connection to the Europeans, and she knew she only had about twenty-four hours of tracking, possibly less.

After she picked up her stylish Opel sedan and drove south along the same highway, she received an update from her inquiry on the video she sent of the Eastern Europeans from the Florence airport. The car didn't have a phone mount, and she struggled to read the report while she drove on the unfamiliar highway. She veered out of her lane, and a large semi blared its horn. The woman's name was Violeta Manolov. Of course, she already knew it was Violeta. Sometimes, the Home Office was so far behind her. Now she had a last name: Manolov. Manolos, the shoes, Amanda told herself as a mnemonic device to remember the woman's surname. *Violet Manolos*. The woman wasn't wearing violet shoes, but the memory trick would work. Amanda could visualize the woman in high-end purple pumps.

Violeta Manolov was Bulgarian. A known member of...

A car came careening toward Amanda's! No, it was Amanda hurtling toward the other car! She regained control of her car and switched to the other window of Rebar, where the tracking of Violet Manolos was displayed. She would have to pull over or read the report later. For now, she decided to continue down the highway and make up for lost time. They were about a half-hour ahead of her. Judging by the increasing distance between her car and theirs, Amanda inferred that they were driving at a high speed. She wouldn't risk driving recklessly herself. And she wouldn't pull over at this point so that they didn't get too far ahead of her. She would rely on the tracking pin and be assured that she could pinpoint their whereabouts.

* * *

Jordan Harrison sat in Pilar's small white Citroën while she drove toward the other edge of town. The streets were totally blackened; not a single streetlight or building illuminated any part of the route. The Citroën had to have been over a decade old, and its interior was well worn. She drove at a fast clip; she was evidently eminently familiar with the roads. They chatted during the drive. He learned that she had worked at the bar since she was a teenager. Her father had opened it decades ago, and he was all but retired. Business was poor. Jordan could tell she was a woman of modest means.

He saw Amanda's message on Rebar that she was heading to Algeciras.

When they arrived at tiny gas station, which had just a single pump and a small convenience store, he said, "Do you think they have a gas can?"

"I have a jar in the trunk," she said, meaning a jug. "You can have it."

"I couldn't do that. I'll pay you." He paused. "Look, I have an idea. I know we don't know each other at all, but I'm work for the FBI in Washington, D.C. Have you heard of the FBI?"

"Yes, of course."

"I need to go back to Algeciras for work. Could I pay you to bring me there?"

"I'm not a taxi," she said haughtily.

He could tell she was offended. "I didn't mean to..."

She interrupted: "What are you going to give me? A pack of cigarettes? I'm not one of your migrants that you can toss to the trash when you're done."

"I'm sorry...."

She interrupted again: "Get out!"

He looked at her, astounded by her harsh reaction.

"I mean it. Get out!" She pointed to the door of the car. "I'll get your jar." She hastily and angrily hopped out of the car and went to the trunk. Jordan followed by exiting the passenger-side door. Instinctively, he put his hand on the gun packed in the seat of his pants. Her sudden volatility made him feel vulnerable, exposed, at risk. She thrust a red plastic gas can toward his chest. The abrupt motion, combined with the sight of the empty red jug, presented an absurdity; instantly, he felt more relaxed. He took his hand away from the gun and took the canister. "Thank you," he said.

As he started to walk toward the gas station, she called out, "I'm sorry!" He looked back and saw that she was practically in tears. She looked shaken up – by something, but by what, he didn't know. She was afflicted with some internal drama – emotional, theatrical, climactic, striking – which caused her to lash out simultaneously at him and herself in some odd way. He stared at her. "Are you okay?" "Yes! No!" she cried. "I'm sorry," he said. Had she been drinking at the bar? Mixing booze with medication? "Everyone is always sorry!" she screamed. He could see she was becoming more emotional, losing more control. "Everyone wants something and then they just leave you. Tell you to fuck off! I'm tired of fucking off!" she roared.

Something had obviously happened to her. He didn't know what. Perhaps some guy had abandoned her. Perhaps a few. Yes, the betrayals, the rejections – whatever they were – had built up and left her stripped, bare, boiling, resentful. What could he say to her? He hardly knew her. Yet she had unleashed on him. Expecting something perhaps. Some measure of comfort. Some understanding. Another apology? No, that wouldn't work. It wasn't his place. He had apologized enough, and she had refused his apology. Now he understood why. She didn't want an apology for his having presumed she might want to give him a ride. No. She had wanted an apology for something deeper, something much more personal, and he had unearthed it, scratched at it like an ugly scab that she had picked time and again, never letting it heal. She wanted to see the blood. She wanted to see her skin crack, peel, and redden. She wanted to keep the chronic wound alive, if only to brandish it to ward others off.

Before he could say anything, she spoke further: "Give me the jar back. I'll take you to fucking Algeciras."

"You don't have to," he said.

"I know I don't fucking have to! I want to! There! Understand?" She reached for the red plastic jug and pulled it from him. He let go of it willingly. He could see that tears had rolled down her face. "Get in the car!"

"Yes, ma'am," he said, moving away from the trunk to the side of the car.

"How much are you going to pay me?" she asked.

"How much do you want?"

"Five hundred. No, a thousand euros."

"Deal." He was carrying with him U.S. dollars. "I'll give you five hundred now. I'll give you the rest when we arrive."

She laughed, eructing an uncontrollable chortle as she tossed the canister back in the trunk, slammed the lid shut, and stuffed the five hundred dollars in her bra.

* * *

Richter had overheard the conversation between Sixtus and Bensaïd. He had managed to shuffle into a side entrance behind the hedges. He was sure that Bensaïd didn't see him. He could have been any of the dozens of people who routinely roamed the grounds of the Vatican, from nuns, to priests, to maintenance workers or security guards. There was never a dearth of do-nothing onlookers spying about, wanting some tidbit of inside information.

So, they were expecting a shipment, and it was on schedule. It was a matter of some importance; they had kept their voices low. They had practically met in secret. What could it be?

As he plodded through the hallways near the nuns' quarters, he wondered if there was any connection between Barranca's death and the shipment. Was Sister Sofija in his room searching for something related to the parcel? Where was she? It was almost 10 p.m.! She shouldn't be out so late! If she were a young nun, the more senior sisters would scold her to no end. But Sister Sofija ruled the roost. She had this imperial air that intimidated everybody. Everybody but Richter, that is. No nun would scare him off.

He was getting tired. He had asked a nun to alert him when she returned. But nothing! He was ready to send a Swiss Guard to patrol the hallways and send Sofija to his office when she returned. Then he heard footsteps coming down the hall. It was the sister! She was wearing street clothes: a knitted sweater, a skirt, flat shoes. She had left the Vatican, gone out into the city. The entire outfit had a hand-me-down air. It was amazing how homely these nuns would make themselves.

She looked startled upon seeing him. "Your Excellency," she said with a hint of a gasp.

"Where have you been?"

"I was tending to an old friend. A woman in need. She is very ill."

"Why didn't you tell anyone where you were going?"

"Who is there to tell?" Suddenly, her tone became haughty.

"I want to know what you were doing in the cardinal's room earlier."

"I heard a noise. As I told you, I went inside. Everything was upside down."

"What were you looking for?"

"Whoever it was who turned the room upside down," she pleaded.

"The cardinal was killed today." He spoke bluntly, to see if she would be shocked or if she had already heard the news.

Her face turned a whiter shade of pale. "No."

"Yes," he retorted. "And I believe his death may be connected to what you were doing in his room."

"I wasn't doing anything. Someone else had been in there."

He grabbed her by the arm and held her firmly. "You don't know what you're dealing with. Barranca's dead. His throat was slashed. That would make you an accessory to murder."

"Murder? I've taken a vow to God. How could I do such a thing?"

He grasped her arm even more firmly, hoping to cause her to budge from her story. "What were you doing in there?"

"Nothing!" She helplessly struggled to pull away. As strong as she was for a woman, she was no match for a man of Richter's size. Nonetheless, her instincts kicked in. She had been in worse situations before and had managed to extricate herself with only scratches and bruises. She was tempted to bite him, but she held herself back. She raised her voice, hoping to draw some attention: "Please, let me go!"

"What were you looking for?"

"Nothing! Please!" she screeched.

He heard noise down the hall. He didn't want to cause a commotion, and he knew he wouldn't succeed in breaking her. He relinquished her arm. "If I find out you're lying, there will be hell to pay. Hell like you've never imagined."

* * *

Amanda continued to drive south through Spain. She saw on Rebar that Violeta and her companion were a way ahead of her, about forty-five minutes. They had been driving for over four hours. She was tired and she hadn't rested well today. She had picked up some coffee at a gas station, which kept her alert, but she wasn't operating at her best.

Suddenly, the light on Rebar for Violeta's car stood still. Had they stopped for gas? They had made a pit stop a while ago. Perhaps they were getting a bite to eat.

She continued to drive, but she couldn't stand not being able to check Rebar more closely and drive at the same time. She took an exit from the highway. It led her to a rotary, and she took an exit that pointed towards Pegalajar. She was in the middle of nowhere and it was completely dark. The roadway continued on and on; there was no place to pull over. "Fuck!" she said to herself. She hated when she got stuck in the interminable labyrinth that was the European road system. It took forever to drive everywhere. The roads made no sense. Half the time, you had to travel out of your way because roadways took you where they wanted you to go and not where you wanted.

This town was so dark, completely lacking life. When she first came to Europe, Amanda was surprised how European villages became ghost towns by 8 or 9 p.m. Now, it was the middle of the night. Even witches would be afraid to show their faces at this hour!

She pulled over as soon as she could. She parked against a stone wall that looked centuries old. A narrow sidewalk separated her rental car from the wall. She took her cell and zoomed in on Violeta's location. She was in Granada, at a hotel called 'The Bishop's Inn.'

How quaint, she thought. They were going to sleep there and presumably drive further down to Algeciras later in the morning.

She held her phone more closely to her face as she read the report on Violeta. She was from Bulgaria. Her father was a leading mobster who spent over fourteen years in prison for racketeering and a bunch of financial crimes. As intriguing and useful as the information was, she couldn't help but yawn. She was human. She was tired, and the bright light from the cell phone screen made her eyes even more bleary. Violeta once headed a racket of nurses in Poland where they siphoned off prescription medications to sell on the black market. Several nurses were arrested, but Violeta somehow managed to elude charges. The last couple of years she was big on illicit arms trades between Russia, Iran, and Arab militants. Last year, Interpol had intercepted a few shipments, but as of late, the trail had gone dead. The report concluded that Violeta was continuing to participate in arms trades but had managed to conceal them better.

Amanda started to read about Violeta's companion. But she could barely keep her eyes open. She could feel tears forming on the edges, and her eyelids wanted to close. She put down the phone. This was as safe as any place, she thought. There was no one around. She doubted this village even had an inn. She looked at the wall. She could only be attacked on her driver's side. She made sure all the doors were locked and reclined the driver's seat. She didn't have the energy to drive back to the highway to find another town. She didn't know this area at all. Granada, of course, she knew, as it was the home of the Alhambra palace. She had never been there but had always wanted to go. Perhaps she might have a chance later in the morning. She would make sure she got just a little rest and then catch up to Violeta before she headed further down south.

* * *

Jordan Harrison and his chaperone Pilar had arrived in Algeciras hours earlier and were now both asleep. He didn't want her to drive back alone during the night. So, he gave her a choice: He could stay with him in his hotel room for the night; he had a room with two twin beds. Or, out of respect for her since they didn't know each other, he could try to get another room for her. She opted for the first. Before they went to sleep, Jordan had given her another five hundred dollars in cash, telling her it was the equivalent of five hundred euros. She accepted it, putting it in her wallet. He had brought five thousand dollars with him in U.S. currency; now he had about four thousand left sitting in the hotel room safe. He put his gun in the safe, too. While he had come to trust Pilar, to some degree, she was an unknown commodity; for all he knew, she might be taking some medication that made her unstable. The last thing he needed was for her to grab his gun, perhaps out of spite for his not making a move on her. After she agreed to stay with him in his room, he had told her, "We'll be strictly platonic. You know what that means, right?"

"You're gay?" she asked, again blurting out a laugh.

During the drive down from Cadiz, he had learned that she dreamed of being a graphic artist. She handed him her phone and told him to scroll through an album. Her designs were quite good: a blend of modernism and touches of nature. He saw numerous depictions of the Iberian lynx, including the picture of the animal that graced the sign of the *El Lince* bar. He also saw the logo that was on the beer that she had given him at the bar which her cousins produced. She had gone to school to study graphic design in Madrid, but her father fell ill when she finished her studies, and she had to take over the bar. Five years later, she was still working there. He surmised she was his age, though she looked older. The unfulfilled years of working at the bar were taking their toll on her. He had asked her why she didn't go back to Madrid and find a job in graphic design. She said she had to care for her father. Her mother had died years ago, and she had no brothers or sisters to take care of him. Later, when she talked more about her background, she mentioned that she was in debt. She said that she had lent money to her sister who never paid her back. Although Jordan didn't want to pry, he made a point to keep talking with her so that she didn't get tired. He asked, "I thought you didn't have any brothers or sisters."

"I didn't say that."

"I must have misunderstood. You said you were the only one who could take care of your father."

"Yes, that's true. It's just that I don't like to talk about my sister. She can hardly take care of herself, never mind our father. She's a drug addict. Meth. She's been to rehab six times. She's lost several teeth. It's difficult to watch."

"I imagine. I'm sorry."

"You're always apologizing, for things you're not responsible for. Are there any drugs in your family?"

"No. My parents were religious and brought us up to avoid drugs. They kept us on a tight leash growing up."

"How many brothers and sisters do you have?"

"Six."

"Six? Wow!"

"My mother was busy."

"They're older or younger?"

"My brothers and one of my sisters are older. I have one younger sister. There are five boys and two girls."

"Wow."

"They're successful like you?"

"Yes. One is a teacher – the youngest. She just started teaching after graduating. Two of my brothers are engineers. I studied engineering too, but I ended up in law enforcement."

"Interesting."

"I have another sister who is a nurse like my mother. One of my brothers runs his own company. He does events, like weddings, catering, that sort of stuff."

"What an interesting family you have."

He could sense the melancholy in her voice. At the same time, there was a touch of hopefulness. It was as if his presence was causing her to rethink how she looked at her life and the choices she could make.

"I'm not really mad my sister didn't pay me back. I guess I owe her. I introduced her to meth."

"You did meth also?"

"No, but I introduced her to the people that did. We went to parties, and one thing led to another."

"You shouldn't feel guilty. People make their own choices."

"I'd like to believe that. Thank you."

When Jordan awoke in the morning, she had already left. As a matter of protocol, he checked the safe to make sure his Glock was there, along with his passport. On the desk below the TV, Pilar had left a note, along with five hundred euros. "500 was enough," she wrote. She had only taken half of what he had promised her. She had signed her name with a heart for the 'a' in *Pilar* and scratched her telephone number.

* * *

Amanda awoke to a pounding on her car window. It was a uniformed policeman, and the sun was just coming up. She motioned her hand to let him know that she was going to roll down the window. She had to start the car first, as the windows were electric. When she lowered the glass about half-way, he started shouting at her in a thick Castilian accent. Although she spoke Spanish, having been startled from sleep, she didn't understand what he was saying. She fumbled some words – none of which really made grammatical sense – and he continued to speak at her in a harsh tone. She came to realize that people were not allowed to sleep in their cars on city streets. It wasn't an unusual ordinance. She explained she had been tired. He didn't ask to see her ID; he just shooed her off.

Amanda drove off, feeling pretty much rested, though she could have used another half hour of sleep. She made a U-turn through the center of town and headed back to the highway. She didn't want to have another run-in with the cop. Reaching the next exit, she pulled off the highway again. She wanted to read the rest of the report on Violeta's companion. This exit led to a mountainous area, and there appeared to be no town in sight. She drove down the road and then decided to pull over, leaving enough room for other cars to pass around her if needed. There were no other cars in either direction. It was only 6:30 a.m.

She opened Rebar and discovered that Violeta's companion was Petar Todorov. Peter To-Do, Amanda told herself to help her remember the name. She routinely came across so many names and, since occasionally a name would resurface sometime later, she found these silly ways of remembering people as a useful part of her personal tradecraft. She was sure her colleagues at Langley would think of her as a complete amateur if she told them of her secret practice. Like Violeta, Todorov was a career criminal with an extensive rap sheet. He started selling drugs as a teenager and grew to be a leading distributor of cocaine by his early twenties. His business was shut down when a rival gang lord threatened to "cut his legs off at the knees." The rival drug dealer was much more powerful and established; so Todorov didn't have a chance fighting against him. He left Bulgaria for Lithuania, had limited success there, and after a few years returned to Bulgaria and landed on Violeta's team. She instantly recognized his potential, and though he never reached the heights he had as a young thug, she considered him a partner and let him know he would take over the entire racket when she retired. It was nice that organized criminals were conscientiously thinking of succession planning, Amanda chuckled to herself.

Having her morning fill of background, she quickly checked the location for Violeta "Violet Manolos" Manolov and Petar "To-Do" Todorov. They were still at the hotel in Granada. She bet they hadn't woken up yet; now she had a chance to catch up to them. She clicked on *Get directions* in Rebar and her maps application opened, telling her to head back to the highway that she had just abandoned.

Chapter 25

Jordan realized he had no car. Algeciras wasn't impossible to navigate without a car, but he knew, as a black man, he would stand out and be an easy target for Sima and her henchman to spot. They were undoubtedly still looking for him. He had to be careful. He still had a dozen rounds left in his Glock, but he would have felt more comfortable had he an extended magazine to hold a couple dozen more. He sent Amanda a note via Rebar. "I'm here in Algeciras. Let me know when you can talk."

She called immediately. "Are you staying in the same hotel room?"

"I didn't have a choice. We arrived late last night."

"You better get a room somewhere else. Don't check out though. Let them think you're still there."

"You think they know where I am?"

"It's better not to take the chance."

"Did you get any more information on her?"

"Nothing yet. I'm not sure why it's taking so long. It's like they're intentionally withholding her background."

"Are you going to be here soon?"

"I'm going to be later than planned. I'm on my way to Granada now. I'm on the trail of two people who flew over from Florence last night. One of them is a Bulgarian woman named Violeta Manolov who is the one who arranged the shipment with Falzone. They made a pit stop in Granada last night."

"You've been following them?"

"I've been tracking them. It's a special method we have. I'll explain it to you later. I'll lose the ability to track them after a day though."

"You have a weapon?"

"Not the conventional type," she said. "Just what I could bring on the plane."

"Sounds very James Bond."

"It actually is," she laughed. "But we've got a safe house in Granada. I'll be able to get a gun there."

"Do you have safe houses everywhere?"

"In just about every big city in the world. Half of them stay empty all the time."

"Is there a safe house in Algeciras?"

"There is. But it's better that you don't go there. Your cover might be blown. There had to be a reason why that woman was able to target you. And it wasn't just purchasing the gun."

"I've been trying to wrap my head around it too."

"She knew you were after the shipment, and she wanted to stop you."

"Why didn't she just kill me at the port?"

"That's too public. There would be witnesses, cameras. She wouldn't want to attract attention, just get you out of the way. She might have just drugged you and dropped you off somewhere once the shipment passed through. That's what I would have done."

"I'll remember that," he quipped.

She chuckled. "I can't say I haven't done something like that myself. I'll call you when I'm heading down to Algeciras."

* * *

Cardinal Richter rose at his usual early hour – 5 a.m. Getting up early was a common habit among the clergy, who routinely went to bed before 10 p.m. Still unsettled by the murder of Barranca, and unconvinced of Sister Sofija's explanation for being in his room, Richter headed to Sixtus's private quarters which were just down the hall from his own. Sixtus was an early riser as well. He knocked quietly on the door. It was now 7 a.m., and the pontiff would have had ample time for prayers and getting ready for the day. The pope wouldn't normally head to the office before 9 a.m., and Richter knew that his earliest appointment was at 10 a.m. with the U.S. Director of National Intelligence, General Jefferson Cheeks. Richter had a pretext for calling on the pope privately: Why was he meeting with General Cheeks? Cheeks wasn't a Catholic, and the American DNI usually met with other Vatican officials, such as the secretary of state – Barranca – or Richter himself. But instead, Cheeks had an audience directly with the supreme pontiff.

There was no answer at the door. Perhaps Sixtus was still in his bedroom and not in the anteroom. Richter opened the door. One of the curiosities of the Vatican was that while many areas were well guarded, the private living areas had little security. Once you gained entry to the private residence, you were free to roam wherever you chose, including the pontiff's quarters.

Richter looked around the anteroom. A small sofa sat against the wall. A couple of armchairs were set around a coffee table, for informal chitchats. For all the wealth of the church, the accoutrements were paltry. Most of the clergy were accustomed to this outward show of poverty. The last thing church leaders wanted to do was to give the impression that they were living high on the hog.

He heard noise – something that sounded like moaning – coming from Sixtus's bedroom. What was he doing? The door to the bedroom was ajar. Richter was going to call out when he heard some additional moaning; he stopped himself from saying anything. But his thoughts were running wild. Could someone be in the room with Sixtus? Could it be some nun or some altar boy? Sixtus wouldn't have been the first pope to have succumbed to such vices. They say Benedict XVI had a stable of young boys with whom he dallied over many decades. Several of them eventually became cardinals and continued the tradition.

Could he be having carnal relations with himself? He wouldn't put it past Sixtus. He seemed so asexual. Perhaps the only person who could satisfy him was someone to whom his hand was permanently attached.

He peeked through the doorway and saw Sixtus on his hands and knees on the floor beside his bed. Sixtus was fully clothed, in the white cassock that popes typically wore inside the Vatican. His hands reached towards the ceiling. "I beseech you. Give me power." He looked overhead. His back was to Richter, who watched in horror. *This* wasn't how one prayed in the Catholic Church.

"Give me strength," Sixtus said quietly. "Let me rule the world in thy name. Please guide me. Please bless me. Oh, hail Satan."

Satan! Richter was shocked, appalled, sickened! A shiver ran down his spine. What was he witnessing? Could he have misheard what Sixtus was saying? The supreme leader of over one billion Catholics was appealing to the Devil? How could he never have suspected such blasphemy?

Richter started to step back when he felt a hand on his back. He turned, and there was no one there. But he could feel the hand pressing against him; it was firm, it was heavy, it was substantial. When he turned back to look through the door, Sixtus was looking at the entranceway. Richter wanted to move backwards, but his body wouldn't allow him. His legs wouldn't budge. His hips could no longer pivot.

"Who is there?" Sixtus asked in a harsh tone.

Richter wanted to disappear, but he could still feel the hand upon his back. It was pushing him through the door. "It is I, Your Holiness." The words slipped from his mouth; he had no control of what he was saying. It was as if the hand that held his body also compelled his speech.

"Were you spying on me?" Sixtus demanded.

"Of course not, Your Holiness. I just wanted to ask you a question. There was no answer at the door."

"Who said you could enter?"

"No one, Your Holiness. Please forgive my intrusion. Are you busy?"

"I'm doing God's work. I'm always busy."

He had just made a mockery of all Christianity. Everyone knew Sixtus was calculating and had an appetite for power – you had to be to become pope. Richter had admired his toughness. But to beseech the Devil and ask for his blessing? What a terrible mistake the College had made in electing Sixtus!

"Why are you looking at me like that?" demanded Sixtus as he rose from the floor.

Richter thought he saw a black shadow as Sixtus's white cassock gathered about him. A smoky darkness was cast over his face, and his eyes seemed temporarily blackened.

"What?" Sixtus said.

Richter heard the voice as a distorted sound that wobbled and reverberated in the room. "Nothing, Your Excellency. Why aren't you using your prie-dieu?"

"What business is it of yours? Get me some more pillows!"

"Of course, Your Holiness."

"What have you come for?"

For a moment, Richter completely forgot why he had come. "You're meeting with General Cheeks. Would you like me to attend?"

"Why?"

"I thought he might ask something that I could help with. He's Director of National Intelligence which oversees the CIA and all the other American intelligence agencies."

"I know what the DNI does," he snapped back. "They don't call the CIA the 'Catholic Intelligence Agency' for nothing."

"It might be technical. You haven't had time to immerse yourself in our intelligence operations."

"I've seen the files," he said. "They know they're being watched and say very little. It's the elections they care about most. But they haven't asked us to intervene for a few years now. I suppose they're content with Foster."

"General Cheeks may be requesting our assistance."

"Perhaps," said Sixtus. "If I need your help, I'll ask."

"Very good, Your Excellency."

"Is there anything else?"

"No, Your Holiness."

"What have you learned about Sister Sofija?"

"She said she heard a noise in Barranca's room and there is nothing more to it."

"You don't believe her?"

"I don't," Richter answered.

"Are you going to ask the Gendarmerie to question her?" Sixtus said, referring to the Corps of Gendarmerie, which investigated all sorts of crimes within Vatican City.

"It's best not to involve them, Your Holiness."

"Maybe so. But it might put the fear of God in her."

"True. Well, I appreciate your support." He bowed to excuse himself.

"One more thing," Sixtus said. "Now that Barranca is no longer with us, I would like you to go to Russia."

"Russia?" he asked.

"Yes. I want to make more inroads with the Russian regime. You can help spread the word. We could use more Catholics in that part of the world."

"Would it be better to wait for Barranca's replacement?"

"No," Sixtus fired back. "Time is of the essence. You will leave this week."

* * *

When Amanda arrived in Granada at approximately 7:30 a.m., she checked Rebar to see where "Violet Manolos" Manolov and Petar "To-

Do" Todorov were situated. They were still in the hotel in the center of the city. She waited. Half of her life as a CIA officer involved waiting. Waiting and seeing; some expectations of movement; some false move that she could capitalize on. And, of course, boredom; daydreaming; thinking about her past and her future while the minutes and hours rolled on. She wished that Rebar had a feature to set an alert when a target was moving; then she could take a nap. But no, she was told that it was too difficult to implement such a mechanism because people were constantly in motion, and though Rebar didn't show the minute details of every movement, the application was sensitive to microactivity. She recalled the conversation she had had with the developers: Couldn't a parameter be set to indicate movement of more than thirty or forty feet, so as not to trigger unnecessary alarms? The I.T. team argued, saying that sort of tracking was problematic; they didn't want to add the enhancement. She gave up. They said they'd add the request to the backlog.

Amanda went for coffee. She had a hard time finding a cafe that was open at this hour. Everything was still closed. That was the Spanish style. Stores opened late, often closed mid-afternoon for a siesta, and then reopened later in the afternoon. But on the outskirts of town, on the way to Alhambra castle, she found a joint that was open. It was run by some Arabs who didn't adapt to the odd business hours, likely out of choice. Many Arab men were in the cafe; they all seemed to have eyes on Amanda as she walked in and ordered. She was tempted to order in Arabic but didn't want to call attention to herself. She got two coffees to go. She didn't know how long her wait would be.

* * *

Sixtus switched to an electronic SIM card that Bensaïd had installed on his cell phone. No one in the Vatican knew that he had this additional card. Bensaïd told him the card would provide the equivalent of a burner phone. No one would need to know of the SIM card's presence. If the Vatican's I.T. team wanted to inspect his phone, Bensaïd advised Sixtus to remove the card, electronically, with the press of a button, and he showed him how.

"Your Excellency," Bensaïd said.

"I think Richter is going to be a problem. I'm sending him to Russia. He's reluctant to go. Can you take care of him?"

"Yes. We can do something."

"It will be temporary, correct?" Sixtus was aware that a murder of another Vatican official would raise serious alarms.

"Yes," Bensaïd said. "You are meeting with General Cheeks today, yes?"

"I am. Has the transfer been made?"

"It will be done before your meeting."

Sixtus hung up, satisfied. Everything was coming together according to plan. Bensaïd had never failed him.

* * *

Jordan did not check out of his hotel room in Algeciras, but he packed all his belongings in his suitcase. A cab took him to the Gibraltar airport, about a half-hour away. He lingered there, grabbing a coffee and almond croissant. The croissant was one of the best he'd ever eaten; it had a syrupy, almond filling. He loved doughnuts and other baked goods with cream, custard, or fruit inside. Following breakfast, he took an Uber to another hotel in Algeciras, a couple of miles from his previous hotel. He was beginning to enjoy practicing tradecraft and being as close to a spy as he'd ever been. At Quantico, FBI recruits were trained to handle undercover missions. He'd taken a circuitous route to prevent being tailed. He'd managed to kill an hour. It was still too early to check in, but the hotel clerk took his bag and said it would be in his room in the afternoon. He paid with his personal credit card.

When he pulled out his wallet, the note that Pilar had left him with her telephone number surfaced from his pocket. He looked at it briefly and stuffed the piece of paper back inside.

* * *

Sixtus met with General Cheeks at his office precisely at 10 a.m.

Sixtus was not known to keep people waiting, no matter how little he desired to see them. He had learned that punctuality, especially among the world's elite, was a cherished quality. In Cheeks' case, it was not a matter of wanting or not wanting a meeting. There was an absolute need, a critical piece of the puzzle that needed to be solidified.

They started their meeting in the papal office, but soon Sixtus led Cheeks into the Vatican. He escorted him past priceless statues and works of art, to impress upon him the power that he was dealing with. While the U.S. maintained supreme military power over the world, and as an American, Sixtus was acutely aware of its importance, he also knew that force didn't equate with power. You could subdue people, subjugate them, but you could not truly reign over them until they became willing believers.

Sixtus sat in a gilt chair that resembled a throne. It was situated in the middle of a hall the size of a ballroom; yet only he and the general were present. Sixtus thought that Cheeks might have some listening device on him. Cheeks had to give up his phone upon entering the pope's office, but perhaps he had some other surreptitious gadget that the American intelligence agencies had outfitted him with. Cheeks was larger than he expected: about six feet three; a supremely solid build – broad shoulders; broad hips; large hands with thick fingers. He was bred to be a beast of burden. In contrast, Sixtus had long, thin fingers that would have been adept at playing the piano if only his mother could have afforded lessons; a slightly protruding belly that made his waist wider than his chest; skin so pale and almost withered he began to covet the chocolate-colored, blood-filled, robust-looking skin of the general to his left.

"I want to make sure that when the weapon goes off, all of Washington will be in a state of shock. There won't be any room for any politician to take Foster's place."

"The city will be in ruins," Cheeks said.

As Cheeks said this, Sixtus visualized the District of Columbia in shambles – a nuclear fallout where the skies where blackened, a multitude of fires blazing, and iconic monuments – such as the Lincoln

Memorial, the Washington Monument, the Capitol Building, the White House – all piles of stone. He had imagined the same spectacle in his prayers: a decimated Washington, D.C. that would be at his mercy. Nothing would be spared. "And you will be where?"

"In Boston or New York. I'll be able to get there quickly and seize power. All the airports will be shut down for days. We will have clearance for your plane to land to hold a vigil, and that is when you will assume power."

"And you will be my Vice President?"

"That is the deal." Cheeks had a resigned tone to his voice.

"Why would you want to associate yourself with the overthrowing of American democracy? After all, you've given your life to defending it."

The question seemed to unsettle the general. "What I signed up to defend hasn't lived up to its reputation. Democracy in America is a dream. The country is ruled by elites – corporate, political, military, academic, ecclesiastical. Money rules everything there, as you know. I am doing this for my family. They will become part of the ruling class, and they won't have to fight or claw their way like I have."

"Bensaïd says you are trustworthy. That he's relied on you for many decades, and that he helped you get where you are today."

"That is true. I am a Muslim. Only my immediate family knows. My brothers and sister don't even know. I go to church like everyone else. But I believe in the way of Muhammad."

"*Allahu Akbar,*" said Sixtus.

"*Allahu Akbar,*" replied Cheeks. "I never thought I'd hear a pope say that."

"What we do in the name of God," said Sixtus. "You will make sure the weapon arrives safely, that it is deployed as expected?"

"The team is ready as we speak."

"They are all Muslims, I presume?"

"Yes. Immigrants. They are eager to topple the government and take over."

"And what will become of them when *I* take over?"

"They will all be dealt with very expeditiously."

"They will try to implicate you."

"They won't have time."

"Won't you be a traitor to them, to your cause?"

"No, because I believe we can live in harmony. Just as the Spaniards and Moors did for almost a thousand years."

"But we know what happened there. What if history repeats itself?" Sixtus was referring to the ultimate conquer of the Moors by Ferdinand and Isabella, the Spanish rulers responsible for discovering the New World.

"Eight hundred years is a long time," said Cheeks. "We'll see what the course of history is over the next millennium. I have one question for you, if I may, Your Holiness."

"Please."

"Is it true that you worship the Devil?"

Sixtus laughed. "Who told you that? Bensaïd?"

"No," he said. "I heard it in prayer."

Sixtus laughed. "If I told you all the things I heard in prayer, we'd both be in an insane asylum right now."

Cheeks chortled in response, uncomfortably.

Chapter 26

At 10 a.m. Violeta "Violet Manolos" Manolov and Petar "To-Do" Todorov still showed on Rebar as being present at the hotel. Did her suitcase remain in the hotel while they left? Amanda didn't think so. She believed they would take it with them. Perhaps they had slept in and didn't need to be in Algeciras until later.

Retail stores were now opening throughout the city. Amanda stopped at a large department store in the center of town. She bought a straw hat, a loose-fitting top, sandals, a backpack, sunglasses, and a long scarf. She stopped at the optical center and bought two pairs of glasses with no prescription lenses. She also bought some simple jewelry – relatively plain earrings, a couple of rings, and assorted bracelets. On her way out of the big-box store, she stopped at a pharmacy, where she purchased both red and dark brown hair dye as well as a pair of scissors and a bunch of bobby pins, barrettes, and hair ties. She also placed an assortment of make-up and bronzers in her cart.

Sitting in her Opel sedan in the parking lot, she stuffed many of the items in her newly purchased backpack. Then she searched for hotels on her phone. She chose a large chain nearby. In larger hotels, hundreds if not thousands of people passed through every day. Almost everyone was invisible.

By 11 a.m., she was at the hotel, checking into a room. She used a hotel loyalty program in the name of one of her false identities to check in early.

While in the room, Amanda dyed her hair dark brown. Desiring only a temporary change in appearance, she opted not to cut her hair. Instead, she used the bobby pins and hair ties to pull her hair up into a sort of French twist. She applied the makeup, making her eye shadow blue, adding mascara to her eyelashes. For her brows, she used the root touch up pen to make them brown. They didn't match her hair completely, but she didn't see that as a problem. When she put on her eyeglasses – a designer-brand, tortoise frame with cat eyes – and looked at herself in the mirror, she told herself that even her mother wouldn't recognize her. With the straw hat and loose-fitting crewneck with batwing half sleeves, her transformation was nearly complete. All that was left was to apply the bronzer to her arms, face, and neck. As she observed herself, she surmised that she looked attractive. She had rarely tried to look pretty, and while no one would mistake her for a model, she was undeniably fair. She stood out more than she was accustomed, but the look fit the locale. She fussed with the shirt – was it too much? No, she told herself. She looked like a tourist, and her look didn't attract attention. That was the key to a proper disguise: to blend in. She looked like scores of young American women who traipsed through Europe on their parents' dime.

It was noon when she noticed on Rebar that Violeta and To-Do were on the move. She was correct in that they were taking the marked suitcase with them. She hastily put her scarf in the backpack; she didn't end up needing the silk wrap at all, though she liked it and looked forward to wearing it sometime. She carried the straw hat as she exited the room and headed to her car which was parked in the hotel structure.

She watched on Rebar as Violeta and To-Do's car moved, slowly plodding through the city toward the outskirts. Yes, she knew where they were heading.

The Alhambra.

Chapter 27

Amanda had always wanted to go to the Alhambra. The majestic Moorish palace, to her, was the most significant and historical monument in Spain. Above all, she had wanted to see the tile work – the intricate geometric patterns that flowed seamlessly into one another, that conveyed the tradition of highly skilled artisans who understood both craft and mathematics. Whether she saw Violeta and Todorov there, she was less concerned. This was an endeavor in which she couldn't fail; connecting with the architecture would be enough to give her fulfillment, regardless of mission.

By 12:30 p.m. she had arrived at the magnificent palace. It was larger than she had expected: more majestic, more serene, more everything. She was truly in awe. How could they have constructed this centuries ago? Was it in the 1500s – she couldn't remember the timeframe exactly. When she checked in, she opted for a self-guided audio tour. That would give her the best possibility of being able to surveil Violeta and Todorov. She learned that that fortress had been built starting in the early 1200s, through 1358. Even more impressive, she thought. Such workmanship, such refinement. Everywhere she walked, she was overwhelmed. She felt so insignificant as a person, hearing on her audio guide that thousands of workers had contributed to the brick, stone, carved stucco, white marble, and tapia structures. *Tapia* was rammed earth, and the name *Alhambra* meant 'the red,' referring to the reddish colors of the walls. She had majored in history and Spanish at Cornell, spending her junior year abroad in Buenos Aires, Argentina. All this study was now coming to fruition as she saw the seeds of civilization and a reverse sort of conquer displayed before her. The *conquistadores* were once the conquered. And while Spain ultimately became an independent state from the union of Aragon and Castile in 1479, the traces of Moorish occupation were never far, including to this day in the Spanish language. The Granada War had been the final confrontation between the Muslims and Christians, and the Spanish victors would go on to their Golden Age, discovering the New World and carrying Christianity there with zeal and fervor.

While ambling through the *Patio de los Leones* – the Courtyard of the Lions, Amanda's tour was disrupted by the purpose of her visit. In a group tour stood Violeta and Todorov, bathed in sunlight, standing around the fountain where twelve lions stood. In her earpiece, Amanda learned that the Moors did not create the stone figures – the Koran forbade the depiction of living creatures. The Christians or Jews, who were forced to convert to Christianity or be expelled, likely created the statues. Columns with intricately carved arches led to halls surrounding the courtyard. Amanda first hid herself on the other side of the fountain, not wanting to be noticed by Violeta or Todorov. She put on the designer sunglasses which she had just bought. She didn't want to risk any eye contact, and the blaring sun made a good excuse. Eyes are the window to the soul, she recalled Cervantes having written. She would not allow these cretins to observe her goodness or quelch her desire to stop them.

She turned down the volume of her recorded guide. She was listening in both Spanish and English, occasionally pretending to fumble with the buttons to simulate listening. But she wanted to hear anything that Violeta or Todorov might be saying. They were being good tourists, enjoying a respite from their journey of evil by listening attentively to the guide in English who gave colorful history lessons without burdening her subjects with onerous detail.

The group moved to the *Salón de los Embajadores,* then to the *Sala de los Reyes,* and to the *Sala de los Mocárabes.* Amanda followed into each of the halls, all drenched in sublime tilework. She made sure that the tour group had already departed before making her entrance. She was determined to make herself invisible; this feat of disappearing was her personal superpower. Eventually, she made her way to the Rooms of Carlos Quinto – Carlos the Vth. He built the addition to the fortress for his intended visits. The temporary lodging, a sort of Airbnb, were as sparse as during his lifetime because he rarely visited. Washington Irving, the American writer, was the chief occupant, and he was serenaded with tales of deceit and deception by gypsies. He turned this experience into the *Tales of the Alhambra,* a worldwide bestseller.

Amanda was getting restless with the history; the sight of Violeta and Todorov had unleashed her training, her instinct to hunt and capture. They were prey to her. The past was a relic, an unfortunate accident, a series of dates, people, and circumstances. She wanted her just desserts.

As she was wrapping up her pseudo-sightseeing of Carlos Quinto's rooms, the tour group entered the room, with Violeta and Todorov in tow. Amanda's back was to them as she meandered outside the square palace. She viewed the circular patio below, with thirty-two columns with bas-relief carvings at their bases. The audio guide noted that the palace didn't have a roof until the twentieth century because funds had dried up. She turned the guide off; she wanted to be with Violeta and Todorov, to hear what they were saying, to know what they were going to do. They'd probably be speaking Bulgarian. She could record them and have their conversation translated. How much time they were wasting. They seemed so chill, so unconcerned. Her own heartbeat was galloping. She could have thrown herself over the balustrade. In her waistband, she pressed the Glock against her skin. This Glock she had hidden in a secret compartment in her suitcase to conceal its contents to X-ray. Only if someone had broken the suitcase apart would they have found it. In her bag, she also had a special pen. She could choose between a fatal injection or one that would merely incapacitate someone for several hours. It was as easy as choosing between red and blue ink. The blue ink contained a high concentration of GBH. The red ink was a Langley secret – one they didn't want to advertise because the chemical was untraceable except through deliberate analysis of the blood of a corpse.

As she made her way down to enter the patio's grounds, the tour came up behind her. She wasn't spending too much time in any one place; she was a true, conventional tourist.

The patio ran around the building, with arches, columns, and alcoves leading to the interior of the palace's first floor. Such a monumental feat of Renaissance architecture. She started to give her own audio-visual narration to the scene.

The tour followed her. Yes, she could have been a paid guide herself. She knew where to go and what to see as well as anyone, even if she was somewhat of a hamster on a wheel, just following signs.

As the guide was giving a florid description of the grandiose palace, Violeta suddenly tapped on Todorov's arm and signaled for them to go. Too soon, Amanda thought. They hadn't seen the intricate tilework in the *Sala de Mexuar* yet. But it must be business. They departed from the group. Amanda lingered behind, observing the stone columns. What intrigue these columns must have seen over the centuries. Someone had scrawled graffiti on the foot of a column: Pedro hearts Ana. No one had the heart to remove his profession of love.

She checked Rebar on her phone. The Bulgarians' location was still indicated as the Alhambra, but they were making their way back to the entrance. Nonchalantly, she traipsed to the exit, following behind. She would keep them on a leash, allowing them to travel ahead of her so that she could safely trail them without being spotted.

As the sun and heat poured down on her, sweat began to gather under the neck of her shirt. She didn't want to lose them. How fast they could move. She checked Rebar. They were now in their car, barreling out of the Alhambra's gates. Had there been some call to action that she had missed? Or were they wired to be in a rush?

As she monitored Rebar, she reached her own car. She took a more careful drive past the guards and tourists who sauntered nearby. She would catch them, and when she did, the pair of assassins would know how powerless they were.

* * *

On the highway driving down to Algeciras, in pursuit of the Bulgarians, Amanda called Jordan on Rebar. "I should be in Algeciras in about three hours."

"That's a long drive."

"Well, they wanted to be tourists. They spent over an hour at the Alhambra."

"I guess there are worse places to have to tail someone."

"I highly recommend it. It's been the highlight of my tour in Europe, besides the private tour of the Vatican that the ambassador arranged upon my arrival."

"Do they really have gold hidden underground?"

"I didn't see that, but I did see rooms and rooms of Picassos, Renoirs, and all other sorts of art just piled against the walls. They're just waiting for someone to rob them." On Rebar, she could see that Violeta and Todorov were only about fifteen minutes ahead. She would have no problem catching up to them should the need arise. "Did you find another room?"

"Yeah, not far from where I was staying. I'm inside my room, keeping a low profile."

"When I get there, I'll tell you where to meet. It should be around four p.m."

* * *

It was mid-afternoon. Cardinal Richter knew that Sister Sofija and many of the other nuns were accustomed to taking short naps during the day. This was their form of siesta, even though it was only 2:30 p.m. He quietly walked through the halls to her room. Upon reaching her sleeping quarters, he listened at the door. No one else was in the hallway. There was not a sound emanating from her room. He opened the door. The room was completely dark inside. He could hear Sister Sofija snoring, mumbling, groveling. She was asleep. He closed the door softly behind him. He used his cell phone flashlight to navigate through the room. He shined it against the foot of the bed, being careful not to aim at her head. The faint glow illuminated her face, and he could see that she was asleep. She lay on her side, facing the wall opposite the door. The room had no windows. Such was the price of being a cloistered servant to the Holy See.

On the bedstand, he found what he was looking for. Her cell phone was within her arm's reach. He snatched it. The model was dissimilar to his own, and he wasn't sure how to wake it up. He pressed several buttons on the side of the phone. Finally, the face of the mobile brightened. A *Face ID* prompt appeared on screen. A mixture of chagrin and satisfaction. Unlocking the phone via Face ID was going to be easier than cracking her password; however, he would have preferred no security. He should have known that this unscrupulous sister would vigilantly guard her phone.

He took the phone and carried it to the other side of the room. There, her face was on its side. He placed the phone in front of her face and waited for the phone to respond. Nothing happened. Drat! The phone probably required seeing her eyes. He held the phone over her face and then softly blew into her eyes. They shook, but still, they did not open. He blew harder. He was tempted to grab her arm and shake her, but he resisted. He took his own cell phone and shone it directly into her face. He held the bright light against her face for several seconds while continuing to blow. Finally, her eyes flickered open. The phone unlocked. He quickly turned off the flashlight on his phone and proceeded to look through her pictures. The most recent picture taken was unusual. It was of a piece of paper, once folded, taken atop a bed. It looked like Barranca's bed! Yes, he recognized the bed coverings the cardinals used. Damn this woman!

He took his own phone and snapped a picture of Sofija's picture. He zoomed in on the photo on Sofija's phone. It was titled a *Bill of Lading* from a company called the Queen of Spades. The package was destined for Johns Hopkins University in the United States. What would she be doing with this? Why would Barranca have it? Was this connected to his death, and to Sofija's mysterious, reprobate behavior? It had to be! Yes, Richter had overheard Sixtus and Bensaïd talking in the garden about a shipment. This must be a very important shipment.

Richter scanned through the other photos on her phone. Pictures of other sisters. Of her daily, sumptuous meals at the Vatican. The wretched woman lived for food. Mere bread and wine weren't good enough for her!

Sofija sniffled, and as Richter looked down, he saw her eyes wide open, staring at her. "What are you doing in my room?"

He grabbed the pillow from behind her head and shoved it over her face. She squirmed and kicked her feet. This woman was a fighter. He knew the type. Unprincipled, corrupt, diabolical. Qualities bred into her as an Eastern European born during the calamitous era of Communism. She wouldn't have survived otherwise, if not for the church.

She seemed to shout something: "Let me go!"

But he held the pillow atop her. He could hear that she was struggling to breathe. He didn't know what to do. His heart raced, and for a moment, he thought he could strangle her. Oh, woe were the fantasies that passed through him! He could hold a hand atop her eyes and force them shut while he took his other hand and squeezed tightly, trying to find the bone that would snap her neck. Yes, he knew there was a way to kill a human, quickly, almost instantly. The Nazis had mastered this technique. Why hadn't he studied those methods more carefully? He should have known that in the Holy See, he would have a need for ultimate acts of survival.

He held the pillow against her face. Underneath, she was hardly breathing. She continued to kick her legs, but the force had dissipated. Her arms flailed, but they were not a threat. He had placed her under his control. Is this what it was like to subdue another human being?

He pulled his hand up from the pillow slightly, as if to give her a passage of air. Then he pushed his hand back down firmly against her face, into her mouth and nose so that she couldn't breathe. Her torso slackened; her neck and head remained rigid. He was in control of the body. He could do with it what he willed.

As he held her down, he could feel himself becoming aroused. How unbridled his carnal appetite had become! He had succumbed to lust and power, and he had not done this in the name of the church. No, he was a man of God. He would not be debased and brought to her abominable level. He had what he needed. He dropped the cell phone on her bed and hastily made a beeline to the door, letting the pillow rise loosely above her face. As he opened it, he heard Sofija gasp, in a whimper, "Richter."

* * *

Amanda saw on Rebar that Violeta and Todorov had arrived on the outskirts of Algeciras. Amanda was only fifteen minutes behind them. She had left just enough room for her to be able to head quickly to wherever they were going. As she observed their location on Rebar, she remarked that it looked familiar. Could they be heading to the same house where Jordan was almost taken prisoner? With that woman Sima and her henchman?

As she drove, she called Jordan through the Rebar app. "I'm only about fifteen minutes from the city," she said. "Our friends seem to be going to your favorite hangout."

He was as stunned as Amanda, though neither should have been. It was just one of those moments when reality kicked you in the ass. "So Sima is just another hired hand?"

"Sure looks like it. There must be a lot of money going around. I'm going to lose tracking of them in a couple of hours. We'll need to put eyes on them. Can you send me your location so we can head over together?"

"Yes, ma'am. I'll let headquarters know where we're going."

"No, don't. I'm concerned there might be leaks."

"From within?"

"Yes."

"Can't they track us on Rebar?"

"It's unlikely anything's being done in real time. Plus, we can turn our tracking off. We'll need to do that before we go."

"Do you think I'm safe here?"

"For now," she said. "But we've got to get on the move."

* * *

Richter stared at the picture of the transmittal notice on his phone. Destination: Johns Hopkins University School of Medicine. Odd equipment referenced. Queen of Spades. What did Barranca have to do with any of this? And why would Sister Sofija go to such lengths to procure such a photo?

He went to the administrative office that was manned by two nuns. They were responsible for the daily comings and goings of the pope's senior staff. They had access to their credit card statements, their emails, their cell phone statements. Little was private in the uppermost echelons of the Holy See. The only thing they couldn't see was each cardinal's individual cell phone and whatever personal texts or emails that would have come in on a personal email account. Richter would have liked to see all that information, to get a full picture of who Barranca truly was.

"Sister," he said to Maria, the head administrator. "I would like to see Cardinal Barranca's schedule the day before he was murdered."

Maria, a Chilean nun who was a favorite of both Barranca and the late Pope Francis, dutifully obeyed. She was the shortest nun in the Vatican, standing at nearly five feet. From the back, with her long black hair flowing from under her veil, she was often mistaken for a young girl. She pulled up his schedule on her computer screen and showed it to him. "Would you like a printout?"

He peered at it. "Can you zoom in on that appointment?" He

pointed to an appointment he had at the American embassy that morning.

As she opened the meeting invitation, the name Bersch appeared on screen along with a telephone number. "A printout of these, please."

"Yes, Your Excellency."

"Thank you, Maria."

Unlike Barranca or Francis, Richter was always a cold man. Perhaps losing both had made him kinder.

* * *

Amanda saw on Rebar that Violeta and Todorov's car stopped precisely at the address where Sima's purported safe house was located. The fact that a network of associates existed across Europe raised her alarms even further. At the same time, she knew that the mission at hand was as critical as she had thought. She wasn't dealing with a run-of-the-mill operation involving an alleged dirty bomb, but a bomb that had purpose and backing. Stopping it, and capturing those responsible, were paramount.

But how could she and Jordan, two ill-armed officers who had never worked together and hadn't met in person, stop this gang? Jordan wasn't even CIA. While he sounded capable enough when she talked with him – and his instincts seemed to be on target, given his doubts about Sima – she didn't have the sense that the two of them would gallop off into the sunset after rousting the outfit. No, whatever she accomplished would have to be hard earned and hard fought. *She* would have to lead all efforts. She would have to use all her training, all her experience, all her intuition, to thwart the crew and stop the shipment.

And if she failed? She didn't want to think of the explanations she would have to give. It wouldn't be right to give a bunch of excuses. Lack of resources, lack of trained personnel, lack of time. No, she would have to take the blame. To complicate matters, she would need to be careful about what she divulged. She was certain there was a leak somewhere, but she had no idea where. Someone on the inside was protecting this shipment, and that someone likely had the proclivity and the power to have her eradicated without any repercussion.

She neared Jordan's hotel. This was their reckoning. They would meet at last. And she would know, once she was physically in his presence, if they had the slightest hint of a fighting chance.

Chapter 28

Richter wasn't a man who took subways. Yet he didn't want to have a Vatican car take him to the American embassy. Once he exited the walls of the Vatican, only telling Maria that he was going on a personal errand, he hailed a cab on a busy Roman thoroughfare. The fabric of the car's headliner grazed against his head, annoying him. His bony knees pushed against the seat in front of him in the compact; this was one of those times when being tall was a disadvantage. Fortunately, when he flew, he was usually in the comfort of the Vatican's private fleet.

As was customary, he wore civilian clothes so as not to attract attention. The sounds of the Roman streets – chirping, hammering, clicking, whirring, high-pitched voices – never ceased to startle him. He had become too accustomed to the peace and solitude of the Vatican walls where a peep might signal big news. The car took him straight to the embassy, where he didn't have an appointment. He showed his Vatican ID to the guard and told him he wanted to see Mr. Bersch. The guard made a phone call. A twenty-foot-high iron fence stood atop a concrete and stone barrier. A puzzled look overcame the guard's face. After a moment, he told another guard to open the gate, and Richter was allowed to stroll through.

Richter was shown to a waiting area off the lobby once he again presented his ID to an official. He waited for five minutes or so in the small conference room which had room for about six or seven people. A camera was positioned in the corner of the room, creating no doubt that he was being watched and the activities being recorded.

He tried not to be nervous. But his throat was parched.

He looked at his watch. Another five minutes passed. He should have made an appointment. But he didn't want to call attention to the matter. He certainly didn't want to be put off and told he couldn't come for a week or so. He was due to go to Russia any day now. Maria kept pestering him.

Suddenly, a man entered with a manila folder. "Cardinal Richter?" he said.

"Mr. Bersch?" Richter was surprised how young the man was – in his late twenties, well-dressed in a suit that was of the fashion – a tailored fit, slim tie, pants that rose above the ankles to show off colorful socks.

"The name is Wilson," he said. "Brian Wilson. Like the Beach Boys."

Richter didn't know what he meant by his reference to the Beach Boys. He didn't bother to pry. "Is Mr. Bersch not in today?"

"That's why I've come. There is no Mr. Bersch here."

"He's not working today?"

"No. We have no one by the name of Mr. Bersch in the embassy. Are you sure you're not mistaken?"

* * *

Jordan was staying in one of the larger hotels in downtown Algeciras. Amanda parked her rental car in the public parking area. She texted Jordan via Rebar as she entered the hotel, asking for his room number. In a matter of minutes, she was face to face with him. They shook hands.

He was taller than she expected, and more athletically fit. He had CNN International playing on the LCD TV hanging on the wall. The news was in English, and it had a story about how President Foster's support of Israel was creating instability in the region. She couldn't attribute any political ideology to Jordan because he was watching CNN; overseas, the available news channels in English were limited. She knew her appearance was disconcerting for him, since she was no longer a blonde. "I dyed my hair to disguise myself. Can I use your bathroom? I want to get rid of some of this makeup."

"Sure, help yourself."

After removing the self-bronzer and eyeshadow from her face, leaving her brows colored to match her hair, she returned to the room. "I see you haven't unpacked." She was referring to the fact that not a single toiletry had been placed on the bathroom counters.

"What's the point?"

"Said like a pro." She was liking him already. In fact, she had an even better feeling about him now that she did when she met him on Zoom. There was nothing like a tête-à-tête that let her know she could rely on another person when push came to shove.

"Does it make sense to go over to Sima's hiding place? It's remote over there, and I barely made it out last time. It might make us sitting ducks."

"What do you suggest?"

"We wait until they make a move. We know they're going to head to the docks at some point. We could hang out there and keep an eye out."

"Knowing how these things go, I wouldn't be surprised if it's a night shipment."

"Why do you say that?"

"Night staff are easier to bribe. They usually have other priorities, and their job isn't one of them. Trust me, I've used a few myself."

"Do you have any contacts there?"

"One main guy. He'll be of help if we need to stop something. But not much help until we get to that point."

"Can we ask him to search everything more thoroughly?"

"Let me make a call." She was liking this Jordan Harrison more than ever.

* * *

"What do you mean, no Mr. Bersch?" Richter roared.

Mr. Wilson seemed to be taken aback by Richter's sudden change in demeanor. He had gone from compliant to aggressive in a matter of seconds. "We have nobody by that name. Cardinal, correct?"

"Yes, I am Cardinal Richter."

"I'm not sure where you got Bersch's name."

"I found it in my secretary of state's calendar. Cardinal Barranca. He was recently murdered."

"Yes, we are aware of that. I'm very sorry."

"He had an appointment with Mr. Bersch the day before he went missing. Here at the embassy."

"Perhaps it was a code name."

Richter thought for a moment. Could Barranca have been meeting with a spy? He wouldn't have put it past him. He was probably selling secrets on the sly. Maybe that's what got him into this mess and why he was killed.

"And what brings you here, cardinal?"

"I wanted to meet Mr. Bersch and find out what their meeting was all about," he said exasperated.

"I see. Unfortunately, I'm not going to be able to help in that regard."

"Is there someone else who can?"

"I'm afraid not." He took a seat at the table beside Richter. "Is there some information you have? Anything you'd like to share?"

Richter didn't like his obsequious tone. Nor did he like the dotted tie the attaché was wearing.

"If the ambassador were in, I would have him see you. But unfortunately, everyone is out now. I could make an appointment for you."

"That's quite all right," Richter said. "Do you have any news on Barranca's murder?"

"I'm afraid we know no more than you do."

"How do you know what we know?" he asked pointedly.

Wilson laughed. "It's a figure of speech. We'll be sure to share any information that comes along. I'm sure you will also."

"Of course," Richter replied, internally bristling at the suggestion. The room gave him the feeling that this was a place where many questions were asked and few answers given.

* * *

As Amanda and Jordan prepared to leave for the port, she stopped him. "I should fill you in the items we have at our disposal." She took out a pair of pens from her backpack. "They look like regular ballpoint pens, and even under magnetic resonance, they appear so. The black ink is real black ink. If you choose the red ink, it's a lethal agent that will kill someone instantly. I've never used it, but I've seen videos. The person will start foaming at the mouth. Their head will start shaking. They'll be completely paralyzed and dead in about a minute. Maybe a couple of minutes if you need a clinically dead determination. Trust me, I've seen the videos."

He believed her without any hesitation.

"The blue ink will render someone unconscious. It's helpful if you want to incapacitate someone but don't want to kill them. All you have to do is prick someone with it. Give them a good jab. Or you can squeeze the solution in a drink. The dye is clear in color, so it will disappear. The plastic holder for the ink makes it look blue."

She handed him a pen. "Keep it on you. Remember, only use the black one if you want to write something."

"That won't be hard for me to remember," he said, half-joking.

"I'm going to give you something else." She took a necklace out of a compartment in her knapsack. A small metal ball hung as a pendant. She opened the toggle clasp to remove the ball from the chain. "Do you have another chain?"

He pulled a gold chain from underneath his shirt. It had a cross at the end. "My mother gave it to me for high school graduation."

"It's perfect. Can you take it off?"

As he removed the ball, she explained: "You have to handle this with care. Inside is a highly explosive substance inside that reacts with water."

"Water?"

"Even saliva. You see, the honchos at the Home Office never want us to go unprotected. You can stick it in someone's mouth, and in about twenty seconds, the person will look like they've gone through a meat grinder."

"You've seen those videos too, I imagine?"

She laughed uncomfortably. "Have you ever seen someone die?"

"No," he said.

She threaded the ball on his chain so that it sat next to the cross. "We should have them make something out of a cross sometime. No one would suspect anything, except perhaps Mossad. Maybe make it a dagger with a poison, or a blinding agent." She reclasped the chain and handed it back to Jordan. "At Langley, they train you to see the reality of death. Most of us aren't accustomed to that. I still have nightmares from some of the images. The faces are haunting. But we're not like emergency medical personnel or other law enforcement where we routinely interact with death. We tend to leave it behind, as a by-product of our mission. But Langley trains us so that in the field we didn't go into shock if we ever encounter death after using one of these implements. The training is meant to desensitize us."

"Did it work?"

"Somewhat. Like I said, I still have nightmares. But funny enough, when I talk about these things, I find myself laughing a bit. Like it's out of my control."

"The laughter or the death?"

"Both," she said, emitting a small chuckle. "See? That nervous laughter? I can't seem to stop it. It must be a defensive reaction. My body telling my mind that it's not okay." She stared at Jordan for a moment, with a curious look. "Have you ever killed anyone?"

"No. But I came close with Sima's bodyguard the other day."

"I haven't either. Maybe today will be our day."

He laughed.

"See. It's contagious." She continued to search through her backpack. She grabbed a bottle of fingernail polish.

"That's a treasure trove of goodies you have in there. What is that?"

"You can never be over-prepared, the boys at Langley like to say. This, my friend, is what we call fingernail polish. My nails need refreshing."

He laughed.

She started to touch up her nails. "Remember, if you need to use the device, you won't be responsible for anything that happens. You'll be asked why you did what you did, but you won't be blamed if things go sideways. You're one of us now. You have carte blanche."

* * *

As Cardinal Richter left the embassy, his head pounded. The noise of the Roman streets prickled his ears, creating a cacophony of sounds and stress. How could people manage to live in a city? He hated going into the city. Even in this neighborhood, one of the most prestigious and exclusive in all of Rome, the constant babble and crackling din left little room for contemplation and soul-searching. But thoughts still ran through him: Should he have given Mr. Wilson the photo he had lifted off Barranca's phone? Would that have made him a target? Was he now a target anyway, having shown up at the embassy? As he strolled down the tree-lined avenue, he felt that someone was walking behind him. He turned back. He saw a woman who looked like a tourist. Down the block behind her, a man in a suit stopped, his body turned one-hundred-eighty-degrees away, talking on his cell phone. Was he paranoid? Now, he felt some semblance of empathy towards what Barranca must have been going through. And he had paid the ultimate price.

Richter scanned the traffic on the boulevard for a cab. None passed. Damn! He felt isolated. Cursed, wretched place. He wanted to call

Maria, to ask her to send a car. But she would ask: What were you doing at the embassy? No one within the walls of the Holy See could be trusted. Dear God, he said to himself, please help me. Then, suddenly, the man who had been standing a block way was shouting at him, in Italian. "*Mi scusi! Scusi!*" Excuse me.

He looked like he wanted to grab Richter's arm. The man was sweating. Richter wanted to get away from him. "Do you know where...?" the man spoke as a car pulled up alongside them. It was a black, four-door sedan. Richter wanted to get away. The man was reaching his hand to grab Richter. No! He wasn't going to let them take him. The man seemed to want to push him toward the car. Richter suddenly started running down the street, away from the embassy. *They* must have sent him. *They* wanted what was on his phone. His slender legs trampled through the streets, rickety-crickety. He took step after step, his knees reaching far in the air; he hadn't run like this since he was a teenager back in Bavaria. He looked behind; he had moved about a block. People on the street were watching him run; what a spectacle he had become. His sticklike legs hurt; his knees ached. The man near the black sedan was gone; so was the car. Blasphemous Barranca! He had led him to this! He had caused all of this!

A sedan passed on the other side of the street! Was it the same one as earlier? Richter couldn't tell. It was black, had four doors. Was it circling him? Why did it want him? What would it do to him? Would it take him to the same place where Barranca had been hauled off to? They wanted every cardinal. Yes, but why? All because of a shipping notice? Something going to Johns Hopkins University? Holy Mother of God! Is this what happened in a world without religion, when atheism was taking root everywhere around the globe? Dear Lord, he cried to himself. And then, suddenly, in an act of God, a taxicab appeared. Richter hailed it, and it stopped. He looked up at the sky. Yes, there was still a place in the world for those who feared God. Yet he knew time was running out.

Chapter 29

Amanda had changed into another outfit that made her look less touristy. Gone were the straw hat, the tacky sunglasses. She had changed into jeans and wore a cream-colored top to match. She could blend in anywhere. She adhered to the one rule that Langley impressed upon all new recruits at the Farm: wear lace-up shoes. Lace-ups were preferred because they held onto your feet better and gave you the ability to run faster and more securely. She opted for a pair of oatmeal-colored oxfords that matched her shirt and had a cushiony sole.

They installed themselves at a small restaurant overlooking the harbor, ordering coffee and a series of *tapas* to pass the time and not raise the suspicion of the owners. Restaurant workers often knew the ins and outs of a location. They could spot strangers who didn't belong, who stood out; they were often the source of valuable information to the police or spies like herself. It was now 4 p.m., and they were both getting antsy and bored. "Do you think we should move on?" Jordan asked.

"We can stay here as long as we need to," she replied.

The waitress came over with a refill of coffee, soda for Jordan. She cleared the plates. "Anything else?"

Jordan as he got up to go to the restroom. While they enjoyed each other's company and learning about each other, she knew the time had come. "Thank you. Just the check," she said in Spanish.

When the check came, she paid in cash, leaving a generous but not oversized tip. Again, the key was to raise as little suspicion as possible. To be forgettable, in Langley's parlance. The best spies were forgettable. Indescribable. They could be your brother or sister or aunt or just the guy or gal mowing your lawn, taking your order at the laundromat, or delivering your mail. They could be anybody. Anybody. But nobody in particular.

"You said you were going to lose tracking on them. How much more time do we have?"

She checked Rebar and saw that Violeta and Todorov's location was still at Sima's. Could they have left the suitcase there, planning to return later? Suddenly, she had the urge to move quickly. "We better get out of here."

"Is something wrong?" Jordan surveyed the restaurant to see if Sima and her henchman were nearby. He didn't see them. He looked out the window toward the harbor. There was no sign of them there either.

"I just got the sense we might have missed them."

"But they're at Sima's."

"Maybe not."

They made their way to the harbor.

"What is it? Did I miss something?" Jordan asked, confused by her impulsive decision to head to the harbor.

Overhead, a small black drone was flying over the water, toward the receiving port.

Chapter 30

"Don't look up," she said. "At two o'clock, there's a drone circling. Drones aren't allowed in this area."

Large ships continued to trudge into the harbor, from the Mediterranean on their way to the Atlantic. The final checkpoint, the only thing standing in their way from escaping Europe, was Gibraltar. Many didn't know that Gibraltar was under the control of the British empire. They would never relinquish control. As long as they held onto this piece of territory known as "the Rock," which had been ceded to them by the Spanish in 1713, the Brits would continue to dominate Europe, even if they didn't belong to that silly program that pretended to be an empire, the European Union. The EU gave dreams of glory to continental Europe, but the hand of Britain was still on its throat, choking it, subjugating it, giving it only occasional air to delay the inevitable death gurgle.

"It looks like it's waiting for something," Jordan said.

Amanda was impressed. She had barely noticed that Jordan looked overhead. "It might be photographing us. Like a live stream. We need to be careful."

"You don't have any drones in your bag of tricks, do you?"

"I'm afraid I didn't pack any. But you know, there are always some at our disposal."

"How so?"

"We keep them in safe houses and warehouses scattered throughout the world. We can activate them at any time."

"I suppose China is doing that in the U.S. also."

"China, Russia, Iran, North Korea. Even our allies – Great Britain, France, Germany. It's the new way of war. We know where many of them are. We know how to deactivate them too."

"We have backdoors?"

"In some. But there are scrambling mechanisms we can deploy. Plus, we have drones that act as drones within the network. Kind of like a queen bee – all the worker bees are dependent on it. When she goes down, the entire hive does."

"Interesting."

"Yes, it's fascinating. Have you noticed how the drone seems to be circling? It looks like it's killing time."

"Yes," he said. "Why haven't the security forces stopped it from flying in the air space? Do you think they haven't noticed it yet?"

"Or maybe they have someone on the inside. Someone who's being paid to ignore it. That's what I would do. It's amazing what a thousand bucks will buy you. People will betray their countries for less. All they have to do is let it pass. Ignore it for a bit, and hope that someone else on the team doesn't spot it."

"Wouldn't it cast suspicion on them?"

"It might. But the person would probably react and help disarm it. That's what I'd tell them to do if their cover was in question. Immediately do the job they were hired to do. Claim they made an honest mistake. Suffer the investigation and ask for forgiveness later."

"They teach you that at the Farm?"

"Yes. They even teach you how to blackmail someone if they

become too uncooperative. Once you contract with us, we don't let you go so easily. That's why we know all about them before we engage – their families, their loved ones, their interests, hobbies. Their secret lives. We'll hold their secrets over them, and the threat of exposing them can keep people in line forever. It's amazing what people do behind closed doors."

"I don't suppose you know my secrets."

"We have files on all the members of our intelligence communities. We only dive into their secrets when we want to exploit them."

"I take that as a *no.*"

"That's a *no,*" she answered. "We don't like to gather dirt on patriotic Americans. It would be too easy for our enemies to exploit. All we need is one rogue officer who wanted to profit from the information. They would have no problem selling it."

"The drone is hovering close to the building."

"It's probably an out of camera-shot. It's an inside job. They know where to keep it from being spotted."

Suddenly, the drone rose higher along the brick building, which was about four stories high. It traveled along the brick areas, avoiding the windows.

Amanda watched it from afar but tried not to stare at it. "It looks like it's taking a more panoramic view. It hasn't found what it's looking for."

"It's not looking for us?"

"I don't think so. I think it's waiting for our friends."

Jordan understood that she was referring to Sima and the Bulgarians.

The drone flew higher up the building, to the roof, disappearing.

"Do you think it found what it was looking for?" Jordan asked, commenting on its vanishing.

"I don't know." As she scanned the area, she saw Sima and her burly body man Todorov walking down the promenade toward the brick building. "Don't look, but at ten o'clock, we have our close personal friends approaching. Let's slow down and see where they're going."

"She might see me," Jordan said. "I'm easy to spot."

"Maybe," Amanda said. "Get your Glock ready just in case. Keep your head down."

Jordan bent over the railing as if staring deep into the water. Amanda stood near his side, in Sima and Todorov's line of sight to help conceal him. She watched as they passed in front of the brick building down the sidewalk toward other buildings along the water. "They didn't go inside."

"Should we follow them?"

"Let's give them a little room." Amanda knew that on the other side of the buildings, ships would dock for inspection. The drone still hadn't reappeared. Sima and her burly man entered another building, one that appeared more of an industrial warehouse. A breeze blew up on the shore, almost blowing Jordan's baseball cap off his head.

As they walked toward the warehouse, a security officer patrolled the perimeter of the buildings. Then, overhead, a large explosion rippled through the brick building, shattering the windows above and scattering glass, bricks, and debris on the road before them. The security guard sheltered for cover. Amanda and Jordan retreated from the brick building, away from the warehouse, covering their ears and their heads as they got out of the way of the falling fragments of brick and concrete. A large plume of smoke fell from the rooftop. Flames ripped outside the broken windows. "Let's go," she yelled, motioning for Jordan to follow her back towards the warehouse.

As they made their way, the security officer held up his baton to stop them. "We're here to help," Amanda said urgently. In her panic, her Spanish wasn't that good.

The security officer looked confused and held up his arm before them. A booming whistle blared from the other side of the building. It sounded like it was coming from the other side of the warehouse, but Amanda couldn't be sure. It was the type of blast that ships would make when they're leaving port, as a warning to other ships nearby to get out of their way. Sometimes, they wouldn't make any sound; but if they were in a rush or making a difficult maneuver, they would.

The security officer stood in their way and tried to corral them toward the water, away from the building. "They need our help!" Amanda yelled through the deafening sounds of the collapsing building.

Before the guard could answer, a large portion of the brick building crumpled before them in large piles of stony destruction. Dust and rubble filled the air, completely obscuring the view of the guard and of each other. Amanda grabbed Jordan's hand and pulled him toward the warehouse.

Chapter 31

Amanda and Jordan tried to enter the cement-and-glass industrial building beside the brick structure that was blown up. Armed security guards stood at the entrance. Amanda and Jordan were covered with soot and ash from the explosion, and they earned wary looks from the security officers. She held out her diplomatic badge and proffered it. The guard examined it circumspectly. She heard him tell the other guard, who was older and likely more senior, that she was from the Italian embassy. "The Italian embassy?" he responded. "Yes, she's American." "From the American embassy in Rome?" "Yes, yes." The dialogue went back and forth in feverish Spanish; Amanda could tell they were unimpressed. "I think we're going to need your FBI credential," she said to Jordan.

He started to reach into his jacket when another of the guards suddenly aimed his pistol at him. "My ID. I'm just getting my ID," Jordan said in broken Spanish. Tense moments always caused one's foreign language skills to deteriorate rapidly. He put his hands at his sides as the guard was not moving the pistol focused on his chest.

Amanda spoke up in more confident Spanish now that some of the shock had worn off. "I'm an American diplomat and this man is with the FBI. He will show you his identification card. We're on an urgent mission to apprehend those responsible for the explosion."

"You have no authority to apprehend anyone on Spanish soil," the senior guard said. "Go back to America."

"Show him your ID," Amanda said.

The guard continued to train the pistol on Jordan as he reached into his inner jacket pocket. He pulled out a plastic covered holder with his FBI badge mounted inside. It was an impressive piece of metal, and the acronym, FBI, was known, feared, and respected worldwide. The junior guard put his weapon down.

Amanda was typing on her phone. "Mr. Iglesias has said he will see us." She held up her phone to the middle guard so that he could read her text message. "Call him, please."

The senior guard motioned to allow Jordan to enter, and Amanda was a step behind him. The middle guard held up his arm to stop her. "Him only," he said.

"Call Mr. Iglesias. He's expecting both of us," she said firmly. She had a way of making ordinary statements commands that couldn't be ignored.

The senior officer signaled for the middle guard to call upstairs. He obeyed; within seconds, he hung up the phone. "He said it's okay."

"Let them pass," the senior officer barked, somewhat annoyed that he might have delayed an important American diplomat as well as an FBI agent and would have to explain this to someone.

Jordan and Amanda entered. "I didn't think there would be a problem," she said. "Iglesias owes us. We got him the job here, and this is way over his head. He's got to be shitting bricks right about now. Don't expect a Julio or Enrique Iglesias look-alike. There's no relation. The only thing they have in common is a bit of a tan."

* * *

Sixtus sat in the courtyard looking up at the elm trees that towered over him. The priestly lore was that these were holy elms, and they called this green pasture within the Holy See the Holy Elms Garden. Everything was holy inside of these damned walls! In their zeal to expand the religion, the Catholics turned their faith into cliché. The sun peered through the elms' canopies, and a dried leaf sat at his feet. If he had a magnifying glass, he could light it on fire. When he was a young boy in Massachusetts, known then as Nicholas Cassella, he used to play with dried leaves, placing them on the ground and holding a magnifying glass over them while the sun bore down. Sometimes, he would hold a leaf by the stem. Other times, he'd place the foliage on blades of grass so that it would float atop them. He would patiently wait while the sun's rays created a black hole in the center, forming an ashy circle. The circle would expand, and a small burgeoning flame would emerge from the leaf. He would take a slender stick and poke it into the fire, causing it to catch fire too. In these times, Nicholas thought he could control fire. He would squint at the sun as its yellow-orangish rays would beam down, blinding him, heating the olive-colored skin of his face and hands. The sun had mighty power, but he could master the star. He could use it how he wanted. It was there, at his disposal, to shape, to summon, to subdue. All you needed was a little will and patience.

Once, he put a leaf atop his palm and let the sun set it on fire. A small flame erupted, and then it grew. Soon, the hot flame burned him. He dropped the leaf to the ground. Some browned grass then caught fire, and Nicholas hastily stomped it out. How quickly fire could get out of control, he realized. How insignificant a boy or man could be. We were all at the mercy of the sun, forces beyond our control. We thought we could control something, but it was more an illusion. We were masters of nothing. Even our will could betray us, go unfulfilled, or lead us astray.

Now, Nicholas was pope, and while being Sixtus made him world-famous and gave him tremendous influence, he had little true power. Is this what it felt like being CEO of a multinational, billion-dollar corporation? Some figurehead, who might be famous and admired, but who was a cog in the machine? Rich, yes, but someone who was still at the mercy of others – a board of directors, consumers, the Federal government breathing down the company's neck. Always being threatened if he didn't comply.

He looked at his watch – it was past 5 p.m., and the call from Bensaïd was late. Articulated cypresses were perched in pots on the sides of his bench. They were kept small, in bonsai form, by nuns who had been sent to Japan to learn the craft. He searched the internet on his phone, for news. The explosion at Gibraltar had been reported. Then his cell phone rang. The initials *A.B.* appeared.

"Your Holiness, the mission has reached its next phase," Ahmed Bensaïd said. "The shipment is on its way. It will arrive in ten days."

"Can't it be sooner?"

How surly the pontiff had become in recent days. "We don't want to arouse suspicion by traveling too fast."

"Don't you think the explosion at the port raised some eyebrows? The media are all over it."

"It will throw them off. They'll be investigating for some time. Besides, it will take Barranca out of the news."

"Don't remind me of that debacle."

"Everything is going according to plan."

"I don't recall Barranca being part of the plan."

"There will always be unwanted casualties. How did we know that man would accost him at Termini Station?"

"How did they know of the connection to the Vatican in the first place?"

"I don't know."

"Someone made the connection. You said nothing could be traced back to me."

"It can't."

"But somehow it already has."

"We don't know that."

"No one reaches out to the Vatican secretary of state for something like this. The post handles private visits to Vatican City. It's like being the Martha Stewart of foreign affairs. Everybody wants a photo op. Something against the backdrop of a white gown and gold leaf. People don't just rush up to accost a cardinal unless they've been tipped off."

Bensaïd weighed his words carefully. "Are you insinuating that I might have been the source of a leak?"

"I'm asking," Sixtus said boldly.

"Why would you suggest such a thing?"

"Because I need to know if you will double-cross me."

"Why would I do that? We've been in this together for years. Since you were a boy."

"Perhaps you were using me."

"You're sounding paranoid. I know that place can do that. You're isolated. You have no freedom."

"And now, I have no cover."

Bensaïd was genuinely confused. "What do you mean?"

"I can't go to the authorities because I've already been implicated."

Suddenly, Bensaïd's tone changed from perplexity to distrust. "What authority would you go to?"

"President Foster."

The thought hadn't occurred to Bensaïd that the American president might help Sixtus were he in some bind. He should have known that Sixtus would consider some way to protect himself should the operation go awry. He would have some card up his sleeve. "Do you think he'd go out of his way to help someone who was suspected of having him killed?"

"Do you think he'd believe that?"

"You know how paranoia clouds one's thinking? He'd never be able to overcome the doubt."

"You've thought of everything," Sixtus said.

"Isn't that what you're counting on, Saint Nick?" Bensaïd would always resort to the nickname he'd given him in boyhood when he wanted to put him in his place.

"If I fail, your whole cause will be doomed for a thousand years." He hung up.

Chapter 32

"*Señorita Amanda!*" Iglesias exclaimed as he saw her walking down the hall toward his office on the second floor. Floor-to-ceiling windows about twenty feet high overlooked the harbor; no ships could be seen in the water. He was a heavy man, nearing 300 pounds, and he waddled from side to side as he made his way toward her. Jordan surmised she was right; there wasn't the slightest resemblance to Julio or Enrique Iglesias except for a pronounced bronzing of the skin. Iglesias kissed her on one cheek as was his custom whenever seeing her.

"This is Jordan Harrison of the FBI," she said.

The men shook hands.

"Is it a coincidence you are here?" His eyebrows danced uncontrollably, moving up and down disjointedly as he spoke, as if to contradict what he was saying. "It can't be," he continued, answering his own question. "What has happened?" He spoke in English, but punctuated his discourse with an occasional *madre mía,* the equivalent of *oh my God!*

She quickly scanned the area for Sima and her burly henchman. They were nowhere in sight. "Can we go into your office?"

"Everything is out in the open here," he said, motioning his face toward the walls and doors of glass. "This is the era of transparency. I have curtains in my office. This way. I'm so glad you've finally arrived. I so appreciate all you've done for me. I hope you can help me out of this mess."

"It's not your fault," she said.

"No, but they will always blame someone. And I am an outsider. From Bilbao, you know. They don't like Northerners here. Least of all demi-Basques."

Amanda had first used Iglesias to help root out Basque terrorists. He was more than willing to help, as he related more to the Spanish than to the Basques. He was gay, and the Basques always treated him as an outsider, an inferior being who didn't belong in their culture. The Spaniards were more welcoming.

"Have you seen this woman?" She showed him a picture of Sima on her cell phone. It was the file photo, obviously a few years old, but it should do the trick.

"I saw her talking to one of the inspectors downstairs."

"Who?" she asked urgently.

"Tigre."

"Tigre?" she repeated, puzzled by the name, knowing that it was the equivalent of *Tiger.*

"That's not his real name, but that's what we call him."

"I need to see him right away."

"You'll see why we call him Tigre then."

* * *

Sister Sofija had all day to let her nerves settle. She waffled between packing her things and finally making a run from her service. She opted to stay at the Vatican. What else could she do? Her nest egg wasn't large enough, and she felt she was at her peak earning years. At least the bribes that she was being paid were larger than she had received before.

She scuttled into the Vatican's main kitchen, where a dozen chefs were in the process of preparing the nightly dinner. She asked for some soda water, saying that she didn't feel well. It wasn't a lie. One of the chefs – an Italian who was always kind to her – offered her some pastry. "The stomach will heal you," he said. She sat at a counter out of the way of all the activity. She ate slowly. She really didn't want the Viennese delight, though it was one of her favorites – *Marillenknödel,* an apricot dumpling.

She pretended to struggle to slice it. She made her way to the drawers where they kept the utensils. She hastily grabbed a steak knife and pushed it up her sleeve.

"Sister, can I help you?" one of the nun helpers asked.

"I need a sharper knife," she said. "I'm having trouble with the dumpling."

"Let me," the kitchen aide said, handing her one of the steak knives that she had just taken.

"Thank you," Sister Sofija said meekly. She lethargically walked back to the counter, almost inadvertently tripping over her feet which she let dangle loosely beneath her. She was taking the sick act too far. She was careful not to let the steak knife fall from her sleeve.

The kitchen aide followed behind her, a look of concern over her plain, rosy face. "Are you okay? Is it that time of the month?"

The aide could do with a little less sampling in the kitchen, thought Sofija.

Sister Sofija laughed. "I haven't had my period in twenty years. Oh, you're so kind. Can I take this upstairs? I can't possibly finish it now."

"Yes. Let me get you a box."

As the aide retreated to the sink area, Sofija grated her forearm against the handle of the knife to hold it in place. Richter will have a surprise coming his way.

The aide returned with a box for the *Marillenknödel* and scooped it into the folded paper takeout container. Sofija departed with it, along with her utensils, including the steak knife that the aide had given her to eat with.

* * *

Amanda and Jordan Harrison rushed downstairs at port headquarters. Iglesias trailed behind them. Amanda could tell that he was out of breath from the brisk walk to the elevator and the trek to the rear entrance. Numerous port personnel and security guards – a blend of port security and Spanish police – were on high alert as they scrutinized the area outside. Sirens could be heard blaring next door. A faint constant beeping, from some alarm system, ship, or vehicle, pulsed in the background.

"Where is Tigre?" Iglesias shouted to one of the men wearing a port security uniform.

"He went home. He wasn't feeling well after the blast."

"Did he get hurt?"

"No. He said he had a headache. He was outside when the blast occurred."

"In the building next door?" Amanda asked.

"No. Here. A ship was leaving right when the explosion happened."

"Which ship was that?"

"I don't know," the officer said.

"I can find out," Iglesias interrupted. "Come."

* * *

Cardinal Richter arrived back at the Vatican. He was beginning to understand what Barranca must have felt like knowing he was being pursued. That shipping notice had to be of great importance. But whom could he go to? He could have left word for the American Ambassador, but how could he be certain he could trust him? This Bersch didn't even exist. He had never even met Perkins, President Foster's ambassador to the Holy See. He didn't think that Barranca had met him. It would be too risky to go to him, Richter deemed, based on the sudden non-existence of Bersch. And was this Bersch tied to Sixtus or Foster? Richter might have found himself in the middle of a power struggle between the two. As both were Americans, they sought to wield their influence around the world. Foster had the American empire behind him, with all its industrial and military might; Sixtus had moral authority, God, and faith. Richter felt that spirit would triumph, in the end, but he had an unsolved murder at his feet. Sixtus was behaving oddly, and now he was being sent away to Russia. How could he avoid going? He could say he had some family emergency. But everyone knew he didn't have any family left. He could say it was a long-lost niece or nephew, someone who needed his help desperately. In the meantime, he had to make sure the picture of the shipping notice was secure. Someone could steal his cell phone. Then the photo would be lost. He would have to email it to himself, and not just to him, but to someone whom he could trust. Who could that be? Under normal circumstances, that person would be Sixtus. But times had changed. He pondered sending it to Father Gómez; but could he be involved somehow with Barranca's murder? He had managed not to be kidnapped, and he was unharmed. Barranca ended up dead. Perhaps he wasn't as trustworthy as he looked. Sometimes the most handsome people had nebulous moral compasses.

Should he send the picture to Cheeks? Say something like, "By the way, we didn't meet, but I have this suspicious letter of transmittal that might have to do with Barranca's murder. Do you think the American intelligence services could investigate?"

Yes, that is what he would do! It would be good for him to foster a connection with Cheeks. And sending the note could serve a dual purpose. It would serve as a sort of insurance policy in case anything untoward were to happen to him.

Chapter 33

President Foster sat at the Theodore Roosevelt Desk in the Oval Office. While many recent Presidents opted for the Resolute Desk, Foster preferred the more rugged and practical association to presidents before him who, like Teddy, used the mahogany piece to let the world know that he was in charge. Presidents such as Warren G. Harding, Calvin Coolidge, Herbert Hoover, Harry S. Truman, and, of course, the man whom he considered to be the best president of all: Dwight D. Eisenhower. Foster adored Ike. He even had a bronze bust of him on the credenza behind his desk. He knew that Woodrow Wilson, that intellectual snob, used the desk too, but he let the matter of that episode slide. Nixon used it too, and after he resigned, it had been relegated to the offices of vice presidents, many of whom signed the insider of a drawer, including Nelson Rockefeller, Water Mondale, George H.W. Bush, Al Gore, Dick Cheney, Joe Biden, Mike Pence, and Kamala Harris. While none of those figures inspired him, he looked at their signatures as a reminder of how only two of them – Bush and Biden – became president. He saw their names as a warning should he fail to live up to the hopes of the people who had elected him.

On his desk sat a gift that had been unwrapped and scanned by the Secret Service. A note from the pope – not handwritten – lay atop the small box. Sixtus sent his blessings and what he called a priceless historical artifact: the original letter that Cardinal Cajetan wrote to Pope Leo X in 1520, protesting the order to arrest Martin Luther. The fragile piece of paper was framed behind glass in museum-quality glazing. On the back, the seal of the Holy See was imprinted upon an English translation of the letter. In his note, Sixtus wrote that not all Catholics at the time were in favor of punishing the Lutheran. He hoped that peoples of all faiths could live together in peace and harmony.

Foster had never received such a thoughtful gift. It truly touched his heart. He even thought he had the perfect place for it: He would get a small display stand so that it could be propped next to the statue of his beloved Ike.

* * *

Back in his office, Iglesias logged onto his computer while Amanda and Jordan waited. He looked stymied. "The network's down. I won't be able to get any records."

"There must be a paper record," Amanda said.

He stood from the computer. "You are right. Let us go see."

They went back downstairs and then outside. Now, the Spanish militia had arrived, and they were blocking entrance to the doorway that led to the harbor. "I'm in charge of this operation," Iglesias told one of the officers.

"This is an active investigation. We can't let anyone outside."

"There are records there and we need them urgently. These good people are with the FBI."

"I can't let you outside, sir."

Jordan thought he'd try his luck with the officer, pulling out his FBI badge. The officer was armed with an automatic rifle, and he immediately pushed it into Jordan's face.

Jordan stepped back. To Amanda, he whispered, "I guess they don't like my kind."

She chuckled a bit uncomfortably, realizing he was referring to his being Black. "Let me try my luck." She pulled out her embassy badge and held it before the officer. She too was immediately met with the automatic rifle in her chest. She didn't budge. "This is an urgent situation," she said in Spanish. "We need to know which ship left the port immediately after the explosion."

"Step back," the officer said to her in English, pushing the rifle into her torso so that she had no choice but to retreat.

"How long will it take you to investigate?" Iglesias asked.

"As long as it takes," came the officer's cryptic reply.

Iglesias looked at Amanda and shrugged.

"Can you get us to Tigre?" she asked.

"I can get you his home address."

"Good."

He started to walk back towards the elevator then suddenly stopped. "I can't, actually. The computers are down. I have no way of getting that information."

"There must be someone here who's friends with him."

His eyes dilated as he came to a sudden realization. "I hope she's still here."

He led them to a receiving area on the other side of the first floor. There, a group of clerical workers circled around a table, gossiping. A couple of them nodded toward the door when they saw Iglesias enter the room. They hushed.

"Viviana. I need to speak with you." He motioned with his finger for her to come.

The youngest of the team – a thin, attractive woman whom Amanda couldn't see earlier, splintered from the group. She had long brown hair, a tight-fitting top, and a skirt that was too short for an office environment. Viviana certainly had some va-va-voom.

"I need you to give me Tigre's home address," Iglesias said to her.

"How would I know?" she said.

"I know you know," he said.

"I've never been there."

"He said you were stalking him, after that..." He let his voice trail off.

"I don't know!"

"Let's not play games with one another. This is an urgent situation. Tell me!"

"It's...." She pretended to search her mind, raising her hand to her face.

Amanda pulled out her wallet and handed her a one-hundred-euro bill.

Her eyes lit up, receptively.

Amanda realized that she had given her too much. She could have gotten away with fifty euros. Yet it wasn't worth tempting the fate of a negotiation. She had learned it was better just to get the deal done and leave everyone more than contented.

Hastily, Viviana spit out the street and cross-street where Tigre lived. "He lives in a blue house with a tile roof."

Amanda repeated back the street names and the description of the house.

"His wife will be there," Viviana said. "Don't tell him I gave you the address."

"We won't. But he might hear about it tomorrow from your co-workers."

"They're my friends," she said. "They don't care."

"Do you have a photo of Tigre?" Amanda asked.

Begrudgingly, she pulled out her phone from her butt pocket. While doing so, she looked back at her group of co-workers who were watching her. She flicked through the photos. As she did so, a few dick shots passed under her long, polished nails as she tapped at the glass screen. Her nails were so long, sometimes the screen didn't respond to her touch. She stopped at a photo of a man's face. His face was tanned. He had a broad smile with gleaming teeth and thick lips. Evidently, a man Viviana longed to kiss and almost certainly had many times. Brown eyes.

Thick eyebrows. A short haircut buzzed at the sides. A very attractive man who appeared to be in his early thirties.

"Thank you."

Amanda turned to Jordan. "A hundred bucks will get you anywhere in this world. All you need to know is whose palms to grease."

* * *

Sister Sofija contemplated sending a message to Violeta. Could she say that Richter had stolen a picture of the transmittal notice? She was supposed to have deleted it. It was a breach of protocol for her to keep it. He couldn't have seen it in her messages. On her encrypted messaging app, all the messages were set to disappear, including file attachments. What could she tell her? She would be blamed.

She clutched the steak knife against her breast as she lay atop her bed. She opened the app and began a message to Violeta. "I think Cardinal Richter knows something. He keeps asking me questions." It was vague enough, but a sufficient warning.

She waited for a response. Violeta wasn't one to respond immediately. But Sofija could see that her message had been read. Then she saw the message disappear on screen before her. She stayed logged in, waiting. She glided her forefinger over the ridges of the steak knife's blade. It prickled to the touch. But it didn't pierce her skin. If Richter were to attack her again, she would use all her force to puncture his body. A cut to the throat would be the most efficient. A bloody mess, surely, but the only way to subdue him without putting herself at risk.

"I'm afraid," Sofija added. While her statement was true, she was also being manipulative. She wanted Violeta to take care of things for her. She preferred not to have to kill him herself.

* * *

When Cardinal Richter arrived at the papal offices, Maria, the chief administrator, said to him, "You look like you've seen a ghost."

"I feel like I have," he said.

"Something must be going around. Sister Sofija isn't feeling well either."

"Is that so?"

"She's been in her room all day."

"Perhaps I should postpone my trip to Russia."

"We're getting the plane ready. You're supposed to leave tomorrow."

"So soon?"

"His Holiness asked us to act with urgency. We have your meetings set up at the Kremlin."

"I'll speak with him."

"I'm afraid he won't be available until tomorrow evening. He has appointments all afternoon and a dinner engagement at the American embassy. The poor man never rests."

"At the embassy?"

"Yes. He has a dinner with General Cheeks and Ambassador Perkins."

"Is there any way I can attend?"

"He already has a date," she said with a hint of gossipy innuendo in her voice. "Ahmed Bensaïd."

* * *

It was nearly 6:30 p.m. when Amanda and Jordan arrived at Tigre's house. Viviana's directions and description were perfect. "You can always rely on a stalker," Amanda quipped.

Jordan was checking his Glock to make sure it was cocked and ready in case they ran into problems with Tigre.

"Let's try to keep the temperature down. I suspect he's just a low-level hired hand who does favors from time to time."

Jordan checked Rebar. "We didn't get the report back on him."

"It always takes a few hours. All someone has to do is enter the name in a computer. They don't seem to prioritize the work we do in the field. They work on Washington time."

"I know the feeling."

"Are you enjoying working at headquarters?"

"It's definitely less stressful."

"That's a question you have to decide for yourself. Do you want the stress and excitement, or a paycheck?"

He thought for a moment.

"No need to answer. It's one of those things I ask myself. When I go back to Langley, I enjoy the routine, but ultimately, I get bored. I can only spend a few months there without pulling my hair out."

"So, you're a bit of an adrenaline junkie?"

"Not at all. I like tracking and capturing those junkies. The world is a safer place without them in the wild." She grabbed her Glock from the center console and opened the driver's side door. "Shall we?"

Chapter 34

As Amanda and Jordan walked to the front door of the blue adobe villa, the front door opened. Amanda recognized the man at the front door, who was wearing a tank top and gym shorts, as the same one in Viviana's photos. Viviana must have called him to warn him that they were on their way.

"Let me do the talking," Amanda whispered to Jordan. "It will be less threatening to come from a woman. These macho men don't respect women."

Tigre was a medium-sized man, about five feet nine or ten, muscular. He appeared to be in his early thirties. As she got closer, she could see a large tattoo on the side of his neck which seemed to go down to his chest. He shouted something in Spanish that she couldn't make out. She waved hello and said, "Hola!" in a cheerful way, as a tourist might.

"*Que están haciendo en mi casa?*" he yelled gruffly. What are you doing at my house? This, Amanda understood perfectly, as did Jordan.

She spoke back to him in Spanish, and she decided to be direct. "Mr. Iglesias gave me your information. I have a few questions about what happened this afternoon."

"Viviana gave you my address. You can't believe anything she says." There were a few *coño*'s mixed up in what he said. Practically every other word. Damn or fuck.

Amanda wasn't going to be rattled. She saw no point in arguing with him. All she wanted was information. She knew this type: a lot of blustery toughness and little to back it up. Besides, there were two of them, both armed, and she doubted he had a weapon. She sensed Jordan surreptitiously reaching around his back, ready to draw his Glock if needed. She quietly warned Jordan, "Don't make a sudden move." They were getting closer to Tigre, and she didn't want to alarm him.

As they were about ten feet from him, she got a clearer picture of the tattoo on his neck. It was a colorful depiction of a tiger, striped in orange and black, its mouth open, baring large white incisors. Of course, that's where his nickname came from. The tiger had a pronounced muzzle and a large brown eye that stared back at her ominously, as if not to say, "I'm watching you," but "I'm hungry." Or "You're my dinner. You're prey." Amanda bet the ladies loved it.

"There was an explosion at the port," Amanda said. "I understand there was a ship that passed."

"I don't know what you're talking about." Again, there was his favorite word, *coño*.

She stood right up to him, and she could see in the front window, a young girl, presumably his daughter, peeking out from behind a lace curtain. "This doesn't have to be difficult. You're not in any trouble."

"Who are you to tell me what I can do or say?" He flailed his arms. He had shaved armpits. She could see his hair was meticulously trimmed also. He was obviously fastidious about his appearance. "Get the fuck out of here!" He continued to swing his arms over his head. It was an animalistic display of strength, of superiority; an attempt to deter Amanda from coming any closer.

"Your daughter is watching. You don't want to embarrass yourself in front of her. Please, be calm." Amanda was reasserting control, redirecting his anger and the conversation to suit her goal: information. All she wanted was information.

"I said, *get the fuck off my fuckin' property!*"

"Where is the paperwork on the ship?"

"I don't have to answer any of your fucking questions!"

Jordan stepped in closer.

"Oh, big man. You want to mess with me?"

"You need to show some respect and answer her questions," Jordan said.

"Fuck you!" Tigre spat out.

"What was the name of the ship?" Amanda demanded.

"Fuck you!" This time, he was practically laughing.

"Your daughter won't appreciate that language," she said. "And she won't appreciate what I'm about to do to you."

He laughed boisterously. As he did, she grabbed his arm and twisted it behind his back. He screamed. Jordan lunged on top of him and pinned him against the cement sidewalk. He yelped as his head hit the hard surface while his arm was wrenched behind his back. Jordan put a knee to his thighs to prevent him from moving. Tigre writhed beneath him. Amanda took her Glock and stuffed it into his face. At that moment, his wife came to the door. She was holding a shotgun, aimed squarely at Amanda, Jordan, and Tigre. If she shot, it would have been anyone's guess whom she might have hit.

* * *

"Get off him!" Tigre's wife hollered.

Jordan lifted his knee off Tigre's chest and he stood. "*Cálmate.*" Take it easy. He kept his eyes directly on Tiger Wife and pointed his Glock at her. Tiger Wife continued to point the shotgun at Amanda. "This is what we call a Spanish standoff," Jordan said to Amanda.

Tigre's wife appeared to be carrying a Benelli pump-action. The gun was much too big for a woman of her size. She didn't look comfortable wielding it. The gun was too heavy for her. She probably wasn't aware that it leaned downward. She held the butt in her armpit rather than against her shoulder; she was an inexperienced shooter and wasn't prepared for the recoil. "Put the gun down and no one will get hurt," Amanda said. "We just have a few questions and we'll leave you alone."

"Get off him!" Mrs. Tiger shouted.

"Not until you put the gun down," Amanda said. "We don't want an accident."

Jordan took a step closer to Tiger Wife, and she looked at him, scared, but she kept the shotgun on Amanda.

"Let's put our guns down together," Amanda said.

Jordan took another step, and Tigre's wife became alarmed and started to point it toward him. In an instant, he lunged at her, tackling her by the shins. She fell to the ground, dropping the shotgun. It didn't go off. When Jordan grabbed it, he saw that the oversized, cross-bolt safety was still engaged. Mrs. Tiger cried out, yelping, "*Suéltame!*" Let me go! She kicked her legs, but Jordan managed to hold them bound together.

Amanda could see that their daughter was still at the window, peering at them behind the lace curtain, watching. "You didn't have to make this difficult."

Tigre stared at her. "What do you want?"

"I want to know the name of the ship that you let pass. And who paid you to do it? Tell me that and we'll end this right here and now."

"Her name is Sima."

"How much did she pay you?"

"Five thousand euros."

"What was the name of the ship?"

"I don't remember."

She pressed the Glock against his cheek.

"I have the name inside."

"Think harder."

"*The Grindon,*" he exclaimed.

"*The Grindon?*"

"Yes, it's a Liberian vessel."

"That wasn't so difficult, was it?" She realized he was afraid of losing his job and had a family to feed. Jobs weren't easy to come by in this part of the world. Yet nothing justified letting a cargo ship pass through for payment of a bribe.

She stood near him, keeping the Glock trained on him. Jordan got up off the ground, letting Mrs. Tigre get up. She scuttled over to her husband and latched onto him, tightly.

"Was any of the cargo inspected?" Amanda asked.

"I signed off on it," Tigre said.

"But you didn't look to see what it was carrying?"

"Drugs, maybe. I didn't care. I did what they asked me. You don't mess with these people. She was there at the port, watching me."

"Where did she go?"

"She was with some guy. He showed me his gun. They walked by the gates just before the blast."

"Did they warn you about it?"

"I don't know."

"What do you mean, you don't know?"

"I can't remember."

"Don't lie to me."

"They said there would be an explosion!" he huffed. "They told me to go inside and stay there. They said I wouldn't get hurt."

"Where did you meet them?"

"A park in the city. El Alcalde Square."

"They gave you cash?"

"Yes. In an envelope."

"All of it, or just half?"

"Just half. I'll get the other half tonight."

"Where?"

"I'm waiting for their text."

"Give me your phone," Amanda ordered. "Carefully."

He took his cell phone from his pocket.

"Put it on the ground."

He placed the phone on the ground before him.

"Now step back, both of you."

Mr. and Mrs. Tigre both took several steps back, toward the house. Amanda could see that the little tigress was still watching them, now more astutely than ever. Jordan strode forward and picked up the phone from the ground. The mobile was locked. He woke it up and held it before Tigre's face, and it unlocked. He saw a text from a contact named "Sima."

"*El Capitán*. 20:30." That was 8:30 p.m.

"You know where *El Capitán* is?" Jordan asked Tigre.

"It's a bar downtown."

"Looks like we have a date," Jordan said.

* * *

Richter debated whether he should tell Sixtus that he was going to the soiree at the American embassy. Why was His Holiness going? It wasn't customary for a pontiff to go to diplomatic functions. Was it because Barranca had been killed? And why hadn't he been invited? Desiring more background on the event, he went to Maria's room, apologizing for intruding on her personal time. "When was this function organized?" he asked.

"It appeared on the calendar this morning. I think General Cheeks arranged it."

Of course, Richter thought. He wanted more private time with Sixtus. "Thank you, Maria."

On his way out from her quarters, which were cloistered at the end of the hall in a secluded area, he passed by Sister Sofija's room. The mere thought of her made him shudder. She had caused much of this. She stuck her nose into Barranca's business, leading to his death! She should be punished! If only he had the means. He would find a way, in time. He paused in front of her door. He heard nothing inside. His inability to hold her to account unsettled him; he wasn't accustomed to being ill-equipped to deal with a situation like this, with some underling whom he should easily be able to dominate. But the circumstances were completely unorthodox. In time, he would have his retribution.

As he passed the room, Sister Sofija appeared in the hallway before him. Both were startled at the sight of the other. He tried to look away, but she stared at him. He caught sight of her death stare and looked back squarely at her.

"Don't come near me or I'll scream." Inside her sleeve, she clutched the steak knife, prepared to draw it and brandish it in Richter's face.

"You love to play the victim, don't you?"

She could feel the blade pressing against her forearm. The prickly sensation reassured her in some way. "I'm warning you!"

"You'll have your time in hell, don't worry."

As he passed by, she let go of the knife and grabbed his arm, pulling him toward her. She spat in his face. "I'm not afraid of you, you bastard!"

He pulled his arm away from her and wiped his face with his sleeve. He considered his own mistreatment of her, having almost strangled her. In part, he deserved how she had treated him. But the lack of respect, her disregard for authority, were unforgiveable. "When I found out what you have done, you will spend the rest of your life in prison."

"You won't come back from Russia!"

Her warning pierced his soul more than any of the venomous hatred that she spewed. She knew something, and the anxiety he felt about the trip, the fear of the unknown, rose in his chest, unnerving him.

From the end of the hall, Maria emerged from her room and saw them both standing there. Richter looked back, uncertain exactly what she had seen. He looked back at Sofija and walked away.

* * *

Jordan sat in the backseat of Amanda's Opel rental with Tigre beside him. Amanda had parked the car along the side of the road, a couple of blocks from the *El Capitán* bar. She looked back in the rearview mirror as she spoke to Tigre. "Remember what I told you. You're only to take the money, say nothing, and leave."

He nodded. For most of the trip downtown, he looked out the window, as if plotting some escape. Amanda didn't know whether she could trust him. "If you mess up, we know where your family lives. We won't hesitate to come back."

"You're threatening my daughter?"

"You put yourself in this situation. Now you need to get yourself out of it. Do as I say and you won't have anything to worry about. Take a misstep and you'll deal with the consequences. Understood?"

He didn't say anything in response. Apparently, he wasn't used to having women tell him what to do.

Tigre opened the car door, got out, and started walking down the street toward the bar.

As Jordan watched him make his way towards *El Capitán*, he asked Amanda, "Do you think he'll listen?"

"We'll see," she said.

Chapter 35

Richter decided not to say anything to Sixtus about going to the event. Was it going to be such a small gathering? A tiny audience for and with the pope? Unlikely for something taking place at the American embassy. Was he that unimportant that he, as chief adviser to the pope, his supposed right-hand man, wouldn't be given the courtesy of an invitation? The effrontery rankled him.

Sixtus would certainly be surprised to see him there. But he would suffer the consequences, come what may. He needed to see General Cheeks. Doing so would help protect him and avoid any repercussions. Sixtus be damned!

He waited until the papal limousine left. He watched from the window as the pope, clothed in his white cassock, got into the car and departed. Then he called for another car to take him to the embassy on Via Sallustiana in Rome. It was only a fifteen-minute drive from Vatican City and a stone's throw to the American embassy to Italy. In fact, it was part of the same compound; the Americans had eliminated the standalone embassy to the Vatican years ago to save money. Richter might even see the man who called himself a Beach Boy, Brian Wilson.

Richter was dressed in his official scarlet robe. He would match the pope in dress. He wanted everyone at the embassy to know that he, though uninvited, was important. The uninvited were often the most important.

He ordered the car to arrive in fifteen minutes. He thought he'd arrive a bit late, to let the embassy staff fawn over the pontiff. That's who they really wanted to see, anyway. He'd make a beeline to General Cheeks while the Americans were being their servile selves.

When he arrived, he saw Sixtus at the center of the room standing near the fireplace, flanked by Ahmed Bensaïd and several diplomats. They blocked Sixtus's line of sight to Richter; Richter managed to gravitate to the other side of the hall, which was the size of a small ballroom. Brian Wilson, appearing like an undertaker in his black suit, approached Richter. "Cardinal, so nice to see you again!" He had an unctuous tone.

"Good evening," Richter said formally.

"No Bersch here," Wilson joked.

The cardinal gave him a blanched smile.

"I'm not sure who gave you that information," he said, prying.

"I would like to speak to General Cheeks. Will he be here?"

"Of course. He arranged this affair at the last minute. He and Mr. Bensaïd."

"Mr. Bensaïd?"

"Yes, the gathering is in honor of him. He is going to be granted American citizenship."

Richter couldn't help but raise his brow.

"At the pope's behest, of course."

"Naturally. They are quite close."

"Indeed." Again, there was a hint of impertinence in his tone.

"Is there somewhere I could speak to the general privately?" As Richter looked around the room, he noticed that the coterie of admirers had dispersed before Sixtus. He now had perfect sight of the cardinal.

Their eyes locked, and Sixtus gave him a curious stare, one that was half-devoid of feeling, and the other half a mixture of curiosity and reproach.

"Of course. There's a study off the entry hall. Would you like me to send him when he has a moment?"

"Yes, please. I'll wait for him there."

A waiter approached them carrying a tray of canapé. Richter, ever mindful of his sticklike figure, declined.

* * *

After Tigre entered *El Capitán* bar, Amanda turned to Jordan. "Let's go."

"Are we going to arrest them?"

"You've got your pen, right?"

"The blue ink, right?"

"Unless you're feeling frosty," she joked, alluding to the red ink that would instantly kill someone. "I'm just kidding. Yes, the blue ink. Just jab it and press the cap at the same time. I'll get Sima. You get the goon."

"What if they're up against a wall and there's no way to get behind them?"

"Then we wait for them to leave."

"What if the Bulgarians are there for back-up?"

"Then we might have to use our guns. Or torch the place." She held out the necklace with the small metal ball that could create a firestorm. "You got yours too, right?"

He reached under his T-shirt. "I wouldn't go anywhere without it."

She laughed, a bit nervously.

"What about Tigre? You think he'll turn on us?"

"Absolutely, if given the chance. But as long as he gets his money, he shouldn't care."

* * *

Richter sat at a small round table across a desk in a library filled with leather-bound volumes. Some of the books were in French, *Histoires Anciennes;* the works of Plato, Plutarch, Pliny the Elder, Cicero, Marcus

Aurelius; they were clearly there for decorative purposes. Richter waited for the general to arrive. He checked his watch. It was nearly 9 p.m. He was anxious. What if they sent him in with Sixtus? Or Bensaïd? Or the ambassador himself? What would he say? "I have information that points to a plot to murder Barranca." No, he would have to come up with some pretext. Tell them that he just wanted to make the general's acquaintance. They wouldn't believe him. He shouldn't have come. He was beginning to have misgivings for having considered the general a potential ally. His stomach turned; he should have eaten something. He stood from the Regency-style table. At that moment, General Cheeks opened the door. "Your Excellency," he said, extending his hand in a warm greeting.

Richter surmised he had had a few drinks. In fact, he was carrying a tumbler that contained what looked like whiskey. He placed it on the table as he sat down heavily on a chair, exhaling. Richter sat back down next to him.

"I should have called on you at the Vatican," Cheeks said. "I understand you're Sixtus's main man." He spoke with a warm drawl.

Richter felt that he could trust the man. "I know you're very busy, so I'll get straight to the point. This has to do with Cardinal Barranca."

"Yes, I spoke with His Holiness about the case. How can I help?"

Richter took out his phone. "I believe he may have been murdered because of this." He showed the picture of the shipping notice to the general.

The general pulled out a pair of reading glasses from his jacket pocket. "The Queen of Spades." He perused the letter for a few moments. "Why do you think it's related to his murder?"

"Because on the day of his death, someone was searching his room and they found this. They thought it was so important that they took this photograph. I have no idea what it means, but it's evidently important to some people."

"If you have it, are you afraid something might happen to you?"

"Yes, I am." Richter was relieved that the general understood how he was feeling. He genuinely seemed to grasp the gravity of the situation.

"How can I help?"

"Could you investigate? I don't trust the Italian police. They're useless. They'll never get to the bottom of this."

"You haven't given them this letter?"

"No. You're the only person who has seen it."

"Could you send it to me? I can do that myself if you allow me." The general waved the phone.

"Yes, of course."

The general texted himself the photo. His phone buzzed in his pocket; he checked that the message and the picture were received. "I have a copy. I suggest you delete this photo immediately."

"Do you think I might be in danger?"

"I wouldn't take the risk. You have the Americans looking into it now. Let us do the legwork. You will feel much better if you rid yourself of this matter and go back to your daily business." He handed Richter back his phone.

Richter stared at the transmittal letter on his phone. The good general was right. It was better to have no connection to this photo. He pressed the *delete* button.

"That's what we call a soft delete. The picture stays in your trash for thirty days. Trust me, I'm the Director of National Intelligence. You have to go to your deleted pictures folder and delete it again. This time permanently."

He spoke with such assurance that Richter dutifully obeyed.

"Do you feel better now?"

"Yes." He let out the word as if having just confessed a major sin and received absolution from the priest.

General Cheeks put his hand on Richter's shoulder. "I could send a security detail to watch over you if that would make you feel better."

"Thank you. But I'm going to Russia tomorrow."

"Are you sure you should?"

"I don't have a choice," responded Richter.

* * *

Amanda entered *El Capitán* from the front entrance. If Sima and her henchman were nearby, she didn't think they'd recognize her. If Violeta and Todorov saw her, they also likely wouldn't make the connection to her. She doubted they even noticed her at the Florence or Madrid airports. People weren't that astute, she learned at the Farm. People customarily didn't recognize others easily, especially in different contexts, unless they had a special interest in you. That interest was usually sexual.

Jordan went in through a rear entrance in the parking lot. He passed by the restrooms. A hall led to the main bar area. Dimly lit tables were scattered in front of booths along the wall. He was nervous; given his altercation with Sima and her burly man, he feared they would recognize him instantly, especially since he stood out as a Black man. He wore a baseball cap, but he doubted it would help disguise him in any meaningful way. He kept a hand on his Glock behind his back as he stepped forward. Before taking a place at the bar, he saw Tigre sitting with Sima and her burly man at a booth at the far end of the restaurant. It was dark inside; he didn't think that they would spot him. He strode toward the other end of the bar, where a bartender stood. He saw Amanda on a stool in the corner near the entrance. She would wait for Tigre to leave and wait for Sima and the burly man to go and then stop them.

As he took a seat, he checked for the pen in his pocket. He was ready when the time came. All he had to do was to remain unnoticed. The bartender approached, and he ordered a beer. At that moment, a hand touched him on the shoulder, startling him. A woman's voice said, "Can I join you?"

As he turned, he grabbed his Glock. He saw Pilar standing before him.

"You didn't think you were going to get rid of me that easily, did you?" she quipped.

He removed his hand from the gun, aware that she hadn't even noticed that he had reached for it. He saw Amanda observing him. She raised her eyebrows and cocked her head. He nodded back to indicate no concern.

"Am I disturbing you?" Pilar asked, looking over to where Amanda was sitting.

"No, I'm just surprised to see you."

"Something for you," the bartender asked her in English.

She replied back in Spanish that she'd have a beer too.

"Why did you disappear?" he asked.

She sat beside him. "I didn't want things to be uncomfortable."

"You didn't go back?"

"I thought I'd spend a couple days here in Algeciras."

The bartender came back with a beer.

"Listen," Jordan said, "I'm actually in the middle of work."

"Oh? Some fascinating FBI stuff?" she replied in a light-hearted tone.

"It's actually quite serious. And dangerous. You should go. I wouldn't want you to get hurt."

"I could use a little excitement," she said.

At that moment, he noticed Tigre walking toward the front entrance. Pilar seemed to notice Jordan watching him also. "He does look dangerous," she said.

"That's not the man we're after. But he is dangerous. Just be on alert."

"Maybe I could help," she said.

"You could sit close to me. I don't want those people to recognize me."

"Who?"

"There's a woman with short hair sitting at a booth with a big, bearded man next to her. She could be Middle Eastern."

As Tigre left the establishment, Violeta and Todorov entered. Jordan saw them walk by the bar and head toward Sima's table.

"Shit," Jordan said.

Pilar instantly recognized that Violeta and Todorov were persons of interest. "Who are those people?"

"They're terrorists. All of them. Extremely dangerous. They will kill all of us without a second thought. I was running from that woman when I met you. They almost killed me. The others are paid assassins. And they pay people to kill too. You really need to leave."

Sima got up from the table and looked over to the bar where Jordan was sitting. He put his head down, staring at the shiny black bar top, fearful that she might recognize him. He leaned in toward Pilar. She crouched her head down too and started to kiss him. She embraced him, letting her arms cover his torso and obstructing him from view. It was as if she was intentionally obscuring him.

While being kissed, he opened his eyes. Sima walked closer. He could see Amanda shift in her seat, readying herself for action. Her arm was extended by her side. He presumed she had the poison pen in her hand.

But Sima took a turn toward the restroom area from where he had entered. Pilar removed her lips from his. "Sorry," she said half-apologetically.

He smiled. "It was nice. Thanks."

"She's gone?"

"Yes. In the restroom."

Amanda got up from her seat and proceeded past the bar to the restroom hallway. With her eyes, she gave a subtle nod to Jordan. He interpreted it as a call to action.

"She's going to the restroom too," Pilar said.

She was very observant. Like a spy.

"Do you need to follow her?"

"No." He kept his eye on the burly henchman, who swigged a beer at the booth, while looking at his cell phone. He had his back to the bar where Jordan was sitting. He raised his arms by his sides, as if to dissipate heat or sweat. Jordan too was feeling overheated in the bar. It might have been adrenaline from the pursuit and the impending charge. It might have been the kiss.

Violeta and Todorov sat at the booth talking to each other, perhaps in Bulgarian. They seemed to have no interest in engaging with the burly man. Jordan noticed he wasn't the talkative type. They sat facing Jordan, but he doubted they would have been warned of him. And if they had, he would take care of them too.

"Maybe I can go see what she's doing," Pilar said.

"You can't put yourself in danger."

"Life is dangerous," she said. Her cat eyes danced in the faint darkness.

He wanted to kiss her again. But he knew he had work to do, and now was the moment to strike. "Give me a minute." He touched her lightly on the arm as he got up from the stool. He calmly sauntered over to the henchman's booth. He didn't want to make sudden movements that would alert him to his presence.

Jordan kept his Glock in the back of the waistband of his jeans and held the pen in his hand, his thumb over the button that would release the ink when he would thrust it into the burly man's neck or shoulder or arm or wherever he could manage to pierce his skin. As he walked toward him, his adrenaline raced. His imagination was running wild. It was as if his imagination was a protective shield against the reality of what he was about to do. He had a vision of the burly man suddenly gasping and foaming at the mouth. Jordan would have injected him with the red ink, but he knew that he would not use that ink. Still, he could see a foamy spittle emerging from the man's mouth. He was trying to talk, but words wouldn't come. His body would shake and convulse. He was like a toy rattle, and his body was rattling itself, shaking, convulsing, unable to stop.

Jordan silenced his mind, steadying himself, telling himself everything was going to be okay. The booth next to the one where the henchman and his cohorts were sitting was empty. Jordan took a seat at it, his back to the burly man. As he sat, he sensed the burly man either raising his arms or turning to him. For a moment, Jordan wondered whether his imagination was playing tricks on him, again as some sort of barrier to this real, unreal, surreal circumstance. No, he moved his head ever so slightly, and Sima's henchman was in fact raising one of his arms, stretching. Without hesitation, Jordan turned and hastily stabbed his bare biceps with the pen. The point of the pen easily penetrated the stocky henchman's thick, burly biceps. The man didn't react. He looked at his arm with a puzzled look. Then he seemed to notice the black skin of Jordan's hand near his own flesh. His eyes jumped in alarm. Jordan's eyes jumped also: Did he select the right ink? Had he punctured the man with the red ink by mistake? Or the harmless black ink? He was supposed to have used the blue ink, to subdue him. As the burly man was about to stand, Violeta and Todorov scuttled out of the booth, perhaps onto the floor – Jordan couldn't see them any longer. But they weren't next to him or at his booth. Suddenly, the burly henchman fell with a large thud. The beer stein splashed across the table, and his arms fell into Sima's wine glass and the drinks that Violeta and Todorov had left. Jordan stood from the booth just as stealthily as he had sat down and cautiously started to walk away, saying to himself, *I killed someone. I just killed someone.* The words repeated in his mind. He asked himself: Was he really one of *them,* as Amanda had claimed? Did he, as the CIA officers did, have carte blanche to kill? Or had Amanda told him that to placate him, to manipulate him, to make him feel better about what he was doing? He looked at the pen which he grasped tightly in his hand, his thumb hovering over the button. He saw that the blue ink was exposed. A sense of relief rushed through him. The burly man was asleep. Perhaps deathly asleep. Very soundly asleep, indeed. The threshold had not been breached. He had accomplished his mission and done exactly as directed.

He looked back at the bar where he had been sitting next to Pilar. She was gone.

Chapter 36

Amanda closed the door of the restroom stall, peering at Sima's body. Sima lay slumped on the toilet and against the wall. Amanda had propped her up so that no one would notice her for a few minutes. She tapped a message in Rebar: "Ready for pickup. Restroom." In the Rebar chat, she saw Jordan's message come through: "Ready for pickup in the bar."

As she exited the lavatory and came down the hall, a sense of urgency permeated her stride. She was pleased that Jordan had succeeded in subduing the burly man. Half their mission was now complete. But they still had to contend with Violeta and Todorov, and she knew that things could get messy from here.

The restaurant crew was agitatedly looking over the burly man's body. They couldn't tell if he was dead. No one thought to take a pulse. Commotion abounded. The bartender left his post behind the bar to assist the waiters and waitresses. Even the kitchen staff came out of the kitchen to see what was going on.

Imagine how they'd react if they found Sima too, Amanda thought.

One of the waitresses was calling emergency services. Amanda saw in Rebar that the call was intercepted by their clean-up crew.

As she scanned the restaurant for Violeta and Todorov, she received a message on Rebar saying, "Rear penetrated. Woman excavated." She understood that the clean-up crew, disguised as emergency medical personnel, had removed Sima from the restroom. At that moment, another trio of technicians entered the bar. They were all armed and trained CIA officers. They pretended to do a little bit of CPR on the burly man before strapping him to a stretcher. They knew he would be out for at least four hours, possibly more, depending on the amount of ink Jordan had injected him with. The lead technician, a native Spanish-speaker whose parents were Guatemalan, told the bar staff that he had suffered a heart attack and that they were transporting him to a hospital. She said he was alive and would probably be okay.

Amanda found Jordan. "Where did the Bulgarians go?"

"They vanished when I stabbed him."

"How did it feel?"

"Satisfying," he said. "But I wasn't completely sure it was going to work."

"This stuff always works," she said. "We've been using these chemicals for years. Where did that girl go?"

"I don't know." At that moment, he received a text on his phone: "I'm following them." He didn't recognize the number, but it was from overseas. He assumed it was Pilar. She must have gotten his number back at the hotel room before disappearing.

"Where?" he texted back. Before he received a response, his cell phone rang from the same number.

"They got in their car and they're heading out of the city."

"You're following them?"

"Yes."

"They're very dangerous. Tell me where you are and we'll send someone. They probably spotted you." He could imagine her in her old, little white Citroën trying to keep chase.

"They're heading to the highway." Suddenly, she screamed, "Oh no!"

"Pilar? What's the matter?" He didn't get a reply. "Pilar?" He heard Pilar scream again, her voice shrill until the line disconnected. "No!"

Chapter 37

Richter managed to avoid Sixtus for most of the evening at the embassy function. The sniveling Beach Boy Brian Wilson attempted to pry more information out of him, to ascertain the reason for his visit to the Italian embassy earlier. "Did you ever manage to find out who this Bersch was?" he asked.

Richter shrugged him off.

"Did General Cheeks know?"

He was certainly a nosy fellow.

Wilson continued, unable to censor himself: "He knows everybody. He's a very well-connected fellow. Even if it is a code name for someone. There are a lot of spies within our corridors, as I'm sure you can appreciate."

"I was mistaken," Richter replied.

"Yes, sometimes people mix up business contacts with embassy personnel. Of course, if I can assist any further in the matter..."

Ahmed Bensaïd broke into the conversation. "Your Excellency. I didn't know you were coming." He cut a very elegant figure, in his finely tailored dark navy Italian suit, his immaculately polished, black leather lace-up shoes and belt, and his tortoise-shell eyeglasses. Sixtus had once told Richter that they were made of actual tortoise shell, crafted in the south of France. Bensaïd's gold wristwatch and gold and sapphire pinkie ring shimmered as he extended his hand to Richter.

"It wasn't planned," Richter replied in a soft voice. He was trying to create a more intimate atmosphere so that Wilson would leave, but the Beach Boy didn't take the hint.

"Well, I am glad you came." Bensaïd didn't have a scintilla of insincerity in his voice. His delivery was as polished as his shoes. "The pontiff and I are leaving soon. I hope you can join us back to headquarters."

"I wouldn't want to intrude," Richter said.

Wilson seemed intently interested in his reply – more than Bensaïd himself – and awaited Bensaïd's rejoinder.

"It will be no intrusion at all. You'll have to tell us all about your little conversation with General Cheeks. He's such a promising leader. Let me get Sixtus. We'll find you. Thank you for your hospitality, Mr. Bersch."

Bersch? Did he hear that correctly? Richter's stomach tossed; he suddenly felt the need to vomit.

"It's Wilson," he said, correcting Bensaïd. Bensaïd walked off toward where Sixtus was holding court. Wilson stared at Richter, seemingly observing his discomfort. "You seem to have become quite pale."

Is this why the embassy sent Wilson to see him when he had asked for Bersch? He was Bersch! Why was he concealing the matter? "He called you Bersch," Richter said.

Wilson chuckled. "I get that sometimes. Must be contagious. Would you excuse me?" He trailed to a room off the main hall.

Richter stood, dumbfounded. Why wouldn't he just say that he was Mr. Bersch when he called on him? Was there some other secret code that he was supposed to have given him so that he would reveal his identity? Barranca had been given his name. But had he actually met

Wilson? Had someone given him the name of a Mr. Bersch to call on? And did Bensaïd know that Richter had gone to see Bersch? Was his name-dropping a way of signaling to him that he knew he was making inquiries? That he was playing a dangerous game? And the car outside the American embassy – he had almost been kidnapped! Had Bersch ordered them to apprehend him? His stomach throttled, and he began to think he had been poisoned. Or had nerves and alcohol affected his empty stomach? He rushed to the restroom.

* * *

"We have to help her." Jordan was typing into Rebar as he and Amanda got into her Opel sedan. "I put in a request to track her cell phone."

"We will, of course," she said. "But we don't have a lot of time. We have a helicopter to catch."

"A helicopter? Is the safe house that far?"

"Yes."

"Shouldn't we get the Bulgarians first?"

"Ideally. But we don't have a ton of time. We need to get whatever information we can from Sima."

"She won't tell us anything," Jordan said.

"I wouldn't be so sure about that."

A military helicopter passed overhead. Jordan looked up at it. It looked British or American, like a Chinook. The twin-rotor craft had propellers on the front as well as the back. "Is that them?"

"It's not safe around here. Especially with the Bulgarians and whoever else they've embedded. Did you get a response back on Rebar?"

He looked at his cell phone.

"Let me," she said. Amanda typed into her phone on Rebar, explaining that this was an emergency, and they needed immediate approval. She knew that her request would get more attention. "Let's head to the highway." She started the car and headed toward the outskirts of Algeciras.

* * *

Richter sat in the back of the pontiff's custom-made stretch limousine across from Sixtus and Bensaïd, who sat side-by-side in the rearmost part of the coach. The windows were so thick you could barely make out the lights from the street. The car was pretty much a replica of the U.S. presidential limousine, affectionately known as the Beast, manufactured by the same team with many of the same safety features. The car could withstand Molotov cocktails and machine gun fire; all the glass was shatterproof; the tires were run-flat.

"Bersch seemed to take an interest in you," Bensaïd said to Richter.

"I didn't notice." Richter tried to hide his nervousness, jamming his hands into his spindly thighs for comfort.

"Had you met him before?"

"Yes. But I thought his name was Wilson."

Bensaïd laughed. "I guess you don't know him very well. He's CIA. Barranca had an appointment with him the day before he was killed."

Nerves shot through Richter. He side-eyed the doors: They were all locked, and he probably wouldn't be able to open them. He'd have limited means of escape. Bensaïd tapped him on his bony knee, startling him. His shoulders jumped up in fright.

"You're with friends," Bensaïd said. "Tell us, what's going on?"

Sixtus stared at Richter with a blank look, expecting him to say something.

"Nothing."

"Were you sore that you weren't invited to the meeting with General Cheeks?" Sixtus asked.

"No."

"But you had a private audience with him?"

"*Private* in quotation marks," Bensaïd remarked. Both he and Sixtus chuckled. "Nothing is ever *private* when you're talking with the Director of National Intelligence."

"Are you not happy with your new role?" Sixtus said. "Would you rather have Barranca's?"

The allusion to the dead cardinal unsettled Richter. "If I am going to Russia, I thought I should play in these circles." Then he asked a more pointed question, endeavoring to keep his tone neutral. "Why would Cardinal Barranca be meeting with Bersch?"

"Perhaps the same reason you were meeting with Cheeks," Sixtus replied.

Richter reflected on Sixtus's comment but said nothing.

"What did he say about me?" Sixtus asked.

"We didn't talk about you," Richter said.

Sixtus laughed. "No? Not a word?"

"I don't believe so."

"Then about what?"

Abruptly, the car came to a stop. Sixtus and Bensaïd were shoved forward in their seats, while Richter was thrown back. The voice of the security chief sitting in the front seat beside the driver came on the intercom: "Sorry, Your Holiness. A stray cat came into the road." The security officer spoke only to the pontiff, as if the others weren't present.

Bensaïd laughed. "We better put on our seatbelts. Or the pontiff might fall victim not to a maniacal, religious fanatic but to an alley cat."

Sixtus gave a nervous laugh, to acknowledge the joke. But still, as pope, his mortality was never far from his mind, especially with the constant security measures the Swiss Guard took, the warnings he was given – even the admonition not to shake hands. For this reason, he was accustomed, as he had been instructed, to hold his hands in a prayer sign as a greeting.

Richter took the opportunity of the near-accident to remain silent. But Bensaïd wouldn't let him off the hook –

"What did you and the general talk about?"

"I wanted to know if there was any message I should convey to Russian officials."

Bensaïd scoffed at the suggestion. "You would have us believe that?"

"That's the truth," Richter answered, mustering a measured amount of indignity.

"What did he say?" Sixtus asked.

"To emphasize the need for peace."

Sixtus burst out laughing. "The general said that?"

"Yes," Richter replied in his most credulous voice.

Now, Bensaïd started laughing too. "What is the penalty for lying in the Catholic Church?" he asked Sixtus.

"A few Hail Marys."

"Everything in the Catholic Church can be washed away with just a few Hail Marys."

"Isn't it the truth?" Sixtus said.

Bensaïd took out his cell phone from his jacket pocket. "Should we call the general to corroborate this story?"

"Go ahead," Richter replied, his eyebrows twitching as he nodded.

Bensaïd clutched his phone and put his other hand on Richter's knee, which caused a slight nervous reaction. "The thing is," he said, "we need people we can trust in this organization. And I'm not completely sure you are one of them."

"Trust is a two-way street," Richter replied.

"That's where you are mistaken. It only flows through His Holiness. You'd do well to remember that."

"You'll be leaving us tomorrow morning," Sixtus said with a downward inflection to indicate finality.

* * *

Amanda and Jordan reached the location where Rebar had last tracked Pilar's phone. Her white Citroën was parked on the side of the road. As Jordan inspected it, he saw her phone sitting on the floor in front of the passenger's seat, as if someone had tossed it back inside. He picked it up with a tissue that he found in the door bin.

Amanda shot him a curious look.

"Trying to preserve prints," he replied.

"Lot of good those are going to do us. You're so FBI."

"Why bother?" he asked semi-rhetorically.

"If you have to ask. It's not like we're going to end up in Federal court."

He looked at her, quizzically. Was she inferring that Violeta and Todorov would end up dead? "What do we do?"

Amanda had checked Rebar earlier and had noticed that the tracking of Violeta's luggage was no longer effective. "I'm afraid there isn't much to go on."

"We can't just let her hang."

"What can she tell them? She probably doesn't even have your number anymore since we've got her phone. Unless she memorized it."

"Unlikely. Then what?"

"They've probably gone to the safe house."

"That could be really dangerous."

"That's this business," she said matter-of-factly.

"Could we get some backup this time?"

"I'll see if anyone hasn't left for Poland."

"That's where they're bringing Sima?"

"You got it."

* * *

Amanda and Jordan headed over to Sima's safe house. Jordan felt he knew the area well, having narrowly escaped the other day. His neck and shoulder muscles tensed as he sat with Amanda in her Opel, waiting for backup to arrive.

"Why do you think she got messed up in this?" Amanda asked.

"Boredom, maybe."

"Maybe she's interested in you. She was following you. How did she know you'd be at *El Capitán*? She had to have been following you much of the day. But I would have noticed. Perhaps she has some tracking device on you. You said you didn't give her your telephone number?"

"That's right." He took his cell phone from his pocket. "It was probably unlocked and she snooped into it. It won't be the first time a lady has done that."

"Some lady!" Amanda cackled.

"You think she put some tracking into it, like Rebar? She's not a spy."

"How do we know?"

"She works at a bar."

"Perfect cover."

"And I just happened to go into her father's bar when I was on the way to Cádiz?"

"True. Doesn't sound plausible. Maybe she is bored. Maybe she likes you. Maybe she wants something more. But how did she find you?"

"We'll have to ask."

"We might not be alive if we wait. Take your shoes off."

"What?"

"Take them off."

He kicked one of his sneakers off his foot and held it by his waist.

"Look inside," she said.

He had a curious look as he peered at the interior cushioning.

"Under the inserts."

He lifted the insole of the sneaker and there, a small tag was practically glued to the side of the sneaker. "It's a tracking device. Like one of those you put in luggage in case it gets stolen. I can't believe she'd do this." He was stunned.

"I don't think it's anything malevolent," Amanda said. "She probably just wanted to keep tabs on you. If she had her phone, she'd know we're here,"

"Seems pretty extreme," Jordan said.

"She probably didn't think you'd ever find out. You wouldn't have if it weren't for me. It's harmless. She probably thought she'd never hear from you again. Or maybe she was going to remove it once you reconnected."

Why was she defending her? She hadn't even talked to her. "How do you know?" Jordan asked.

"Just a hunch. Besides, we're trained to use commercial means whenever possible, so as not to alert anyone that we're under cover. I've used those tags myself. They're great to slip into books. People just think they're a security device to prevent theft. If you can get one into someone's laptop bag, you're golden."

"Now I feel like I really owe her."

"I wouldn't go that far. She wouldn't be in this mess if she weren't snooping around."

At that moment, Amanda received a notification via Rebar that *The Grindon* had disappeared. Dumbfounded, she stared at the screen, re-reading the message. Did it say what she thought it did?

"How could it disappear?" she wrote back.

A response came back: "All radar was turned off. Emergency tracking was disabled. The ship has gone ghost."

American submarines were a master of this technique, but commercial vessels usually didn't have the knowledge of how to hide itself from radar. There had to be somebody highly trained, with a military background on board.

"Where was the ship last seen?" she wrote.

"Entering the Atlantic."

"Where was it headed?"

"Baltimore."

Baltimore was too close to Washington, DC for Amanda's comfort. Even an explosion at Baltimore Harbor could cause massive damage and disruption. The ship had to be stopped.

"Something wrong?" Jordan asked.

"We lost our ship."

"You're kidding?"

"I wish I was."

The backup team arrived. The team consisted of one person – a woman whom Jordan recognized from *El Capitán*. She had posed as an EMT. Jordan learned she was an American CIA officer born to Guatemalan parents in the U.S. Her Spanish had been flawless; yet she didn't have the Castilian accent. Jordan found her easier to understand than the local Spaniards.

The woman was named Monica, and she stood just over five feet two. Jordan didn't want to be sexist, but when he saw her, with no one accompanying her, he didn't have the greatest measure of confidence. Violeta and Todorov were world-class terrorists. They held a hostage he cared about and felt didn't deserve to be put in this situation, even if she did put a tracking tag in his sneaker. His neck muscles tightened. He tried to shake it off, loosening his jaw by cracking his mandibular joint to little avail.

"Are we gonna do this?" Monica said.

With this one statement – this question that was half-inquiry and half-challenge, Jordan's perception of Monica changed. She had transformed from the caring, nurturing medical technician he had seen at *El Capitán* to a rough-and-tumble, "let's-do-this" sort of chick.

She took out a Sig Sauer pistol that she had concealed under her shirt.

"What's our plan? We have to make sure she doesn't get hurt," Jordan said.

"It might already be too late for that," Monica replied.

Amanda lifted her pendant from her shirt, brandishing the silvery-brass ball that contained the explosive material she had prepped Jordan on. "We might have to smoke them out."

Monica laughed. "I like your way of thinking."

"They'll kill her," Jordan said.

Monica rolled her eyes.

"No," Amanda said. "We'll blow up the front, and they won't know what hit them. They'll either head out the back or a side door. They'll want to get to the car."

"Why don't we just blow that up?" Jordan asked.

"That might not draw them out. We need to make sure they get out of the house. If it's half on fire and ready to blow up, they'll leave Pilar. They probably realize by now she doesn't know anything anyway. Sound like a plan?"

Monica nodded in agreement.

"You guys are the experts," Jordan said.

They walked from their car down the street toward the house. Amanda recognized Violeta and Todorov's rental car sitting in the driveway. As they approached the front yard, Amanda took the ball of the pendant and moved it closer to her mouth. "Get ready." She licked her tongue over it and threw it at the front door. It ricocheted against one of the front steps and stopped near the side of the house, in front of a large casement window. Jordan recognized that this was where the living room was. They waited several moments.

Nothing happened. No explosion. Nothing.

Chapter 38

"You think it needed more spit?" Jordan was crouched alongside them behind a tree on the side of the road.

Before she could answer, an enormous explosion occurred, blasting the casement window and creating an earth-shattering sound that sent smoke and debris through the air.

"I think that got their attention," she said. "Let's go."

Monica and Jordan rushed to the side yard toward the rear of the house. Jordan knew there was an entrance there – the French doors where he had managed to escape. Amanda watched the smoke clear from the front of the house. Todorov opened the front door. Leaving the door open, he shouted something unintelligible back inside. Violeta came running out. Amanda steadied herself against the tree as they hopped into the rental car. They backed out at a crazy high speed; Todorov was driving. They almost backed into the tree where Amanda was standing! Then they made a hasty turn, avoiding it. She aimed to fire at the car. She wanted to hit the tire's wheels. She didn't want to kill them; they had too much valuable information. She shot a few times. In the blaze of dust from the dirt that spun up from the road, she saw the car continue to hasten away. She had only managed to hit the car's frame. They drove in the direction toward the highway, opposite where Amanda had parked her rental car.

She knew that they only had a minute or two to escape before Violeta and Todorov would muster the courage to return. Jordan and Monica emerged from the back with Pilar. Pilar had zip ties around her hands. The three of them dashed toward Amanda. Then the four bolted to the rental sedan down the street.

As they drove off, Jordan could see that Pilar's mouth had been gagged. She was silent for a while. Then she finally spoke, her eyes tearful, her tone imploring: "They know who I am. They have my name. My address. They'll get me. My father. They told me so. I have to go home. I have to save him."

"We can put you in hiding and give you protection," Amanda said.

As she said this, Jordan noticed that Monica shot her a look. He looked back at Pilar, wondering if she noticed the look also. It was as if Monica was saying, "Why are you promising her this? We can't help her!"

But Pilar just stared ahead, with a blank expression, as if recalling being at the hands of Violeta and Todorov and suffering the recollected acts and words they used to torture her. She was free now, but she sat still, resigned, like a caged bird.

Chapter 39

The next morning, Richter was awakened by a gentle knocking at his door. A Swiss Guard told him that the plane was ready. While he had a private jet at his disposal and, theoretically, he could have flown at any hour, a slot was provided to the Vatican to depart Rome's Leonardo da Vinci Airport at 6 a.m. The flight would last six hours; he would arrive in Moscow around noon. The guard passed him his official itinerary which he placed on his dressing table while he took a shower. He barely glanced at it. Everything was being staged, choreographed, for him. He could feign illness – his stomach was still in knots – but he decided he must go through with it. Besides God, he had General Cheeks on his side. He would come through for him. God would see to it.

When Richter emerged from his shower, he took a towel and rubbed his face dry. When he looked up, he saw Sixtus standing before him, a shadowy figure. He rubbed his face again, and Sixtus was gone. Then he reappeared. But he could only see Sixtus's face; his body was merely a faint background image under a robe. He was imagining him. From the corner of the pontiff's eye, a bloody tear fell, rolling down his cheek, leaving a crimson trail that seemed to sparkle against his pale skin as it disappeared. Richter shook his head and shouted a visceral grunt – nothing that was German, English, or Italian, merely a monosyllabic roar. He lifted his hand and started to make the sign of the cross before his bare, graying chest. Sixtus burst out laughing; there was no sound, just his mouth widening in an engulfing blackness. Then he was gone, a phantasm that had vanished as quickly as it had appeared and reappeared. He had to be death itself, the living incarnation of the end, the embodiment of the fatalistic call to which he would succumb. Richter had to get out of the Vatican. The place had become so unholy in the last few months. He looked around the room, praying for the Church's salvation as much as for his own, and asked, *Will I ever come back?*

* * *

Pilar didn't want to leave Jordan's side. But he explained she would be safer that way. She couldn't continue to straggle alongside them. She would be sent to Madrid where Interpol would put her in a safe house. They would pick her father up, too. Before the car came to pick him and Amanda up, he asked her, "Why did you put that tag in my shoes?"

"I didn't want to lose track of you."

"You didn't think I'd call."

"I knew you wouldn't call," she said. "You're on business. You're working. Your career is the most important thing to you. You don't have time for people like me."

"That's not true," he said.

"I know it is. Now I regret it. I could never have a future with you, not with people like *them* in the world."

Jordan knew she was referring to Violeta and Todorov, and perhaps even Sima.

"I wanted to help. To do my part."

"You *have* helped," he said.

"No. I've made a mess of things. That's all I'm good at, you know? That's what we Spaniards do."

He chuckled, touching her shoulder. "I'll see you when I come back, before I leave."

"Tell me one thing, Jordan Harrison." She took a pause and didn't say anything for an uncomfortable beat, looking at him stilly. "Tell me you'll get them for me. That they won't get away."

"I promise," he said. With a quick hug, they said goodbye.

Chapter 40

A military helicopter took Amanda and Jordan from Algeciras to Seville. There, they boarded a military plane that took them to a base in Lask, Poland. The trip was under five hours. They arrived in Poland just after noon. From the base, they took a car to a small town called Spadadz. Located an hour south of Lask, the town was once a center of textile manufacturing, but all the facilities had been abandoned during World War II and had largely remained unoccupied. Post 9/11, the Pentagon leased one of the warehouses for *cooperative military activities*. The intelligence apparatus used this relatively benign description as a euphemism for a black site. DoD spent over one hundred million dollars refurbishing the warehouse, fitting it with state-of-the-art electronic surveillance systems, anti-aircraft defense systems, and drones. Dozens of drones flew through Spadadz, patrolling it for signs of countersurveillance. The townspeople soon realized what was going on in their once-quaint village: interrogations, torture, kidnappings, disappearances. While the occasional terrorist still found inhospitable accommodations at the site, the warehouse was largely unoccupied, playing host to special VIPs only once or twice a year. Most of the black sites within Europe had been shut down, but the Americans worked with their NATO counterparts to keep this one open. The U.S. promised it could be the crown jewel in their fight against terrorism, specifically jihadism. But the reality was, these days it usually welcomed only uncooperative CEOs and politicians who refused to toe the line, thinking they were untouchable.

Last evening, Sima and her burly henchman arrived as special guests. The proverbial red carpet was rolled out for them. Amanda and Jordan agreed that it would be more difficult, i.e., bloody, to make the burly henchman talk. So they opted to choose Sima as their more cooperative target. She had been subjected to alternative sessions of blaring rock music and ear-piercing Carnatic music from India, which to the Western ear might be kindly described as annoying, particularly if you were stripped naked, blindfolded, and given drinks that left an unpleasant, rusty taste in your mouth. Not to mention the urge to pee, though, fortunately for the captive, nary a trickle came.

Amanda was given the option by facility staff to enter with a utility cart that housed a host of fearsome-looking, Inquisition-style steel utensils. She declined, believing they wouldn't be necessary. Half-jokingly, she said, "I might be tempted to use them." She knew how these secretive interrogations could incite the worst of human nature in the interrogator, particularly when they weren't yielding the intended results. She didn't wish to unleash this side of herself. She didn't want to be faced in the mirror of memory with the deep regret that she had allowed herself to become debased. "They're going bareback," came the announcement on the comms devices as she and Jordan were led to Sima's room.

As they entered the cavernous room, which had fluorescent lights blaring down from the ceiling beneath the woofers and subwoofers that provided concert-like sound fit for an amphitheater, she said to Jordan, "Do you want to do the honors?" She was referring to taking off the hood and mask that covered Sima's head.

He approached her cautiously, even though her legs and hands were chained to a chair. The metal chair looked like it belonged in an automated operating room. It could convert itself into a table, straight or Z-shaped, and could rise or lower electronically by remote control. When Jordan removed the hood and blindfold from Sima's eyes, reflex forced her to close her eyes. The light was so blinding her eyes needed time to adjust. Jordan could see that she had red marks on her face, scratches on her arms. Bruises had already formed about her neck, where it looked like a collar had earlier been placed. Yet there were no signs of blood. She had been fully showered, likely against her will. Her dark hair was glistening. He had never seen her without makeup and was startled by how young she looked, like a girl of eighteen or nineteen. He knew she was twice that age. His eyes too were playing tricks on him. It must have been the light, the atmosphere, the anxiety. Cognizant of the interrogation – or *interview,* in Agency parlance – he was about to have with Sima, he felt a pit in his stomach, an unmistakable hollow, as if his entire core were empty of guts, blood or organs. Reflexively, instinctually, he put a hand over his midsection to calm himself, to fill the void. Sima's dark brown eyes seemed to bore through him, as if to say, "*I may be shackled and at your mercy. But have no mercy on me because I will kill you. I need my revenge.*"

Amanda watched as Jordan stood by Sima's side. He didn't move. She could tell he had been seized by a catatonic stupor. He didn't know what to say or what to do. He hadn't been trained to handle these types of interrogations. She hadn't prepared him. Rain pattered down onto the metal roof, creating a broken, stuttering drumbeat. "What's the name of the ship that you're using?"

"I don't know," responded Sima.

Without hesitation, Amanda stood behind her and grabbed her hair, twisting it in her hands over Sima's head. Sima shrieked. "I hate to mess up your beautiful hair." Amanda pulled the hair tighter, forcing Sima to look up at the lights overhead. "There are cameras up there and they are filming everything," Amanda said, lying. She knew that the agency did not tape their interviews to provide officers with plausible deniability. Whatever happened in this room stayed in this room. Some agency personnel dubbed the chambers *Caesar's Palace*. They were the CIA's version of Vegas.

Amanda pulled her hair harder, and Sima's bulging eyes had nowhere to look but at her. "Don't lie to me about something I already know!"

"Then why did you fucking ask?" Sima shot back.

"Because I want to know what kind of piece of shit I'm talking to! You want to play this the hard way or the easy way? It's up to you. I've done it both ways. I don't get pleasure out of seeing people bleed, or lose their teeth, or get their fingernails ripped out. But if that's what you want, tell me and I'll get some guys in here who'll fuck you up real good."

Jordan was shocked at what he was hearing. He didn't think he had ever heard Amanda swear before. The rain suddenly became fiercer. He looked up at the ceiling, wondering, *Was water going to pour down on them?*

"I'll cooperate," Sima said.

"Smart girl." Amanda was relieved, as she knew that the information received through torture was less reliable than that given freely. She removed her hand from Sima's hair and stood in front of her. "Where is *The Grindon* going?"

"Baltimore," she said.

"What's it carrying?"

"An almost fully assembled nuclear device using highly radioactive cesium-137."

"Who's going to receive it?"

"I don't know," she said.

Amanda took a step closer toward Sima.

"I don't know!" Sima repeated. "All I know is that it will be in good hands. They kept parts of the plan secret, so that none of us knows what is completely going on. In case we're captured."

"The irony," Amanda said.

Sima let out a laugh.

"Who's funding the operation?" Amanda asked.

"You have to know that," Sima said.

"You're in no position to tell me what I know. Say it to the cameras," Amanda shot back, motioning her head toward the corner of the room where a dummy camera was positioned.

"KZ," she said begrudgingly. When Amanda didn't respond, she announced what the initials stood for: "Khalid Zahir."

"Why is he doing this?"

"He doesn't like the United States, obviously."

Her matter-of-fact tone didn't rattle Amanda. "He's made millions – billions – off the United States."

"Then call it ideological. From what I understand, he doesn't want to be in a master-servant relationship. Even if he's being well paid."

"He wants power?"

"Yes."

"How will this achieve anything? Destroying a city, killing innocent people?"

"It will certainly get people's attention."

"It will put a target on his back. He has to know the U.S. will hunt him down and kill him, like it did with Osama bin Laden."

"Either he doesn't expect he'll be implicated in the plot, or he doesn't think he'll fail."

"Fail at what?" Amanda said. "Blowing up a city?"

"He wants to take down the U.S. government. He'll finish what bin Laden failed at doing, destroying Washington, D.C. Baltimore's not far from the capital, you know. I don't know all this for a fact, but it's what I've heard through the proverbial grapevine. I'm just a girl for hire."

"If something happened to President Foster or Congress, the American people wouldn't fall in line behind a Middle Eastern billionaire. There would be a revolt. Tremendous resistance."

"Of course they wouldn't," she said. "They'd need somebody they could trust. Someone American. Christian. Pious even."

The Christian reference made Amanda think of how Cardinal Barranca was specifically targeted. "What are you insinuating?"

Sima shrugged. "It's just what I heard."

"Say it for the camera," Amanda said, nodding her head toward the decoy camera.

"The pope could swoop in and save the day. Nobody suspects a pope."

Chapter 41

"Do you believe her?" Jordan and Amanda sat before untouched cups of coffee in a small conference room.

"What incentive would she have to lie?" Amanda answered.

"But the pope?"

"The truth is sometimes stranger than fiction."

"The henchman's story pretty much lines up with hers. It makes me suspicious."

"But it lacks the details. He said they were only paid a million dollars. She told us two. It would make sense she would lie to him about how much they were being paid so she wouldn't have to share it all. He didn't know about the cesium. It lines up if these are rumblings they've heard. They've been kept in the dark. They've had to fit the pieces together. But they don't really care as long as they get paid. It's typical for these kinds of people. They're not terrorists but they're happy to facilitate terrorism. They're not ideological, but they're just as dangerous."

"So do we go interview Sixtus?"

Amanda laughed. "You're so FBI. And what, arrest him?"

"What's the alternative?" Jordan asked.

"I'm afraid ultimately," she hesitated for a moment, "we'll have to kill him."

Chapter 42

Richter's plane landed in Moscow just before 1 p.m. All through the flight, he wondered whether the jet was going to have a malfunction and require an emergency landing. Nobody else of any importance was on the flight; all were disposable. Then he landed, somewhat rockily, but safely, nonetheless. There must be some other way they'd kill him. Some Russian sniper. Some lethal cocktail. A mysterious heart attack.

He didn't want to get off the plane. But he had no choice. What would he face in Rome? No doubt a similar fate. In either place, he had no support system that he could rely upon.

No fanfare awaited him at the airport. What was he expecting? A royal welcome? But there wasn't a single Russian envoy present to greet him. The Holy See had made all the arrangements, including the car that would bring him to his hotel. For each single thing that the Vatican controlled, he felt more at risk. They could micromanage his movements, off him whenever they wished, make him disappear into the Russian ether. There was something more. Richter knew that if Sixtus sensed that he was trying to free himself from Vatican control, he would meet a sudden, untimely end. When he made his move, he would have to be certain of success. If not, death was a certainty.

* * *

The Grindon cruised at a speed of fifty knots, almost twice the speed of larger transatlantic shipping vessels. *The Grindon* was much smaller than those, and it was outfitted with special motors that Queen of Spades used to prioritize speed over fuel efficiency. Many people didn't realize that the reason large shipping vessels took so long to cross oceans was a result of trying to be more efficient with gas and oil, the most expensive expenditures in shipping. Centuries ago, Chinese ships traveled the globe powered only by wind at higher speeds than the typical cargo ship of today.

The parts of the bomb were kept in separate compartments. The detonator was stored at one end of the ship, along with pallets of mechanical drones. The detonator itself was indistinguishable from the other drones. The radioactive part of the weapon was located in a more precarious part of the ship, near the engine. It was held securely in the center of an airtight, stainless-steel box, which itself was stored within another metal box. The outer box was six feet tall by five feet wide. Around the outer container, polyethylene foam insulated the boxes from movement. Between the foam and the outer box, a layer of silica ensured dryness. Between this layer were placed bags and bags of glazed ceramic chips. They were poker chips, all emblazoned with the Queen of Spades logo. Ceramic and clay were widely known to be radiation barriers. Cat litter was frequently used to camouflage radioactive material and was flagged internationally as a substance that port authorities should inspect carefully. Queen of Spades opted for the less common poker chip, as it fit better with their alleged brand. The boxes of chips were added as a precautionary measure. If the contents were X-rayed, the radioactive material would be less likely to be discovered. Clay, like cat litter and glazed ceramics, was slightly radioactive; so any alarm would be deemed a nuisance. If anyone asked why the boxes were being stored in the engine room, they had a plausible response: The chips were deemed too valuable to be stowed along with other cargo. Despite these subterfuges, Khalid Zahir's team didn't think they'd be able to evade authorities if the boat were put under inspection. But since Queen of Spades had an inside man at Algeciras, the fear of detection was quelled.

The outermost box was made of military-grade, synthetic materials that provided barriers to air and moisture. Queen of Spades had purchased, in bulk, the foil-and-nylon coating from one of DoD's major suppliers. Queen of Spades had affixed a label on the box: *Master Controller.*

* * *

"Kill the pope?" Jordan asked incredulously.

"It might be a first, even for CIA. But if he's become a political figure, that makes him a viable target."

"It seems extreme."

"Overthrowing the U.S. government isn't? We have a duty, to the Constitution, to preserve, protect..."

Jordan interrupted – "... and defend the Constitution. Yes, I know."

"That's our obligation."

"How do we know he's really involved? We have the word of someone who's a terrorist? She tried to kill me. How much credibility should we give her?"

"Let's boil it down. We have a shipment of cesium headed toward the United States. She knew the name of the ship. We know that the ship was contracted through the Queen of Spades. We have the receipts. She admitted to being paid. She's given us the account, and we're tracing that money now. She told us it came from an LLC in the Cayman Islands. If we can trace that to Khalid Zahir, we know he has, through Ahmed Bensaïd, been a chief proponent of the pope. He's been supporting Sixtus since he was a boy. We have the money trail – going all the way back to Williams College and Harvard Divinity, his missionary work in Paraguay, his mother's medical treatments when she was dying of lung cancer. The oxygen tanks were paid for by Bensaïd. I've personally seen the receipts."

"How would he get mixed up in something like this? Isn't he on friendly terms with Foster?"

"Foster is a Lutheran. I don't think it's religious zeal. Sixtus has always been a relatively neutral player when it comes to religion. That's what made him an easy choice within the ranks. Our personality profile suggests his true passion is power. There's only so far you can go when you're pope.

"Why would Sima lie?" Amanda continued. "What's in it for her? Do you think she has some vendetta against Sixtus? Or against the Catholic Church? She wants to save her skin. She knows how to survive. And she knows information – true, reliable, accurate information – is currency. This isn't the first time she's been in this situation."

"What do you mean?"

"Remember when she told you she was with MI6?"

Jordan listened attentively but didn't answer.

"She wasn't lying. She used to be one of us. She went rogue. She got a better offer, as they say, and she took it. She first came on our radar shortly after she resigned five years ago. Highly enriched uranium had suddenly made its way to Tehran. She knew the backdoors in the Persian Gulf. It was an access point that the Israelis would use. Only the Agency, MI6, and Mossad knew about it. We traced the leak to her. She decided to play nice, knowing the Iranians wouldn't save her. Besides, she wasn't interested in living a life in exile on the Arabian Peninsula. She prefers Harrods over hiding out in the desert. So, she gave us the information we needed. We arranged a sting, and we got our guys."

None of this was in the report she had shared with him. Why had she concealed this information? Was this part of the game? He cast aside his suspicions. He could – he should – trust Amanda. He wasn't familiar with this world. "So, she thinks we'll let her go in this case too?"

"She knows we will. And we will," Amanda said resignedly. "That's the way of the world. Remember that, if you ever get trapped in a tight spot. At the Farm, they teach us no secret is worth our life, even if someone else will die as a result. There will always be others to take their place. But not us. We're special, and we deserve to be protected, to be saved. The Agency won't fault us for giving up even the most secret information, unless we cross the line and willingly betray our country. That's what Sima did. For that, she'll always be out in the cold."

"I need to send a report back to Washington."

"You can't do that," Amanda said. "Sixtus isn't operating alone. Bensaïd isn't either. They're working with somebody. You can't just take over the U.S. government unless you have someone highly placed within. Very highly placed. I'm talking, VP, Speaker of the House-level. We need to identify that person and stop the shipment."

"How much time do we have?"

"A few days, a week at most."

"Are we going to brief the president?"

"Only when we have to. We don't want more eyes on this than we need."

* * *

President Foster sat inside the White House's Situation Room, officially known as the John F. Kennedy Conference Room. General Cheeks was providing an update to the National Security Council on the whereabouts of *The Grindon*. "We have our submarines on high alert. Given what we know, it will take about two weeks for it to reach Baltimore."

"Are we sure it's headed to Baltimore?" Foster asked.

"We have information from a reliable source whom we've worked with before," Cheeks said, "though there's always the possibility that it might deviate from its current destination."

"Who's behind it?"

"We believe it's an Arab militant group out of Yemen. Highly funded, through oil tycoons. They've wanted to retaliate against us since we bombed them in 2025. We suspect Khalid Zahir is behind it."

"What do we have on him?" Foster asked.

"He has his tentacles in real estate all over the world. Investments in hotels, resorts, casinos, that sort of thing. They say he's worth a hundred billion. He's a Sunni. He's opposed to U.S. support of Israel as well as our ties to Saudia Arabia, Jordan, and Egypt. He's tried to sow discord among our Middle Eastern allies. It hasn't worked. This might be a last-ditch effort. He's certainly raised the staked with a radiological dispersion device." Cheeks was using the more militarized name for a dirty bomb.

"What do we think his intention is?"

"One of our greatest fears is that the ship could reach the port of Baltimore and explode there before we have a chance to intercept it. That would be catastrophic. A loss of life in the thousands, depending on the potency of the explosive material."

"And it's cesium?"

"Yes. So we're much better off than if they got their hands on uranium, which would cause damage like we haven't seen since Nagasaki or Hiroshima. We just have to make sure it doesn't come close to heavily populated or sensitive areas."

"Like the Pentagon?"

"Or the White House."

"What are the chances of that?" Foster asked.

"Slim, given our advance knowledge."

"Any political ties that we can call on?"

"There is one, but not a conventional source." Cheeks exhaled as he took a pause. "Pope Sixtus."

"The pope?" Foster exclaimed.

"I met with him recently. We know he is connected to Ahmed Bensaïd, who has an affiliation with Zahir."

"What kind of affiliation?"

"Business. Bensaïd is more measured. Sixtus considers him very trustworthy. He said he could intervene on our behalf."

"Does he know anything about the bomb?"

"I didn't tell him anything yet. I just wanted to feel him out at this point. But if you allow me to, I can enlist his help."

"We're not there yet," Foster said. "Let's give it a week and if we don't track the ship down by then, I'll get him on the phone. In the meantime, I'll send him a very thoughtful thank-you note for his recent gift. It's something I'll treasure forever, unless the Archives makes me put it in the Smithsonian."

Cheeks chuckled, presuming Foster was making a joke. Foster, for his part, observed him with a stone-faced, somber demeanor.

* * *

Richter had never been to Moscow before. Prior to his meeting with the Russian delegation, which included Russia's ambassador to the Vatican, Vitaly Chertkov, he asked his driver to pass by St. Basil's Cathedral. He wanted to admire the colorful, onion-shaped domes of the Orthodox church. Ivan the Terrible had built the vibrant, red-brick structure. He had the builder blinded after it was completed so that no other church would ever compete with its beauty. As Richter's limousine passed by it, he gasped at its sheer splendor. He recalled how Napoleon had scornfully ordered his troops to burn it to the ground after they couldn't disassemble it and take it back to France. A spontaneous rain shower, a manifestation of divine protection, saved it.

"Magnificent," Richter uttered to himself. He felt that it was the most beautiful church that he had ever seen. He longed to go inside, but there wasn't time. Chertkov, the young whippersnapper ambassador, was awaiting him. He recalled how Barranca had told him that in Russian, Chertkov was derived from the word *chort*, which was a demon in Russian folklore. But Chertkov had a smooth, polished demeanor, with a full, dark beard that glistened in the light; and brown eyes that looked at you so warmly, you couldn't help but smile upon meeting him.

The limo entered a side gate to the Kremlin. The Kremlin had a much more imposing and foreboding presence than he expected. Fear crept over Richter. His stomach wrenched into a gurgling knot. He thought he was going to have an accident. He was about to ask the driver to stop, but the car zoomed on, as if being pulled by some mysterious force, leading Richter to his fateful destiny.

Richter wore a black cassock, which he preferred for non-liturgical function. His meeting with Chertkov went without a hitch. The typical smiles and pleasantries, Richter had managed to find a quiet bathroom beforehand with little embarrassment, and soon it was off to a sumptuous lunch. Chertkov tried to tempt him with a series of fine vodkas, but Richter waved them off, saying that his stomach was bothering him. An exchange of gifts followed, and Chertkov was surprised that Richter didn't even have an aide with him to handle the letter from the Russian president or the modernistic depiction – almost graffiti art – of St. Basil's Cathedral. Chertkov graciously had one of his aides assist with attending to Richter.

He is being too nice, Richter thought.

He was given a private tour of the Kremlin that lasted over an hour. There were security guards everywhere, all with earpieces connected to mobile communication devices. *They can't kill me here,* he thought. Or could they? Although he tried not to show his nerves, he was petrified. When something rattled or a sudden noise sounded unexpectedly, his head turned sharply to examine the room. At one point, he heard a female security officer behind him laugh in response to his abrupt head-turning. He glared at her, and she stared back, scowling, undaunted by the challenge. *If anyone shall kill me,* he thought, *it will be that unnatural woman.* As he thought this, she seemed to smile at him in response.

Once he had seen all the trinkets and baubles and listened patiently to the guide's palaver, he was thanked for his visit. Richter left, unimpressed, despite the countless times he had heard "priceless treasures" from the lips of the Russian-to-English interpreter. The basement in the Vatican was many times more impressive. Yes, the days of Russian glory had passed. Perhaps next time he would go to St. Petersburg, where he heard the most stunning works were supposedly held.

Just when he was about to leave, Chertkov gave Richter a private tour of the Russian imperial jewels. They had saved the best for last. He found that the Romanov's royal jewels rivalled the crown jewels of England in their lure and elegance. Chertkov asked if he wanted a private tour of the grounds. Richter politely declined. God knows what might happen to him outside.

Upon leaving the Kremlin, Richter's limo drove him back toward the hotel, but it took an unexpected stop: St. Basil's Cathedral. "You must see," the driver said in broken English. "It is just as magnificent inside."

Richter looked out the tinted window. He was titillated by the prospect of going inside.

"I will wait here," the driver said.

Richter couldn't resist. He stepped out of the limousine. As he walked down the sidewalk through the crowd toward the entrance, a young man in his mid-twenties wearing an athletic track suit rushed behind him. Richter heard a high-pitching yelling. He became alarmed. The youthful Russian man was pushing a woman and her tourist companion. They were shouting at him. The man held up his arm at Richter. All Richter could see was a needle staring him in the eyes. He held up his arm and grabbed the man's forearm as he attempted to stab him with the syringe. Richter watched the yellow fluid shake inside the hypodermic needle as the man forcefully tried to get it closer to Richter's shoulder and neck. He screamed, "No!" The woman tourist and her companion grabbed the man's arm and torso from behind. He tried to wriggle free, but the woman's male companion was strong. A throng gathered, yelling at the man: "What are you doing?" "Who are you?" "Get out of here!" The mob encircled him. The woman's companion managed to subdue the young Russian and tackled him to the ground. As the companion hovered over him, his arm pressing against the athletic man's neck, the youthful Russian choked. He gasped for air. In a fit of fury, the youthful Russian jabbed the needle in the man's forearm. He fell, gasping for breath. The young Russian athletically jumped up and pushed his way through the crowd as the woman stared in horror at her dying companion, screaming.

Richter ran as fast as he could back to his limo. As he reached it, he saw his driver standing outside it, looking at him. Richter peered back, scrutinizing him. In less than a second, his instinct screamed, "No!" He stopped in his tracks. Did his driver deliberately bring him to St. Basil's? Did he know that he would be attacked? Never had Richter been confronted with such a resounding message to act. It was pure intuition. A sign of divine intervention. He continued to run past the limo onto the street. There, a taxi was parked, waiting to pick up a small group of tourists when they exited the cathedral. Richter opened the door to the cab, motioning for the driver. "Hurry!" he shouted.

Chapter 43

"Where to?" the cab driver asked Richter in Russian. Richter understood what he was asking but didn't know enough Russian to respond. He blurted out in English, "There! Go there! Straight ahead!" He didn't know where to go or what to do. He didn't want to go back to his hotel. What if it was compromised? Surely, Bensaïd and Sixtus's men would be looking for him. The young man they sent to kill him would be, too.

They had hired a Russian. Someone who wanted to inject him with a deadly poison. How could he go back to the Vatican now?

The cab drove forth, and the driver asked him something in Russian. His eyes looked beseeching.

Additional directions? Yes, Richter assumed.

They were heading into a commercial district. There were many stores nearby. He would have to get out of his clerical garb and change into something that would draw less attention. "Here!" Richter said.

The driver looked back in the rearview mirror, confused.

"Stop!" Richter said.

"Here?" the cab driver seemed to ask in Russian.

"Yes," Richter replied.

The cab stopped. Richter handed him his credit card.

"Card no," the driver said in English. "Cash."

Richter had no Russian rubles.

"I don't have any money," Richter said, extending his hand with the card.

The cabbie shook his head. "Cash please."

Richter looked through his wallet. He only had euros. He took out a ten-euro bill. Surely, the fare must have been a fraction of that. He handed it to the cab driver and said, "That is all I have." Quickly, he got up out of the backseat and exited the car, rushing toward a shopping center.

* * *

By evening, Richter had a new set of clothes and a new hotel room. But what could he do? All his belongings were still at the hotel. Fortuitously, he had brought his passport with him in case he had any trouble getting into the Kremin. And he had his phone. Oh, his phone! Couldn't they track him through his phone? The police had known where Barranca was by analyzing his phone's data. Should he shut his off? Should he throw it away? Perhaps he should get a new one.

And the hotel room – he was paying by his Vatican credit card. The accounting team at the Holy See might be monitoring the charges he was making. Oh, he had made a terrible mistake, coming to this hotel, to Moscow. But what could he do? He had that secret offshore account where he pocketed the bribe to vote for Sixtus. That damned vote! No wonder all the cardinals were paid such a high price! A million dollars. Normally, two-hundred fifty thousand would suffice. The College of Cardinals had been hoodwinked! It would take days to get the money, though. And he couldn't do it from Russia. He didn't have a Russian account and, even if he opened one, his Swiss bank wouldn't wire money to an unregistered account. He would have to get back to

Western Europe, avoid the Vatican, be on his own for a while. And he couldn't take the Vatican jet back. He'd have to find another way. These thoughts continued to pour through him, overwhelming him, exhausting him. Finally, somehow, he managed to fall asleep.

A few hours later, an intruder was at his door. The door to his hotel room opened. Richter didn't even notice.

Chapter 44

"Cardinal Richter? Cardinal Richter?"

Someone was poking at Richter's side. He looked up and saw a woman hovering over him. He anxiously looked back at her. What might she do to him?

A Black man was standing at the foot of the bed. Inside the room were Amanda and Jordan.

"Who are you?" he demanded. "What do you want from me?" At least they didn't appear to be Russian.

"My name is Amanda O'Brien. I am with the Central Intelligence Agency. This is Jordan Harrison. He is with the FBI."

"How did you get into my room?"

"We have a special card. It allows us to get into any hotel room anywhere in the world." Amanda was telling the truth. CIA officers had a plastic card that would bypass the lock of any hotel door. Only a lock with a chain or a manual deadbolt could secure a hotel room door. In Russia, China, Iran, and other countries, the CIA used a different card for access. Those locks were programmed with different technology. But all the technology emanated from the United States, and lock manufacturers were required to keep a backdoor open for the American intelligence community.

Was she telling the truth? He couldn't argue with her. "What do you want from me?"

"We're here to help. Your life is in danger."

"I know that! That's why I'm here! How did you find me?"

"We tracked your cell phone. Others may be doing the same. We need you to come with us. We'll bring you to safety."

"There is no safety for me!" he yelped. "Sixtus wants me dead!"

Amanda turned to Jordan, raising her eyebrows as if to ask, *Now do you believe me?*

* * *

It was past 9 p.m. Richter had no choice but to gather his few belongings and go with these alleged intelligence officers. He had forsaken his ecclesiastical robe and now wore street clothes. Amanda and Jordan showed him to their car, which Amanda had gotten from the Moscow chief of station. They drove through the darkened streets of Moscow to the suburbs. Once they left the city, it became eerily dark. What had he gotten himself into? There was just a smattering of buildings along the roadway, occasionally a gas station or small store. This is how people disappear, Richter thought.

He wasn't going to go without a fight, he vowed to himself. Even though Jordan Harrison was tall, strapping, muscular, and would easily be able to subdue him, Richter wasn't the type to lie down and take it. He wasn't Barranca. He'd get his money's worth, even if it meant only getting scraps of DNA under his fingernails.

"Tell me what is going on," he said from the backseat. Jordan sat beside him, on guard.

He told himself he could pull at Amanda's hair and make her swerve and lose control of the car. He could cause lots of trouble. He had God on his side.

"Have you ever heard of a radiological dispersion device?" Amanda asked.

"No. What is that?"

"A dirty bomb," Jordan answered.

"Yes, that I've heard of."

"There is a shipment on its way to the United States."

A shipment, thought Richter. It must be connected to the shipping notice he had found on Barranca. Of course!

"And what does that have to do with me? With the Church?"

"We believe Sixtus is helping facilitate the shipment. Through Khalid Zahir."

"I never heard of him. Who is he?"

"He is a Kuwaiti billionaire."

"Is he connected to Bensaïd?"

"In fact, he is."

"I never liked him." Richter tried to cast his dislike of Bensaïd aside. "What has this got to do with me?"

"They obviously think you know something or they wouldn't be trying to kill you. We heard about the incident at St. Basil's."

"How?"

"Through the Moscow station. They've been watching you since you arrived. Except while you were inside the Kremlin. There, we had to rely on third-party reports."

"But I'm not involved with any of this."

"You must know something."

He should have never gone to the U.S. embassy in Rome, he told himself scoldingly. "Whatever I know, I told General Cheeks."

"The Director of National Intelligence?"

"Yes."

In the rearview mirror, Amanda shot a look of concern at Jordan, who maintained a poker face. However, she was certain that the revelation resonated with him. Turning to Richter in the mirror, she said, "What did you tell him?"

"I didn't have much to tell him. I just sent him a photograph."

"A photo?"

"Yes, something I got in the Vatican. Barranca had a shipping notice in his room. I didn't have the original, but I sent the general a picture of it."

She tried to steady her breathing, to remain as composed as Jordan as she drove along. "Do you have a copy of it?"

"No," he said. "I deleted it. That is, General Cheeks did. He said it was better if I didn't have it."

"Do you remember anything about it?" Jordan asked.

"It had an unusual name. The Queen of Spades."

Now, Jordan shot Amanda a look. Their eyes met in the rearview mirror.

"How did you send it to him?" Amanda asked.

"I texted it to him."

"Then you must have a copy on your phone. In your text messages," Jordan said.

Richter pulled his cell phone out of his pocket. "I probably do." He scrolled through his text messages. "That's odd. It's not here. There's no text to General Cheeks."

"Maybe he deleted that, too," Jordan said.

"Possibly." Richter continued to scroll through his phone. "I do still have his contact information here. Should I call him?"

In unison, both Amanda and Jordan said, "No!"

Chapter 45

On the darkened roadway, Amanda started driving faster, reaching a speed of eighty miles an hour.

"What is going on?" Richter said, panicked. "Where are we going?"

"We have to get you somewhere safe. The place where we were heading isn't safe anymore."

"I thought you said it was a safe house."

"It is. But it might not be as safe as we thought." She knew, however, that they didn't have other options. Russian suburbia was no place for American intelligence to be wandering.

"What do you mean?" Richter asked. "Should I call General Cheeks? I'm sure he can sort this all out." He took his phone to his ear.

Amanda shook her head. Instantly, Jordan took the cell phone from Richter.

"What are you doing? What is going on?" Richter screeched.

"You've compromised the security of our mission by involving

General Cheeks," Amanda said.

"He's a four-star general!"

"That may be. But perhaps he wants something more."

"I don't understand," Richter said exasperatedly.

Amanda looked at Richter. "What did the shipping notice say?"

"Queen of Spades, I told you."

"What else? Where was it going?"

"Someplace in the United States. John Hopkins University School of Medicine."

"What were the contents?"

"I don't know."

"When was it due to arrive?"

"I don't remember."

Amanda was getting frustrated. "Think!"

"I don't know!" he retorted. "I didn't pay that much attention to it."

"Why don't you have the original letter?"

"I only got a photo of it from a nun who was in Barranca's room."

"A nun? What was her name?"

"Sister Sofija. Listen, I didn't think it was important. Then I remembered Sixtus talking to Bensaïd about some shipment."

"Who else besides General Cheeks did you talk to about it?"

"No one. I went to the American embassy and was looking for someone named Bersch, but there was no one there by that name."

"Who did you speak to?"

"He said his name was Brian Wilson. But I later learned his name was Bersch. I think it was his code name."

Jordan shot him a look.

"Look, I know this all sounds crazy, but I am telling you the truth!"

As she kept her foot on the gas, Amanda didn't address him directly. Instead, she looked at Jordan in the rearview mirror. "I don't think we're safe with Rebar. They can use that to track us."

"You think they know where we are?"

"They definitely can track us through it. Whether they've bothered, that's another question."

"What do we do?"

She slowed the car and took a rough turn onto a side street. The car crawled along. Up ahead, a dirt driveway was barely visible. She turned off the headlights.

Richter gasped, startled by the blackness that enveloped them. "What is happening? Why are we in the dark?"

"We're going to need you to be quiet," Amanda said, inching forward into the driveway. "We need to see if we're alone."

A car was parked in front of the house, which was a wooden, farmhouse-style cottage.

* * *

The safe house was located in the middle of nowhere. Before getting out of the car, Amanda checked the note she had taken. Yes, this was the correct address. "You stay here," she said to Cardinal Richter as she opened the driver's door.

Jordan exited the car from the back. "Do you know whose car that is?" He nodded his head toward the vehicle parked in front of the house.

"No idea." Amanda hadn't been told that anyone else was staying at the house. But in the Russian Wild West, everything was unpredictable. An American officer's cover might be blown and emergency shelter suddenly needed. Or was someone waiting to ambush them? Someone who might have been tipped off by General Cheeks? Walking past the car, she held out her arm to see if she could detect any heat. The air was perfectly cool, either on account of the nighttime or the fact that the car had been parked for some time. She grasped her pistol, which she had retrieved at the CIA station. "You have your gun ready?"

"My pen too. And the powder ball on my cross." He was referring to the explosive device he had dangling on his necklace. "Should I take the back?"

She nodded. When he had made his way to the rear of the house, she knocked on the front door and waited for an answer. Nobody came. Whose car was it? She waited a few moments longer.

The door had an electronic locking mechanism with a combination keypad entry. It was a special lock that had had its card reader disabled so that the station could monitor who entered the home. She checked her phone for the code. She punched in the eight digits. Every officer who was granted entry was given a unique security code. The door buzzed and opened.

The entryway was completely dark. Amanda used her cell phone flashlight to guide her. A man stood opposite her in the hallway, brandishing a gun at her.

Chapter 46

Amanda kept her gun under her jacket, out of view as she faced the unknown man.

"Amanda?" the man asked in English. He had an American accent.

His use of only her first name gave her some comfort – it was CIA custom. "Yes," she answered.

"I'm Bob. Bob Goodman." Bob was in his mid-to-late fifties with short dark brown and graying hair. He was just shy of six feet, with a medium-to-heavy build, and wore gold-framed glasses. He had a benign, friendly expression. "Yes, I know it's a funny name. Everyone knows me as *Bob G.* The station chief told me you'd be coming. Forgive me for not answering the door. I didn't know if it was the mobsters who were chasing me."

It was odd that the station chief hadn't mentioned that someone else would be in the safe house. Perhaps he didn't know, thought Amanda. And yet, the man was literally in the dark, with all the lights out. How odd. How long had he been standing there, waiting for her? Even if Bob's visit was unplanned, wouldn't the station chief have sent her a message on Rebar that someone named Bob Goodman would be there? He knew *she* was coming. Yet he hadn't opened the door. He had left her standing outside and instead risked a dangerous situation. What if she had trained a gun on him when she had entered? One of them could certainly have been killed.

Then, in the darkened hall, someone grabbed Bob by the arms, seizing his gun.

* * *

In the middle of the Atlantic Ocean, a few dozen miles west of the Azores, *The Grindon* met up with a superyacht named *Das Kapital*. *Das Kapital* had left Ponta Delgada on São Miguel Island earlier in the afternoon. It was capable of traveling at speeds of almost fifty knots. When the two vessels met on the open ocean, the precious cargo of *The Grindon* was carefully transferred onto *Das Kapital*. *Das Kapital* had been purchased earlier in the year by Khalid Zahir. He had registered it in Panama to a fictitious Russian oligarch. The captain, Yuri, an actual Russian, played the role of this oligarch. His crew, all Russians, were fellow terrorists for hire. Besides the crates of casino chips and drones, the other cargo on the ship consisted of dozens of military-grade machine guns, PKMs and Dushkas. Their mission: deliver the cargo safely to the United States as fast as they could. If any vessel were to stop them, they were to pose as friends of the Russian billionaire Yuri. They had even hired a few models to pose as their girlfriends.

* * *

In the darkened hallway, Amanda stood as Jordan held Bob tightly against his chest. Amanda had secured Bob's pistol and placed it in her jacket pocket. She took out her own gun. She knew from training that she should never rely on someone else's weapon, only her own.

"This really isn't necessary," Bob said. "I'm CIA."

"That may be the case, but I don't know why the station chief didn't advise me that I'd have a welcoming committee."

"I wasn't sure I'd make it here. Would you please let me go?" He tried to wriggle free, but Jordan held him securely against his body, placing his leg between Bob's so that he could trip him in case he tried to flee.

"If I wanted to hurt you," Bob said, "I would have done it when you knocked on the door." As he said this, he continued to tender a half smile.

"Why didn't you answer?" Amanda asked.

"You always have to be careful in this business."

She wasn't satisfied by his answer. And that smile, which was a mismatch to the circumstances, further provoked her suspicions. "You pulled a gun. Why escalate things if you didn't know who you were dealing with?"

"Instinct. This is Russia. You haven't been here before, have you?"

"Didn't you research me before I came?"

He emitted a slight chuckle, but Amanda could see that he was wriggling his arms, resisting Jordan slightly. Again, there was a mismatch between his facial expression and his behavior. It was a sure sign of deception, she had learned at the Farm.

"There wasn't a need," Bob G. said. "I got filled in by the station chief."

"I'll get the handcuffs," Amanda said, knowing that all safe houses were outfitted with restraints. She turned on the lights in the hallway and proceeded by Bob and Jordan. As she passed, Bob G. thrust his body at Jordan to tackle him to the floor. The swift maneuver almost worked, but Jordan managed to keep his balance. Instead, he pushed his weight atop Bob and brought him to the floor.

Bob's face was contorted sideways against the parquet-patterned wood. "This isn't necessary," he said.

"You got him?" Amanda asked Jordan.

"Yeah," he said.

She retreated to the kitchen where she found zip ties. When she returned to the hall, both Jordan and Bob were gone.

Chapter 47

"Jordan!" Amanda yelled.

"In here," came his reply.

The sound emanated from a room on the other side of the house from the kitchen. Amanda entered the arched entry and proceeded into the living room, holding her gun before her. Before her lay Jordan on an oriental carpet on the floor, covering his eyes. It looked like he had been pepper-sprayed. Atop him was Bob, who held a gun to Jordan's head.

* * *

"I'm only going to ask you once," Bob said very calmly, but obviously disheveled and out of breath. "Put the gun down or I will blow his head off."

"Okay, take it easy," Amanda said, sliding her gun on the floor toward him. Because of the carpeting covering the ceramic-tiled floor, it only went a few feet from her. "We don't want anything untoward to happen."

"The other gun too," Bob said, referring to his own gun which she had seized.

She took that gun from her jacket pocket and slid it on at a slight diagonal trajectory from the other gun. She glided the gun cavalierly, seemingly without giving it any thought, so as not to arouse Bob's suspicions, though the truth was she had made deliberate moves to scatter each of them in the room. Depending on where she was standing, she would improve the probability of access to one of the guns, either by her or by Jordan.

A knock sounded at the front door. It must have been Richter. He was getting anxious sitting all alone in the darkened car. He wasn't the type you could leave solitary for too long. In that way, he was like a stew that needed constant stirring to prevent over simmering.

"That must be our guest of honor," Bob G. said. "The Cardinal."

"Yes," Amanda said in agreement. "He won't understand what's going on."

"I'm not sure any of us do," Bob G. said.

"What do you propose we do?" Amanda asked.

Bob yanked at Jordan's neck. "Perhaps I kill him now, so we don't have too much of a crowd at our party."

"I wouldn't do that," Amanda said. "He's FBI."

"I know. But he's so new he won't be missed. He's hardly had time to grow any chest hair. Besides, he let a fifty-year-old man take him down. He can't be that good."

Another knock sounded. Richter was growing impatient.

"Go get the door," Bob ordered Amanda. "And bring him here."

It was a risky move, and one that Bob G. would regret.

* * *

As Amanda went to the front door, she slipped the pendant off her necklace. She put the silver chain in her jacket pocket while she kept the pendant in her hand. She couldn't use the explosive device just yet while Bob G. still had Jordan subdued. But if she could somehow manage to relinquish him from his control, she stood a much better chance of extricating them from the situation.

She opened the door.

"I have to go to the bathroom," Richter said.

"Bring him in!" Bob G. yelled.

"Who is that?"

"Trouble," Amanda said curtly. "Come inside."

"Your Excellency," Bob G. exclaimed boisterously upon seeing Richter in the arched entryway of the living room. "Please have a seat."

"I must use the restroom," Richter responded.

"There'll be time for pissing and shitting later. Sit down."

"Do as he says," Amanda advised.

Richter took a seat on the settee facing Bob G. Opposite was a fireplace, over which a mirror hung. On the mantle stood a porcelain vase and a pair of faux Fabergé eggs on immodestly gilded stands. Amanda stood behind Richter.

"Are you one of Sixtus's men?" Richter asked.

"Even better," Bob G. retorted. "I'm one of General Cheeks' men. I know what you're up to and I'm going to stop it."

At that moment, Richter held his chest and stomach and groaned loudly. It was just the kind of distractful disturbance that Amanda needed. She took the brass pendant and put it in her mouth and then threw it at the far end of the room, near the fireplace. Bob G. saw that she threw something. As he looked, Jordan pushed with all his might against Bob's arm, lifting it to the ceiling as he fired. Plastic dropped in the corner of the room. Glass shattered, from vases or knickknacks. Almost instantaneously, a massive explosion erupted. Jordan got up from under Bob. He yanked the gun from his hand and pushed him toward the fire that had erupted. Plumes of smoke filled the room. Richter sat in shock on the settee. Amanda grabbed him and pulled him toward the door. As they retreated from the living room, Jordan took his pendant, put it in his mouth, and threw it at Bob, who was still on the floor. Jordan and Amanda covered their ears as they ran into the hallway with Richter toward the door. Another explosion detonated and Bob erupted into flames.

His screams and cries could be heard echoing as the trio escaped from the safe house. In a matter of seconds, there wasn't a single sound that emanated from the living room except for the popping of the fire and items falling from the walls, ceilings, and tables.

* * *

Amanda headed to Bob's car and opened the door, which was unlocked.

"You want to take his car?" Jordan asked.

"I don't think ours is safe. They're probably tracking it."

"And they're not with Bob's?"

"We'll find out."

Bob had a relatively late-model car, about five years old or so. Amanda knew it couldn't be hotwired. Hotwiring cars, which the Farm taught all new recruits, was essentially a thing of the past, though the movies made it seem as though it was still possible. Nonetheless, CIA officers would sometimes be in a situation, depending on where they were in the world, where hotwiring a car or truck was possible. So she, like all recruits, had had dozens if not hundreds of hours of training on this most basic escape technique. The Farm insisted it be mastered at all costs. You couldn't leave the Farm without being able to hotwire a car successfully. Every car, truck, and motorcycle model was slightly different, but the technique was the same. Come graduation time, each recruit would have to hotwire some unknown vehicle as part of an escape challenge.

Modern cars, however, were different. They operated through an ECU, an electronic control unit, which controlled the security of the car as well as the transmission and engine. Obtaining control of the ECU was the key. Fortunately, the CIA, through agreements with all major car manufacturers, had a backdoor into all cars made in the West or sold in the Western world. So, Korean car makers qualified, and Bob G.'s car, which was Korean, could be hacked. Amanda took out her cell phone and opened an app. New officers were always amazed that the CIA had an app for everything. The app had a benign name, *HomeLock*. All she needed to do was to enter the VIN, the vehicle identification number, into the app. She found the VIN of Bob's car on the door jamb. "Can you light this with your phone?" she asked Jordan anxiously.

"Sure." He aimed his cell's flashlight on the metallic plaque of the door.

Letter-by-letter and number-by-number, she entered the code into HomeLock. When she finished, the app had full control over the car's ECU. She started the car. Sitting in the driver's seat, she electronically lowered and raised the windows. Everything seemed to be working. "Now comes the hard part," she said to Jordan.

"What's that?" he asked.

"We need to ditch our phones."

* * *

"Ditch our phones?" Jordan asked.

She knew that leaving their phones behind would be a risk. They wouldn't have access to Rebar. They wouldn't have access to HomeLock. They wouldn't be able to call or text anyone. But she knew it had to be done. "They're tracking us. We've got to slow them down."

"But they'll be tracking this car too," he said.

"Yeah, and we're going to switch it for something else. We just need a little time." She called out to Richter, "Cardinal, get your things out of the trunk. Leave your cell phone in the car. You don't have an Apple Watch or anything like that, do you?"

"No," he said. "If I leave my phone, how will anyone find me?"

Even he was concerned about not having a cell. "That's the point," she answered. "Just get your things and we'll get you a new phone soon enough."

Ever the dutiful servant, he obeyed, gathering his small suitcase and leaving his cell phone in the backseat. Amanda followed, putting her cell phone in the backseat. Jordan dropped his there, too.

"We can't just leave them there," she said. "The Russians could get in and access Rebar."

"Aren't we supposed to wipe them?" Jordan asked.

"I have something better." She took her necklace and pulled off another round ball from the chain.

"How many of those do you have?" Jordan asked.

"I have one left after this," she said. "Let's see if we need it. Everyone, get in the car." Turning to Jordan, she said, "You drive. Remember, don't turn the car off under any circumstances. Without the app, we won't be able to start it up again. Go down the road. I'll get in once I light this baby up."

After he and Richter got into Bob G.'s car, Jordan proceeded to back it to the street. Amanda waited until the car was safely out of the way. She took the ball on the pendant, spit on it, and tossed it into their car. She ran to Bob G.'s car. As she reached it, an explosion set their car ablaze. They watched the fire as they took off down the road.

* * *

Jordan drove as fast as he could along the darkened streets, approaching speeds of seventy and eighty miles per hour whenever it was safe. They headed west of Moscow. Richter was exhausted, and Amanda, from the front seat, could see him drift in and out of sleep along with the occasional car bump or unanticipated turn. She knew he was a liability. Too rickety; untrained; untrusting. But he could be left alone; he wouldn't cause much trouble. He was the type of collateral you could jettison to help improve your mission's odds of success. But leaving him behind would expose them and lead to their capture. She couldn't see him holding up in an interrogation. He wasn't Barranca. He didn't believe in *the cause*. He didn't even know what *the cause* was; and his instincts for self-preservation were not well tuned. He was too accustomed to having everything his way without so much as a tussle. He was a church bureaucrat, through and through.

They had driven for about an hour. They reached a small city where there were actually other cars on the road. Jordan had to slow to a reasonable forty or fifty miles per hour. "We've got to switch cars," Amanda said.

"You think they're onto us?"

"They might be getting to the safe house. We can't risk it."

"Should we steal something?"

Now he was talking. There were some businesses around, but most of the parking lots were empty. And there was an occasional person – an employee or security guard – that might interfere. "Why don't we head up there?" She pointed in a westerly direction that appeared to lead them out of the city.

They proceeded up the road and soon found themselves in a remote part with an accessway to a main route. "Pull over here," she said. "We'll pretend we're broken down."

They got out of the car and lifted the hood. Jordan put the hazard lights on. Richter woke up, confused. Amanda grabbed her jacket and as a car passed by, she waved it like a flag. A car passed. They waited a few more minutes. Another car passed by. Amanda looked at the tailpipe of the car; fortunately, there was no noticeable exhaust. They had left the car running in case no one stopped. They didn't want to turn it off as they would have no way to restart it. Passing cars wouldn't be able to tell it was running. A few more minutes. A car passed, and as it did, it pulled over to the side of the road. Then it started backing up.

Amanda grabbed her gun and placed it so that it was hidden under her jacket. Jordan readied his gun also, keeping it hidden. Amanda could see that Richter, still in the backseat, was awake and watching.

From the car parked on the roadside, an elderly woman emerged. Jordan's heart sank. Amanda wasn't feeling all too positive about what they'd have to do either. What was a woman in her early sixties doing pulling over to help stranded motorists? The woman called out something in Russian to them. Amanda and Jordan didn't understand.

"English?" Amanda said.

The woman shrugged, saying something back in Russian.

The language barrier proved a suitable check to the moral quandary that faced them. Amanda pulled out her gun from her jacket and aimed it at the woman. The woman shrieked and started running back to her car. "Go after her," Amanda said.

"Me?" Jordan asked.

"She doesn't know you have a gun," Amanda said.

"Okay," Jordan said reluctantly. He chased after her, and as the woman reached her car door, Jordan got in front of her and held his arm on the car door. She screamed again and held up her hand to his face. Then she sprayed him directly into the eyes with pepper spray.

Chapter 48

Jordan had managed to raise his hand as the stream of pepper spray squirted into his eyes. But he was too late. While his hand caught some of the spume, most went directly into his eyes, nose, and cheeks. He turned from the woman in anguish. Now, it was his turn to scream. "Ugghhh! Owww!"

The woman was about to get into her car when Amanda grabbed her hand. She forced the pepper spray canister out of her hand. Holding her gun to her head, she said, "The keys."

The woman started to kick Amanda.

Didn't she see that she had a gun to her head?

A true ballsy Russian woman. A true survivor.

Amanda held the gun carefully. She didn't want to risk it going off by mistake, especially if the woman struggled. She didn't want to hurt her. She put the woman in a bundle submission hold. She felt bad, even though Jordan had been maced. He kept rubbing his eyes while Amanda held the woman steady, looking out on the street, fearful that a car would pass. Fortunately, none were in sight.

"Your keys," Amanda repeated, more urgently. Then she looked into the open car door and saw them sitting in the cupholder. "Can you see?" she asked Jordan. "They're inside the car."

"No! Goddamn it!" he replied in anguish.

His face was reddening. Tears rolled down his cheeks.

"We'll get some milk," Amanda said. Then she looked in the backseat. "Actually, it looks like she has some there. Go into the car and grab it."

Jordan stumbled to the passenger side of the car and opened the door.

"The back door," Amanda said.

Jordan opened the rear door and found the bag of groceries. He took out the bag and let the items – a loaf of bread, a box of cereal, the milk – fall to the ground as he scoured for the milk.

"It's on the ground," Amanda said. She watched the woman look in dismay at her groceries on the ground. Amanda felt a twinge of regret. "We're sorry."

"Sorry?" the woman repeated.

Now she speaks English!

"Yes, sorry."

The woman spat back something in Russian while Jordan rinsed his face with the milk. The creamy milk helped soothe his porous skin and eyes, and he could see better.

"Should we let her have our car?" Amanda asked Jordan. Her initial plan was to swap cars, but now she was having second thoughts.

"No!" he roared. "Leave her stranded!"

Amanda could see that he was riled by having been pepper-sprayed. Holding the gun aimed at the woman, she went to the other side of the car to gather her groceries. The woman waited. Amanda bent down to retrieve the items and put them back in the bag. When she got up, she started to say, "Here are your groceries," but before she could finish, the woman was running down the road.

"Leave 'em," Jordan said spitefully.

"Let's get out of here," Amanda said.

They walked back to their car. There, they turned off the engine as well as the hazard lights. If the woman came back, she wouldn't be able to drive off with it. Jordan could see better now. "We're leaving," he said to Richter. Jordan marched back to the woman's car. His stride had lost much of its momentum. He didn't seem the same person since he had been sprayed.

Inside, though, Amanda thought the situation was funny, almost farcical. The woman's ambushing of him had been so unexpected!

* * *

They drove onto a highway, and fortunately, the woman's car had a built-in navigation system. Without a cell phone to guide them, they relied more than ever on alternatives. They had been driving for a couple of more hours, about five hours in total, and were now almost at Smolensk. It was 11:30 p.m. Amanda hadn't wanted to put an exact address in the navigation system. She didn't want them to be easily tracked, and she didn't want to put her friend at risk.

"Where are we going?" Jordan had asked her. His listless voice couldn't conceal the fact that he was tired.

"To see someone who can help us," she answered vaguely.

"I could call headquarters," he said.

"You can't. We have no idea who's working against us."

"And you're sure this person we're going to isn't?"

"Yes," she said.

There was no additional explanation. Her word was final.

They arrived at the center of the city. Smolensk seemed like a mini-Saint Petersburg. It had historical charm, colorful buildings, green spaces, medieval churches and fortresses, expansive parks, picturesque bridges crossing the Dnieper River, all dotted with, or marred by, gargantuan apartment blocks and other examples of Eastern Bloc architecture.

"Take a left here," Amanda said to Jordan.

Richter had fallen asleep in the back seat.

"Do you know where we're going?"

"Not exactly." She was tempted to enter the name of the business in the navigation system but didn't want to create a record of it. Several youngsters in their early twenties – all tattooed with leather jackets, dyed and spiky hair, and skinny jeans – were walking along the street. "Pull over here." When Jordan stopped, she quickly got out of the car and approached the group, asking them in English for directions. They motioned to go straight and then take a left. When Amanda was sufficiently satisfied that she knew where to go, she told Jordan to head north. The area became sketchier, with fewer people on the dimming streets.

After following the given directions, Amanda saw the building that she was looking for. A neon sign with green, red, and white lights – a bit of a Kermit the Frog motley – along with a blue palm tree hovering over the name of the business: Kokomo. Svetlana had sent her a picture of the shop when she had opened it. Svetlana had always loved that song; Amanda found it grating, but, somehow, perhaps through Svetlana's sheer will, it had become *their* song. Svetlana had loved its bouncy feel, its optimism, its reverence for love; she found hope in that song and a dream within it. Her dream, to own a tattoo shop, was embodied here, back in her hometown of Smolensk. Amanda hadn't seen her since she had moved back, their relationship having ended because Amanda told her it could never work. She would always be traveling; she would always be working; Svetlana had told her she was in love with the CIA; the truth was, she was. The CIA was her dream, her passion, *her* Kokomo. She didn't need palm trees or the beach or some beautiful woman to pine after; she only needed the gray, murky world of people she could never trust or rely on; the feeling that she was making a difference in the world; the feeling that her country needed her. Besides, she had told Svetlana, she didn't even know if she was a lesbian.

"So, I am just an experiment?" Svetlana had said. "A phase?"

"I don't know," Amanda told her.

"I won't be played with."

"I'm not playing."

"You are."

Amanda could recall the conversation as if it happened not much more recently than three years ago when they were shacking up in her apartment in Fairfax, Virginia. "I don't like Virginia anyway. I don't really like the U.S. either. I'm going back to Russia," Svetlana had pronounced in her definitive way. And within the week, she left. They had spoken occasionally, but now it was only through texts and social media. It was as if Kokomo had been swallowed up by some vicious tsunami, and Amanda was thousands of miles away, only conscious of the memory.

"This is it?" Jordan asked.

"Yes. Let me go inside. You wait here." Amanda exited the car and walked to the front door. The shop was closed. She pressed the button on the intercom. She didn't know if there would be any answer.

Chapter 49

Das Kapital raced forth through the Atlantic towards the United States. The superyacht could hold approximately a quarter of a million liters of fuel. At the speed it was traveling, it burned through 2,500 liters every hour. Much of the kitchen equipment and other amenities – spa, gym equipment, beauty salon, bars – were removed to make the ship lighter and able to travel at high speeds. Only the swimming pool was kept intact, for appearances' sake. The fuel was slated to last a week. That would be more than enough to get it to its destination at its current traveling speed of forty knots. The crew knew they wouldn't be stranded; Khalid Zahir had made sure his oil tankers would be in the region to assist should there be a shortfall.

* * *

Amanda could see a light in the windows above the Kokomo tattoo parlor. Svetlana had told her she had an apartment above the shop. She had bought the building using the money she had earned working as a graphic artist in the U.S. and Europe. As Amanda waited for her to answer the intercom, she perused the list of services that Svetlana offered and thought back to the time when Svetlana had offered to give her a tattoo. "You can't. You're not licensed here," Amanda had told her.

"What do you need a license for?" Svetlana had scoffed. "Everything is more regulated here than in Russia. And you say you're a capitalist society? You're run by the government. Of the government, by the government, for the government. Fuck the people."

The truth was, Amanda had never wanted a tattoo and didn't like the thought of being permanently branded. Besides, she'd have to disclose it to headquarters. She didn't want Langley to intrude in her life more than they already had. She already had to report her acquaintance with Svetlana to the Agency because Svetlana was a foreigner. They had to vet her, make sure she wasn't a Russian spy. Amanda had to be extra careful not to leave any devices near her that could be compromised. That was no way to carry on a relationship. But that is what the Agency wanted – they preferred their officers to date one another and not to venture outside the intelligence community for companionship. It was a life destined for solitude.

Amanda rang again – this time, once, twice, three times. Svetlana used to ring her like that too, as if to say, *It's me!*

The intercom buzzed back. Amanda immediately recognized Svetlana's voice. She asked, in an annoyed voice, "Who is it?" in Russian.

"Svetlana, it's me, Amanda. Can you let me and my friends in?"

She seemed to utter, "My God," in Russian.

A pause ensued. Amanda wondered: *Is she going to open the door?*

Then, the intercom buzzed to unlock the lobby door.

* * *

In his sumptuous, South Kensington, London townhome, Khalid Zahir met with Ahmed Bensaïd for an update on, what he called, their 'project.'

"Everything is on schedule," Bensaïd told him.

"And our friend?" Zahir asked, referring to Sixtus. "He's being cooperative?"

"For the moment."

"We won't need him forever, you know."

"No. But we shouldn't jettison him unless it becomes necessary."

"After he makes his speech, calms everybody, he will have done what we need."

"It might behoove us to keep him around."

"Perhaps. On a tight leash. He can have an accident."

"But that will just leave our other friend," Bensaïd said, referring to General Cheeks.

"He, we will have to keep around. On an even tighter leash. But we can't let him out of our sights. I don't trust him not to betray us. He has no real power or influence, not like our protege. He could double-cross us; then where would we be? A religious man and a military man, that would be a formidable antagonist. But if we take the religious man out of the equation, that just leaves the military one. America has no appetite to be led by a military strongman. And we will fill their religious zeal, whether they like it or not. They didn't give our people a choice, did they not?"

"So, he must die?" Bensaïd asked.

"On that, we are in agreement. It is Allah's will."

* * *

Amanda, Jordan, and Richter sat in Svetlana's living room. It was a busy, colorful environment, much like the tattoos that covered her arms, torso, and legs. Plants in woven baskets hung from the ceilings and walls. Amanda had never known Svetlana to be such a lover of foliage. But it did make her think back to when Svetlana had given her a small tropical plant. The gift had made her feel slightly uncomfortable – she had to have it inspected for listening devices. There were none. Under Amanda's benign neglect, the little weed died within the year.

"Can you help us?" Amanda asked. The question at hand: Could Svetlana provide them with safe passage to Belarus?

"I can make some calls," Svetlana said.

"We don't have much time. We have to go tonight."

Svetlana scoffed. "It's the middle of the night. That will make border patrol suspicious. A midnight crossing."

"We can wait a few hours," Amanda said. "We need to ditch the car and get another one."

"You want to use mine?" Svetlana asked with an indignant tone.

"Or maybe someone you know."

At that moment, a woman in her late twenties or early thirties, wearing a long T-shirt as pajamas, emerged from the hallway into the open-concept living area. She said something in Russian to Svetlana, and Svetlana responded back. Amanda heard her name in the middle of the explanation. The discussion between them seemed quite animated, especially considering the girl was half-asleep. The dialogue continued back and forth for a minute or so, during which time the girl shot Amanda an occasional look. It wasn't a look of contempt but more of bafflement. Amanda assumed she was Svetlana's new girlfriend. Svetlana didn't bother with an introduction. Ultimately, her girlfriend relented, seeming to say, "Whatever," or something to that effect, and retired back to the bedroom.

Svetlana turned to Amanda. "I have a car for you. I will drive you myself."

"It could be dangerous. I don't want to put you in jeopardy."

"If you didn't, you wouldn't have come," she snorted.

Chapter 50

Amanda, Richter, and Svetlana were driving towards the Belarus border, cramped into her girlfriend Zhyuli's – the Russian equivalent of *Julie* – compact car. They had finally managed to depart from Smolensk around 5 a.m. Jordan had ditched the car he and Amanda had stolen from the pepper-spray-yielding, Russian woman near a strip of warehouses on the outskirts of town. Svetlana had followed him in Zhyuli's car. When they returned, she gave him the keys to her car and told him to follow her. The plan was that Svetlana, Amanda and Richter would drive in Zhyuli's car. Then when they were relatively close to the border, Svetlana would take her car back from Jordan and drive it back home while Amanda, Jordan, and Richter continued into Belarus. But before they could leave Smolensk, they had one final issue to take care of: Richter's identity.

During their relationship, Svetlana had once told Amanda that she had traveled to the United States on a false passport. Amanda didn't disclose this fact to the Agency. Svetlana had told her that she had previously traveled to Washington, D.C., New York, and Chicago. Amanda was surprised to learn of this, because Svetlana's passport had never been used to enter the United States before. That is when Svetlana confessed. She told Amanda that she had gotten a fake passport from someone she knew back home. Her reason: she was considering moving permanently from Russia and didn't want her travel to the U.S. to be used against her. This excuse didn't sit well with Amanda; so, she pried further. Svetlana revealed that she didn't have the money to travel to the U.S., but that if she posed as a tourist and sent back a series of photographs and videos, the Russian government would pay for her trip.

"So you were spying for the SVR?" Amanda asked, referring to the Russian intelligence service.

"Yes. But I'm not a spy. Why do you care? How do you know so much about Russian intelligence?"

Amanda had never told Svetlana that she was a CIA officer. She used a cover of working for the World Bank in Washington. For all Svetlana knew, she was a senior financial analyst researching distressed economies at the bank.

"We have to be careful about who we associate with," Amanda rejoined.

"I'm not good enough for you?"

"I didn't say that."

"Then what? What's the big deal?"

She couldn't tell her she was a CIA officer; she never would. Not until the end.

* * *

"What kinds of pictures did you have to send back?" Amanda had asked her.

"There were pictures of one man in particular," Svetlana said. "He was a general."

"What was his name?"

"I don't remember," she replied with an off-handed manner.

Amanda could tell she wasn't telling her the truth. She could read Svetlana like a book. "You don't remember?" she asked in disbelief.

Svetlana paced around the room. "Let me think." After a few moments, she owned up. "Yes, now I remember. He had such an odd name. General Jefferson Cheeks."

At the time, General Cheeks was not yet Director of National Intelligence. But he was on the Joint Chiefs of Staff.

"Why did they want pictures of him?"

"I have no idea. All I know is I got a free trip in exchange for some pictures and video."

"Where did you see him?"

"He was giving a talk at the United Nations. All I had to do was wait where he and the other diplomats entered the building. I walked all around the building. Taking pictures of everything, pretending like I was interested in architecture. It wasn't hard. I actually do like architecture. In Chicago, he gave a speech at the University of Chicago. I showed up there too. They got me tickets under someone else's name. I don't know who. I was so nervous about it, I left my fake passport back at the hotel. I was afraid someone was going to stop me and say the name on the ticket didn't match my passport. But I learned that things don't work like that in this country. Americans are so trusting." She almost seemed to say this as an indictment of Amanda.

"I sent the pictures and video back using a secure link. That was it. I never heard from them again."

"The FSB arranged the fake passport for you?" Amanda asked.

"Yes. I kept a screenshot of it in case something happened to me, since I wasn't traveling under my own name. I wanted my family to know I was safe or if I went missing."

* * *

Before setting out on their journey to Belarus, Amanda asked Svetlana to call the man who had provided her fake passport. Svetlana said, "Are you crazy? It's one a.m."

"It's not for me. It's for our friend. He's a cardinal."

Svetlana didn't respond.

"With the Vatican."

"And?" she said.

"His life is in extreme danger. We need to bring him to safety. He only has his real passport. Jordan and I have fake ones."

"We do?" he asked, interjecting.

"I got them in Poland. Before we left." She took them out of her jacket pocket and handed Jordan his. "Put your real one away. From now on, make sure you only use this one."

"Yes, ma'am," he said.

He was always so polite.

"Fake passports?" Svetlana said. "What's going on? Some undercover operation?"

Amanda chuckled. "It's just a precaution. Your man is in Smolensk, right?"

"He was. But I haven't talked to him in like forever."

Amanda was always impressed how fluent Svetlana's English was, even if she did have a thick accent.

"Can you call him? We can't leave the cardinal. They'll kill him. You do still have his number, don't you?"

"I think so," she said. She took her cell phone and started scrolling through the contacts. "Yes." There, she found his name, Dmitry. She started typing into her phone.

"What are you doing?" Amanda asked in a tone of voice that was familiar, as if they had seen each other daily for the past few years.

She shrugged. "I'm sending him a text."

"Call him." She could see that Svetlana was annoyed with her, but she knew she would acquiesce. "Please."

She let out a little huff; then she hit the *call* button.

The phone rang. Soon, Svetlana was having a conversation in Russian. She was doing a lot of talking. Amanda didn't grasp any of it. After a minute, Svetlana turned to her.

"What country do you want the passport from?"

"Germany," she answered. "And it needs a visa stamp."

Svetlana went back to talking to Dmitry in Russian. Then she turned to Amanda, "He said, no problem. Germany's easy."

"How much will it cost?"

Svetlana asked Dmitry. Then she turned to Amanda. "Four hundred thousand rubles."

Amanda took out her phone and searched for the currency exchange rate. "That's fifty thousand dollars."

"You want it tonight, right?"

"Yes. But I don't have that kind of money."

"He probably takes Bitcoin. Can you get that?"

Amanda thought for a moment. "Yes."

Svetlana turned back to her mother tongue to talk to Dmitry. Then she turned to Amanda and said in a flat tone, "He takes Bitcoin."

"Get his account info." In part, Amanda was relieved. The truth was, she didn't have any Bitcoin. She would have to think fast.

* * *

"Do you have a laptop I can use?" Amanda asked Svetlana.

In a matter of minutes, Amanda was online. She logged into a private VPN to prevent her activities from being tracked. She opened her wallet, which had a laminated card with her emergency contact at the Agency, her supervisor Veronica. These laminated cards were standard issue for CIA officers. In the heat of a mission, critical contact information might be needed, to help an officer in trouble or in case the officer was killed. On the back side of the card, there were two credit cards listed with their expiration dates and three-digit CVV codes. In a bind, she could use these cards for purchases. She logged into her account for the first credit card. It had a limit of $25,000. She went to her second card, that one had a limit of $30,000. For the first account, she transferred $25,000 to her bank account. Then she did the same on the second credit card. In about thirty minutes, after verifying her identity through her email, she had fifty grand at her disposal, ready to be converted into Bitcoin when Dmitry's masterpiece was completed.

Svetlana, Amanda, and Richter headed to Dmitry's studio. He had a stationery shop as a front. They waited in the car until Dmitry arrived. As he unlocked the door, he waved them in.

Dmitry looked to be in his early sixties. He had long, graying black hair that flowed to his shoulders. He wore black-framed eyeglasses that covered only half of his bushy eyebrows. He looked like he had been roused from sleep – he wore sweatpants and a T-shirt. With his hoodie and foam clogs, he looked perfectly grandfatherly.

When they got to the backroom, he was all business. Amanda was amazed how slim his operation looked. In the front room, he had the photo studio set up to take pictures for anyone who came in, including his black-market clients. In the back, he had a computer and a 3D printing machine. All sorts of paper stock lined the shelves. When it came time to fix the personal details onto Richter's passport, Dmitry went to a shelf and pulled out a box. Behind the box was a second box that contained the card stock for the Federal Republic of Germany. He rifled through the contents until he found a card that looked just about right. It was worn enough, its edges slightly frayed. In about a half an hour, Richter had a new passport and a new German name.

Dmitry waved the new passport. "I'll need payment."

"Yes, I have your Bitcoin details. Let me make the transfer." Amanda took Svetlana's phone and installed her VPN app on it. She then logged in with her credentials and chose the same location she had used at Svetlana's apartment: Madrid, Spain. This way, the bank would recognize her location as the one she had just confirmed. She transferred $50,000 to her Bitcoin account. She then purchased $50,000 worth of Bitcoin. Immediately, she transferred the same amount to Dmitry's account.

As soon as the transfer was complete, a notification buzzed on Dmitry's phone. He logged into his Bitcoin app and smiled. "All in a night's work. I love doing business with Americans. They are much more generous than the Russians." He handed Richter his new passport.

"He needs a Russian visa stamp," Amanda said. "And a visa to go to Belarus from Russia."

"Oh yes." Dmitry went to another box on the same shelf. He took that box to his desk and took out a rubber stamp and an inkpad. He affixed the visas on pages five and six. On the other pages, he stamped various countries – England several times with different dates, France, Italy, the United States, Mexico, Brazil – places that he thought a man like this freshly denominated Herr Schulz would have traveled to. Dmitry had dozens of stamps in the box, and he intuitively seemed to know what color ink to use for each country. "Now you have a passport that matches the man. It's valid for a few more years." He closed the box of stamps, gathered the remaining stock, and carried them back to the middle shelf. No doubt he was in a rush to get back to bed.

Chapter 51

Amanda sat in the passenger seat of Zhyuli's car while Svetlana drove. Richter was in the back seat. Again, he drifted in and out of sleep. All he did was sleep. He must have had a mean case of jetlag. Every so often, Amanda would look through the rear window to make sure Jordan was still following them, in Svetlana's car. He was always close behind, managing to keep up with Svetlana's rather erratic driving. She was always in a hurry when she drove. In this case, she couldn't be faulted for her haste.

They had been driving for almost an hour and a half and were fast approaching the border. Soon, it would be time for Jordan and Svetlana to switch cars. Amanda knew that now was the time to have the conversation with Svetlana that she had wished she had had years ago. This might be the last time they saw each other.

"Do you remember when I asked you to leave?"

"I certainly do," she said defensively.

"I wasn't completely truthful why."

"You mean you weren't confused about your identity?"

"No. Well, maybe. I was. Maybe I still am. I don't really know. I don't like to define myself like that."

"You want to be gender-fluid? That's what they call it, right?"

"Something like that. But that wasn't the real reason."

"Does it matter?" Svetlana asked. "You can see that I moved on."

"To me, it does. I would like to give you more closure."

"Trust me, I have all the closure I need." She made no attempt to conceal her prickly tone.

"Then maybe I need more closure."

"That's more like it."

"The real reason we couldn't be together was my work."

"Yes, when the World Bank came calling, you never hesitated. You worked so many hours. I knew you were seeing somebody else."

"I wasn't," Amanda said.

"Don't bullshit me. I know you."

"You do, yes. But not everything. The reason I had to break things off was that I didn't want to pull you into my work. I'm with the Central Intelligence Agency."

Svetlana looked at her, quizzically.

"I lied to you. I wasn't with the World Bank. Ever. I've always been an officer with the CIA since I graduated from college. They recruited me out of Cornell. I couldn't tell you because I knew you wouldn't want that life. You were in some ways so anti-American. And I knew that if things continued, I'd have to disclose a romantic relationship. They would have pried into your life. A lot. And it might have jeopardized my career."

"So you really were in love with your work?" she asked sarcastically.

"I was. I am. I'm sorry I couldn't fit you into it. I go abroad every few years. The Agency wouldn't have let you come with me."

"How do you know?"

"I know them. They are extremely distrustful of Russians. They would be scanning our devices constantly. They'd probably put listening devices and cameras in our apartment. That's how suspicious they are."

Svetlana looked in the rearview mirror at Richter.

"He knows I'm with the Agency, too," Amanda said. "That's why I have a duty to get him out of Russia."

Svetlana pulled the car over to the side of the road, suddenly. The car jerked to a stop. Jordan slammed on the brakes behind them, not expecting to stop so soon. He managed to stop just behind them on the dirt embankment.

"I don't want any part of this shit!" Svetlana said. "I don't want to help the CIA!"

"I know you don't," Amanda said. "That's why I'm telling you this. Do you understand now?" Tears filled her eyes. Svetlana stared at her, her eyes glaring.

Jordan stepped out of his car and made his way to the driver's side door. He looked confused as he saw through the window that Svetlana was in tears. She rolled down the window.

"Is everything all right?" he asked.

"Get back in the car," Svetlana said. "We'll almost there."

He shot a look at Amanda, raising his eyes in concern. She nodded, to let him know that everything was okay.

Svetlana put the car back in gear and slowly pulled back onto the road. There was no traffic in sight. She watched in the rearview mirror as Jordan proceeded behind them. "Thank you," she said to Amanda.

Amanda understood what she meant. She had spared Svetlana from being an Agency wife who would never truly be accepted. "Can I borrow your phone for a second?"

Svetlana nodded to where it was sitting, in the cup holder.

Amanda searched the internet. After a few moments, the song "Kokomo" started to play. As the tropical, percussive beat pulsated, Svetlana hummed along with some of the infectious tune. The feel-good melody echoed through the car's speakers. When the song reached the exuberant chorus, Amanda started to sing along. Svetlana then joined in. They sang away to the nostalgic, uplifting anthem. Richter woke up. When the second verse came on, they listened to the Beach Boys sing.

But when the high-energy chorus returned, they piped in again, singing loudly over the band. Even Richter learned some of the lyrics. By the end, he was singing along, albeit in a whispery bass. He was probably embarrassed.

When the song was over, Amanda turned to Richter and said, "We're sorry. That's our song." She turned to Svetlana. "We'll always have Kokomo."

"Yes, we will," Svetlana said.

"I guess this is our Kokomo."

"Could be worse."

"I always hated that song."

"I know."

"But I learned to love it. Because of you." Amanda could feel her throat tighten as she spoke.

"There are worse things in life."

"I would have never remembered the name of your shop if it weren't for that song."

"I like it," Svetlana said. "It's catchy."

"So are bed bugs and scabies."

"Sometimes you're too much."

"I know," Amanda said.

They drove in silence for a few minutes. Amanda knew she had to get back to business. This brief foray into her past had been enriching on a personal level, but her private life was always a lower priority. "I have another favor to ask," she said.

"What now? Haven't I done enough?"

"You have. This is something I just thought of. You mentioned the man you were surveilling, General Cheeks."

Amanda could see Richter listening attentively from the back seat. She continued: "Do you still have those pictures?"

"I do," Svetlana said. "You want them?"

"I'll pay you for them."

"You don't have to do that."

"I want to. I know it will help. I'll give you five thousand dollars for them. Do you have a pen or paper here?" She started to look through the side bins of the passenger door.

"Look in the glove compartment," Svetlana said.

Amanda opened it. Inside was the car manual along with a paper pad and some pens. She wrote a URL down. "It will be a secure site where you can upload them. I'll write it down for you. Just put a comment that it's to the attention of Amanda O'Brien."

"Okay, I'll do it when I get back home."

"Do you want the money in Bitcoin?"

"I probably should. I wouldn't want my government to track this."

"I can arrange cash if that would be easier."

"I'd rather not have a visit from some CIA operative, thank you."

"Okay, when you upload the pictures, put in your Bitcoin account number. I'll arrange the transfer. Be aware it might take a few days. I just blew my wad on that passport."

"I thought you said we couldn't trust General Cheeks," Richter chimed.

"That's right. That's why I want to look at those pictures. I want to see what the Russians were so interested in."

"I'm sorry I've been so much trouble," Richter said.

"None of it is your fault. You happened to get caught up in things. Trouble is my business anyway," Amanda replied.

"Thank you again," Svetlana said. "If there was anyone I'd want to be in trouble with, it would be you."

"You might just have your chance," Amanda responded.

Chapter 52

They drove for twenty more minutes, and then Svetlana said, "I think it's time for me to leave you."

Svetlana saw a desolate part of the road with an embankment ahead. She tapped on the brakes a few times to flash them, to give Jordan a signal that she was going to pull over. She stopped on the side of the road, leaving enough space for Jordan to park behind.

"It was good seeing you," Svetlana said to Amanda. "I hope you find some happiness in your life."

She had a sweet tone to her voice; Amanda did not take her statement as unkind. Svetlana was Svetlana; she would never be the optimistic, joyful woman that Amanda was. She would always have Mother Russia in her soul. "I do too. It was great seeing you too." Amanda lightly grasped her hand.

Jordan was approaching the car. Svetlana watched as Amanda took her hand away.

Svetlana opened the car door. As she got out, she popped her head back in the window. "Should I have asked for more?" Her voice had a bit of New York grit and gumption.

Amanda reveled in her uncharacteristic spunkiness. "No. I gave you top dollar."

"Top Dollar Amanda. That's what I'll call you from now on."

"Bye Kokomo," Amanda shot back. To her surprise, Svetlana laughed.

* * *

While Svetlana drove back to her home in Smolensk, Amanda, Jordan, and Richter proceeded onward in Zhyuli's car. Jordan drove. Amanda told him that he would have to drive because the Belarusians, a rather patriarchal society, would expect a man to be driving and if she did, they would distrust them. Richter, it went without saying between the two of them, couldn't be relied on. There was no telling how nervous he might become from the most routine of questions.

"I told Svetlana I'd let her know where we'd leave the car in Belarus," Amanda explained. "We'll have somebody drive it back to where it's closer for her. We'll be going north. To Vitebsk. It's an hour from where we'll cross. It's the birthplace of Chagall. They dedicated a museum to him there after the fall of the Iron Curtain in the early nineties."

"You're just full of information."

"I did my research before we left. Thank God for the internet," she said.

"You've never been?"

"No. But I know from there, we can get anywhere in Western Europe. Just wait."

"We need to get across the border first." He looked in the rearview mirror toward Richter, raising his voice. "Cardinal, how are you doing back there?"

"About as well as can be expected."

"We hope to have you back home as soon as possible."

"I can't go back there!" he said indignantly.

"I know," Jordan said apologetically. "I mean, anywhere you want to go in Western Europe."

"Yes," Amanda said. "We'll put you somewhere safe, don't worry."

Richter grumbled.

"Just remember," Amanda said in an attempt to cheer him up, "we'll always have Kokomo."

"What's that about?" Jordan asked.

"Nothing. Listen," she said, addressing both, "I need your passports. Your real passports. I'm going to hide them."

Both Jordan and Richter handed her their real passports.

She opened the glove compartment and took out the manual for the car. It was in a plastic case. Along with the manual were the original bill of sale, car registration forms, and repair receipts from the dealership and other repair shops and tire shops. She took a few of the receipts out, then stuck the passports inside some of the folder receipts. She put the manual back in the glove compartment and then scattered the remaining receipts on top and in front of the manual. It looked a bit of a mess, the way a glove compartment should.

She now addressed Richter, speaking more loudly as a teacher would to a class. "You have your passport ready, right?"

"Yes," he groused. "I'm old but I'm not deaf. You don't have to yell."

"I'm sorry. I just..." She realized she was still speaking loudly and needed to lower her voice. "I want to make sure you don't get nervous. Take a few deep breaths and relax. There's nothing to be worried about. These passports should get us through."

"Famous last words," he muttered.

In less than ten minutes, at 6 a.m., they arrived at the border checkpoint. A Belarusian soldier in a camouflage-patterned uniform, flagged them to stop. Jordan slowed the car, halting before the soldier, who was already scanning the car as he stared Jordan down. Another soldier opposite from him held a Russian-style automatic rifle. The soldier who flagged them down was also armed with a similar rifle, but he wasn't aiming it at the car. Amanda noticed in the side mirror another soldier behind them had another automatic weapon pointed at them.

"We've got a welcome party," she said.

Jordan quietly agreed. Then he rolled down the window. The Russian guard barked at him.

"I think he wants you to turn the engine off."

Jordan complied.

The Russian barked another order at him.

Jordan didn't understand, saying, "I don't speak Russian."

The border guard took his rifle from his side and pointed it at Jordan. He motioned it back and forth along the side of the car. "Out of the car!" he commanded in English.

As Jordan opened the car door, the guard yelled, "Hands up!"

Jordan obeyed the officer's commands, cautiously getting out of the car.

"All of you!" the guard shouted. "Out of the car!"

"Party time," Amanda whispered.

* * *

Amanda and Richter proceeded to get out of Zhyuli's car, keeping their hands in the air as the Belarusian border guard had instructed them. "Your passports!" he commanded in English. Amanda took hers from her pocket, and Richter retrieved his. They held them in the air over their heads.

"Against the wall!" the guard shouted, pointing his rifle at a cement wall. The wall divided the car lanes from the administrative offices. It was topped with barbed wire.

Amanda slowly made her way to the wall. It looked like the perfect place to execute someone.

Richter followed behind. "They don't seem happy to see us. I hope these passports work."

"Shh," she said, annoyed by his lack of discretion. "They might have listening devices near."

The guard was quickly behind them as they made their way to the wall. "Turn around!" he ordered.

They obeyed, twisting to face him. He reached his arm toward their raised hands and took their passports. The other guy who was serving as patrol came to get the passports. The patrol officer ran to the station at the gate.

All this fuss, Amanda thought. They are just going to run the numbers in a database and see that there are no international warrants on them. They are going to check the visa stamps that allowed them to enter Belarus from Russia and conclude that they are genuine. They must not like Americans. At least they will learn that Richter is not American.

"Where are you coming from?" the senior guard asked.

"Smolensk," Amanda said. "Sightseeing."

"What did you see?"

"The fortress, the cathedral, the garden, the deer."

"The deer?" he asked.

"Yes, the sculpture of the deer," she answered, referring to the large bronze structure of a deer that she had searched on the internet in preparation for questioning. She knew she had to be prepared. As the Farm had taught her, she would play the role like an actor on a stage who had researched the back story of the character she's playing, to give the character life and make her seem believable.

"Did you rub his balls?" he asked.

Amanda had read that rubbing the genitals of the deer was a superstition among locals, to bring luck. "No," she answered, "but they did."

The guard gave a short grunt of a laugh. "You don't look like tourists. Where is your luggage?"

Amanda saw that another guard was inspecting their car. "We have our bags. But we travel light. We only stayed in Russia for a few days."

"And why have you come to Belarus?"

"We're on a pilgrimage," she answered. "We're Catholics, and we're going to visit some holy sites." Amanda had read that there was some history of repression against Catholics in Belarus. Today, there was a softness toward the religion. Catholics represented ten to twenty percent of the population. "Herr Schulz is a priest."

"He is?" the guard asked in disbelief. "Say the Apostle's Creed for me."

Richter didn't hesitate. He rattled it off, starting with "I believe in God, the Father almighty, Creator of heaven and earth, and in Jesus Christ, his only Son..." and ending with "the forgiveness of sins, the resurrection of the body, and life everlasting. Amen."

The guard yelled something back to the guard inspecting the car. Amanda assumed it might have something to do with Richter being a priest. "Yes," came the answer from the other guard. The more junior guard then returned with their passports. He had Jordan's in his hand. Amanda saw that while he spoke anxiously, and rapidly, he didn't look concerned. The passports all checked out. In fact, Amanda had arranged for her and Jordan's fake addresses to be within ten miles from each other in Virginia. This way, they looked like they could very well go to the same church and be friends.

Richter said, "Would you like me to recite the Nicene Creed also?" Without waiting for a response, he instantly launched into it – "We believe in one God, the Father, the Almighty, Maker of heaven and earth...."

The guard interrupted – "Stop! Get back in the car!"

His order was directed only at Richter; Amanda remained standing against the wall. No one was tending to Jordan; she threw him a glance. They both knew that they were at a standstill. Amanda thought it was ironic that Richter, whose passport had the least quality in terms of a fake, was the first to be cleared. Amanda's and Jordan's passports were so well contrived, in fact, that if the border agents verified any of the stamped entries with the border services of any of those countries, all the records would have come back authenticated.

Another security officer was inspecting the outside of Zhyuli's car, holding an under-vehicle inspection mirror and camera to the underside of the chassis. Accompanying him was another guard who crouched under the car. He examined and felt around all the tires. Was he planting a tracking device? Amanda wondered.

The senior guard snapped some orders at the one who was standing over Jordan. Soon, he was ushering Jordan to the wall where Amanda was standing. They didn't say anything to each other. The guards stood close. Amanda motioned to indicate listening devices posted along the wall.

They both watched as the officer who was inspecting the underbody of the car turned to closer scrutiny of the interior. He was looking under the front car seats. Richter sat in the backseat. Such an odd way to perform a vehicle inspection, Amanda thought. They were certainly grasping at straws.

The guard crouched under the steering column. Amanda could then see him rifle through the compartment between the front seats. He slid over to the glove box. Amanda couldn't see his head. He seemed to disappear for a few moments. Jordan and Amanda stared forward without looking at each other, trying not to display any hint of concern. When his head emerged, he held up a small envelope. It was the car registration. The guard came out of the car and handed it to the senior officer, who said to Jordan, "This is not your car."

"No, it's a friend of ours," Jordan said.

"Where is she?"

"She's at home."

"How do I know this car isn't stolen?" the guard asked.

"She hasn't reported it stolen. You could call her, but she's probably still asleep."

Hearing this, Amanda became alarmed. They didn't have cell phones on them. Wouldn't the officers find that suspicious? Of course, they could hide behind their 'pilgrimage' excuse. But it might not pass muster.

"She won't awake for a call from the police?" the guard said.

"I'm sure she will," Jordan replied.

The line of questions and answers sat uneasily with Amanda. They didn't even have Zhyuli's phone number! Suddenly, it looked like their cover story was falling further apart. They could come up with some excuse about knowing where she lived or being too nervous to remember the number. But the arguments wouldn't hold up with this aggressive guard.

"We have the authority to impound the car," said the guard.

For a moment, Amanda thought that she could offer some money to the guard to extricate them from the situation. Then she realized that the officer was laying a trap for them: by offering a bribe, they could be legitimately detained and charged. At this point, they really had no grounds. If the American embassy were to become involved, the guards' behavior would be criticized. It would be better to let things play out, she determined. The guards likely didn't want any unnecessary scrutiny or to have their judgment second- or third-guessed. Bureaucracy still held an important role in the post-Communist society, and administrative procedures and decisions could have profound effects on the constituents of former Soviet-bloc nations. In some respects, the effects today were more severe than under the Communist regime.

"If you impound the car, we will have nowhere to go. We will have to stay here," Amanda said.

"We have jail cells," the guard answered.

"You'll put a priest in jail?" she asked.

The guard thought for a moment and looked overhead. He knew that security cameras were recording all their interactions. The priest had been allowed back in the car. And now, they might take him out and put him in jail? Amanda sensed that he was not liking the situation. He had been put in an uncomfortable situation, one which had an unpredictable outcome if it were subject to scrutiny.

The senior guard brandished their passports in his hands. "We will be watching you while you are in Belarus. You should make your trip quick to avoid further trouble." He handed their passports back to them. The junior guard came up from behind and held the car keys for Jordan to take. Jordan and Amanda were silent as they walked back to the car. They knew that any statement, no matter how innocuous, might be used against them. It was better to take the win and be on their way.

* * *

"Do you think they'll be following us?" Jordan asked.

Amanda put her index finger on her lips to shush him. She raised her arms, pointing to her ears and then to the sides of the car, suggesting there might be listening devices implanted in the vehicle. "They said they would. But we're not doing anything wrong."

Jordan seemed to understand her admonition. "No."

"Are we going to be able to get out of here?" Richter asked.

Again, Amanda hushed him silently. "There's no reason we can't continue on like we planned."

After driving for another hour, they reached the northern Belarusian city of Vitebsk. Vitebsk had the charm of medieval Russian cities with its picturesque churches and civic buildings. Richter seemed to appreciate the surroundings through admiring glances. They continued through the center of town, to the outskirts. "There," Amanda said, pointing ahead.

"There?" Jordan asked, seeing a yellow, Gothic Revival church up ahead.

"Yes," Amanda answered.

"We're going to a church?" Richter asked.

Amanda again hushed him silently. "Of course. We need to pray, don't we? Besides, our guests will meet us there."

Jordan drove into the parking lot for St. Mary's Cathedral, a magnificent example of eighteenth-century architecture. The window and door had pointed arches, and the steeply pitched roof made the building tower over the surrounding neighborhood. A castle-like tower stood at the side of the cathedral.

Jordan parked. As they walked toward the church, Amanda said, "Sorry I couldn't say much in there. I didn't know if we'd be listened to. I have a contact that we're going to meet here. They'll get us to Lithuania. From there, we can go anywhere in Europe." She handed them their real passports, taken from the car manual case. "You won't need these yet."

As they went into the cathedral, Richter stopped, making the sign of the cross and kneeling before a stone fountain containing holy water.

He had a solemn look as he passed inside.

Jordan followed Amanda as she strolled toward the altar of the cathedral. She went through a side door that had a Russian *Do Not Enter* sign. Amanda didn't care; she knew she would find Eddie there. She looked inside the office; Eddie was not there. Suddenly, a voice rang from behind –

"Are you looking for somebody?" an Irish accent rang out. Eddie was short with red hair, green eyes, and freckles all over his face and hands. He looked like a forty-year-old schoolboy.

Amanda turned around. "Eddie?"

"Amanda?"

"Yes," she said relieved.

"What is the code word?"

Amanda knew that he had to confirm her identity. She had set the code word herself. "Kokomo."

Eddie rushed out his hand. "Welcome to the center of the resistance."

* * *

Resistance was an overstatement. The cathedral served as a refuge to those like Amanda who had been stranded in Russia. It was a classic smuggling operation. Eddie was a member of MI6, as he held dual British and Irish citizenship. British citizenship was a requirement to join the elite British intelligence service.

"Is everything ready for us to get to Lithuania?" Amanda asked.

"The birdy will be ready in a couple of hours." He had a thick Irish brogue. It gave his voice a playful edge.

"Great. Where will it take us?"

"We have an airstrip. The Lithuanians are much more friendly to us than these Belarusians." In fact, Lithuania had joined both the European Union and NATO in the early aughts.

"Is it safe to leave our car here?" Amanda asked.

"It's okay. I had it checked. There are no tracking mechanisms on it. Leave it here."

"Where do we have to go?"

"Our airfield is on the outskirts of Vilnius."

Amanda had never been to Vilnius, or Lithuania, for that matter. "How long will it take?"

"I'm afraid it will be over five hours. Are you ready for another long drive?"

"We have to get going. We can always stop somewhere if we need a rest."

"Very well," Eddie said.

She went to talk to Jordan and Richter, who were sitting in the waiting area outside of Eddie's small office. "Are you boys ready for the next leg of our trip?"

"I can't say I am," Jordan said.

"Neither can I," said Richter. "I suppose we don't have much choice."

"No. It wasn't really a question," replied Amanda with an apologetic tone.

* * *

Das Kapital continued its relentless run towards the United States. The seas continued to be unusually calm, allowing it to cut through the ocean at top speed. Through a satellite connection, Yuri the captain messaged Bensaïd that all was proceeding ahead of plan. Three more days of traveling would bring the superyacht to the American shores.

* * *

Eddie drove all the way to Vilnius. He planned on returning to Vitebsk tomorrow or the next day. He wasn't in a rush; there was little for him to do except rescue the occasional MI6 or CIA spy that came his way. He doubted he'd see one for another six months.

As they approached the majestic capital, Eddie asked, "Shall we drive through Old Town? It's a medieval wonder. A UNESCO World Heritage site complete with cobblestone streets."

"No." Amanda was determined to get out of Eastern Europe as soon as possible. They would have to be satisfied by the glimpses from afar of the city's Baroque architecture.

"Can you tell me what the rush is about?" he asked impishly.

"I'm afraid it's highly classified."

"Of course."

Like clockwork, Amanda, Jordan, and Richter left the Vilnius airfield in a Black Hawk helicopter, the mainstay of U.S. military transport. They landed in Prague, Czechoslovakia a couple of hours later at an airport that used to be the primary airport for Prague but now was used as a military base for NATO. At the airfield, Amanda arranged a car to go to the city center. They would spend the night at a non-descript hotel in Prague's Old Town. She had gotten a cash advance on her personal credit card and paid for the room in cash to avoid being located. "We're going to leave tomorrow," she said to Richter. "Jordan and I. You will stay here in hiding. You'll be able to order room service. There's enough variety, so you shouldn't get bored for a week or so. You shouldn't leave the apartment."

"I can't stay cooped up that long!" Richter said.

"You have to be patient, for your own safety. We'll send somebody by to check on you."

"Where will you be?" The uneasiness and anxiety in his voice were difficult to miss.

"I'm not sure quite yet," Amanda replied. "But I'll be in touch. We got you this burner phone. Don't use it except for emergencies."

* * *

That Sunday, Sixtus led mass at St. Peter's Basilica. He spoke of the need for world peace, for the end to hunger, and for compassion for those who were less fortunate. He preached that the more developed Western countries of the world had a responsibility to assist those countries that were struggling. His reasoning was that their struggles were in many ways caused by continued domination of Western economies. He was careful not to place outright blame on the Western nations but said the developing world's desperate need was an impossible cycle to avoid. The West accumulated wealth at a capitalized rate, and it could easily dominate the Third and Fourth World. He called on the need for mercy, for tolerance, and for justice for all peoples of the world, of all faiths and creeds.

News of his speech was reported throughout the world. While a video of Sixtus giving the speech played quietly in the background of the Oval Office, President Foster read the translation from Italian, studying it carefully. As he read it over several times, he glanced at the letter from Cardinal Cajetan to Pope Leo X urging caution against the arrest of Martin Luther. Who was this man he was dealing with? Should he really be making political statements like this? After all, Sixtus was a religious leader. But now he was stepping into the secular realm, and his words were fighting.

While the pope's recorded speech played out on the television, Foster glanced at the classified brief on his desk. *The Grindon* had returned to port in the Canary Islands. No suspicious contraband was found in the search.

As he watched the pope on screen pontificating – yes, *pontificating!* – before a crowd of supplicants, he recalled the words of Karl Marx: *Religion is the opiate of the masses.* There was nothing more powerful than an assembled crowd bent on change and reform. Foster knew how tenuous a government's hold on the people was. It was a contract that the people innately acquiesced to, through education. Some would say through indoctrination and propaganda. But if the people no longer wanted to obey, if they had a need to revolt – as they had done in France against their government – the people would win. No army was strong enough to withstand the will of the people. Many pointed to the American Revolution also. But that event was different: the people were revolting against foreign control. The French Revolution was the true turning point in history. The people had decided enough was enough and demanded regime change. Even the U.S. couldn't withstand such a challenge today. All it would take is a hundred thousand or so people to stand up to cause change. And with over fifty million Catholics in the United States, mustering up a hundred thousand would be a piece of cake. When you considered that many of the adherents of the Church were immigrants and of lower social status, it would be easy to arouse them and turn them against the government.

Yes, Foster concluded. The pope was dangerous. He would have to be reined in, subdued. Foster knew the adage about keeping one's enemies close. He rang his secretary and asked her to set up a meeting with General Cheeks and the Security Council for the morning. She asked what the subject was. He came up with a code name. He thought of *Quiet Suppression,* but that could become controversial if ever leaked or declassified. As he watched the video of Sixtus giving communion wafers to the faithful, a different name came to mind: *Sleepwalker.*

Chapter 53

On Monday morning, Bensaïd called to congratulate Sixtus on his speech. Media coverage was non-stop, causing all the commentators in the U.S. and Europe to ask, *Are we responsible for the decline in other countries?*

Much of the polemic was inconclusive. But the talk continued. If one thing was certain, Sixtus was a pot stirrer.

"I don't know why I had to give that speech," Sixtus said. "Shouldn't I be lying low? I just put a target on my back."

"You've got your name in the news; that's the important part. People need to start looking at you like a world leader. Besides, this news cycle will be over in a few days, and the media will move onto something else. Everyone will forget what you said."

"I'm not so sure about that," Sixtus answered. In front of him, a TV cable news program had American bishops and university economists fiercely debating the issue. The news commentator took a stance, saying, "Doesn't the pope have a point?"

* * *

On Monday afternoon, President Foster met with his National Security Council in the Situation Room. "I called this meeting to discuss a potential threat to our government," Foster said. "I assume you all have read or heard the pope's comments about Western civilization."

Many in the room nodded. General Cheeks looked puzzled.

"We need to learn more about what's driving Sixtus, and how he ended up with the viewpoints that he has. We'll call this *Operation Sleepwalker.*"

"Isn't it a bit premature to launch an operation?" General Cheeks asked.

"When the spiritual leader of one and a half billion Catholics around the world calls out the U.S. and Western Europe for actively and passively suppressing the rest of the world, I think we, or at least I, have an obligation to stop the spread of such dangerous propaganda."

"Was he just calling on us to do more to lift other nations up?" Cheeks said.

"If you want a productive dialogue, you pick up the phone," Foster answered.

Cheeks realized that Foster and Sixtus were now in a bit of a pissing match. "I just met with him. He didn't say anything at all like this."

"That's what concerns me. He says one thing to your face, and then he goes public with inane accusations. What is he saying behind our back?"

"He sent you that nice gift." There was a hint of a question in Cheeks's voice.

"Yes, it was very thoughtful. But who put him up to it? Who put him up to making statements like he did yesterday? He can't be acting of his own accord! Is he some sort of puppet? Is some committee pulling the strings? His actions don't correlate with his words. He should know better!"

"He was plucked out of nowhere," the secretary of defense said.

"Precisely," Foster said. "Or maybe not. You don't just wake up one day and become pope. There's a trajectory. And I believe his rise runs afoul to everything we stand for. Are we all in agreement on that?"

Secretary of Defense Orozco nodded in agreement as did many others on the Council. Cheeks looked around the room, capturing all the reactions. It was clear that he was one of the odd men out.

"This is why we need a deep dive into his background, a thorough investigation of what he really thinks about the United States."

"The CIA has already done an exhaustive personality assessment," Cheeks offered.

"I don't care about his personality. I care about his politics!" Foster challenged.

"We have that information in the report. He cares about the downtrodden. He's no different from the popes we've had for the past fifty years."

"But he's an American!" Foster interjected. "There's a difference."

"He's barely lived or visited the U.S. since graduate school," the secretary of state noted.

"Exactly!" chimed Foster. "What kind of American barely visits his home country?"

"He has no family here," Cheeks said.

"And possibly no real ties to us or our way of life anymore either," Foster said.

"This has all become a bit overheated. It will pass in a few days."

"I'm sure the news cycle will chew and spit it out soon enough. But if these are his real feelings, or the views of the people propping him up, I can't let it go. I don't understand why you're so reluctant about this, general. I'm not asking for him to be assassinated."

"No, of course not," Cheeks said.

"Then by the end of the week, I'll have a comprehensive report, no?"

No answer came. The president's statement was understood to be an order, not a question.

* * *

Amanda and Jordan flew from Prague to London on a commercial plane. While flying coach was customary for all but the highest-ranking

CIA and FBI officers or when a particular cover required business or first class, the cozy seating felt downright comfortable. After driving in Zhyuli's cramped compact car for endless hours and being transported in booming military aircraft and helicopters where legroom was offered at the expense of unremitting, ear-splitting engine and propeller rumbling, the commercial flight felt luxurious. They had checked into a hotel in Shadwell, in London's East End. While not posh, the neighborhood was trendy with an up-and-coming air. Amanda chose it because she needed a relatively cheap, by London standards, place to rent that provided easy access to public transportation. She also knew that American and British intelligence would consider it out-of-the-way and that it wouldn't be on their radar. She had only booked a room for a couple of nights, using her personal credit card. She wasn't even sure they would stay that long. The suite wasn't inexpensive, and Amanda was getting close to her credit limit. Again, she took a cash advance on her credit card, and while she knew this could be tracked by the Agency and MI6, her exact location wouldn't be known. Their first order of business was to get new burner phones, and that proved eminently doable; Jordan had also taken a cash advance on his credit card.

Since Amanda had been out of touch with headquarters for a few days now, she knew that she'd need to send a message to let them know everything was okay. She felt she could trust her direct supervisor, Veronica. She had reported to Veronica since she joined the CIA seven years ago. While they didn't work directly on operations together, Veronica was aware of all her activities. She was more of a mentor or career advisor than anything else. In the early years, Amanda could go to her to figure out protocol or to navigate a difficult situation. For the last few years, they spoke rarely, only when necessary. When Amanda would send her a message today, she would likely be surprised, unless Langley had already sent the equivalent of an all-points bulletin to track her down.

She logged into her VPN service and composed the email, which she sent from an encrypted, CIA messaging service:

"Hi V." Amanda always referred to Veronica as *V*. "I'm still in

Europe and things have gone haywire with Double Bogey," she wrote, referring to the code name for her operation. "I'm in deep cover with Jordan Harrison from the FBI. We've uncovered a serious threat to national security, and we believe someone in the highest echelons of U.S. intelligence is assisting. For that reason, we no longer have our government-issued phones or access to our usual tools." Amanda knew that V would understand this as a reference to Rebar. "We believe a world leader with the help of an international terror network is planning on detonating an atomic bomb in Washington, D.C., to overthrow the U.S. government. I can't give you more specifics at this point. We have to stop the ship from reaching U.S. shores. Do not go to the NSC." By referring to the National Security Council, Amanda thought this would give V an indication of who may be assisting with the plot.

She signed the note *AOB,* for *Amanda O'Brien.* Veronica would recognize this as the way Amanda typically signed off on communications. Amanda also knew that the *V* and *AOB* would give Veronica comfort that Amanda wasn't writing under any duress.

Jordan, who had the news on in the other room in the suite, had also logged into the VPN and was sending a message to Larry, his supervisor at the FBI. He was equally cryptic:

"We believe someone at the highest level of our government is working with the terrorists to deploy a dirty bomb in Washington, D.C. Do not go to the NSC or it will jeopardize our mission to stop them from detonating it."

When he saw Amanda standing in the doorway to the room, she looked less assured than he had ever seen. "What now?" he asked.

Chapter 54

When Larry received the message from Jordan, he was shocked. He sat before his computer for several minutes, reading and rereading the message. "*Do not go to the NSC.*" The words reverberated through him repeatedly as he reread the warning.

"*Do not go to the NSC.*"

What was he thinking? This had to be some sort of joke. He couldn't afford to have one of his men stranded God-knows-where in Europe on a mission that was bound to fail. Jordan needed backup. He was a junior agent, for Chrissakes! He needed expert advice and guidance. He couldn't possibly understand what was happening or why.

He should have known better than to send an unseasoned officer on a joint mission with the CIA. He was doomed from the beginning. Now, Larry had to extricate him from the situation. Larry was always the one doing the rescuing, taking care of those who couldn't take care of themselves. Of course, he couldn't do it *himself*. He needed to call in the big guns. The NSC would know what to do. They could coordinate activities over all branches – the CIA, FBI, NSA, DIA, you name it. *They* would make sure Larry came home safely. And he would never – even when the DNI insisted as they did in this case – send a fresh recruit to do a more experienced agent's mission again.

So, he did what any rational FBI supervisor would do. He went to the National Security Council.

* * *

In less than three days, *Das Kapital* would reach the shores of the United States. Yuri was pleased: Fuel capacity was still high, and there was no need for refueling.

His million-dollar payday would set him up well for retirement. Never again would he have to be a bootlegger for arms terrorists. No matter what they offered him, he could say no. He would shack up in a place in the Caribbean, live out the rest of his days in the U.S. Virgin Islands like Robert Oppenheimer, the father of the atomic bomb, or in Bermuda, where Michael Douglas and Catherine Zeta-Jones were known to hang their hat. Easy Street was just beyond the horizon.

* * *

Amanda and Jordan spent the night and the next morning sleeping off their jet lag after having traveled non-stop for the past few days. Their bodies couldn't take the perpetual onslaught. They would awaken, look at their phones or the alarm clock to see what time it was, find it unbelievable, at times comforting, but regardless, their reaction was always the same. Sleep. More sleep was required. And more sleep they got.

Practically, twenty more hours of sleep. At 7 p.m., the day after their arrival, Amanda awoke. She and Jordan hadn't left the hotel room since they had arrived. She sauntered in the living area of the suite, finding Jordan sleeping. He too, as if on some shared biorhythmic schedule, awoke near the same hour.

Amanda sensed that it was time to go. Where exactly, she didn't know. But she knew they needed to find out where the boat was that was carrying the bomb headed toward the United States. *The Grindon* could still be tracked.

She saw that Jordan was awaking. "We need to make a call."

"Who to?"

"No, not who. Where," she said, correcting him. "We can't call from here. They'll be able to track it. But if we go somewhere in town, we'll be safe."

"Are we checking out tomorrow?"

"Depends on what we learn in the call. You want to come with me or shall I go alone?"

"I'll go with you," he said. "We're a team."

"Yes, we are," she said.

* * *

It was 8 p.m. when Amanda and Jordan arrived at Piccadilly Circus. The area was very much the Times Square of London, with busloads of tourists, neon lights, and various entertainment outlets and restaurants catering to voracious hordes. Amanda chose a Middle Eastern joint that served typical export cuisine, such as shawarmas, kebabs, and falafel. Jordan had no objection as he too liked Middle Eastern food. Mostly Arab men, young and old, congregated in the spot, which had a window overlooking the side street to the main circle. They ordered and sat down at a booth away from the windows, taking ginormous sodas with them, the kind you typically found in the United States. The entire restaurant was decorated in white and chrome; perhaps in an earlier incarnation, it had been home to an American-style fifties diner. The raucous men around them were chattering non-stop; the setting was perfect. On her burner phone, Amanda dialed her supervisor. It would be 3 p.m. back in Washington.

Veronica didn't pick up.

Amanda dialed again.

Again, no answer.

She called a third time. This time, Veronica answered with a meek

"Hello."

"V, it's me, Amanda."

"I thought so," she said. "Glad you remembered our little game."

"Yes, of course. I need your help on something." Amanda had to be careful that someone might be monitoring V's cell phone.

"What's going on? I have leadership crawling up my butt trying to get answers on you."

"Tell them you haven't heard from me."

"I will. What's going on?"

"I need to track a ship called *The Grindon*. It left Algeciras a few days ago. It got rubber-stamped. It's carrying a dirty bomb destined for the United States."

"You're shitting me?" Veronica was always so colorful with her choice of language.

"I'm afraid not. It will arrive any day now."

Amanda and Jordan's food arrived on plastic trays, in Styrofoam, to-go boxes. Jordan, so ravenous, set out to eat his. Amanda left hers untouched.

"When you make the inquiry," Amanda said, "can you do it under my name?"

"You know I can't do that," she said, scoldingly.

"I know," Amanda laughed. She took this as a cue that V would indeed perform the search using Amanda's ID and password, which she had once shared with her. "This is probably the tenth time I've asked." The *ten* that Amanda referred to was a clue to her latest password, which she incremented each time a reset was required. V would understand that her current password would now end in *10*.

"And this is the tenth time I'm going to say, *go fly a kite*."

Amanda chuckled. "Just be prepared for some questions because somebody is going to ask why I'm looking that up."

"Any idea who that might be?"

"I don't want to get cheeky with you," she said. "I don't."

Veronica understood the reference to General Cheeks. "Got it."

"How long will it take?" Amanda asked.

"I need at least an hour," Veronica said.

Amand hung up and said to Jordan, "We gotta go."

"You think they're tracking her calls?"

"We can't take the chance." She grabbed her to-go box and Brobdingnagian drink and started toward the door.

They took a cab to Camden Town, a trendy neighborhood to the north where Amanda was certain a pub would be open to receive them. They had a beer. "I really want to eat my shawarma," Jordan said.

"We can reheat them back at the hotel. Let's get some food here."

They ordered typical pub grub – fish and chips and a shepherd's pie. The food was meh. The waitress asked if they wanted dessert. They passed. They ordered another round instead. Amanda called V back. "Did you find anything on *The Grindon*?"

"As a matter of fact, it turns out it's been sitting in the Canary Islands for several days now. Reported mechanical failure."

This was not good news. Amanda knew that highly sensitive nuclear material wouldn't just be left sitting in port. *The Grindon* had to have met some other vessel for an exchange of cargo, to create a more clandestine delivery. But with whom? Where? This operation was obviously elaborately planned. The terrorists hadn't left any detail to chance; they knew that *The Grindon* might be compromised at some point, and they decided to hedge their bets. What could she do now?

"You know, they've already asked about you," Veronica said.

"Since we talked an hour ago?"

"I had a call from the DNI. Of course, I told them I don't know anything that's going on."

"Could they be monitoring your phone?"

"If they were, I would know about it."

"How?" Amanda asked.

"One day, I'll tell you. But we're safe so far. They've got to be tracking my outgoing calls, though."

"We better get moving," she said to Jordan.

"You know you can only hide for so long," Veronica said on the phone.

"I don't plan on hiding that long. I'll talk to you soon." Amanda hung up. "Come on, let's go," she said to Jordan, who had barely touched his new pint. She left some money on the table to cover their food and tip and hustled out the door with her takeaway from the Middle Eastern restaurant. As they exited the pub, she placed her cell phone on the window ledge where the menu was showcased. Let them find it, she thought.

"Do you think they know where we are?" Jordan asked.

"They will soon enough," she said. "And with all the cameras in this city, it's not going to be easy to hide. We're going to have to get out of London soon."

Chapter 55

Back at their Shadwell hotel, Jordan downed his shawarma.

"We have to find the boat," Amanda said.

"But how?"

"I don't know. But if *The Grindon* was in the Canary Islands, it had to have met some other boat nearby. "Zahir has to have yachts at his disposal."

"Would he use one of his own? Or would he hire one out?"

"I don't know," Amanda said. "Your guess is as good as mine."

"Do you think Richter would know?"

"Let's call him," she said. "We should check in on him anyway."

* * *

"Hello?" Richter's voice answered weakly.

"It's Amanda," she said, using Jordan's burner phone. "How is everything?"

"Okay," he said. "I really want to get my old life back."

She realized that might be a hard, if not impossible, goal. "Hang tight. Listen, are you aware of any other ships that Bensaïd or Zahir might have access to?"

"Zahir has a superyacht. Sixtus was on it before he got elected."

"What's it called?"

"*The Lady Slipper*, I think."

"How big is it?"

"A monstrosity, of course. He cruises the Mediterranean with it any chance he gets. A couple of months ago, Bensaïd was on the Amalfi Coast and asked Sixtus to join him. He couldn't, though."

"Any others of note?"

"Nothing I can think of. Why? What's this about?"

"We're just watching all angles."

"Don't tell me you've lost track of the ship!"

"No, we know exactly where it is," Amanda replied. "We'll check back in a couple of days."

Richter started to mutter something, but Amanda hung up. She knew he was lonely and needed someone to talk to.

Amanda continued to pack her things; Jordan followed suit. She had told him they needed to leave the hotel suite. It was just a matter of time before the NSA, if Cheeks were directing them, would be able to patch into all the cameras within London and piece together their relative location. She couldn't take the chance that they'd be apprehended. She had to stop the shipment.

But *The Lady Slipper*? She'd need V's help once again.

* * *

This time, they took a cab to the fashionable Chelsea district of London. An assortment of restaurants and cafés were still open. They chose a crêperie that was off the beaten path. They loaded up on sugar – whipping cream, raspberries, blueberries, and delectable hot chocolate to wash everything down. Amanda placed the call to V –

"Can you help us track a yacht owned by Khalid Zahir? It's called *The Lady Slipper*."

"Are you on the move?" Veronica asked.

"Yes."

"Good. Give me a half hour."

* * *

As they were halfway towards Chinatown, in Soho, Amanda called V from the cab as it snaked through London traffic.

"Sorry, *The Lady Slipper* is sitting in the Côte d'Azur," Veronica said, referring to the French Riviera. "It's been docked there for over two weeks."

"And there's no way it's being spoofed?"

"You know we have backdoors into that sort of thing. They would have to take the ship apart, chop it up, and practically reassemble it for it to drop off our radar. And if we caught someone doing that, we'd send Interpol after them and make their life hell."

"Gotcha," replied Amanda.

"Why don't you come back to Washington? We'll figure out a plan here?"

Was she trying to reel her in? Had Cheeks gotten to her? Now, Amanda was beginning to question the veracity of the information V had provided. Was she lying about the location of *The Grindon* and *The Lady Slipper*? No, V wouldn't do that to her. She would only want to help. She had to be thinking they could act more covertly in person. But there was too much risk. Cheeks had too much power, and even an experienced senior officer like Veronica wouldn't be able to contravene his authority. "Let me try to work things out here," Amanda said. "I'll touch base if we don't get anywhere."

"Be careful," Veronica warned.

Chapter 56

As they approached Chinatown, Amanda took the SIM card out of Jordan's phone. It was getting late, and they had no need to call anyone else. She needed to think, to plan. Tomorrow, they'd get a new SIM card. She felt safe enough spending the night in Chinatown. They'd check into a cheap hotel. There were plenty of other tourists around. They wouldn't stick out.

While she knew her plan wasn't foolproof, she felt she was practicing her tradecraft.

* * *

General Cheeks stood by the Theodore Roosevelt Desk beside President Foster in the Oval Office. The president read the preliminary report that Cheeks had brought for him. "This isn't the report I asked for," said the president. "It's the same rehashing I've seen before."

"Yes, sir. The report isn't new. I didn't know if you had seen it."

"I have. And it doesn't tell me what I want to know. I want all the analysis we've got on Sixtus's political motivations. His ambitions. His worldview, politically speaking. No American becomes pope unless he has an ace or two up his sleeve. I want to know what those are."

"Very good, sir. The end of the week we'll have it." Cheeks meekly showed himself out of the president's office.

Foster watched him leave, aware that this wasn't the first time that Cheeks's work product was off the mark. Foster couldn't consider his efforts to be substandard. But he wondered if the misdirection was intentional. He told himself no. This was another example of the shortfalls of bureaucracy and government deficiency.

* * *

Sixtus's *Warning to the West* continued to make headlines throughout the world. Sixtus watched cable news in multiple languages – English, Spanish, and Italian – to hear firsthand what commentators were saying. Overall, the message was positive. The West deserved to be scolded. Sixtus was demonstrating leadership. The U.S., European, and Canadian governments would be well advised to create closer partnerships in the developing world. A few commentators criticized Sixtus's delivery. He could have been kinder. He could have advocated for 'being a good neighbor,' rather than admonishing the West for being exploitative. "He's never been known for his soft touch," one commentator said.

What does she know? Sixtus thought. She's never even met me.

But Sixtus knew that all this was a distraction. The real business at hand had to do with the explosive change that was about to occur in the United States. His nerves were taking hold. He couldn't wait, after all these years, all these dreams, all his machinations and imaginations, to see his destiny be realized. Besides the media, the other distraction in the Vatican was the arrival of three hundred children for summer camp. The children ranged in age from six to twelve. The perfect age, he had learned as a young priest. As he was being initiated, the priest at his parish told him a secret about the Catholic religion. He told him it was the holiest of secrets. The holy of holies. He told Sixtus that while other religions and faiths, such as Freemasonry, coveted youth and saw the very young as a path to immortality – you could drink their blood; you could vampirize them – the secret of the highest of highs within the Catholic Church taught a different approach. The priest said that it wasn't necessary to sacrifice children, to kill them, to touch them, to abuse them. No, that was evil. All that Sixtus needed to do was to put mental images in his mind – a movie of sorts – of him tapping into their energy and draining them of it. The images – the dream – would be enough to sustain him. In time, the children would replenish what had been taken.

Sixtus didn't know what to think. He had never heard of such a thing before. But he followed the priest's advice. He didn't notice any change. He was tempted to stop. Then one day, he got severely ill with pneumonia. There was a risk that he might not make it. In his withered state, Nicholas Cassella – the pope-to-be – mustered all his might. He imagined the young children who attended church. Then more specifically, he thought of one of the altar boys. He focused all his energy on him. He became one with the boy. The next morning, when he awoke, the illness had cleared. It was as if he was never sick in the first place.

He didn't see the altar boy in church for a couple of weeks. Soon, he received word from the priest that the boy was deathly ill. He had suffered kidney failure. His family was stunned. They had no inkling he had any such malady. In a matter of weeks, the boy was dead. He was buried in the churchyard.

Now that three hundred children filed through the Vatican, filling the halls with their spirited laughter, their playful connections with one another, their exuberant chatter, Sixtus had the necessary infusion he had hungered for. He gave a speech before them in the Paul VI Hall. How silent they were. How they hardly let their eyes drift off him. How they were mesmerized. They looked at him as an apostle of God. As a magical figure. Sixtus could feel their energy. And as he spoke, he inhaled the air from the room. He created images in his mind of these children. He sucked everything from them. Suck. Suck. Suck. They would never know what they were losing. He imprinted several of them in his memory, so that he could recall the color of their hair, the shape of their heads and arms and hands and legs and eyes and noses. He drew concrete pictures of several of the boys who sat nearest him. While they remained seated, he could feel them drift closer to him. They were moving toward him, like a magnetic pulse. They were all becoming one. As he continued to speak to them, he could hear his own words reverberate in his mind as he held the boys close to him in a circle. They boys hovered about his head like angels. Yes, they were angels. Soon they would fall.

* * *

In the early morning, Jordan was startled awake by sounds he heard in the hallway. He was a light sleeper, and the walls and doors in this hotel were paper thin. He listened to the thudding at the door. It sounded as if someone was trying to open the door! He grabbed his gun off the bedstand, got up, and went to the bed where Amanda was sleeping. They had separated the two twin beds before they went to sleep. He woke her, shushing her before she could make a sound.

She too could tell someone was at the front door. If they're CIA or MI6, she thought, why don't they use the plastic key card to unlock the door?

They had no time to gather their things, and no way to take them. There was a window that faced the back of the alley. They hurried to it, opening it. As Amanda first crawled through it, onto the ledge that was no wider than a Juliet balcony, she heard the door electronically unlock. Yes, they had the special card that gave them access to any hotel room in the world! The chain on the door kept the door closed. But suddenly, whoever was on the other side barreled against the door and pushed it open, tossing it off its hinges and pulling the chain from the wall. While they did this, Jordan hustled out the window onto the ledge. They both jumped onto a fire escape attached to the corner of the building. As they made their way down, Jordan looked back up at the hotel room and saw someone crawling out the window. He shot at them. They jumped back into the room. The maneuver was enough to hold them off for a minute while he and Amanda made their way to the bottom of the fire escape.

But they knew it would only be a matter of minutes before they caught up to them. What if one of them was waiting for them below? Sure enough, a gun shot them, ricocheted toward them off the iron railing of the fire escape. Jordan fired back. He and Amanda dashed down the street. The street was desolate. They wouldn't be able to hail a cab – there were none around at this hour. All they could do was run. Run. Run. Run. Like their lives depended on their escaping.

They made their way down one street onto another. They turned onto one that was more residential. Jordan was right behind Amanda. "How did they find us?" he asked.

"Probably through the cameras and facial recognition. They followed us through the streets. There are cameras all over London, you know. And they have our pictures in government databases."

She saw that a light was on in one of the basement apartments that they approached. She rushed down the stairs. Jordan stopped at the top of the stairs, watching behind them to see if anyone was on their trail.

A woman opened the door to Amanda. She was elderly and Chinese.

"Please, we need help," Amanda said.

The woman wanted to close the door, but Amanda put her foot against it. She hadn't wanted to pull out her gun, but she had to. She pointed it at the woman's face. The woman was stunned into silence. Amanda motioned for Jordan to come down and join her.

Amanda turned the lights off in the apartment so that it was dark like all the neighbors. Jordan quietly locked the door. The morning sunlight lit up the apartment sufficiently so that it was easy to observe the interior.

Amanda held her pistol out toward the woman. "We won't hurt you. We just need to hide for a bit."

"Please, take my money," the woman said. She started to go toward her stovetop where she was cooking something. The kitchen and living areas were all open to one another in one relatively small room.

"No!" Amanda said sternly. "Stay there!" She couldn't take the risk that the woman was going to grab the pot of boiling water or broth or whatever it was that she was cooking and throw it at them. People would do anything when cornered like a wild animal. "We don't want your money. We just need to hide. Calm down. Don't be afraid. Sit down over there."

The woman obeyed, taking a seat on the tattered, flower-patterned, upholstered sofa that looked to be half the woman's age. Amanda turned off the burner where the woman was cooking. It was a broth. Amanda didn't want the light from the stove to light up the apartment from the street. On the end table, she noticed a framed picture of an elderly Asian man. "Is that your husband?"

"Yes."

"He passed on?" Amanda asked, partly out of sympathy, partly because she wanted to know if he was in another room of the apartment.

"He is in hospice," the woman answered.

"I'm sorry," Amanda said. "We won't hurt you. Are you cooking him something?"

"Yes. His lunch. Egg drop soup. His favorite. But he might not remember. He has Alzheimer's." The woman's English, though accented, was good.

The woman reached over to the end table where the picture stood, startling Amanda, who retreated. The woman opened a drawer on the end table. Was she going to pull out a weapon? Fortunately, people weren't well armed in England. At most, she would have a knife, and unless she was some sort of martial arts expert, Amanda or Jordan could easily subdue her.

"Look," the woman said.

In the drawer were stacks and stacks of bills, all euros. There could have been ten or twenty thousand euros.

"Take it," the woman said. "Please."

"We don't want your money," Amanda said. "We won't harm you."

"It's yours," the woman said, giving her an entreating look.

* * *

General Cheeks was speaking into a burner phone that he used to communicate with Bensaïd. "I won't be able to hold off inquiries much longer."

"The shipment is due to arrive in two days," Bensaïd said.

"And the detonation is still planned for Friday?"

"Yes. That's when the leaders of all the South American countries will converge in D.C."

"There's been no change in venue?" Cheeks was referring to the Pan American Union Building which served as headquarters to the Organization of American States. The building was notable as the site where President Jimmy Carter signed the treaty granting Panama control over the Panama Canal.

"No. We want the president, Speaker of the House, Secretaries of State and Defense to be there."

"You know the vice president won't be in attendance."

"She'll be easy enough to take care of later."

"She'll try to usurp authority."

"You can handle her, no?"

"I suppose I can."

"We've gone over this," Bensaïd said. "People will be in such a state of shock they'll believe anything. Let her assume she'll take power. All you need is a couple of days and Sixtus will be there. He'll take things from there."

"Some people won't want to accept leadership from a religious figure."

"They will if they see this as an attack on Christianity, which it is. The American people will want order and stability after half their government is wiped out. That's what Sixtus will give them."

"But he just gave that speech that was so critical of us."

"Not to worry. He'll play up the virtues of the United States. He can pivot like the wind."

"If there's resistance?" Cheeks asked.

"There *will* be resistance. It will be your job to contain it. One of the first acts has to be a declaration of martial law. The vice president must issue this proclamation immediately. Once she does, get the military firmly under your control. Sideline her. Then we'll be able to set up Sixtus's interim government."

"Interim?" Cheeks asked.

"That's what we'll tell the public. Of course, we won't have any plans to vacate until Washington is firmly in our control. If there's open rebellion, we'll turn America's nukes on the people."

"You said that will be a last resort."

"It is!" proclaimed Bensaïd. "But it doesn't mean we shouldn't plan for it. Listen, I understand how you're getting cold feet now that we're close to achieving our aims. But you have to let things take their course now. There's nothing – or no one – that can get in the way of the plan."

"I'm concerned about those two intelligence officers," Cheeks said.

"One is a brand-new FBI agent on his first mission abroad. The other is a junior case officer who has been essentially cut off from the home office. There's not much two people can do."

Chapter 57

Amanda and Jordan stayed in the Chinese woman's apartment for an hour. The sun had risen completely, and now the light inside was perfectly normal. No one could see through the windows because all the curtains were closed. At one point, Amanda addressed her host as 'Mrs. Wu'.

The woman said sharply, "How do you know my name?"

Amanda explained, truthfully, that she had seen a piece of mail with her name on it. The woman was satisfied.

While they sat in silence, a knock tapped at the door. Mrs. Wu did not rise; she looked nervous as she sat beside Amanda on the sofa.

Amanda took out her pistol, as did Jordan. Mrs. Wu became more nervous. Suddenly, someone was putting a key in the door and unlocking it. A middle-aged Chinese woman entered. "Mom? What's going on? Who are these people?"

Realizing that the person at the door was Mrs. Wu's daughter, Amanda kept her gun behind her back to conceal it. Jordan did the same. "We're social workers checking on your mother's health," Amanda said.

The daughter looked confused. "You're not her normal social worker."

"No," Amanda said.

"Why are there two of you?"

"He's in training," Amanda replied nonchalantly. "Please, come join us."

The daughter closed the door. At that cue, Jordan motioned for the daughter to sit on a chair by the sofa. He, in turn, secured the door. As he latched the door, the daughter looked up in concern. She stood.

"Please sit," Amanda said.

"Listen to them," her mother advised.

Amanda brandished her pistol. Mrs. Wu's daughter looked up, terrified. She turned toward Jordan. He was holding a gun aimed at her as well. She raised her voice: "Mom, tell me what is really going on!"

"There is no reason to be concerned," Amanda said. "We're with the FBI and we're conducting a criminal investigation."

"Of my mother?" the daughter asked.

"No, nothing to do with your mother. We sought refuge here. We were being chased by the criminals. We just need to hide out for a while, and we'll be on our way. We won't hurt you."

"I should call the police," the daughter said, pulling out her cell phone.

Jordan immediately grabbed it from her. "No."

The daughter started crying. Then, without hesitating, she screamed at the top of her lungs. Jordan put his hands in her mouth. She started biting him. He yelped. He jammed his hands further against her mouth to prevent her from making any more noise. Amanda went to the stove where she grabbed a kitchen towel hanging off the handle. She stuffed it in the daughter's mouth as she rasped, reaching her hands out to stop Amanda. Amanda was undeterred.

"Please don't hurt her," Mrs. Wu said.

"We won't. We just need you to be quiet," Amanda said.

The mother had tears in her eyes, too.

"Please, just be calm. We'll be gone soon enough."

"Take our money," Mrs. Wu said, pointing to the end table drawer that was still open.

Amanda looked at the pile of bills. The cash could come in handy. She went back to the kitchen and took out a notepad and pen from a drawer. "Please, write your name and address on this piece of paper." As she handed Mrs. Wu the pen and paper, she went to the end table drawer and started counting out bills. "We will only take five thousand euros. We will pay you back."

Mrs. Wu's daughter's eyes bulged as she saw Amanda pull out a stack of money. She didn't want her to take it.

Amanda reiterated, "We will pay you back. We are only taking this temporarily."

"Keep it," Mrs. Wu said. "Please, leave us alone."

* * *

Amanda had asked the daughter, whom she learned was named Nancy, if she had a car, and Nancy responded, somewhat hesitantly, that she did not. Mrs. Wu looked at her urgently, as if to say, "Tell the truth." Amanda picked up on the interaction and asked the daughter to empty her pockets. Of course, there was a key fob with a Toyota emblem.

"You shouldn't lie to me," Amanda told her. "We'll be getting off on the wrong foot."

"We already have," Nancy replied drily.

Amanda took Nancy's cell phone from her. "I'll need your cell phone, too," she said to Mrs. Wu.

"It's on the counter, over there," Mrs. Wu, her hand shaking, pointed to the edge of the kitchen countertop.

Amanda went to retrieve it. She tossed the Toyota key fob to Jordan. "Why don't you drive?"

After spending an hour and a half in Mrs. Wu's apartment, Amanda deemed it safe to leave. The people tracking them had likely already left the area or were scanning it. Before they left, Amanda took a scarf from the elderly woman's closet and wrapped it around her hair. Jordan took a Manchester United cap from Mr. Wu's side of the closet. He also put on a hoodie that he found there. Anything to help change their appearance. When Mrs. Wu saw him, she winced. She must have been reminded of her husband wearing the same clothes.

Nancy's car was parked down the street. Amanda and Jordan cautiously scanned the block to make sure the men following them were nowhere in sight. The car lights flashed as Jordan unlocked the car.

Jordan got in the car while Amanda opened the front passenger door for Mrs. Wu to step in. Nancy hesitated behind them, near the passenger rear panel. Her mother shot her a look. Amanda thought it was funny how much communicating they could do with each other silently. She interpreted the look as telling her daughter that she must obey and get in the car. Nancy seemed to resist.

"Leave us here," Nancy said to Amanda. "Take my car. I won't call the police."

"You have to come with us," Amanda said.

"Please," Nancy said.

"Come," Mrs. Wu said from the passenger seat.

"We need you to come with us."

"You have our phones, our car, our money! Why do you need us?" Nancy yelled.

"Please, be calm," Amanda said, observing a couple who strode on the opposite side of the street. "We need you to come with us for a little while. I told you we're in a lot of danger and we can't risk any loose ends."

The couple walking their dog on the street stopped and seemed to be watching them while their dog sniffed a trash receptacle.

"We're people, not loose ends," Nancy said. Nonetheless, she opened the passenger door and got in.

"On the other side," Amanda said, pointing to the driver's side of the car. She wanted her to sit behind Jordan. This way, they'd have coverage from both sides if Nancy tried to interfere with his driving.

As Jordan pulled away, the couple on the other side of the street watched them depart down the street.

* * *

Amanda took Mrs. Wu's cell phone and downloaded a commercial messaging app. She entered V's number and sent her a message. All communications were encrypted; their texts and calls then couldn't be tracked as long as they were done on the app. Amanda asked her to call her back on the app.

"Where are you?" Veronica asked.

"In London still. But we got tracked."

"I was afraid that would happen. They're monitoring my calls. I'm glad you contacted me this way."

"I need you to do a couple of things," Amanda said. "I'm going to send you some videos and pictures of our friend. Russian intelligence was tracking him a few years ago. I need to know who he's meeting with. Can you see if we have any matches for anyone else who's photographed?"

"Okay," Veronica said.

"I'll upload them to a secure site for you. The other thing I need is a plane. A private plane. I need to get to the Canary Islands. I'm sure we're flagged, so I don't think we can fly commercial."

"That's not going to be easy," Veronica said. "Do you know how much that will cost?"

"A hundred grand? Is our country worth it?"

"I'll see what I can do," Veronica answered. "But the request is going to raise some eyebrows."

"Can you do it through one of our partners?" Amanda asked, referring to one of the hundreds of corporations that the Agency had close affiliations with.

"I can make some calls. But you need to be ready to go."

"We'll be standing by," Amanda replied, hanging up.

Nancy snapped at Amanda, setting Jordan on alert and causing his ears to perk up. "I have to go to the bathroom."

Chapter 58

Cardinal Richter had left his hotel room and was walking the cobblestone streets of Old Prague. He wandered aimlessly, looking into the shops, traipsing across one bridge and returning via another. His burner cell phone was in his pocket. He had used it a few times to call Amanda's burner in the U.K., but there was never an answer. He pulled it out once again, return-dialing her number.

Still, no answer.

He grumbled to himself. She didn't want me to leave the hotel room. *What did she expect? That I could stay in there for days on end without seeing anybody? It was worse than a monastery. There, at least fellow companions would be suffering in solitude.*

He had to get back to Rome. He had to alert the other cardinals of Sixtus's intentions. They would have to stop him, somehow. But whom could he turn to? Barranca would have been the logical choice. The rest were a bunch of sycophantic cowards. Even the few that had a chance to be pope wouldn't threaten the orthodoxy at this point. No, they'd need some serious cajoling and likely something to grease their palms to action.

It was now past 11 a.m. and all the vendors had set up their wares alongside the bridge. He had gotten his share of exercise, and it was time to turn back to the hotel where he could rest. Walk, rest, rest, walk – his body couldn't decide what it needed. But his mind knew – he had to get out of Prague. There was nothing here for him. No one, either. He looked over the bridge and saw a tall spire jutting amongst a bunch of buildings. Yes, he thought. There must be a Catholic Church nearby. He stopped to ask one of the vendors. The man spoke English and directed Richter back toward town.

Richter made his way, unaware that he was being followed.

* * *

Jordan stopped the car at a gas station on the outskirts of London. Amanda escorted Nancy to the restroom. They reached the grimy-looking door to the restroom on the side of the station. "Do you really have to follow me in?"

"I want to ensure your safety," Amanda said.

Nancy snickered.

Amanda tried to open the door, but it was locked. The handle had a combination-keypad on it.

"I'll go inside to get the combo. Can I trust you to stay here?"

"Where would I go?" Nancy scoffed.

"Your mother needs you here," Amanda said.

Nancy didn't respond. Amanda went inside. As she was speaking to the clerk at the counter, who gave her the combination, she heard a horn honking from outside. She looked at the car. Jordan was flashing the headlights and honking the horn. Amanda realized that something was amiss and ran back to the restroom, fearing that Nancy had taken flight. No doubt, Nancy was no longer standing outside the door. Amanda saw that she was running back down along the highway, trying to flag someone down with the sweatshirt that she had removed.

She looked like a complete lunatic.

No one stopped. Amanda raced after her, but Nancy noticed that Amanda was making chase. She ran further down the highway. A car pulled over. Nancy got into it. Within seconds, she was gone.

* * *

Richter found the Catholic Church that he was looking for. He got lost after asking for directions on the bridge but had managed to locate the church after searching for it on his cell phone. He entered the church, dutifully making the sign of the cross. A few people were sitting at the pews, some kneeling in prayer. He did the sign of the cross once again as he slipped into a row in the middle of the church and sat. He stared at the depiction of Christ on the cross behind the altar. The cross was adorned with gold; blood trickled from his nailed palms. Richter closed his eyes.

A man in a black coat sat in one of the rearmost rows behind Richter. He didn't bother to make any signs of the cross when he entered the nave or the pew. He watched Richter pray.

Richter asked for God's forgiveness for being greedy, for taking the bribe to vote for Sixtus – Nicholas – for pope. He asked for forgiveness for taking bribes in the two prior elections also. He told God that he had excused himself because he considered it 'par for the course,' but he realized that he had erred. He should have known that the amount proffered for the Sixtus vote was exorbitant; he shushed his mind as it wandered – he wasn't there to rehash the circumstances but to offer contrition.

He told God that he had always tried to be a faithful servant, but that he was imperfect. As he prayed silently, he realized that he had said the same things, hundreds if not thousands of times. As he said the words now, they rang hollow. There had to be something more, something deeper. He sensed that a sort of finality was creeping in on him. He was not the same man that he was years or even a few months ago. He had had an awakening. A reckoning, perhaps. And now he was alone with the sound of his voice. He listened silently for some sign, some indication that God had heard him and would pardon his indulgence. But no words came back for him. God was not speaking back. He quieted his mind for the next couple of minutes; still, no response.

He heard a sharp sound from behind him – a screeching sound as if someone was moving something across a floor. But he didn't open his eyes to see what had made the noise. Now, he was alone with God. He wouldn't let anything earthly interfere with this moment. He prayed waiting for word. Then he drifted off to sleep.

* * *

"What has she done? You have to go after her!" Nancy's mother said to Amanda as she got back in the car.

Amanda received a message back in the secure app. It was from V. "I have found a plane. Be at Heathrow at 3 p.m." As she read this, Veronica sent another message. "Look for the sign for Dalloway." Amanda knew that this was a reference to *Mrs. Dalloway,* the novel by Virginia Woolf and one of V's favorites. Amanda and Veronica had bonded over books. Amanda had never read the novel but had put it on her list. V had warned her: *Women who don't work end up like Mrs. Dalloway.*

"You can't let her leave!" Nancy's mother bellowed.

"It's too late," Amanda said. "We have to get to the airport."

"No!" Mrs. Wu howled in a fearful roar.

* * *

Richter awoke, startled from his nap. He looked up at the vaulted ceiling, where angels were suspended, their arms outstretched to one another. Through his restful slumber, he felt as if God had given him some answer. He looked at his watch – he didn't know how long he had slept. He had to have been there for at least a half an hour, if not longer.

He stood from the bench, unaware that the man who had been sitting in the rearmost row had moved to a pew a row behind him on the opposite side of the nave.

Chapter 59

"Please!" Nancy's mother pleaded, looking through the rear windshield for some sign of her daughter.

"Mrs. Wu, you'll catch up with her later. You must be patient." Amanda knew that Nancy would be slowed as she didn't have her cell phone.

"What have I done?"

"Nothing. Sometimes you end up somewhere and something happens to you. That's life."

"My husband will be worried," she said.

"You will see him soon. I promise. We won't hurt you. But we need to make sure we're safe. We're being pursued and that puts all of us in danger."

"So I might get killed too? Why would they want to hurt me?"

"Again, sorry to have gotten you mixed up in all this. I'm afraid we had no choice."

"You could have left me at home. My daughter too. We wouldn't..." She hesitated.

"You know Nancy would have called the police."

"Yes," Mrs. Wu answered. The skin on her face relaxed as she admitted the truth to herself. Nancy would not have allowed Amanda and Jordan to have intruded into her mother's apartment. She was too high-strung, too much of a warrior to let others trample on her rights.

They were nearing Heathrow. They were a couple of hours early. Amanda watched as Jordan looked at his watch. Amanda sent a message to V. "Is there any way we can get on the plane earlier?"

She got no response.

"Should we go in and park?" Jordan asked.

"It's probably best."

He took the exit off the highway leading to Heathrow.

* * *

Rested, and feeling more refreshed than he had in the past week, Richter made his way back to his hotel, following the guide on his cell phone app.

Unbeknownst to him, the shadowy figure in the black overcoat followed a block behind.

Just as Richter was about to enter the hotel entrance, he turned back, startling the man behind him who was now about a dozen yards away. The man looked down and pretended to look at the flowers growing in a pot outside a restaurant.

Richter barely noticed him, but he did, in fact, notice the man. Richter continued walking toward the man. He stepped beside him, not making eye contact, as he entered the restaurant. He asked for a table for one. He was tired of the food from room service. He needed something fresh. And the Czech fare here seemed to fit the bill.

* * *

As they parked the car in a lot near the private terminal, Amanda received a message back from Veronica: "Plane will be ready at 2 p.m." That still left an hour to kill. In the time Nancy had escaped, she would have had the opportunity to go to the police. They might be looking for

Mrs. Wu.

As they all exited Mrs. Wu's car, Amanda took a picture showing it parked in the space with the column number beside it. "This will help you tell the authorities where your car is. You have your wallet, right?"

"Yes," Mrs. Wu answered.

"Do you have enough money?"

"Yes," she answered dutifully.

"How much?"

"Twenty euros," she said.

Amanda took her wallet out and gave her back five hundred euros. "I don't want to take all your money. I need a favor. Can we leave you in a restaurant for a couple of hours while we board the plane? Then you can call your daughter. But not before. Will you do that for me?"

"I will."

Amanda trusted her. She knew that in the world of a spy, trust was more important than anything else – money, connections, power, weapons, secret gadgets. Trust would allow you to continue in your course of action. Without it, you were dead. "Thank you."

In the private terminal, they found a restaurant that catered to the business elite. Amanda could tell that Mrs. Wu felt out of place: She wasn't dressed for the occasion, having been roused unexpectedly from her apartment and only planning a visit to the hospice center with her husband. Amanda regretted having involved her and placing her life at risk. She looked around the restaurant – everybody looked suspicious. Globetrotters were out in full force from every European capital: Swiss, Germans, Russians, Ukrainians, Swedes, Danes, English, Americans, Chinese, Koreans, Japanese, Mexicans, Brazilians. It was a true melting pot: the worst of the worst gathered to spend their spoils as their hearts desired, doing no good in the world except pumping money through the consumer economies that kept the West afloat. You couldn't tell a business tycoon from a spy; that was the problem today. But the true spies, Amanda knew, were people like her: people who had come from modest means; led simple, god-fearing lives; tried to do good with their work; tried to provide a better life for their families. But these people –

these were the ones who all they had to do was wake up and check the multimillion- and multibillion-dollar investment portfolios that they had inherited. Life wasn't fair, she knew; but it didn't have to be so imbalanced. If she could only do one thing in this world, it would be to help correct this imbalance. Not take away anything from others, but to give others all over the world an equal opportunity to share in the spoils of capitalism. Helping others was once the province of religion, but now, increasingly, the burden fell to governments while religion turned the other cheek. Or it offered crumbs which it called faith. No, Amanda thought, something had to change. Unfortunately, with Sixtus at the helm, the Catholic Church would provide little relief. Who knows what he would do once he consolidated power. A true world government would take hold; Christians would meld with Muslims, and the world would be like Spain under Moorish rule. Art and culture could flourish. If it weren't for the wars between the Christians and Muslims, Spain would have been the consummate paradise. Is this what Sixtus and Zahir planned? Another bite of the apple? A *conquista* where there would be no resistance and, hence, no *reconquista*?

What if she let things run their course and didn't interfere? No, that wasn't an option. The people should decide, and not because of an attack or an explosion. They should decide by ballot box.

Their drinks came. Iced tea and lemonade. Jordan ordered a beer. An assortment of haddock, cod, Brussel sprouts, fried zucchini, and mozzarella sticks. Amanda felt guilty; she was paying for this unwanted meal with Mrs. Wu's hard-earned money. Mrs. Wu hardly touched the food. "Eat," Amanda said. "It will do you good." She nibbled. Amanda nibbled, too. Jordan, like most men, had a heartier appetite.

How could Amanda right the wrongs of the world? She knew she couldn't. She stuck her fork in a piece of haddock, chopping it this way and that – hashways. She wasn't keen on eating it, even though it looked perfectly edible. There had to be some other reason for this life, her existence. Stopping Sixtus and Zahir. Even with the fate of America at stake, this raison d'être didn't seem enough. Or was it her fate that they would slip through her hands? That she couldn't stop them? Oh, she thought. *Is that what is happening? Am I the one who can't stop the wheel from turning? From the fire taking root and spreading throughout the forest? Am I the one who is going to be buried under an avalanche of snow while trying to hike up the mountain? I am nothing and yet, I am all.*

"Hey, are you okay?" Jordan asked her.

Mrs. Wu stared at her.

"Yes," Amanda said.

"She is thinking," Mrs. Wu said. "About the fate of the world." She stared into Amanda's eyes. "It doesn't ride on your shoulders. It rides on all of us."

"I suppose," Amanda said.

"I lied to you before. I was going to call the police after you left. But I won't anymore. I will give you time to leave. I think we need you." She placed her hand on Amanda's hand, the one that wasn't holding the fork picking apart the fish. "I will do my part."

* * *

It was 8 a.m. in Washington, D.C. President Foster, who routinely woke at 5:30 a.m. no matter how late his night was and how many gin and tonics he had, was already settled in the Oval Office. He told his secretary to send a message to General Cheeks asking for the status of the report on Sixtus. He was growing impatient. As he took the framed letter gifted by Sixtus and tried to decipher the Latin script, he told himself this artifact had no place in the White House. The U.S. prided itself on the separation of church and state; Sixtus would have known this. Why was he parting with an object of such historical significance? Why was he unnecessarily obsequious? He had to have some ulterior motive. Did he want to create some special relationship between the U.S. and the Vatican, like the U.S. had with Great Britain? Possibly. But the letter was clearly an attempt to ingratiate himself with Foster. Beware of Greeks baring gifts, thought the president.

* * *

Jordan had purchased new SIM cards using the cash that Amanda had taken from Mrs. Wu. They couldn't risk MI5 or the CIA tracking them or having any access to their whereabouts or communications. Waiting in the terminal lounge, he swapped the cards into Mrs. Wu and Nancy's cell phones, placing the old SIM cards in his pocket. He would toss them away after they left London to prevent them from being found.

"I will reimburse you for the cell phones," Amanda said.

"Are you sure?" Mrs. Wu was suggesting that Amanda might not successfully complete her mission.

"I will send a note to the home office authorizing them. You don't have to worry."

Mrs. Wu emitted a hmm.

"Take a taxi to your husband," Amanda said, handing her some more cash. "Call Nancy from there." It was almost 2 p.m. They could now board the plane and wait a short while before takeoff.

"Will those people come after us?" Mrs. Wu asked.

"I'm afraid they could," Amanda said. "Whatever they ask, just tell them the truth. That we stole your money, your daughter's car, and took your cell phones. Tell them we swapped out the SIM cards. Tell them we ate at this restaurant and tell them that I gave you money for the cab and that I said I would reimburse you. Tell them the truth about everything. That way, they won't suspect you of being involved. Don't wait to get the cab. Get one right one we leave because they will know the time we took off. If you hesitate, they will suspect you. They will have us on camera throughout the airport. Tell them that we were nice and that you tried to be cooperative. That reminds me, I need to get you the picture of where we parked your car." She realized they couldn't send the picture via their new cell number or they could be tracked. "Jordan, we'll have to swap the SIMs back."

"No need," Mrs. Wu replied. "Column 8A in Lot 7."

Amanda looked at the photo stored on the phone. Column 8A was right. She showed the picture to Mrs. Wu. She figured she was right about the lot number also.

* * *

After his splendid meal, Cardinal Richter returned to his hotel room. He had spent much of the day outside. It was a welcome respite from what he considered his prison cell. He lay on his bed when his burner phone buzzed. He hoped it was Amanda. He answered, but no response came.

"Hello?"

Still, there was only silence on the other end.

"Hello?"

The number was blocked. "Is anyone there?" Perhaps there was a bad connection.

At that moment, the chime on the door sounded. He went to the door, still holding the phone, believing that Amanda was calling him. "Amanda?" he said into the phone.

Without thinking, he opened the door. The man in the black overcoat stood before him, pointing a gun as he pushed his way, forcing Richter back.

Chapter 60

Amanda and Jordan got onto the private jet without a hitch. Veronica had arranged use of the plane, promising to reimburse the corporate client for all expenses. The jet headed toward the Canary Islands, where it would arrive in four and a half hours, in the evening. Since Amanda had made the plans while the Wus were present, Jordan hadn't had a chance to find out what her plan was. "How are we going to find out what happened to the Queen of Spades shipment?" He sipped a beer that the flight attendant had served him.

"V said *The Grindon* was still there. Someone has to know what happened."

So, she was taking a stab in the dark. He was afraid that it might be the case. "What if they won't talk?"

"We won't give them a chance." As she said this, she typed a secure message into her phone, sending it to Giuseppe Falzone, who owned half of Queen of Spades. Her Sicilian friend had taken a liking to her. She hoped he would force his team to cooperate.

To her surprise, she instantly got a reply: "How is my beautiful spy doing?"

She chuckled. He was a real charmer. As she pecked away at the virtual keyboard on her smartphone, she turned to Jordan: "I'm texting Giuseppe Falzone. The Leopard."

Jordan nodded. "You think he'll help?"

"I'll do it the old Italian way. Grease his palms and make him an offer he can't refuse." She typed this message: "I need your help on what happened to *The Grindon's* shipping contents. They disappeared. I'm headed to the Canary Islands now and want to talk to the captain. Can you help?"

"That is going to cost you," he wrote back.

"What are you thinking?"

"I need Interpol off my back. They interfere with my business."

"You want carte blanche?"

"Yes."

"I'll see what I can do."

"For three years," he wrote.

She swallowed. He wasn't making this easy. The Leopard was a hard-nosed negotiator. He certainly understood her need for the information and was capitalizing on it. "Give me a couple of hours."

"Thank you, beautiful," he signed off.

She hated how men always seemed to reduce women to their looks. Besides, she knew she wasn't beautiful. But any woman, attractive or not, would succumb to such manipulation. She took a sip of her juice while speaking to Jordan. "He wants free rein for his drug business for three years."

"We'd never do something like that, would we?"

"We've done worse." She asked herself: *Do we really have a choice?*

*　*　*

Cardinal Richter sat on the edge of the bed while the man in the black overcoat stood before him. "Please don't hurt me," Richter said. "I don't want to die."

"Who are you working with?" the man asked.

Richter looked at the man's hair – it was shoulder-length and stringy and ran down his forehead almost into his eyes. He seemed to be wearing a wig. "I'm not working with them."

The man jabbed the butt of his pistol against Richter's cheek.

"I just met them," Richter said. "In Moscow. A woman named Amanda who said she's from the CIA. And a man named Jordan. He's from the FBI. I have no idea if they're telling me the truth. They put me in hiding here."

"How can I reach them?"

"I can't. She calls me. She changes her number all the time."

"Your phone," the man said. Although he spoke in English, Richter could tell that he too had a foreign accent. Richter handed him his burner phone, and the man looked through it.

"Did Sixtus send you?" Richter asked.

"You could say that." At that moment, the man stepped a foot back and fired his pistol to the side of Richter's head. The sound was muffled by a silencer. But the mess it left on the LCD screen of the TV opposite them was unmistakable.

* * *

By the time the plane landed at the Gran Canaria Airport in the Canary Islands, Amanda received word back from Veronica. She hadn't contacted Interpol to make the request to give Falzone what was essentially immunity from prosecution for three years, but she gave Amanda permission to make the deal. She, like Amanda, understood what was at stake.

As Amanda and Jordan made their way in the cab to the chief commercial port in the islands, the Port of Las Palmas, which was about a half hour north, she wrote back to V: "What if Interpol doesn't approve?" In part, as much as she trusted V, she wanted to have a record of her concern.

Amanda barely paid attention to the rolling green hills, sweeping ocean vistas, and the lush tropical landscape. She was singularly focused on her work at hand.

Veronica responded: "They'll agree. One way or another."

Amanda took a screenshot of the exchange. Then she immediately emailed the photo to her private email. She doubted the NSA had broken into it yet. "Looks like we're all good," she said to Jordan.

"Langley approved the deal?"

"V did. That's all that matters."

"Does she have the authority?"

Amanda didn't answer. She continued punching into her cell phone browser. She accessed the secure site where she had asked Svetlana to upload the pictures of General Cheeks. Dozens of photos were uploaded. Amanda spent the next several minutes downloading them. She scanned through them. Many were amateurish, showing the top of Cheeks's head and a crowd of security and media around him. Amanda could tell they were media by their badges. She zoomed in on some of the names, but they were hard to decipher when she enlarged the photos on her small cell phone screen. There were so many photos to go through. As she perused them, they started to look the same. Washington, New York, Chicago – she had a hard time distinguishing between the cities. Then, one picture captured her eye: A woman in one of the photos looked familiar. Had she seen her in one of the other photos? She looked back through them. Yes, there appeared to be the same woman, at the United Nations Plaza. She had a journalist's badge, but Amanda couldn't decipher the name. Then she looked at the picture of the woman near Cheeks at the event in Chicago. It took place at some large convention hall. It was the same woman. Yet, in Chicago, she wasn't wearing a journalist's badge. It looked like she had some other I.D. given to her by the convention center. However, other people in the photo did have badges that clearly said *media*.

Yes, the woman was familiar. She showed the photo to Jordan.

"Isn't that...?" he said. "The hair. It's blonde, and the skin has been lightened. But isn't that Sima?"

"Oh my God." Amanda held the picture closer to her eyes so that she could see the woman's face more clearly. Sima? Yes, the cheekbones were the same. The shape of the eyes, too. "I think you're right. Why would she be traipsing around Cheeks? And what would the Russians want with that?"

"Could it be some sort of kompromat?"

"Do you think the Russians hired Sima to follow him?"

"She is working for the Bulgarians. It wouldn't be a surprise. She's an agent for hire."

"Aren't we all?" Jordan joked.

Amanda chuckled. "Do you think the Russians could be involved with this plot? Did they pressure Cheeks to cooperate?"

"If they did," Jordan said, "he didn't have to. He could have blown the whistle on them."

"Unless they had something highly incriminating on him."

"Perhaps. But even then, what could be more incriminating than committing treason against your own country?"

"Fair point." Amanda twisted the phone in her hands. "I was going to send the photos to V for analysis, but now I don't think I have to."

"She's still being detained, right? Why don't we have the interrogators ask her what she was doing?

"Good idea," she said. "By the way, you haven't mentioned anything about the black site in your reports, have you?"

"What reports?" he said. "My boss isn't real interested in what I'm doing."

"Good. Let's keep it that way."

They arrived at the port. While a commercial center, it was quite picturesque, with a smattering of billowy white clouds gleaming overhead. The port wasn't gritty and dirty like more bustling ports.

Amanda turned to the cab driver: "Where do crews tend to congregate after hours?"

"There's a string of bars on that alley over there," he said, pointing. "I can drive you there."

"That's okay. We'll walk."

* * *

"Does The Leopard have a way to contact the captain?"

"That's a good idea," Amanda replied to Jordan as they walked down the alleyway east of the port. "I told him we had a deal, but I haven't heard back. It seems like he's playing coy."

"Or is he talking to his men? Like, telling them what to say and what not to say?"

"There's always that risk. But if they're not forthcoming, we can always cancel the deal. That's how this stuff works. We have a way out if we want it."

"Or we could just renege."

"That's a difficult one to pull off. If we get too cocky, no one will do business with the Agency. There's a certain amount of honor we have to uphold." She paused for a moment. "You seem to have the instincts of a good officer. You should think about transferring to the Agency. It's not that common, but I could put in a good word."

"Let's see this mission to its conclusion first," Jordan replied.

Amanda pinged The Leopard on the messaging app again. "We're in CI," she wrote, referring to the Canary Islands. "The captain's name and location."

No answer came.

Amanda and Jordan headed into a pub, *La Cabeza del Pez,* the fish head. They ordered beer and finger food at the bar. Amanda lipped a hundred euros in front of her plate. "I'm looking for a crew," she said to the bartender.

The bartender swiftly swept up the bill with a bar towel in hand as if he were cleaning the counter.

"It's *The Grindon,*" she continued.

"That's nothing but trouble," the bartender said in broken English.

"I'm looking for the captain. You know him?"

"Hristov?" he said.

"Yes, that's him. You've seen him around?"

"He comes here, usually later, looking for girls." The bartender nodded toward the corner of the bar where a throng of young women clad in tight-fitting, glittering outfits congregated. "Eleven p.m. is the best time. He'll be with a group of men from the ship."

"What does he look like?"

"Tall, thin. A wiry, scruffy beard. In his late fifties. High cheekbones. Brown, graying hair. He'll be vaping. It's not allowed, but we don't enforce it against him."

"Thank you," Amanda said.

"The men will be armed," the bartender said. "Nobody here will protect you. Watch out."

* * *

Das Kapital was only a day and a half away from the shores of the United States. The captain checked the fuel gauge. He had more than enough fuel to get to Baltimore. He would refuel there before heading down to Miami. From there, he'd fill up again to top off the tank before heading to the Bahamas. He expected to stay in Bermuda for a few weeks before heading off to the Virgin Islands. The more he thought about his future, he wondered whether it would be wise to stay in the U.S. Virgin Islands, where he would be subject to American jurisdiction. The British Virgin Islands were little better, as he'd be under British rule. Damn! All these Caribbean islands were under the thumb of some Western nation! Bermuda was more self-governing, he had learned. Perhaps that was a better spot to pitch his tent.

After the delivery was made and his pay was wired to his account, he could relax. He would see what island life offered in terms of weather and women, the two most important things to him at this stage in life. He didn't care about the health care system – he'd been a smoker since he was a teenager. He had a cough and a scratchy throat for the better part of the last ten years. Only after a heavy round of drinking would he cough up blood. He needed to slow down and enjoy things from now on. In the Caribbean, he'd have no problem finding a woman who'd cling to his side and enjoy the trappings his newfound riches offered. Bitches were like dogs; they'd cozy up to you as long as you fed them and pet them once in a while.

* * *

General Cheeks waited in the Oval Office's reception area for President Foster to return. He had the report on Sixtus that the president had requested. It wasn't fully finished yet, but he knew there would be little change from its overall findings. Sixtus was self-centered and arrogant. He had little affiliation to the U.S. since he had spent most of his adult life abroad working for the church. Besides, his upbringing in America was a constant struggle against poverty and what he perceived as an unjust capitalist system that rewarded those who came from privilege. Why hide this information from Foster? He wanted to know; now, he would get a more complete psychological profile on the man who recently warned the world of American imperialism. It didn't matter that Sixtus was now part of the elite, a world-renown leader of millions who pledged blind faith. He wasn't in control of an actual government, though according to intelligence analysis, this was a natural next step. The Catholic Church had always aspired to be a temporal power as much as a spiritual one. Of course, the intelligence concluded that despite these ambitions, Sixtus would likely fall captive to the trappings of the Vatican and abandon his ambitions in time. He would continue to sound the rhetoric of injustice and inequality of men, but he would end like those before him: neutered, resigned, ever watchful of his historical legacy.

Cheeks watched as Foster read the report. When he finished, he said, "This isn't what I was told. Why have they been hiding this information from me?"

"I don't think they've been hiding anything. It's nothing new, as far as church leaders go. The intelligence services didn't think you were interested."

"I'm not like other leaders. I believe that the spirit creates the health and wealth of our people. It's the source of our greatness. It's what's made the American experiment successful. Many think we can't be beholden to our churches. But I believe if we don't, we won't have any government left. Sixtus seems to be of a similar mindset. But it's dangerous when religious leaders try to govern from the pulpit. Thank you for bringing this to my attention, general."

"Certainly. May I ask," Cheeks said, changing the subject, "if I may be excused from attending the event on Friday at the Pan American Union. My wife's birthday is coming up, and I want to surprise her with a trip to Niagara Falls. She's never been."

"How is Liz?"

"She's doing well. In good health. Staying active volunteering."

"Good for her. It's not a problem. We've got practically half the government coming. I don't know why we need to make such a dog and pony show of it. All we're doing is ensuring free trade in the Americas."

"It's a big deal," Cheeks said. "It will help quell anti-American sentiment in Central and South America. Besides, we haven't had many victories on the diplomatic front for a while."

"Yes," Foster agreed.

"You don't think there's a security risk having much of the line of succession present, do you?"

"The vice president won't be there. She's the most important one. Besides, it will be in Washington, D.C. What can happen here?"

Chapter 61

Although it was late, Jordan placed a call to Richter. He and Amanda had time to kill before Hristov would appear at the bar. They sat at a restaurant where they picked over some *papas arrugadas* – wrinkled potatoes – and *queso asado,* grilled cheese. Each had a beer in front of them. "No answer," he said to Amanda.

"He's probably asleep."

"It's not that late."

"We'll try him in the morning."

"Perhaps we should send someone to check on him," Jordan said.

"I don't want the hotel staff to get suspicious."

"Do we have an officer who can do a welfare check on him? We said we'd send somebody by."

"I know," she said. "But we have to be careful. I don't know if any of our people in Prague have ties to Cheeks. All the intelligence services must be looking for Richter since he disappeared from Moscow. All it takes is one person who wants to impress the higher-ups, and we've got another body on our hands."

The idea of leaving Richter hanging didn't sit well with Jordan. Is this what the secret world of espionage was all about? Get the information you need from someone and then move on? What about protecting one's assets? But Amanda's judgment had been sound throughout the mission. Who was he to second-guess her? She had the experience, the training. Besides, what purpose would it serve to talk to Richter and hear that he was bored and wanted to get back to his normal life? Such a return was unlikely.

"The captain's going to be at the bar soon. We need to find out what Sima knows." She took out her cell phone and called the black site in Poland.

"How do you know they don't have a back channel into Cheeks?"

"I don't. But we don't have much to work with."

First, Richter, and now, Sima. Jordan was beginning to question whether a certain sense of desperation was leading Amanda. But what did they have to go on? Leads had dried up; increasingly, they were on their own. They were being targeted themselves. Veronica seemed to have their back, but how much longer could she help? He and Amanda would either have to expose the conspiracy or be killed.

"Shepherd," Amanda said. "What did you learn?"

"Something that scared the shit out of me," he said.

Chapter 62

"What's that?" Amanda asked Shepherd.

"Our friend says she's been working for the Russians off and on since her days at MI6. She's done assignments for them here and there."

"Nothing earth-shattering about that."

"She's not the only one. She said General Cheeks has also."

So Shepherd was exposing information about General Cheeks. He surely wasn't in his back pocket. "Like what kind of stuff?"

"She said he facilitated an arms deal a few years ago. He met up with some Russian agents in New York and eventually the shipment came through from Canada to Chicago."

"Why was she spying on him?"

"It was part of a honeypot operation. She was there to document the interactions between Cheeks and the girl. She wired up the girl when she went to Cheeks's room that night. The girl was posing as a journalist."

"They have video?"

"Video, audio, everything. Sima said he was careless. He disclosed classified information to show how important he was. She said the whole operation was about documenting his activities and making him look bad in case he ever tried to double-cross the Russians."

"So that's how they got me in Moscow?"

"She said he's very well connected with the FSB. Between his contacts with the Agency, MI6, and the FSB, there's no escaping him."

"Does Sima have copies of the videos?"

"She said she never got copies. But she knows the girl they hired. She still poses as a reporter in the U.S. She offered us her name for her freedom."

"I don't think we can take her up on that deal. Get the info from her. You know how to do it. Give her until tomorrow. Check it out. See what you can find on Sima's interactions with Russia. But you're going to have to be super-quiet. If Cheeks gets an inkling that you're snooping close to home, he'll put the kibosh on the operation."

"Got it," Shepherd said, hanging up.

"Sounds like we got confirmation that Cheeks is no good," Jordan said to Amanda.

She placed her cell phone on the table. "If we can get proof to the president in the next twenty-four hours, that will take care of him." She looked at the television screen on the wall, nodding to Jordan to look. A newscaster was mentioning a conference of world leaders in Washington this Friday. The volume was turned down, and Amanda followed the closed captioning:

"*World leaders from Latin America will meet with President Foster in Washington to sign a sweeping accord reducing trade barriers and increasing military cooperation. Foster has touted this as a major expansion of the Monroe Doctrine and will help place all countries of Central and South America on equal footing with the United States. European leaders have suggested it may be the first step in creating an American union that rivals the EU.*"

"Do you think this is when they plan to strike?" Jordan asked.

"It would make sense. There must be a sizeable diplomatic contingent present. Besides the typical high-level government officials."

Jordan pecked at his cell phone, searching the internet for news on the conference. "It's going to be held at the Pan American Union Building this Friday. The presidents of Mexico, Columbia, Argentina, Brazil, Chile, and Panama will be there, among others. It doesn't say anything about the U.S. delegation." He hunted more through the internet, finding another article. "It says the secretaries of defense and state will be there along with the Speaker of the House and the president pro tem of the Senate. Except for the vice president, that pretty much wipes out the line of presidential succession. Do you think she's in on it?" Jordan added.

"She's a Foster loyalist. She's going to be his successor when he terms out. Why would she take a risk now? He plucked her from nowhere and has insulated her from anything that's gone wrong. She's bulletproof. She'll be our first female president."

"Maybe she's part of the plan, at least as far as Cheeks is thinking. They'll install her, but usurp all the power and put her on the sidelines. He'll have de facto control of the military. She won't be able to step in. If she tries, she'll be easy enough to dispose of."

"Interesting theory," Amanda said.

Jordan looked at his watch. "The captain's got to be there now."

"Right. Let's go."

* * *

When Amanda and Jordan returned to the bar, Hristov was already holding court. He and his men occupied a couple of booths in the corner, where a bevy of women, both young and middle-aged, clustered around them. "Here we are again," Jordan said.

"I can't tell you how many bars I've been in since I joined the Agency," Amanda quipped.

"Let's get a couple of beers. It's always helpful to have an extra weapon on hand," Jordan said, alluding to the bottle.

When they ordered their beers, the bartender that they spoke with earlier nodded toward Hristov's booth. They left him another tip, in case things got out of hand. It never hurt to have allies around.

Amanda and Jordan headed over to Hristov's booth. Before they reached it, Hristov, who sat in the center of the booth with men on each side, called out to them: "You looking for me?"

"As a matter of fact, we are," Amanda answered. "I understand you're the captain of *The Grindon*."

"What about it?"

"Can we sit down?" Amanda asked.

"You better not."

His henchmen nodded menacingly towards them. They kept a close eye on Jordan as he was larger and a greater physical threat. Of course, they didn't know how lethal Amanda could be.

"The ship returned to the islands for some reason. Empty." She let that final word stop with a thud.

"What's it to you?"

"The Leopard assured us you'd be cooperative. Mr. Falzone, you know him, correct?"

"He doesn't control me," Captain Hristov snapped. The men about him laughed. The scantily clad women looked on, with heightened interest.

He was being difficult. Amanda glanced at Jordan, to see where his hands were. One held the beer bottle; the other was beside his side so that it could easily reach his gun.

"We don't need any trouble," Amanda said. "Mr. Falzone doesn't either. All we need is some information. You're responsible for that ship, right? It would be terrible if something happened to it before you brought it back to base." She took out her cell phone and tapped the screen, pretending that she was typing a message.

Hristov understood that she was insinuating that she could blow it up. "Let us talk." He waved his arms for his men to leave the booth and the women to scatter.

Amanda took a seat at one end of the booth while Jordan sat at the other, edging Hristov in so that he moved to the center. "We appreciate your cooperation," Jordan said.

Hristov groaned.

"What happened to the contents on board?" Amanda asked.

He hesitated. "We delivered them as we were supposed to."

"To who?"

"I don't know. I didn't ask for I.D."

Amanda put her hand on his forearm, applying gentle pressure. The move seemed to take Hristov back by surprise. "I don't need a name. I need a what."

He harrumphed.

"So the boat is only worth so much to you? And your allegiance to Falzone is questionable. How about your family?"

"You come here to threaten my family?" His eyes rose in anger.

"I came for information. When I don't get that information, I'm prepared to do anything at my disposal." She squeezed his forearm.

He forcibly wrested his arm from underneath hers and took a sip from his large stein of beer. Jordan was surprised by the sudden movement and kept his hand on his gun, prepared to draw it out.

"Perhaps we didn't introduce ourselves," she said. "We're with the CIA. Our capabilities extend far and wide. You can take that as a threat if you like. All it takes is a little cooperation to avoid knowing what I'm referring to. I could make one phone call and have you and all your men swept up to a black site if that's what you prefer. And The Leopard will not be happy when I report back what you said about him."

"So, you will make things up?" Hristov said indignantly.

"No need for us to lie. But I can tell by the look on your face what you think of him. I'll let you keep that mask. If you just give us a name."

He took a sip of his beer. Amanda followed with a sip from her bottle.

"A ship by the name of *Das Kapital*," Hristov said. "It will be on your doorstep any day now. Then tell me what kind of power you have."

"Is this another one of the Queen of Spades' ships?"

"It's part of Khalid Zahir's fleet. We're just middlemen. You really think you got what it takes to stop a nuclear weapon from blowing up

Washington, D.C.?"

"What do you mean, blow up Washington, D.C. How powerful is this weapon?"

"I have no idea," Hristov said.

Amanda grabbed his arm. "I think you do."

"What is the weapon?"

"It's a nuclear weapon. I told you already."

Why was he saying that it was a nuclear weapon? Yes, a dirty bomb had a nuclear component, but it was much less powerful and destructive than weapons-grade nuclear material like uranium or plutonium. "A dirty bomb?"

He chuckled. "No, not a run-of-the-mill dirty bomb. We had to be very careful. I'm glad I got rid of it. It's a full-scale nuclear bomb. Uranium-based. An atomic bomb."

So, he was confirming that it was fissile material. "Where is it going?"

"Baltimore."

"How will they get a weapon like that past security?"

"That's not my problem."

"Tell me," she ordered, grabbing his arm.

"I heard the systems won't be working. They have ways of disarming them and no one notices, you know?" His eyes flickered, then looked furtively away.

Yes, Cheeks would have the connections to see that this was done. All he needed was one person on the inside who would take a big payday. "How do I know you're telling me the truth?" Amanda was trained to ask that question when she didn't notice a sign of deception but couldn't find a motive for the person to lie.

"Fuck you!" he retorted. Indignance rose through his eyes, causing his eyebrows to rise and wrinkles to overtake his forehead.

She had her answer.

* * *

Amanda and Jordan returned to the area of the Gran Canarias Airport where they found a rather seedy motel. She chose this one because she didn't want to be asked for a passport; even though she had a few fake ones with her, she thought they might already be flagged by Interpol. All during their drive, they chatted about what Hristov had told them. A nuclear bomb? A uranium-based bomb? It would have the power to kill fifty thousand people in densely populated D.C. It could easily jeopardize the president's life and other national political figures. Nuclear fallout would leave the city in ruins. The entire city would have to be evacuated, even parts that weren't destroyed. Recovery efforts could take a decade.

"But Sima had said it was cesium," Jordan said.

"I don't think she was lying. She would have no reason to lie. She doesn't know. Besides, I don't think she'd get involved with something like that. As bad as she is, I think she has limits. A bit of a moral compass not to kill tens of thousands of innocent people."

"We have to tell the president."

"Yes." Amanda considered the option. With Cheeks against her, there was no way she could get a message to President Foster. For all intents and purposes, he had her isolated, a *persona non grata* within the Agency. She couldn't give up and try to go to some 'authority'; Cheeks would have her killed before she could get through the door. No, she would have to finish the mission. If she failed, she'd never be able to forgive herself.

Jordan sensed her wheels turning. "Can Veronica track *Das Kapital* down?"

"She should be able to. It's a large, seafaring ship. They were able to make *The Grindon* disappear for a little while, but a larger ship is much harder to conceal. There are a lot more hidden components that the owners of the vessels don't even know about. I doubt Zahir's team would know how to make it completely untraceable."

"You trust her?"

"I do."

"Can she get the go ahead to stop it?"

"That's going to be the hard part. We're going to have to step in."

"What can the two of us do?"

Chapter 63

Amanda tossed and turned all night, but she had managed to get some rest. Both she and Jordan awoke at 5 a.m. First, she searched the internet for the time difference between the Canary Islands and Prague. It was earlier there – too early. She didn't want to awaken Richter. She would call him later.

A response had come back from Veronica with the location of *Das Kapital*. She reported than an aircraft carrier was not far from the American coast. She requested that Amanda and Jordan go to the Gando Air Base from which NATO conducted operations. Amanda wondered whether they'd have to trek halfway across Gran Canaria Island; fortunately, the base was only a five-minute drive from the airport. Veronica told them that a jet would be waiting for them. She had pulled in a favor from a NATO contact. She told him that she needed to transport two highly valued assets to the aircraft carrier *USS Franklin,* which was named after Benjamin Franklin and was the successor to the aircraft carrier that was bombed in World War II.

Veronica asked for the names that they would use. Amanda gave her two names taken from their fake passports.

She and Jordan wasted no time in getting a cab that took them to the air base. They were greeted at the gate by NATO security and escorted to the landing strip. There, they took a Japanese-made military jet that traveled at approximately 570 miles per hour. They were due to arrive at the aircraft carrier in seven hours. Before they took off, she placed a call to Richter.

"Still no answer?" Jordan asked.

"No." Now, she was as concerned as Jordan. She doubted she would have service on the aircraft carrier to call Richter again.

When they landed on the *USS Franklin* in late afternoon, a Lieutenant Commander greeted them on the flight deck and led them to the captain's office. As she suspected, her cell service was non-existent.

A junior officer sat next to the captain's desk. Captain Buck wasn't told of any details of the operation by Veronica. Amanda would have to use her powers of persuasion. "We need a guided missile to destroy a ship," she said bluntly.

He laughed. "We can't just go around blowing up ships without authorization."

"I'm giving you authorization," Amanda said.

"You don't have the authority," he scoffed. "This Veronica doesn't either."

She could sense the disdain in his voice. Buck was a tall, lanky man in his early sixties. She could tell that he was nearing retirement. "Captain, we wouldn't ask you unless it was absolutely necessary."

"It's out of the question! Absolute hogwash!" he roared. "You can't just come on a ship and order us to do something that is contrary to every military convention. I have no legal basis for attacking another ship."

Amanda knew that he was right. "We need to inform the president."

He laughed more boisterously. "Do you know how preposterous this is? I can't just pick up the phone and get the president! I've never spoken to him in my life."

"I know this is unusual," she said, "but thousands of lives are at stake, including the president's."

"I have a good mind to throw you both in the brig!" he clapped back.

"We need you to call him!" Amanda said.

"Just call him!" joined in Jordan.

Captain Buck stood, readying to pick up the phone on his desk.

Jordan instantly pulled his gun from his waistband and pointed it at Buck. The junior officer beside Buck stood, and Amanda reached for her weapon and pointed it at him. They had rehearsed the maneuver while on the transport plane.

"We need you to get the president on the phone," Jordan said. "This is a national emergency. His life is at stake."

Amanda could see that under Buck's uniform his knees trembled. "No one will get hurt if you make the call."

"I don't have a direct line to the president," he said. "There are channels."

"You have two channels," she said. "One to the secretary of defense. The other to the chairman of the joint chiefs of staff. Secretary Orozco can probably get him on the phone more quickly. He'd be a better bet."

"You guys have lost your mind? Do you know your careers will be over with this stunt?"

"We're aware of that," Amanda replied calmly. "Just make the call. If we get him on video, that would be better. I want to know who's in the room with him."

"You sure have your demands ready," he said indignantly.

While he spoke, Amanda noticed that his body shifted forward at the desk. She could tell that he hit a silent alarm button. "You shouldn't have done that."

Jordan rushed to the office door, which he locked using a deadbolt, chain, and a bar that he placed across the door. The extra security was present for the captain to barricade himself in the office in case the ship was under attack.

Amanda kept her gun trained on both Buck and his assistant. "Sit down, both of you." Her eyes bore into Captain Buck's. "Call Orozco now and tell him you have an emergency. Tell him you are being held captive and that he needs to arrange a call with the president immediately. Am I making myself clear?"

His throat parched, the captain swallowed. "Yes."

He called his command center and told his crew that he was being held captive in his office. He asked them to call the secretary of defense and to arrange a video conference with the president. "That is an order."

The crew member who took the call started to raise some concerns, but the captain hung up.

"That wasn't so difficult, was it?" Amanda said.

Pounding could be heard against the door.

Amanda took out her necklace, where the round explosive ball hung. "This is an explosive device that will blow up the ship if I activate it. The CIA uses it to create diversions. We use it to blow up buildings. Don't think I'm bluffing. Order your men to stand down."

Captain Buck watched her for a moment; then he picked up the phone and called the command center, ordering all men to stand down.

"Sir, you pressed the alarm? Are you in danger?" the crew member asked.

"Of course I'm in danger!" he bellowed. "This is a direct order! I don't want to get killed!"

After a pause, the men outside the door became as quiet as mice.

Amanda raised her gun to the captain's head. "Ask them what the status is."

"They just put the request in!"

"We don't have time!"

Irritated by being ordered around, which was an uncommon occurrence for him, the captain obeyed, shouting into the phone. "This can't wait! I need this done right away! Get the secretary's office on the phone and patch him through!"

"Yes, sir," came the crew member's answer.

After a moment, the crew member came back on the line and said,

"We've got the secretary but are still waiting for the president to get into the Situation Room."

"How long?" the captain asked.

Another pause. Then the crew member returned. "Not sure."

"Get the video link up," the captain said, motioning to his assistant.

Jordan aimed his gun at the assistant. "Let me."

"The remote is in the drawer," the assistant said.

Jordan opened the desk drawer and took out the remote. He pressed the power on. The TV screen turned on, and an unfamiliar interface appeared. There were selections for SatCom – for *satellite communications*, Command and Control, Navigation, Weather, and others.

"Go to SatCom," the assistant said.

The app launched. A globe spinned while the connection was made. After only a couple of seconds, a message appeared, announcing, "You're connected!"

"Go to the menu on the right," the assistant said. "You'll see a Video Conference option."

Jordan proceeded to select the menu. A prompt appeared, asking for a code. "What now?"

"We wait," the assistant said.

"You didn't have to do this," the captain said to Amanda.

"You didn't give us a choice."

After several minutes of silence, during which Amanda asked herself whether she had made the best decisions – finally telling herself that she had, that there was no need to second-guess herself, a message announcing *Incoming Call* beeped on screen.

"Answer it," the assistant said to Jordan.

Jordan couldn't find the option. "How?" He gave the remote to the assistant, who answered the call.

"Let me talk," Amanda said to the captain. She addressed the screen. "Captain Buck is fine. I'm sorry for the way we've had to handle this, but we have an urgent situation on our hands, Mr. President."

The president sat at the head of the Situation Room's table. The camera lens widened, and the Secretary of Defense Orozco became visible. On the President's other side sat General Cheeks.

"I'm Amanda O'Brien," she said, unsure whether they had deciphered her real identity yet.

"We know who you are," President Foster snapped. "I demand that you release the captain from your custody."

"I will." She hesitated for a moment. She knew the next thing she was about to say would make her sound like a lunatic. "But I need you to blow up a ship on the way to the United States."

"Are you crazy?" he shouted.

"I'm beginning to think I am, a little bit. But we had no other choice."

"There's always a choice," he said, lecturing.

"There wasn't," she interjected. "Your life is in danger, as is American democracy. Tomorrow, a nuclear weapon will land near Washington, D.C."

"I know about this. It's a dirty bomb. Cesium-based."

"No, that's not correct. It's a uranium-based atomic bomb."

"Is that correct?" Foster asked Cheeks.

"No. It's only a dirty bomb. We're certain."

"That's a lie," Amanda interjected. "You're being misled, Mr. President. This bomb will be detonated at the Organization of American States event Friday at the Pan American Union building, where you and many other leaders from our government will be in attendance." She took a pause, giving the president a moment to digest the information and to respond.

The president seemed to be at a loss for words. "A nuclear weapon?"

"Yes, we have it confirmed." She didn't have any qualms bluffing the president. He couldn't possibly be more informed than she was. "The general sitting beside you knows all about it."

"Cheeks?" he asked incredulously. "Why haven't I heard about this?"

"This information is completely unverified!" he roared.

"That's not true," Amanda said, remaining calm. She knew she could lose credibility if she became overly defensive. "We confirmed the information through extensive intelligence. The weapon is on a yacht owned by Khalid Zahir. It's named *Das Kapital*. This is an international conspiracy involving Zahir and anti-Western leaders seeking to overthrow the U.S. government."

"What anti-Western leaders?" Cheeks scoffed.

Amanda knew he was trying to set her up. Would she name the pope? How ludicrous might that sound if she said Sixtus was part of the plot? Would Foster be receptive to the information, or would he dismiss her as some crackpot? "We will address that in due course. There are national security concerns that we need to deal with first."

"Might I remind you that we're in the Situation Room!" Cheeks roared. "This is the place to have those conversations! Why are you stringing us along? And what gives you the right to hold a captain of one of our ships captive for your wild conspiracy theories?"

"This isn't a conspiracy theory," Amanda shot back. "This is life and death. We can't take the fate of our government lightly. Would you like me to tell the president of your involvement in the plot?"

Cheeks was reeling. "Now you have gone off the deep end! This is the most insubordinate accusation I've ever heard!"

"So you deny working with Zahir and Ahmed Bensaïd on facilitating the shipment of this weapon and having Pope Sixtus take the president's place and you taking the place of the vice president?"

"This is the most ludicrous thing I have ever heard!"

"Mr. President, the general sitting next to you has been the nexus between Zahir and the plot. Not only that, we have evidence he has worked as an asset for Russia over the years. My supervisor at Langley can provide you with all the details."

"This is an outlandish accusation!" Cheeks bayed.

But Amanda could tell the president wasn't fully convinced of Cheeks's loyalty. Where did that distrust come from?

Jordan spoke up: "Mr. President, you don't know me, but I am with the FBI. I can vouch for everything that Amanda is saying. I've been working with her on this operation since I arrived in Madrid. Everything she said has been truthful. This plot extends far and wide. It has led to the death of one of Pope Sixtus's cardinals."

"That is absurd!" Cheeks spat out. "One of his cardinals? Which one?"

"Cardinal Barranca," Jordan answered.

"What about Cardinal Richter? I suppose I'm responsible for his murder, too. I plotted with the pope? Do you know how ridiculous you sound?"

Jordan looked at Amanda as they both took in the news of Richter's death. They had located him. Jordan thought he must have been careless. He had gotten too antsy; he didn't like being cooped up. He was used to his routine. The events of the past week must have upended his entire life.

Compartmentalizing the shock, Jordan turned back to the screen, addressing General Cheeks. "I couldn't believe it either, at first. Then I, along with Amanda, saw the evidence. I'm new to the FBI. I wouldn't stake my reputation and career if I wasn't one hundred percent certain. Mr. President, the man sitting next to you is not the man that you think. He has a plan of his own. But soon he will find that Zahir will betray him. He is being used, just as the pope is. I'm not excusing their behavior. They're certainly not innocent. They need to be punished. We've sent a tranche of information to Langley. It supports everything we say. Our first order of business is to destroy *Das Kapital*. We respectfully ask for your permission."

Cheeks quieted his voice as he spoke to Foster. "That is a private vessel. If it's owned by Zahir, he'll have a legitimate claim against us. It will create an international scandal."

"Who is on the vessel?" the president asked, addressing Amanda and Jordan.

"Terrorists," Amanda said. "They deserve to die. You cannot let them reach the shores of the United States."

"Captain," the president said, "what will it take to disable the ship?"

"We could take it out with one missile," Captain Buck said. "But I don't believe these folks. I think you should listen to the general."

"I'm glad one person has some common sense," General Cheeks said derisively.

The president turned away from him, interpreting his comment as a personal slight.

"Mr. President, your life is on the line. We must act now. This is the defining moment for you and our country. It's your divine mission." Amanda knew, from the Agency's extensive psychological profiles of the president, that the religious reference would resonate with him.

"You can't possibly listen to these fools," General Cheeks huffed.

"Destroy the boat!" the president clamored.

"It is a violation of international law!" General Cheeks said.

He was showing his true colors, Jordan thought.

"I will deal with that! We can't take the risk. I want the boat destroyed immediately! And you, Amanda O'Brien, need to be in my office in the morning."

"Certainly, sir. Thank you."

"Captain," the president continued. "You heard my orders. Send a missile and blow up the ship before the hour is out."

"Yessir," the captain replied.

The teleconference disconnected. The captain got on the line with his command center and ordered an ESSM, a RIM-162 Evolved Sea Sparrow Missile, to be launched against *Das Kapital* off the Atlantic coast. He hung up the phone. "You'll get your wish in twenty minutes. The missile flies at Mach4+. It's almost hypersonic."

"We'll wait," Amanda said.

"You know, making an enemy of General Cheeks isn't going to do your career any good."

"I'm here to uphold the Constitution. It's the oath we took. I have no allegiance to him, only to my country. I expect you feel the same."

"I've heard this bluster before. It always ends the same, with a thud," the captain replied.

Chapter 64

Amanda and Jordan waited in the captain's office, continuing to hold him captive. They weren't going to take the chance of being sent to the brig for their blatant acts of mutiny. Just as Captain Buck promised, the call came approximately twenty minutes after giving the order. He listened to his command center on the line. Amanda could see that his face was losing color. Holding her pistol, she said, "Put them on speaker phone."

Captain Buck complied. "Repeat what you said to me."

"Excuse me, sir?"

"I said *repeat what you just said to me!*" He yelled with such force his voice became shaky; he was short of breath. It was as if his command was the last utterance of a dying man.

The seaman spoke: "Our satellites show that a nuclear explosion occurred when *Das Kapital* was struck. It was not a full-scale explosion. It does not appear that the chain reaction occurred successfully."

Amanda spoke: "Has that been reported to the president?"

"It has."

She looked at the captain. "Now do you believe me?"

* * *

Amanda and Jordan were about to board the same Japanese-made military transport plane that had flown them to the carrier. Amanda had confirmed with Veronica that they could travel safely with the pilot. She assured her that he had allegiance to the Agency and not to the Department of Defense. Amanda asked what happened with Cheeks. "Don't know," came her reply. The lack of news unsettled Amanda.

They held the captain at gunpoint until the engines roared and the plane was seconds from takeoff. He wouldn't dare shoot down the plane, Amanda thought. Or would he? No, the president had authorized the destruction of *Das Kapital*. The commander-in-chief thus gave tacit approval of their mission. Her imprisonment of Captain Buck was justified. He wouldn't be able to successfully argue otherwise, no matter how much his feelings and ego were bruised.

Jordan closed the hatch after he and Amanda passed through. The plane took off.

Now that Richter was dead and retrieving him in Prague was unnecessary, there was only one place to go.

Rome.

Chapter 65

"The president has to act," Jordan said to Amanda as they sat on the plane en route to Rome.

She understood that he meant that Foster had to take some action against General Cheeks. "He's one of the president's men. They all have a certain amount of protection. Plus, he's a military man. He'll put up a fight. They'll have to drag him away in chains."

She continued: "V is putting all the evidence together now. It's only a matter of time before they see what a traitor he's been."

"And Zahir?" Jordan asked. "He has men everywhere. Are we going to be safe in Rome?"

"One thing you'll learn about this game," Amanda said, "is that you're never safe anywhere."

* * *

Sixtus received a phone call on Wednesday morning that the ship bound for the U.S. had been destroyed. Bensaïd had called him from one of Zahir's private jets. He was on his way to Rome and requested a private meeting.

The Vatican was in a state of uproar over Cardinal Richter's death. The media began reporting that the pope's life was in danger because, now, two cardinals close to him had been murdered. Pundits opined that it was only logical that the pontiff would be their next target. But who was behind the shootings, they asked? Why were they being targeted? Was it a byproduct of some sort of palace intrigue?

Sixtus didn't want to deal with any of the questions or the media scrutiny. Now that Richter had been eliminated, he was completely isolated at the Vatican. There was no one he could count on as an ally. He should have known not to sacrifice Richter. Now, he could only rely on Bensaïd. But now that their plan had been blocked – and his involvement likely exposed – he was more vulnerable than ever.

In his room, he kneeled at the prie-dieu where he had placed a compact mirror on the shelf facing him. He took a vintage Chinese cloisonné bowl that he kept ashes in. The nuns had wondered what the ashes were for – Were they some kind of incense? Was Sixtus smoking in private? They never dared ask the pontiff. Sixtus took the ash and threw it at the mirror, silently and prayerfully beseeching for his master to come. Sixtus looked at his distorted image in the mirror. The ashes were in the way of one eye; his lip was split. "Come to me," he said in a low tone. "I need you, Master."

Suddenly, the image of Sixtus turned into an almost reptilian creature. It had a long, protruding beak of a mouth; a pointy, scaly forehead; black, birdlike eyes that blinked rapidly.

"I do not want to fail you, Master."

The Devil's mouth opened, revealing not one but six or seven rows of teeth all massed together and connected to one another. The mouth opened and the teeth receded, folding into themselves as they disappeared. A tongue that extended beyond the mirror seemed to be a foot long. It lashed Sixtus across the face, entering his mouth and causing him to gag. Sixtus wanted to plead for forgiveness, but he couldn't speak because his tongue was twisted with the Devil's. A fork of His tongue went down Sixtus's throat, not just down his esophagus but all the way down to his intestines. Sixtus could feel his belly bursting. He was about to vomit.

The Devil removed his tongue, and Sixtus gasped as air reentered his lungs.

"You thought you were God," the Devil said. "*I* am God. I am the only God. I am the true God."

A lucite pyramid stood on the far corner of the prie-dieu's shelf. Sixtus saw that flames gathered around a tower. The tower became the Vatican, and fire engulfed it. The crystal turned red. Sixtus could feel heat burn against his face. His eyes stung. He had to close them. The scent of chemicals burning caused him to cough. "I know," he tried to say, but he couldn't enunciate the words completely.

"You want to be God on Earth, but Earth is just a prelude. There is no afterlife. There is only true life, an everlife that I am lord of."

The heat subsided. Sixtus could open his eyes. The stench of chemicals still reeked in the air.

"I gave you everything and now you must return the favor. The millions of souls who listen to you must come to my door. They must beg for my allegiance."

"How?" Sixtus said.

"The power of the pulpit. It is the only power you have. Tell them Jesus was a heretic, and they need to be heretics too. Tell them to find refuge in the voice that comforts them. That voice will be mine. Tell them that they are all brothers in the fight. I will come to support them. Tell them when they pray to ask for the secret knowledge of the world. I will show them the abyss of the downtrodden and the sinful. I will lift them from their misery with everything their hearts desire. Tell them not to fear because an angel will be guiding them, and that angel will be me. When they pray, tell them to deliver their souls to that angel with one simple word." The Devil paused. "*Amen.*"

Sixtus knew that prayer was the key. Everything he had was the result of prayer. You could pray to a demon or an angel. The only difference was that the demon would give you want you want and need, while the angel would tell you to have faith, to be meek and humble, and to believe in One True God. But Sixtus knew there was more than God. Yes, man was caught between the two of them, and one day one would vanquish the other.

"I will give you one more chance," the Devil said, "because I believe in you." The tongue disappeared and the rows of teeth flashed before his mouth. Then the mirror turned back to the ashy reflection of Sixtus. Now, Sixtus's eyes were black like the Devil's.

An alarm in the room sounded, and Sixtus looked overhead, to the ceiling. The smoke alarm had been triggered by the chemical fumes. He stood from the prie-dieu. He attempted to pick up the crystal pyramid so that he could close the lid. But the hot crystal scorched him and fell against the wooden shelf, burnishing it.

The Swiss Guard patrolling the entrance to Sixtus's suite entered the room. Following him, several cardinals and nuns came in. "What happened?" the guard asked.

"I don't know," Sixtus said. "The smoke alarm went off."

"Let's get you out of here."

"Come, Your Holiness," one of the cardinals said.

As Sixtus exited the room, he noticed that Sister Sofija was eyeing the prie-dieu. Did she see smoke coming from it?

* * *

Amanda and Jordan landed in Rome in mid-afternoon. During the flight, they had discussed how they might handle the situation with Zahir, Bensaïd, and Sixtus. Their options weren't good. The Vatican was a sovereign state. To place Sixtus under arrest was legally impermissible. Nor could they detain him. The Agency wouldn't like that approach anyway. Of the three, Bensaïd was the easiest to handle. He was a middleman. Without Zahir, he had little power. He could be easily apprehended. Zahir would be beyond arm's reach; having had his yacht blown to smithereens likely put him in hiding in Kuwait or some non-cooperative Arab country, like Yemen. Regardless, Sixtus was the key; he was the one who had to be subdued. Without him, Zahir and Bensaïd had no avenue to assume power.

Matters were complicated because they still didn't know what was happening with General Cheeks. Had they detained him? Had they cut off his communications? He could have warned Zahir and Bensaïd. Who else might have been working with the general? He might not be a lone wolf. Co-conspirators might be hunting Amanda and Jordan as they trekked across the continent.

Upon landing, Amanda contacted the black site in Spadadz, Poland. She asked for Sima to be transported under protective custody to Rome this evening. While there was no similar type of facility to hold her in Rome, she would be placed in a safe house and guarded at all hours.

"Do we have to be careful about using safe houses? Cheeks might be alerted," Jordan had asked Amanda during the flight.

"We won't mention that there's a prisoner. The Spadadz officer will book the house in his name."

"Will he get suspicious?"

"I think Cheeks knows his goose is cooked. We've put things in motion that getting rid of us won't stop."

Nonetheless, Amanda knew it was prudent to be cautious. She and Jordan had left their cell phones back on the aircraft carrier to prevent any tracking. Upon landing in Rome, they secured new burner phones. She then immediately contacted V. "We just landed in Rome," she wrote.

They initiated a secure call through a messaging app.

"The shit has hit the fan," Veronica said. "Cheeks is in a military holding cell facing charges of espionage."

"What about treason?" Amanda asked.

"They haven't gotten there yet. There's some talk that they don't want to expose the public to the threat the country faced. Here's the good part. The president has given us the authorization to take out Sixtus."

"Take out as in..."

"Assassinate," Veronica interjected. "He wants it done now. We need someone on the inside. We could poison him."

"That will take too long. We'd have to create a false identity and get them into the Vatican. The pope has to be on high alert by now. I doubt he'd allow personnel changes. He won't let anyone get anywhere close to him. I have another plan. We use Sima." She didn't bother to explain that she already had Sima en route to Rome.

"You think she'll kill for us?"

"She will if we let her off the hook."

"So, she goes back to being an agent for hire?"

"Yes. She's an expert shot. She could shoot him."

"She'll face prison time. Look what happened to the man who tried to kill John Paul II. We won't be able to intervene."

"Only if she's suspected."

Chapter 66

When Amanda and Jordan received word that Sima had been safely transported and secured, they immediately went to see her at the Roman safe house. Now that General Cheeks was in custody, they felt safer traveling in the city. It was unlikely that the Agency or MI6 would be targeting them, even if Cheeks had other collaborators. They would know that they were also being watched and would be hesitant about proceeding. They would know that substantial evidence must have been gathered against Cheeks. They would know that he no longer had President Foster's confidence. They would know they were doomed.

Yet for Amanda and Jordan, time was not on their side. They had to act quickly before they were stopped. They understood the threat that Zahir and Sixtus posed. If they didn't take care of them immediately, Foster might change his mind. It wasn't every day that he'd allow the assassination of a pope. Aides would speak to him and try to change his mind; he was known to listen to those who had contrary opinions. He was known to be a compassionate man. How would it look if it were revealed that a nation-state like the United States, under his command and direction, killed a sitting pope? His name would go down in infamy.

Amanda and Jordan were escorted to the windowless room where Sima was held. The room was more of a cell than a bedroom. The walls were made of concrete; a prison-style bed was the only furniture; the steel toilet had no lid and was bolted to the floor. Nothing in the room could be converted to a weapon. The safe house was used invariably through the decades to transport gangsters, terrorists, drug dealers, and enemy spies. Sima, as skilled as she was, would not be able to escape.

She sat up on the wafer-thin mattress when Amanda and Jordan entered the room. "I should have known it was you who sent me here."

"We need your help," Amanda said.

"This is a funny way to ask."

"We had to act quickly. And we weren't given many options."

"What can I possibly do for you? I've given you all the information I have. I've been truthful. I haven't held anything back. And now what? I face detainment and a jail term of at least twenty years?"

"It's likely to be a much longer sentence," Amanda said. "That's what I want to spare you from."

Sima's body loosened in anticipation. "You could just let me go."

"You know we couldn't do that. But we could if you did something for us."

"A quid pro quo. Of course."

"We want you to kill someone."

"I usually don't do the killing," she said.

"You're trained. We know you're an excellent shot."

"You want to send me to kill The Leopard?"

"He's on our safe list," Jordan said. "No. Someone much more important. The person behind this operation."

"Zahir?" she scoffed. "I don't have a prayer of getting anywhere close to him. He stays in his private layers and is guarded all the time. He's an impossible target. You might as well sentence me now."

"He's working with someone," Amanda said. "Perhaps you know

this. Sixtus."

"The pope?" She laughed.

"Yes."

"You can't be serious."

"We are. We want you to do it this Sunday. It will be his birthday. He'll be parading through the streets of Rome, trying to cultivate public favor. He has to know he's on shaky ground."

"I won't get near him. He has the Swiss Guard around him. The Popemobile is bullet proof."

"Our intelligence shows that he'll mingle with the people. It's his birthday. The flock will want to cheer him on. He's not going to hide behind glass. He'll go through St. Peter's Square and shake people's hands. We'll get you there. We'll get you out safely."

She stood from the bed and shouted. "Are you crazy? I'm not going to be set up for killing the pope!"

"Please, Sima."

"Don't *please* me! I've done horrible things, but I'm not going to go down in history as the crazy woman who killed the first American pope!"

"I told you, we will get you out safely. No one will suspect you. Your slate will be clean. We'll get you settled anywhere in the world that you want to go."

Sima grasped her hair and pulled at it. Her time under interrogation was taking a toll on her. She kept shaking her head. Amanda looked at Jordan, giving him a concerned look. Perhaps Sima's emotional state was at such a point she couldn't be relied on. Or did this decision weigh too heavily on her? Was she contemplating it? Did she realize the predicament she was in? She had no way out without being tried, convicted, and sent to prison. The certainty was one hundred percent that she would be found guilty. She had to know this.

"Sima, please calm down. I understand how you're stressed about this. You need to understand this is the best way for you. I know what happens when you don't cooperate. The system is stacked against you. A jury will convict you. They'll send you the harshest prison in the middle of nowhere. They'll limit visitations. Don't do this to yourself."

"Don't do this to *me*?" she screamed. "*You* are doing this to me!"

"You are the one who left MI6 and began working for enemy states! Don't pretend you're innocent in all this!"

"Do you know why I did it?" she yelled.

"For money."

"Yes. For money. And do you know why I needed the money?"

"Your mother was sick," Amanda replied.

Sima seemed surprised. Amanda knew and she didn't care. "She was going to lose everything she had!"

"I understand. But there are limits, Sima."

"You're talking to me about limits, and you want me to kill someone?"

"It won't be the first time," Amanda said. "Your mother died under suspicious circumstances, didn't she?"

Sima's eyes widened. "You're accusing me? Of killing my own mother?"

"She was dying. You justified it. But I don't know if the courts will see it the same way. It's life in prison or this. I can't do any better."

"I've made mistakes," Sima said. "Yes, I admit it. We all have. We do what we must. Don't pretend you're a saint."

"I've only killed under the color of law," Amanda said.

"Justify it any way you want. You're a killer too."

Amanda couldn't deny her past, but all acts she had committed were done under the color of law. "Do we have a deal?"

Sima's eyes went from Amanda to Jordan, back to Amanda, and then back to Jordan. Finally, they rested on Amanda. "How will you get me out?"

Chapter 67

Sixtus met with Bensaïd on Saturday morning. They sat in the garden where tulips and roses grew in colorful abandon. Bensaïd brushed the cement bench where they sat, to ward off speckles of dirt lest they attach to his impeccable suit. While Sixtus welcomed seeing his old friend, he wanted to hide from everybody else. Even within the confines of the Vatican, the world seemed unwelcome. But then he remembered his instructions. He needed to tell his flock that they were heretics like Jesus, and an angel would comfort them. They needed to give themselves and offer their souls to that angel.

What would they think? The guidance was unconventional and lacked support within doctrine. But his words could *make* doctrine. Who would dare oppose him?

"My brother," Bensaïd said, "I'm sorry things didn't work as planned."

"There has to be something more we can do."

"In time," Bensaïd said. "But you need to pretend that nothing has happened. General Cheeks has been arrested."

"My God!" exclaimed Sixtus. "There will be no one to protect us."

"Not for the moment. But we must be patient."

"They must know the plan. But how?"

"I don't know," Bensaïd said. "But Zahir is not happy. He can now no longer venture out of Kuwait. I must go to him."

"You can't leave me stranded like this!"

"It's better that we don't talk or see each other. The Americans have a way of eavesdropping into all conversations. You know that they have tiny drones that look like flies but are actually listening devices? Some are so small they can go through a cracked doorway or an open window. Then they can expand like a flying insect and disappear behind paintings, books, television sets, anything. Or hide under furniture. They can send whole swarms of these insects into places and even escape if an electronic sweep is conducted."

"Why are you telling me this?"

Bensaïd pointed up and around the garden. "This is an open space. You know how easily they can monitor a place like this?"

"They might be listening now?"

"Probably. They say Allah or God is always listening. What's the difference?"

"Should I stay inside?"

"It would be better."

"I don't want to go out anymore. I'm going to cancel my appearances for the next few weeks."

"No. Pretend nothing is wrong. Don't show fear. Your flock needs to see you."

"You think this will pass?" Sixtus asked hopefully.

"I don't know, Your Holiness."

"Then what can I do?"

"You don't have to do anything," Bensaïd said. "They can't arrest you. You're on Vatican grounds."

"You as well as I know we have no army. We are here at the pleasure of the Italians. They'll give into the Americans without a whimper."

"Italy won't want its reputation tarnished. It won't want the papacy interfered with. It's the last thing it has, even though it doesn't really have it. The Vatican is the main draw for visitors to Rome. Italy would be nothing without it."

"There's the Mafia," Sixtus said.

"Yes, and you must keep them on your side. There's no telling how useful they might be."

"This sounds like goodbye," Sixtus said.

"Only for a little while. You know me. I can't stay away too long. Have you been praying?"

"Yes," Sixtus replied.

"And?"

"He said I have one more chance."

"Listen to Him," Bensaïd said. "He will never let you down."

"Maybe not. Everyone else has."

"Don't doubt. That will only cause you more trouble. You need to be steadfast, now more than ever." Bensaïd reached into the interior breast pocket of his suit jacket and pulled out a small, rectangular box, about eight inches long and five inches or so wide. It was wrapped with a gold and black ribbon. A black stone in the center held the ribbon together. Sixtus recognized it as an onyx. He thought of Ezekiel 28:13, which listed onyx and other stones that Lucifer was associated with. Before Sixtus opened the box, he asked himself: Was there some piece of jewelry inside? Some expensive wristwatch which he knew he could not wear? Or a ring?

He opened the box. Inside, there was a whitish and yellow bone, as long as the box and curved, lying atop satin lining.

"It's from Jesus's exorcism."

Sixtus knew the story of the exorcism of the Gerasene demoniac, which Mark, Matthew, and Luke recounted in the Bible. In the story, Jesus exorcised an evil spirit from a man and changed the spirit into two thousand swine, which he cast into the river and drowned. The man wanted to follow Jesus, but he was told to stay in his village and proselytize the miracle that Jesus had performed.

"It's a birthday gift," Bensaïd said. "It's the remnant of one of the ribs of the swine, preserved for these thousands of years. I was finally able to track one down and have it authenticated. They say the bones are those of swine and humans, intermingled. We had it sent to a lab, and the DNA was confirmed. It is indeed half-human and half-pig. The miracles of science. Jesus had the power, Sixtus. We do, too. Do not forget that."

Sixtus rubbed the tip of his index finger against the bone, caressing it. "I will cherish it always. Thank you, my friend."

"I really wanted to get you a hoof," Bensaïd said. "But it appears none might exist anymore."

"It's probably better," Sixtus said. "The nuns would ask what it is. This, I can explain to them." He paused. "I don't know. I'll think of something."

"I'm sure you will. You always do."

Chapter 68

On Sunday morning, June 6, Sima was outfitted with a blonde wig, a hat, sunglasses, and blue denim overalls that were fastened by Velcro patches at the shoulders, waist, and legs. The overalls could quickly be removed and discarded; she would be able to appear in completely different clothing that was hidden under the overalls. This way, if, after the shooting, police were looking for a blonde woman with blue overalls, she wouldn't match the description. It was a typical CIA trick: misdirection. Something they used in the media, interrogations, and routine operations.

She wore white gloves that reached her forearms so that she wouldn't leave any fingerprints or DNA on the weapon. All the clothing she would remove yet keep with her in an expandable bag that she held in her pocket. None of the clothing could be left behind because traces of sweat could be traced back to her.

In a final touch, the CIA crew applied a wafer-thin face mask made of synthetics. This would transform her honey-olive complexion into the fairer and paler hue of a Caucasian. She was playing the role of a British tourist, there to see the pope and to shake his hands. She would sing "Happy Birthday" if the crowd decided to, though they might sing it in Italian. In that case, she would just watch and smile.

She looked at herself in the mirror. Staring back at her was the reflection of a woman whom she used to dream of being as a child. Not the cast-out, poor, brown girl with hand-me-down clothing that her mother would get from her sister who had already had a daughter. As she looked at the black boots that were like tactical gear that she now wore, she recalled how she was once given a pair of brown shoes with a thick rubber soul. They were a little too small for her feet, but she loved them. She called them her 'shit kickers.' She was determined to beat up the other girls who, when they weren't ostracizing her, made fun of her in class. She never got into a fist fight, though. The fights only played out in her mind.

What would all those girls think of her now? She barely recalled their names, but a few of them still clung to her. Bethany. Astoria. Astoria – how could she forget her? Who would name their child 'Astoria' except parents who felt that their daughter was destined to be a queen or a model or a glamorous posh girl at Oxford or Cambridge? Astoria ended up being a waitress. Sima had looked her up when she was at MI6. This fact gave her glee.

Now she had license to kill. She shouldn't care. But she knew it gave her power, and this power had fueled her for many years, all through her career. People could mess with her, but the weapons she wielded no longer were shit-kickers. They had bullets. They were truly lethal. She didn't have to fantasize any longer. She could take her revenge on every person she targeted. This was her retribution. And for every person that she ever killed, she would imagine the face of Bethany or Astoria staring back at her. She was freeing those girls, her nemeses, from their miserable, unfulfilled lives.

* * *

Amanda and Jordan were in the other room as the disguise artists applied finishing touches on Sima. "I can't believe this is happening," Jordan said. "Do you think she'll go through with it?"

"She doesn't really have a choice. Even if she fails, it will scare Sixtus into submission. He knows it won't be the last attempt."

"Do you think he knows the CIA has a target on him?"

"He has to. Who else could take out *Das Kapital* like that? Who else could have pieced together all the evidence? Plus, he has to know what's happened to General Cheeks. He knows he's been cornered."

"Could there be another way?" Jordan asked. "Short of killing him?"

"When you go up against someone with that kind of power, there's only one option. Unless you want to end up with a Hitler. You take him out the first opportunity you get, before his power and influence grows. Don't tell me you're having second thoughts?"

"This wasn't my plan," Jordan said. "It all seems so unreal."

"Social media has made death seem unreal," Amanda said. "What do they say? *Unalive* someone? To get around the censors? It's murder, suicide, abortion, the death penalty all rolled into one. How unfeeling we've become."

"I'm not ready to give in."

"No. Sometimes you have to fight. That's what we're doing."

"Is it? Or are we becoming like them?"

"I thought you were a natural officer, Jordan. Maybe I got ahead of myself. Sometimes the only way out of the gray is to look at everything as if it's black and white."

"But killing."

"This work isn't for the squeamish. You have to have guts. Maybe you're rather AI take over. Make the decisions for you."

"There's no telling what it might do."

"Exactly. So we make the best decisions and move on."

"We assassinate a pope and just move on?"

"Sixtus isn't the first," Amanda said. "The first pope, maybe. But there have been many others. You've heard the stories of JFK being taken out by the CIA. Other world leaders. We play for dominance. We play to win. There's too much at stake."

So, she was insinuating that the CIA was behind Kennedy's death? He had seen videos from JFK's nephew, Robert F. Kennedy, Jr., who also claimed they were responsible. "You're probably right. This is all new to me."

"Remember, you give someone like Sixtus an inch, and you end up with Hitler invading all of Europe. It's a calculated risk. It will be a shock, but everyone will move on. Very quickly. You will see. It's amazing how little people think of what's happening outside of their everyday lives."

Was she right? Jordan didn't know. She had a point. Some catastrophe would happen and then in a week or so, something else would turn up on the news and dominate the headlines, causing everyone to forget. Was it all planned? Was there some master system of mind control at work? Was he now part of 'the game'? Is this how people got sucked into the secret world? He had gone on a seemingly innocent mission, and now he was at the center of an operation that would change the fate of the world. He had to see things to their end. Despite his moral discomfort, he couldn't turn back. His own life had been threatened. Just on the other side of the wall was a woman who didn't give a rat's ass about his life. She was going to kill *him*. Why should he care about any of them? If it weren't for Amanda and the Agency, he would have been dead. He *owed* them. *They* weren't asking for his life. They weren't even asking him to take another's life. They were just asking him to help protect the United States and Western democracy. What he was doing was heroic. Then why did it feel like a crime? Because Sixtus was the pope? A religious figure? Yes, there seemed to be a line that was being crossed. But Sixtus himself had crossed that line first. He wasn't an innocent victim. His intentions were evil. Then why did Jordan care? His mother had always told him, "You care too much." Yes, you can't care. Not in this world. Not anymore. You have to go with the flow. Stop questioning things. Give a smile. Play along. Everything will be fine. Don't rock the boat. Nothing good will come. And if things go wrong, no one will blame him. The mess will be cleaned up. All he has to do is commiserate. Yes, the pope must die. If he learned one thing through working with Amanda is that she had his back. She wouldn't let him down. He was no longer little Jordan the kid with the world stacked up against him. He was part of a team now.

* * *

Before Sixtus left his room to deliver his Papal Mass, he took the box that Bensaïd had given him and opened it. He held the thin, yellowing bone between his fingers. Whereas he would have once been excited by the rarity of such an item, this morning he felt little as he grasped it. It seemed devoid of power. It lacked significance. The only connection he felt to it was due to Bensaïd's gifting it to him. How much things had changed over the past couple of days. What was once a certainty, a fulfillment of all his dreams, now seemed a futile fantasy. And he was left alone, abandoned. He twirled the bone in his fingers. It was so brittle he could break it with his thumb and forefinger. He could smash it under his foot and turn it into powder. Any form it took, it would be equally useless.

He had a few moments before his assistants would arrive to dress him. He opened his prie-dieu and placed the bone next to the cloisonné bowl. He stared at the instruments for a moment; then he closed the panel.

He thought of the sermon he would give as his aides entered the room, carting a rolling garment rack replete with the traditional papal vestments. As he undressed, they placed an undergarment, the alb, over his own. They fastened it with a cincture, a belt. Then they placed a stole around his neck, which had narrow bands of cloth laying down his chest. A cape-like mantum covered his torso. Buskins, or stockings, embroidered in gold for the pope, were placed over his socks. Sandals came next. Then a subcinctorium was fastened to the cincture and hung by his side. The pectoral cross and the fanon, a large collar, were fixed about Sixtus's neck. Pontifical gloves were placed on his hands. The chasuble was placed over his head and fitted over his torso, with the fanon readjusted over it. The pointy, cone-shaped mitre was placed on his head. Then the pope's ring was placed over his gloved finger.

The high priest had been adorned.

Almost everything was in the color of the day – purple, which denoted penance and was customarily used during Lent, Advent or funeral services. Green would have been the usual color, as the church was in Ordinary Time, but Sixtus requested purple. The staff were surprised, but they were reminded that it was his birthday and they would not fuss over his wish. Since he was American, they understood he would forge his own traditions.

In less than a half hour, he would deliver his sermon. The staff pestered him about notes, offering to write them up for him. He declined. He told them to leave him. He still didn't know what he would say.

* * *

Amanda and Jordan each secured tickets to the Vatican's 12:30 mass, using connections at the embassy. They would sit in separate areas of the basilica. Jordan would be closer to the front, while Amanda would be behind him on the opposite side. Neither would have guns, as they did not want to circumvent the airport-style security that they would have to pass through to enter St. Peter's. Yet each had a few defensive tools that they could use to create diversions if necessary. Sima would not attend mass; she would wait outside until Sixtus toured the plaza in his Popemobile.

A full crowd of approximately 15,000 was in attendance. Cardinals assisted Sixtus in performing the rites of service, including the readings of the Gospel and the responsorial psalm. Sixtus then delivered his homily. He spoke in a soft voice, and his message of brotherly love and being a peaceful neighbor related to the passages read, including Hebrews 13:1 and Matthew 22:39. Then he communicated his vision of what it meant to be a faithful servant of God. This part of the homily did not directly apply to the scripture read. But no one seemed to notice, as Sixtus deftly weaved his message into a personal appeal to everyone in attendance. He implored everyone to beware of false prophets. As he stood at the papal altar, a crow landed atop Bernini's Baldacchino, the massive bronze canopy with twisted columns that soared almost ten stories high. Sixtus didn't notice the crow as it was over his head, but several in the crowd did, including Jordan.

Sixtus exhorted the crowd not to succumb to the needs of today, but to look inward and upward. He told them to pray to the one true savior, Jesus Christ. "Our one and true perfect lord." As he said this, the crow let out a grating rattle. A slight chorus of laughter erupted, and Sixtus looked overhead. Amanda noticed the crow also. Sixtus couldn't see anything except the ceiling of the Baldacchino, which was made to look like cloth though it was a combination of bronze, stone, and wood. Jordan swore that the crow was scratching its feet atop the column. "Fear the Devil," Sixtus said, "for he will take many forms, promise you your dreams, and lead you astray. Jesus is our only redemption."

The crow took a brief perch atop one of the angels in the corner of the Baldacchino facing Jordan. Then it flew toward the rear and disappeared.

After communion and the sign of peace, Sixtus was due to give a final blessing. However, he stood with his mouth dry, unable to speak. The cardinals looked with concern. The crowd observed him in anticipation, in expectation of the rite. One of the cardinals finally stood next to him and spoke into the microphone: "*Benedicat vos omnipotens Deus: Pater, et Filius, et Spiritus Sanctus.*" "May Almighty God bless you: the Father, and the Son, and the Holy Spirit."

Sixtus listened, bewildered. He looked pale. He had the absent expression of a man twenty years older who had suffered a lapse in memory and didn't know where he was.

The accompanying cardinals escorted Sixtus into the private area of the basilica. "Are you okay?" one of them asked.

Sixtus answered in his normal voice, not in the feeble tone he used at the altar. "Yes, I'm fine. I got hot in there."

The cardinal put the back of his hand against Sixtus's forehead. "You seem to have a fever. Is the mitre too tight?"

"Possibly," Sixtus said. "But it might fall otherwise."

"We can have a larger cap installed." The cardinal lifted the headgear to take it off. It wasn't held by any straps, only by the cap and skullcap underneath. He handed the mitre to an assistant. "We can cancel your appearance," the cardinal said to Sixtus.

"I wouldn't dream of it. They expect to see me. The plaza is full."

"Yes, eighty thousand people are waiting," another cardinal chimed in.

"Come, sit down," the other cardinal said. "We will fetch you some juice."

"I'm fine," Sixtus said defensively.

He sat for several minutes. He could hear the rustle of the crowd milling about. But the hullabaloo was normal. He never saw crowds at St. Peter's Square grow restless or agitated. They were the most well-behaved assembly any leader saw, a testament to the neighborly affection and mutual respect of Catholics.

He finished his juice. Another ten minutes elapsed. An aide returned with his mitre. "Are you ready, Your Excellency?"

Sixtus turned toward one of the cardinals. "Another juice, please. Could you have them spread the word that I will be outside in ten minutes?"

Chapter 69

Amanda and Jordan stood near, but not next to, each other along the route that the Popemobile would pass through the square. They watched Sima, fully disguised, taking her position. She stood back from the front of the line, installing herself near a smattering of tourists who were there on solo trips. She determined she would be able to insert herself more easily between them when the pope passed to take her shot. One was an Asian woman – Filipino perhaps – and the other a woman in her twenties who looked to be from some Nordic country. An elderly couple stood next to them. There were not many men in this area, which would help Sima avoid capture. The entire audience was cordoned from the route by fabric-covered barriers placed throughout the square.

Word soon rang through the crowds through announcements by several aides that the pope would soon be making his way through the plaza. The crowd became noisier in return, spreading the word amongst themselves, their cheer brightening amidst the anticipation. Some began to sing psalms.

After ten more minutes, word came that the pope would appear in ten minutes. Aides passed spring water in plastic water bottles to the public. The bottles had a plain white label adorned only with a gold cross.

Both Amanda and Jordan became anxious. Jordan wondered whether Sima would go through with the assassination. Part of him wished she had chickened out earlier. But he knew that she was in a desperate situation, and the performance of this act was her salvation. Then he reminded himself, repeating the words in his mind, to convince himself of the veracity, "The pope deserves to die. The pope deserves to die."

From the other side of the plaza, the crowd began to cheer. Sixtus had arrived in his white Popemobile. A dozen security officers wearing black suits with grey-blue ties walked along each side of the vehicle. Another trio of officers followed behind it, and an additional pair of officers were in front of it. Finally, a third man, who was dressed in the same black suit, led the procession, walking backwards as he held a camera over his head, recording the van's movements.

The Popemobile was built like a truck, with a covered cab and an open bed behind it. The vehicle was a bit of a bastard between a truck and a jeep. Everything about the auto, except the tires, was white. A large chair, upholstered in white leather, was positioned behind a podium where Sixtus stood. He waved to the crowd. Amanda and Jordan watched him. He lifted his hands in a praying motion. He bowed to the spectators. He smiled. He looked alert. A bald man drove the Popemobile. The crowd soon burst into the Italian version of 'Happy Birthday'. The melody was the same as the English version, and the song was unmistakable to any English-speaker in attendance. A few attendees near Amanda and Jordan sang the lyrics in English. Others hummed. Church bells rang out. It was a happy moment.

Members of the crowd brandished flags from their countries: the American flag, the Canadian, the English, the French, of course the Italian. Flags from many other lands as well. Yes, Catholicism was a worldwide movement and had roots everywhere.

Jordan's eyes roamed the crowd. Several in attendance wore ball caps, some with Boston Red Sox and New England Patriots hats, Sixtus's home teams. One woman nearby sported a hijab.

The Popemobile made its way toward the fountain designed by Bernini, in front of the colonnade. Numerous security officers wearing bright yellow vests stood as barriers between the public and the passing pope. Parts of the crowd could rush in relatively empty areas of the square behind the line to follow the vehicle. In each of these barren lots, the spectators moved in waves to follow the vehicle. Sima stood in one of these areas. She took her pistol from the sheath at her side; the sheath didn't conceal the weapon from the metal detector, but Amanda had had the CIA hack into the detector and disable it. Everyone passed through this detection system without issue. As people passed, only stock images appeared on screen. Bensaïd passed through this same detector. The security team deemed nothing unusual. Many of the machines throughout the plaza rarely picked up any item of concern. Keys, cell phones, and wallets were the usual culprits. While security personnel advised everyone to empty their pockets, a few would always forget. Five minutes after Sima had passed through security, she sent a text to the Agency team. Her location was verified, and they turned off the bypassing mechanism that had put in place. The occasional alert began to ring out, catching the stray wallet or keychain that a devoted servant carried. Bensaïd passed through before the detection system was restarted.

The Popemobile was a couple of squares, or blocks, away from Sima. Perhaps fifty yards separated her from the vehicle. Soon, it would come her way. She held her hand on the gun. The Filipino woman and the Nordic girl looked over in anticipation of the pope's arrival. Sima knew she needed to get closer to get a clean shot. As they twisted to get a better glimpse of him, she inserted herself between the Nordic girl and the elderly couple at the front of the line. While she encroached in their space, they had no option but to make room for her as the movements of the Filipino woman and the Nordic girl had unintentionally created a space.

The Popemobile stopped. A yellow-vested security officer lifted a baby from the crowd and handed it before Sixtus. He placed his hand on the baby's back, in a blessing, and the officer instantly took it away. A different officer took another baby from someone at the front of the line. This child was much younger than the previous one, more of an infant, less than a year old. Sixtus couldn't see where the baby had come from. His senses were overloaded. As the baby was presented to him, he looked at the baby's eyes. They were closed. In a flash of a second, as the baby was held before him, he was tempted to have his touch drain the baby of its energy. As he reached his hand behind the baby's back, the baby's eyes opened and suddenly flashed red. Sixtus was startled. A second later, the baby was whisked from him back to the crowd. As the Popemobile moved on, he scanned the crowd where the baby was placed. All he could see were black shadows. The rush of the cheering throngs, the parade of security, the bright Roman sun, the circuitous route of his vehicle overwhelmed him.

The Popemobile made its way closer to Sima. Forty yards. Then thirty. Then twenty.

Sima could feel her heart racing. Never had she had such a rush. Usually, she had to act on impulse, at the whim of the moment. Now, everything was pre-planned, calculated. Normally, others did this kind of work for her, not herself.

Fifteen yards. Ten yards.

It was time to act.

The pope waved to the crowd. He looked at the rushing throng behind Sima that was following his movement in the block. Sixtus wasn't even looking at Sima or anyone else in the front line. She held up her gun and aimed it at him. She would hit him, she told herself. She would fire several times as she had been counseled, to ensure that he would be killed. She was ready to pull the trigger. At that moment, another shot rang out from behind her. Then an additional shot, and a third. Tourists nearby instantly cried out in shock from the sound of the bullet. Dozens ran for cover. Sima lowered her gun back by her side and looked in the crowd. She saw someone in black – a black sweatshirt, black joggers, a black cap – making his way through the crowd. In the rear of the running crowd, one man stood still. She recognized him. A man she had seen in photos. It was Bensaïd.

Chapter 70

Sixtus had been shot in the chest. Blood splattered over the white leather chair behind him and the white roof of the cabin. The bald driver's head was mottled with blood. Numerous security officers tried to prop Sixtus's slumped body in the leather chair, but he had no life within him. They held him in place. Sima was shocked as much as the rest of the crowd. Numerous officers rushed around the Popemobile, standing atop it, holding out their weapons. Sima extracted herself from the area. The Chinese woman was frozen, her hands over her mouth. The Nordic girl beside her was taking video with her cell phone. When Sima turned back into the crowd, Bensaïd was gone.

When Amanda and Jordan heard the shots, they assumed Sima had fired. But as they made their way through the fleeing crowd and saw her standing still, and no one rushing her, they realized that there had been another gunman. Sima walked slowly towards them.

"What happened?" Amanda asked.

"I don't know. Someone from behind shot him. He was in black. I saw Bensaïd. He was behind me, from where the shots rang out."

"Bensaïd?" Amanda said. "Are you sure?"

She nodded.

A block away, shouts emanated from the crowd. People gasped. They cried. They shuffled to the side. As Amanda, Sima, and Jordan made their way to the back of the block to investigate the commotion, a throng of security officers hovered in the block adjacent. Amanda wanted to move in, but there were too many onlookers. She couldn't push her way through.

"I'll lead," Jordan said. "I'm good at this." He instantly set forth, gently putting his hands on backs and shoulders and moving numbed people aside. "Excuse me. Excuse me," he kept saying. Sometimes, when someone wouldn't move, he'd give them a little shove. If it was a larger man, he'd give a larger shove. "Excuse me. Excuse me." He was relentless. Soon, he, Amanda, and Sima were about ten feet from where the security officers had tackled a man in black. The guards formed a circle around him. Amanda could see that the man appeared to be bleeding. The church bells rang out. They kept ringing, as if they couldn't stop. The looping tolling combined with the cries and shrieks of women and babies created a din. Amanda saw that the man had had his neck slit. A bloodied knife lay near his feet.

* * *

Amanda and Jordan arrived in Washington, D.C., on Monday morning. They had taken a red-eye overnight. On Tuesday morning, they were to meet with President Foster.

Sixtus was pronounced dead at 2:20 p.m. on Sunday. The entire world was shocked. Stories of the "beloved pope" ran non-stop in the media. His bloodied, purple cassock was being preserved, both for evidentiary reasons but also ontological and spiritual ones. Hearts on social media were shattered. Gutted. The first American pope was dead. Sixtus had never been so popular. Behind the scenes, the White House pushed forth the narrative of Sixtus's indomitable faith as well as his redoubled patriotism after he became pope. A remarkable man was the message. *A lionhearted pope*, they called him.

Upon arriving at the White House, Amanda and Jordan were escorted into the East Room, the large banquet-hall-sized room used for formal events. Foster's chief of staff told them that there would be a private ceremony, closed to the press and to officials who did not have the highest level of security clearance. Each would receive the Presidential Medal of Freedom. Amand and Jordan were shocked, and they sat in disbelief until the president arrived. In bestowing the medals upon them, he commented that the pair had "changed the course of world history and saved American democracy and our republic. None of us would be here if not for them." His words rang true.

After the ceremony, a small luncheon was held. Veronica attended, along with numerous cabinet secretaries. All profusely thanked Amanda and Jordan for their service. Of Amanda, they asked, "What's next?" She could only answer, "A little R and R."

Veronica informed Amanda that Sima, even though she didn't perform the act they contracted her for, was given a complete and unconditional pardon. She was being settled under a new name in her chosen destination. "Santa Fe, New Mexico," she whispered. Jordan overheard her.

"What about Zahir?" Amanda asked.

"What can we do?" said Veronica.

"He and Bensaïd get off scot-free?"

"They did us a favor. We don't have blood on our hands. They sacrificed one of their own. They wanted him dead. I'm sure they've paid off his family handsomely. They found a patsy just like when John Paul II was shot. It's not hard in those parts of the world."

Amanda knew that V hated the Middle East more than any other part of the world. She had been stationed in various parts – Syria, Lebanon, Israel, Jordan, Saudi Arabia, Turkey, Afghanistan. Amanda had never heard the full stories of what had happened to her, but whenever Veronica spoke of the region, a look of disgust overcame her mouth and eyes. One day, she would get the lowdown.

For his part, Jordan felt out of place among all the high-level officials. They shook his hand, but the small talk made him feel uncomfortable. They seemed to be in a celebratory mood, and while there was cause for celebration, there was cause for concern. He found it difficult to process the whirlwind events of the past week. A dead pope. An averted nuclear explosion in our nation's capital. He had expected to work on important matters, but this assignment was beyond any possible aspiration. His supervisor, Larry, was in attendance. He had never been to the White House before. "I guess we're going to lose you," he said to Jordan. Jordan didn't know how to respond. He just gave a short chuckle of acknowledgement. He wasn't ready for his career to skyrocket.

As the ceremony was winding down, Amanda and Jordan found themselves in an increasingly empty room. The president and his cabinet had left. Before she left, the chief of staff told them, "The president really likes you." She handed each of them her card. They now had a direct line to the Oval Office. Staff were clearing plates and glasses. "I guess this is the end," Jordan said.

"I'm sure our paths will cross. Some place and time when we least expect it."

www.ingramcontent.com/pod-product-compliance
Lightning Source LLC
Chambersburg PA
CBHW020247120726
47904CB00001B/115